PRAISE FOR Syd Arthur

"Syd Arthur's journey toward enlightenment is a laugh-out-loud adventure full of wisdom and wit. This book will touch your spirit and funny bone, awaken your senses, and nourish your soul."

JOAN BORYSENKO, PH.D., author of the *New York Times* bestseller
Minding the Body, Mending the Mind

"Written with wit, wisdom and compassion, *Syd Arthur* invites us to discover the spiritual opportunity beneath our obsessive relationship with food and our bodies. Syd's journey illustrates how the process of opening your heart is much more satisfying than the project of controlling your body."

DR. MICHELLE LELWICA, author of *The Religion of Thinness*

"Every once in a while you read a book that provides you with such a deep connection the story's heroine that you wish she would simply step out of the pages and become your best friend (think Helen Fielding's Bridget Jones, or Jennifer Weiner's Cannie Shapiro.) Ellen Frankel's Syd Arthur joins their leagues with her warm sense of humor, acute eye for social nuance, and infinitely relatable search for meaning in her life. Buy a few copies—I guarantee you'll want to share 'Syd' with the readers in your life!"

WENDY SHANKER, author of
Are You My Guru?
How Medicine, Meditation & Madonna Saved My Life

"...a truly touching book with great spiritual insights to carry you long after the last page has been read."

RABBI BARUCH HALEVI
Congregation Shirat Hayam

Syd Arthur

Ellen Frankel

PEARLSONG PRESS
NASHVILLE, TN

Pearlsong Press • P.O. Box 58065 • Nashville, TN 37205
1-866-4-A-PEARL • www.pearlsong.com • www.pearlsongpress.com

© 2011 Ellen Frankel
www.authorellenfrankel.com
A **Book Group Discussion Guide** for this novel is available on the author's website
& at www.pearlsong.com/sydarthur.htm.

ISBN-10: 1597190268
ISBN-13: 9781597190268

Book Design by Zelda Pudding. Cover art by Joanna Gammel.

Life Holds On • Words and Music by Beth Neilsen Chapman • © 1990 by
Universal Music—MGB Songs • International Copyright Secured • All Rights
Reserved • *Reprinted by permission of Hal Leonard Corporation*

I'm Free • Words and Music by Pete Townshend • © 1969 by Towser Tunes, Inc.,
ABKCO Music and Fabulous Music Ltd. • Copyright renewed • All Rights for
Towser Tunes, Inc. Administered by Universal Music Publshing International MGB
Ltd. • All Rights for Universal Music Publishing International MGB Ltd. in the
U.S. Administered by Universal Music—Careers • International Copyright Secured
All Rights Reserved • *Reprinted by permission of Hal Leonard Corporation*

Galileo • Words and Music by Emily Saliers • © 1992 EMI VIRGIN SONGS,
INC. and GODHAP MUSIC • All Rights Controlled and Administered by EMI
VIRGIN SONGS, INC. • All Rights Reserved • International Copyright Secured
Used by Permission • *Reprinted by permission of Hal Leonard Corporation*

Library of Congress Cataloging-in-Publication Data

Frankel, Ellen, 1961–
Syd Arthur / by Ellen Frankel.
    p. cm.
    ISBN 978-1-59719-026-8 (original trade pbk. : alk. paper)—ISBN 978-1-59719-
027-5 (ebook)
    1. Jewish women—Fiction. 2. Self-actualization (Psychology)—Fiction. 3. Sub-
urbs—Fiction. 4. Jewish fiction. I. Title.
    PS3606.R386S93 2011
    813'.6—dc22
                                        2010027993

To seekers everywhere:
May your spiritual search bring answers to the age-old questions—
"Where do you find your bliss?"
"How do you attain enlightenment?"
and
"What's for dinner?"

Prologue

The man we know as Buddha was born in the sixth century B.C.E. in northern India. His given name was Prince Siddhartha, the elder son born to a wealthy king who ruled a small country. When Siddhartha was just days old, his father, King Suddhadhana, invited a group of Brahmins or priests to a palace feast to foretell the future of the newborn prince. The Brahmins predicted that Siddhartha would either be a great and powerful ruler of the land, or a wise spiritual teacher and leader. King Suddhadhana had no desire for his son to become a spiritual leader. Instead he dreamed of his son becoming a powerful ruler over his kingdom and land. Therefore, he decided to protect Siddhartha from a spiritual path by keeping him sheltered in the palace, and lavishing upon him a world of luxuries and privilege with no exposure to the realities of suffering in life.

As a member of the elite in the caste system, Siddhartha lived a pampered existence in his father's palace. He enjoyed the best of everything: fine clothes, excellent education, including tutoring in the Hindu classics, and servants at his disposal. All who surrounded him were young and healthy; anyone who was sick, or elderly, or dying was not allowed within the palace walls. At the age of 16 he married a young princess named Yasadhara, and they continued to be showered with every extravagance. His life was so sheltered that he knew nothing about the inevitable suffering in the world. However, as he grew older and ventured outside of the palace gates, Siddhartha encountered what we all must face: the sorrows in life that come from aging, sickness and death. Confronted with this, he was unable to enjoy the luxuries of his sheltered life and could not ignore the reality of the suffering of mankind. Therefore, at the age of 29 he chose to renounce his royal title and leave his wife and only child, a son named Rahula, to become a seeker of truth and to find freedom from suffering.

He wandered as an ascetic, denying the needs of the body, looking for answers and meaning. He met famous religious teachers and, being a good student, quickly mastered whatever he was taught. But he found that these austere practices brought him no more freedom than his years of living in the midst of the worldly pleasures of his palace. So he set out to discover the truth on his own. In time, he discovered that an end to human suffering and the beginning of true freedom came from practicing a life of inner and outer balance, what he called the Middle Way.

One evening, at the age of 35, Siddhartha sat himself under a Bodhi Tree and vowed to find liberation among the forces that bring suffering. He sat there through the storms brought by fear, attachment, greed, hatred, delusion, doubt and temptation. And there, under the tree, Siddhartha attained enlightenment and became known as the Buddha.

Soon after his enlightenment a fellow traveler passed the Buddha on the road and was struck by the Buddha's radiant, calm and peaceful manner. The man approached him and asked, "My friend, what are you? Are you a god?"

"No," replied the Buddha.

"Are you some kind of magician?"

"No," the Buddha answered again.

"Are you a man?"

"No."

"Well, my friend, then what are you?"

The Buddha replied, "I am awake."

And so Siddhartha became known as the Buddha, which means, "one who is awake," and spent his life teaching others that everyone has a Buddha nature and the potential to awaken.

2,500 YEARS LATER in the cloistered world of suburbia…

Chapter One

"Syd, are you awake?" Gary whispers. I am, potentially, but if I answer there is little chance of falling back asleep and finishing the incredible dream I was having where George Clooney and I are sipping dirty martinis in this sultry jazz club, his fingers inching up my thigh. It must have had something to do with the fact that I fell asleep watching a rerun of ER.

"Hey Syd, are you awake?" Gary asks again. I can hear him getting his briefcase, opening and closing the closet door. I close my eyes tightly, trying to imagine how much further George Clooney's fingers might have traveled if I'd been allowed to keep sleeping. I pull the quilt up to my chin and rub my feet along the warmth of the blanket, content to stay blissfully groggy.

"I'm up," I manage to say, opening my eyes and looking at the clock. 6 a.m. Really, I don't know why I bother looking at the clock. Gary and I have been married for twenty years, and every morning he leaves for work at the same time. At 5:15 I ignore the alarm he sets, but I'm aware that he doesn't procrastinate getting out of bed. Actually, he kind of bolts out of bed, like he's eager to start the day, which I guess he is. He loves working at Global Investments, loves advising other people when to buy or sell. I'd be awful at that job. I'd tell people to buy, they can always return later.

Gary sits down on the bed beside me, looking like he just stepped out of J. Crew and bought the sales pitch from head to toe. As he leans down to kiss me good-bye I smell his just showered freshness, his Georgio Armani scent, and try to keep my morning breath to myself by kissing him somewhere on his shoulder.

"What time will you be home tonight?" I ask, thinking how I have nothing for supper, and maybe he has a dinner meeting and then I can just make myself a Lean Cuisine.

"Early, definitely in time for dinner," Gary says with a smile. "What are

9

you up to today?"

"Oh, a million little things," I answer. How many of us housewives say that? A million little things can be anything from a pap smear to watching talk shows all day. You know that husbands don't really want the details of a million little things as long as one of those things is picking up his dry cleaning, so you're pretty much free to do what you want with your unaccounted for time. Of course, when your kids are little the million little things become a zillion little things, and having a pap smear actually begins counting as some "quiet time." I mean, just think about it. In the doctor's office there's usually coffee and some good gossip magazines. Then you get your own room where you get to lie down and put your feet up. So really, it's practically a spa day.

"I'll call you later, then," Gary says as he ruffles my hair. "Love you, Syd."

"Love you too," I say as I watch him walk out of the room, hear his footsteps down the stairs and listen for the garage door to open and close. 6:05 a.m. *I should get up now,* I think, imagining all the things I could do. I could get on the elliptical trainer downstairs and watch the Food Network. I could get on the treadmill and watch HGTV. I could get on the bicycle and call Jodie Gordan, my best friend, and tell her that George Clooney has incredible fingers, and that we really should go out for drinks more often instead of counting either our Weight Watchers group or our Mah Jongg evenings as "girls' night out." Also, note to self: Find out how many calories are in a dirty martini.

My feet are the perfect temperature now, after all that rubbing against the soft, warm blanket. But I fight the comfort. "If I get up now and work out," I reason, "I'll have an early start to the day, and I'll feel so good." I know me—it's much harder to work out later in the day, and I'm absolutely committed to losing ten pounds by Thanksgiving. That leaves me somewhere in the neighborhood of ten weeks to go.

There's really nothing magical about Thanksgiving being my time framework for losing weight. It's just that I tend to pick holidays as markers, and this being mid-September, it's the next biggest holiday. (Let's be real. Have you ever heard someone say that they want to lose weight by Halloween)? Trust me, by Thanksgiving I'm sure I'll be setting my weight loss goal for Hanukkah, and after that—well, you get the idea. My weight seems to be like the seasons; the pounds come and they go. Ah, the weight cycles of life.

I was thinking about my last diet where I'd lost ten pounds quickly and gained fifteen back even faster, and when I opened my eyes again it was 10:18 a.m. I had fallen asleep and now was behind in my day, because, after all, I had a million little things to do.

Chapter Two

They say it hits you in unexpected ways. The sudden grip in your stomach, the tear at your heart. It all sounded a bit dramatic to me, to tell you the truth. After all, it wasn't like my daughter, Rachel, our only child, fell off the face of the Earth. She was only beginning her freshman year at the University of Wisconsin, for God's sake. A mere three-hour car drive away. So why am I standing in the aisle at Super Shop with tears running down my cheeks? It has to be about something more than not being able to buy pasta because I just started the Atkins diet. I'd been fine the other week, loading the Range Rover with boxes full of books and comforters, clothes and CDs, her laptop and DVD collection of the entire series of *Friends*. Gary and I imparted words of wisdom to our daughter as we drove from our home in Highland Ridge, a suburb on the North Shore of Chicago, out to Madison.

We reminded Rachel that she should find a good dry cleaner for her sweaters, and that she should make sure to change her sheets every week. We insisted she should never walk home alone at night after studying at the library. We reminded her to stay away from the bratwursts, that nothing good could come from consuming such a thing. That she should be aware that "the Freshman 15" is not a myth, that many a trim girl gains the unwanted pounds before mid-terms are over, and before you know it, you're vowing to lose at least five pounds before you come home for Thanksgiving.

"Keep up your running and you'll have nothing to worry about," Gary had told our daughter. "You've always been able to eat anything because you've inherited my metabolism."

"Well, I gave her my thick, silky brown hair," I defended. "And my adorable nose."

"Syd, you had a nose job."

"Yeah, but I gave Rachel the same plastic surgeon. And about this metabolism thing. It's not my fault that I inherited from my mother an uncanny ability to gain weight just by smelling the dessert."

I looked at Rachel and realized that she had her iPod on. "Can you even hear what we are—" She cut me off.

"—saying? Yes, I can multitask. I'm listening to Dave Matthews and you guys without missing a beat."

Then Gary started telling Rachel about when he met me in college our first year at Madison. "Your mom had the perfect figure. But too many pizzas and not enough running and here she is at age 43, obsessing about her weight and still trying to lose at least ten of the freshman 15. But I have to say, your mom turned heads then, and she turns heads now."

I had shot him my evil eye, which he thought was uncalled for.

"Hey, it's a compliment. You're a beautiful woman and the envy of a lot of people. You're tall and leggy, and those big hazel eyes drive me wild, and—" Gary had taken one hand off the wheel and started rubbing my neck and pulling my head close to him.

"God," Rachel said. "Enough. You're freaking me out. Dad, after you set up my computer, you can just go and get a room or something." Rachel turned the volume up on her iPod and began staring out the window at the rolling farms rushing by.

But I had to admit Gary struck a nerve. I have always felt that the only thing standing between me and perfect bliss were these extra pounds. When I was younger I had a faster metabolism, more willpower, and could lose weight more easily. I kept the scale down by spending more days on my diet than off and going for a jog almost daily. But over the years the pounds crept back, I discovered tiramisu, and jogging felt as unappealing as attempting to summit Everest.

Gary runs almost every day, and every now and then he tries to convince me to join him, but I decline. To tell you the truth (not that I've shared the explicit details with Gary), I have tried, on occasion, to go for a run. But the thing is, I was in labor with Rachel for two full days. I had to push that child out of me for more than three hours, and I don't think my organs have ever fully recovered. My bladder actually seems to move further south each year and, well, you can imagine the unpleasantness of pounding the pavement with your bladder pulsating lower with each step. Worse yet is running during allergy season, and you've got the bladder pushing downward and the pollen in your nose and you sneeze an innocent sneeze and you pee a little in your pants, Kegel exercises be damned. So mostly when Nike entices me with the slogan "Just do it," I say, "I did, and it wasn't pretty."

Gary would agree. He doesn't like to hear of any problems, any messes. He doesn't want anything out of order, anything out of control. Not household matters and not bodily matters. Take my stretch marks. No really, please take my stretch marks. Someone. Anyone.

I remember Gary bringing home cocoa butter creams meant to prevent, or at least reduce, stretch marks during pregnancy. He would lovingly rub it all over my swollen tummy, telling me that after our daughter's birth I'd be able to wear my bikinis with the best of them, with a nice, smooth, belly. I think I'd disappointed him when I didn't share his enthusiasm over swimwear, and when I'd get up in the middle of his massage to make a pan of fudge brownie mix he'd demand, "What do you think you're doing?" And I'd try to explain that the cocoa butter smells like brownies, and that this cocoa butter was a tease, making my mouth water in anticipation and then not delivering.

"You'd save calories by licking your stomach," he'd say.

"Can't reach," I'd respond.

"It's a dog's life," he'd say.

But I digress. Rachel fell in love with the campus, her roommate and her dorm immediately. When school began she called to say that except for botany she loved all of her classes and was running almost every day along the path beside Lake Mendota. She was happy, so we were happy. But then, if we're all so happy, why do I taste the salt on my lips from the tears that have traveled down my cheeks in the middle of the supermarket?

It's the shopping cart. It's the contents, or lack thereof: a bag of Red Delicious apples, romaine lettuce, skim milk, dog food. Aisle after aisle, my hand starts to move to a shelf and then my mind jumps alert and reminds me to bring my arm back to my side. No need for macaroni and cheese, salami, pizza rolls, Pop Tarts. No more Mountain Dew, pretzels, or Ben and Jerry's Cookie Dough ice cream.

"She's gone!" I want to cry out to the pimply faced stock boy, to the other women pushing shopping carts loaded with groceries. I especially want to yell this to the women who have their small children sitting in the front of the shopping carriage eating a slice of American cheese from the deli.

"They were right," I want to tell these young mothers. I wouldn't listen to the wise older women who went before me. They used to tell me the children grow up so quickly, in a flash. I used to counter, "If they grow up so fast, how can the days go by so slowly?" But it's true. Suddenly they're all grown up, and they leave you and your heart breaks into pieces when you least expect it.

"Sydney Arthur! I thought that was you!"

I pull myself back and see Cynthia Goldberg rushing toward me.

"Hi there, " I say, touching under my eyes to make sure there are no signs of tears. "My allergies are driving me crazy," I venture just in case. "I've got to remember to pick up some Benadryl."

"We should all retire to Arizona, land of no pollen," Cynthia offers, her red manicured nails drumming along the box of cinnamon toast waffles she is holding in her hands. She still has children at home; she might as well buy the economy size box and stock up. "Though I hear," she continues, "that the people who retired to Arizona in search of relief from their hay fever missed the old blooming foliage from home, so they brought back their favorite plants and then introduced them into their new neighborhoods and now they're all sneezing their way through Phoenix and Scottsdale."

"Probably good for Benadryl's stock," I say, thinking how good a Belgian waffle would be right now. With tons of strawberries and whipped cream.

"Yeah, you know, you might want to share that tip with Gary. Maybe some clients out in Arizona would be interested! So tell me, is Rachel all settled in?"

"Yep, and she's doing just great," I tell her.

"How wonderful," Cynthia says as she drops the waffles in the cart on top of the chocolate vanilla swirl pudding that's rubbing against a bottle of apple juice. I think I feel my uterus contract.

"I'm late for my golf lesson, but I'll see you tomorrow at the club for the fashion show luncheon," Cynthia says.

"Yes, absolutely," I tell Cynthia as I spy a bag of Oreos peeking out from under a bag of carrots. We squeeze each other's hand like comrades going off to battle, nodding and smiling at each other, knowing, but not speaking, about the awkwardness sure to follow, as we will continue to pass each other in aisle after aisle. I watch her push her shopping cart forward with purpose while I stand frozen, as frozen as the pizzas that beckon from behind the iced-up shelf doors.

I realize I look a little crazy standing in the middle of the aisle, so I start moving. "There must be something else I can put in my cart," I think. Then I wonder: Am I facing a crisis of the empty nest, or a crisis of the empty fridge? Is it my heart that's aching or my stomach that's growling?

I add a dozen eggs to my cart, orange juice with calcium, and a box of Special K. (I'm still hoping that I too, may someday reach the goal of Kellogg's old jingle and say: "Thanks to the 'K' you can't pinch an inch on me.") I am resigned. This is, perhaps for the foreseeable future, the way my grocery cart will look.

As I walk toward the checkout line at the register I glimpse the bakery to my left and see a table filled with braided challah breads for the Sabbath.

And then it hits me.

I leave my place in line and push my cart with a purpose. My heart quickening, my head drumming with the mantra "It's Friday, it's Friday, it's Friday," I make my way to the bakery and pick up a braided challah bread, squeezing the soft, doughy curves in my hands. I place the bread in my cart, admiring its perfect form. I decide then and there that on Fridays religion trumps the Atkins diet, and eating carbohydrates is not only permissible but damn near virtuous. It's the Sabbath, after all. And as a not-so-observant Jew, I decide it's time to pay more attention to the commandments. Honor the Sabbath. What have I been thinking? How have Gary, Rachel and I spent so many Friday nights at Ming's Garden eating General Gau's Chicken and Moo Shoo Pork (that dish must be a two-for-one in commandment breaking). How long has it been since I said a prayer before I ate? (And let's face it. "Please God, don't let this chicken Parmesan go to my hips," doesn't count.) After all, we are told to thank God for bringing forth the bread from the Earth. And I don't think God meant a blessing for the low-carb or no-carb or tastes-like-cardboard bread, but this, this braided yeast that has risen to usher in the Sabbath. I commit myself then and there to filling up my shopping cart with the ingredients for a real Friday night dinner: matzo ball soup, brisket, roasted red bliss potatoes, green bean casserole, challah and wine.

I'm back in the aisles, but this time with a purpose. I'm pulling things off the shelf, filling my cart with the ingredients and items needed for celebrating the Sabbath. I get back in line feeling my stomach (or is it my heart) relax a bit. I breathe in and out, feeling something I can't quite put my finger on.

On my way home I stop at the liquor store to buy a rich Merlot. You can't pay me enough to buy that Mogen David kosher wine most of us grew up with. Of course, my Uncle Abe used to tell us that the most popular Jewish wine was really a whine: "I want to go to Miami." And Aunt Selma made sure that's where she and uncle Abe retired. But she's no fool. She's lounging in the Florida sun on her deck drinking a full-bodied Kendall Jackson Chardonnay.

Chapter Three

Okay, I have to confess here. More than rediscovering the peace of the Sabbath last week, I rediscovered the pleasure of a full meal, fat, carbs, sodium and all. And I haven't looked back. Not when I ate the entire chicken breast stuffed with spinach and feta at the club's fashion show luncheon, and not when I was running late for an appointment last Tuesday and drove through McDonald's for a quarter pounder with cheese, large fries and a Diet Coke.

So here I am, listening to the rain pounding against the skylights overhead like a spray of bullets. Not that I've ever heard a spray of bullets, what with living in suburbia and all, but if I had, this is, I'm sure, what it would sound like.

I'm so exhausted it feels like midnight, but when I consult my trusty Omega it reads 3:30. I have four more hours until I have to be at Jodi's for our weekly Mah Jongg game. The rest of the afternoon looms ahead of me, and all I want to do is put on my old gray sweats with the drawstring, the pair I can adjust with the waistband tied to fit loosely around my stomach, making me feel like I'm barely bloated at all. That would allow me a brief respite from the raging war I've been having with the zipper and snap of what used to be my favorite pair of jeans. I'm working on the premise that my housekeeper, Marina, washed them in hot water and tumbled them in a hotter dryer and therefore they must have shrunk at least a size. But the fact that my non-stop eating has included not one single Slim-Fast shake makes me think that perhaps I have contributed in no small way to my current discomfort.

Looking across the kitchen into the family room, my eyes find and challenge Levi, our five-year-old dog who is stuck in perpetual puppyhood. Ever since Rachel was four, maybe five, years old, she had wanted a dog. I knew for certain I would never give in.

For starters, my house was meant to be a show house. In a welcoming way, of course, but a show house nonetheless. I spent years as a teenager poring over *House Beautiful* and *Better Homes & Gardens*. I take after my mother in this way. She, too, loves to shop and decorate, and taught me how important it is to have a perfectly appointed home. When my friends and I used to go to the mall, I'd beg them to go with me to the furniture section of the department stores. When we'd have sleepovers, I'd listen to my friends imagine whom they would marry, how many children they'd have, what their names would be. I, on the other hand, would use my moment of fantasy to share my decorating ideas, filling the imaginary rooms with sleek, contemporary furnishings or sparse, rustic notions.

I was forever changing my decorating plans, but always and forever in my mind my house was as spotless and perfect as the rooms featured in my glossy magazines. Every counter gleamed, every piece of glass sparkled. Every Waterford crystal bowl was filled with apples or lemons. Gerber daises and roses filled vases throughout the house and a fire roared invitingly in the parlor. Chenille throw blankets adorned the arms of sofas and chairs, adding color, texture and warmth to the open, airy rooms.

Of course there would be a husband and a child, but the house of my childhood dreams lusted first and foremost after plush fabrics and window treatments.

Don't get me wrong. I happily grew into my role as wife of Gary Kaufman, mother of Rachel Kaufman. I would have been proud to become a Kaufman myself, but being the only child, I felt it was my duty to keep my maiden name, Arthur. After all, my parents, especially my dad, claimed I would always be his princess, Princess Syd Arthur. I need to carry on his lineage. It's not so easy to walk away from royalty. And "Princess Kaufman" lacks the aristocratic image that I think "Princess Arthur" conjures.

One of the best delicatessens in Highland Ridge is called Kaufman's (no relation), and hey, I'm all for lox and bagels, but I'm thinking lox and bagels are not making you think "palace" and "kingdoms." But Arthur? "Arthur" makes me think of King Arthur and Queen Guinevere, of Excalibur swords and knights.

But again, I digress.

I grew into my role as suburban wife and mother (though sometimes Rachel came close to seeing my princess-like qualities when she got mad at me for something and called me a royal bitch). But I digress yet again. Which is something you'll have to get used to, though I'm not sure Gary ever has.

I also grew into my spacious, contemporary home on beautiful Cherry Street with its manicured lawns and reassuring cul-de-sac. I threw myself into my work with our decorator, appointing every room with a mix of elegance and comfort and charm. The Bible says God created the world in six days and on the seventh He rested. Well, I'm thinking that God didn't use the same contractors we did, because forget creating the world, it took us close to three years just to renovate. And after enjoying this perfection for a few years, (you know, the Gerber daises and roses in the vases, blah, blah, blah), Rachel turned 12 and began preparing for her bat mitzvah when, at age 13, under the laws of Judaism, she would become a woman. Forget that she still didn't make her bed, preferred me to cut her steak, and still loved fleece pajamas with feet. According to the Jewish powers that be, she would be an adult in the eyes of the Lord.

Well, the trouble really started when she got her Torah portion, the verses of the Torah that she would read and interpret the following year, in front of the congregation. Rachel, Rachel, who loved animals more than anything, who had been begging for a dog for at least seven years, my poor Rachel—her Torah portion came from the book of Leviticus, and it dealt with animal sacrifice. *Oy vey.* She was beside herself. Gary would try to comfort her, would tell her that there are no more animal sacrifices, just really big temple dues, but that didn't appease. She would tell us, her grandparents, her Hebrew teacher, that she didn't want to have a bat mitzvah anymore, didn't want to learn—in Hebrew or in English—how the Jews were supposed to bring animals to sacrifice at the Temple.

One Sunday evening after my parents had joined us for dinner, we all sat in our family room while my dad tried to explain to Rachel why becoming a bat mitzvah was so important.

"L'dor va dor," my father, Max, had told Rachel. "From generation to generation we pass on the teachings of the Torah, the love of the Torah, to our children. And you, my Rachela, are the next generation, the only grandchild. You must receive and then carry on our traditions."

My mother, Estelle, said to Rachel, "Yes, that's important, but honey, darling, think about the fun you'll have. Think of the party, the new dress! Your parents have had the club and the band booked for three years already. Everything is in place. You have to have your bat mitzvah."

Rachel had just stood there, her arms crossed in front of her chest and her face holding the same expression she had as a toddler when I would try to get her to eat her peas.

"Party shmarty!" My dad had said to my mom. "It's tradition, it's her heritage." My father walked over to Rachel and cupped her chin in his hands. "Rachel, honey, listen to me. There were children, children your age, murdered in the Holocaust, killed in the concentration camps just because they were Jews. In their name, Rachela, you have to become a bat mitzvah."

"Hey, slow down," I said to my dad. "Let's not bring the Holocaust into this. That's not her burden. Rachel—"

But Gary had interrupted me. "No, I agree with your dad. That is her burden. It's all of our burdens. And Rachel is going to get bat mitzvahed even if I have to—"

"What, kill me?' Rachel had jumped in. "Kill me like those poor sacrificed animals?"

"Achhh! Enough! This is nonsense. Rachel, you are going to have a bat mitzvah, and you are going to do a lovely job reading from the Torah," my dad pronounced.

"And you'll look beautiful," my mom added. Gary and I looked at each other and then at Rachel. Her lips quivered and she looked like she was about to cry, but then you could just tell something happened, something in her changed. She pulled out a stool from the bar and jumped up to sit. Swinging her dangling legs, she began to move in for the kill. Using that pre-teen voice where everything sounds like a question, she began.

"The other week in Hebrew school? Our teacher taught us about *Tikkun Olam*—about how it's each of our duties to repair the world?"

At this, my parents were beaming. Gary looked like he could burst with pride. I knew something was up, and that we were all about to be played like a fiddle by a 12-year-old fiddler in the family room, if not on the roof.

She continued, "We need to take care of each other, to love each other and help to make the world a better place for everyone; our family, our friends, our teachers and neighbors—"

More beaming from the proud grandparents and father and then, drum roll please, Rachel is getting ready to reel them in—

"—and even the animals," she had stated with the wide eyes of an accomplished fiddler. "After all, they're just innocent creatures in this world, and they need protection." Then, as if this thought had only just occurred to her, she jumped off the stool and stood facing all of us as if she was part of a presidential debate, just getting ready to offer the solution to global warming.

"Hey, because I'm going to have to read about animal sacrifices? And because that makes me feel so sad? How about for my bat mitzvah to be really meaningful I show my love and my efforts to repair the world by getting a dog and taking care of him and—"

"Hold on a minute," I said, as I took in the beauty of my house, Oriental carpets and all.

"No, no," my father said. "She has a point."

"She has been wanting a dog since she was a little girl," my mom added.

"Gary," I began, trying to catch his eyes, which were looking everywhere but at me in that moment. My heart began to sink as Rachel's spirits began to rise. She could see where to pursue her efforts.

"And dad, you could maybe take him out on your runs? And I could teach him to bring in the newspaper for you?" Gary ruffled Rachel's long brown hair, and my dad put his arm around my mom's shoulders.

"Has everyone gone mad?" I asked

"No mom really, it will be great. I promise, I'll walk him and feed him and—"

I interrupted her. "Oh, honey, every child who wants a dog says that, but believe me, they don't follow through. I'll be the one walking him and feeding him and cleaning up after him, and it won't be about you repairing the world, it will be about him ruining our house."

"Now Syd," my mom said. "Don't you think you're being just a bit dramatic? How hard can it be?"

I gave her my evil eye. "Hey, you refused to get me a dog because of all the work involved!" I shot back.

"Well, things are different now," my mom had said.

"Really, Mom, different? Different how? It's not like the Internet can walk the dog, not like the remote control can feed the dog. How are things different?"

"Oh, I don't know, Syd, they just are. And look at Rachel, look how much she wants a dog."

I had looked over at Rachel, who had assumed "the position." She was on her knees, her hands in prayer, making her eyes as wide as possible with just the right mix of hope and innocence across her face.

"And we'll buy the dog for her," my dad added, as if it were merely a financial issue. Before I could open my mouth Rachel jumped into her grandfather's arms and he twirled her around and around. My mom clapped her hands together and Gary, sensing an impending disaster had been averted, gave Rachel two thumbs up and then turned on the TV to check the score of the Bulls game.

So here I am five years later, with Gary at work, my parents in Florida, and Rachel at college, leaving me to take Levi out in this miserable weather for his walk. "Thank God you're cute," I say to Levi, "otherwise all bets would be off."

My parents had bought Rachel the puppy before her bat mitzvah, and to their credit they actually found a breed that, thankfully for me, was hypoallergenic, a rare breed called a Coton De Tulear. They're cousins of the Bijon Frise and were originally the palace dogs of Madagascar, so I was hoping that through evolution, what with being palace dogs and all, they had inherited a gene that ensures that they refrain from relieving themselves on imported plush carpets. He weighs only 12 pounds—as I look at him I think of how I'd love to lose the equivalent of a Levi—and is just one big ball of long white hair and floppy champagne colored ears.

The evening they brought the dog over to our house, a month before the bat mitzvah, Rachel was ecstatic. She held the puppy in her arms and smiled as she was licked from eyelids to throat.

When the subject about his name came up, Rachel declared she had it covered. "We'll name him Levi."

"'Levee' like what keeps a dam from bursting? What kind of name is that?" my father asked as my mother stood taking pictures of this momentous occasion.

"No, no. I want to spell his name L-E-V-I—it's just pronounced 'levee.' It's short for Leviticus. You know, where my Torah portion about animal sacrifice is from. See, it's all part of *Tikkun Olam*. By naming him Levi, we take away the horrible stuff about animal sacrifice and instead take care of our innocent puppy and help to heal the world."

"Achh, she sounds like a rabbi already," my dad said, pinching her cheek. "I'm so proud of you, my Rachel."

"Thanks, Grandpa," she said, as Levi began licking my dad's hand.

"You know, you might want to include that idea in your bat mitzvah speech; that sounds good—" my mom was saying as Gary jumped in.

"Yeah, honey, have you begun working on your speech yet?"

"A little. I'll finish it, don't worry. Levi here will help me," Rachel said as she patted and kissed her new best friend and apparently now her co-author. She put Levi down on the floor, where the new puppy promptly walked over to the Persian rug in the foyer and peed. Apparently I was wrong about inheriting the palace gene thing. And so it began.

So now here I am, with Levi cocking his head in that humanlike way that melts your heart, and I resign myself to pulling on my rain slicker, digging out my rain boots from the back of the closet and getting Levi's leash. The minute I take down his leash Levi begins jumping up and down like a lunatic, something he's done since he was a puppy. I step outside and the rain is pounding my face, making *thump, thump, thump* sounds against my hood.

"C'mon Levi, go potty," I tell him, hoping this will be quick.

I venture through puddles on the street and a gust of wind throws my hood off, drenching the top of my head. Meanwhile Levi is getting soaked, his paws turning wet and dirty as he travels over grass, mulch, and patches of mud. Thankfully as we reach the stop sign at the end of Cherry Street I see him lift his leg and relieve himself. He pulls to continue further, wanting to roam down Maple Street, but I refuse his request and tug the leash back towards home. The street names in our neighborhood—Cherry, Maple, Cedar, Sycamore, Birch, Willow—remind me of a bumper sticker I once saw that read: *Suburbia: Where they tear out the trees and then name the streets after them.*

"Let's go home, Levi, hurry!" I pull him into a slow jog until I reach my house and open the garage door, grabbing a towel to dry him off. I am soaked and a mess, and the only thing I can think of that will warm and cheer me is the Godiva chocolate bar sitting in my kitchen drawer.

I hang up my raincoat, kick off my rain boots, and pull my wet hair back into a ponytail. Eating the candy bar is not going to help me get back on track with my diet. I know this. And yet I can imagine the feel of the chocolate soften and liquefy in my mouth, the silky, smooth texture, the warmth of the melting on my tongue. I go to the drawer and take out the chocolate, and even though I want to tear off the wrapper I undress it slowly, finding the golden wrapper underneath the outside packaging. Sometimes I think I engage in foreplay and make love more sensually to chocolate than I do to Gary.

And here is my dirty little secret. So bad that if the vet knew, I probably would be deemed an unfit mother and Levi would be taken away. It's too fattening to eat the whole bar by myself, even though God knows I want to. Anyway, Levi and I like the same foods. He can match me calorie for calorie, though he never seems to gain an ounce. I break off squares of the chocolate that I feed to him, while I savor the rest for me. He loves it.

I know, I know. They say chocolate is poison for dogs, but I've been doing this for years, and he's fine. Okay, the other dirty little secret is that if my feeding him some of what I eat to save calories—you know, when I feed him some cookies, lasagna, popcorn, cereal, bagels—if when I do this it shaves a little bit of time off his lifespan, would it be the end of the world? Okay, I realize for him, yes, it would be. But for me? Well, I'm reminded of one of the few jokes I can actually remember the punch line to.

A priest, a minister and a rabbi were talking one day about when they believe life begins. The priest said, "I believe that life begins at the moment of conception, because therein lies the potential for human life." The minister said, "I believe that life begins when the fetus becomes viable." The rabbi said, "Well, I have to disagree with you both. I believe that life begins when the kids go to college and the dog dies."

So here I am, with Rachel at school and Levi sharing my Godiva, and I'm wondering, I'm midway through my life, but where is my life taking me? And wherever that is, could I please go there as a size two?

Chapter Four

"Six crak," Jodi says, throwing out her Mah Jongg tile and adjusting the remaining tiles on her yellow rack.

"Eight bam," I say.

"Red dragon," Margot says as she throws her tile into the mix.

"Four dot, and will someone please move this bowl of chocolate pretzels away from me?" Donna says as she eats another one. Jodi moves the bowl across the table and throws out a nine dot. Donna's hand finds the bowl of cashews to her left and starts eating them by the handful.

"North," Jodi declares.

"South," I say, throwing out my tile hoping that no one is playing the winds. "Hey, Jodi, I like your new serving bowls," I tell her, helping myself to some cashews.

"Thanks, I bought them at Crate and Barrel the other week," Jodi tells me.

"Five crak," Margot says, throwing the tile out with one hand and grabbing a handful of chocolate pretzels with the other.

"That's it, Mah Jongg!" Jodi declares, picking up the tile and adding it to her rack, exposing her winning hand. We all tell her what a beautiful hand it is while secretly making sure she hasn't made any mistake in her tiles, which would mean one of us would still get a shot at winning this hand.

"Shit! Look, I was only one tile away. I needed a one bam," Donna says as she reaches across the table for the chocolate pretzels.

"Okay," Jodi says. "That was a 30-cent hand from you guys," looking at Donna and me, "and Margot threw me Mah Jongg, so that's sixty cents from her."

We throw our coins over to Jodi with sighs, as if she's broken our banks. Jodi counts up the change. "That's $1.20!" she reports cheerfully, scooping up the assortment of quarters, dimes and nickels and putting them in her beaded coin purse.

"Great! You can afford your Dunkin' Donuts coffee tomorrow morning!" Margot teases.

"Yeah," I say, "but you can't afford it from Starbucks unless you win another round."

We all throw our hands from the last game into the middle of the card table and start mixing the tiles.

Have you ever heard the sound of Mah Jongg tiles being mixed? It's a wonderful, soothing sound of clicks and clacks that all of us except Donna grew up with, having had mothers who also played Mah Jongg.

I can remember, when I was little, my mother hosting Mah Jongg games when it was her turn to have the girls over. My mom, who was always dieting, would bake lemon cheesecake squares, would buy chocolate covered almonds and M&Ms and display these snacks on fancy serving plates and etched crystal candy dishes. I'd enjoy taking bites here and there before the ladies arrived, and sometimes my mom did too.

Once, when I was about eight years old, I watched her sneak some cheesecake squares and eat them quickly. I asked her if that meant she had ruined her diet. I remember her pulling me close to her, and how good she smelled. I think the perfume she used to wear then was Chanel No. 5. And she asked me, "Syd, honey. If a tree falls in the forest and no one is there, does it make a sound?"

"Huh?" I had asked.

My mom had taken a fistful of M&Ms and I watched her open wide and throw the colorful candies back into her mouth, making clicking sounds against her molars not unlike the glorious sound of the Mah Jongg tiles.

"Darling, if you're eating something while you're busy doing something else, and no one is around watching, the calories don't really count."

Things started to click for me. "Is that why you don't eat the bread with Daddy and me at dinner, but when you're cleaning up and washing dishes, you pull out big chunks from the loaf and eat them?"

My mom had looked alarmed. "You see me do that?" she had asked.

"Yeah, all the time," I answered. Then I got worried. "Wait, Mom. If I see you eating the bread every night, does that mean that the calories do count for you? Is that why your diets never really work, and why you haven't lost weight? If I look the other way next time, will that help?"

My mom changed the subject, but I remember noticing that she had moved the bowl of M&Ms away from her.

My mom would show me how to set up the Mah Jongg racks, and she'd teach me about the tiles belonging to the different suits—the craks, bams and dots—along with showing me the winds, dragons, flowers and jokers. When the ladies arrived they'd all hug me and tell me how grown up I was getting. They'd ask me how school was, how my art lessons were going, and then I'd have to go upstairs to my bedroom. There I would hear the murmuring of their voices interspersed with bursts of laughter, and every fifteen minutes or so, the sound of the tiles being mixed for the next Mah Jongg game.

It was such a reassuring sound. A women's sound of laughter and secrets. A world where husbands didn't belong (my dad always went out when my mom had Mah Jongg at our house) except as a topic of conversation, but where daughters would one day enter, not as "helpers" who set up the game with their mothers and then went upstairs, but as inhabitants of chairs at the table, saying goodnight to daughters of their own, who in turn had helped set up the tiles, and who had sampled the snacks.

Only Donna hadn't grown up with these rituals, being what we call a "New Jew." When she married Joel Bernstein she converted, and along with learning to make a brisket, she learned to play Mah Jongg. It's a very strange thing—Mah Jongg is traditionally a man's game played in Asia, but in America it became a woman's game played by Jews. And a surprising choice it is, because these are women who take their nails very seriously and have manicures on a weekly basis. How they chose a game that requires the shuffling of tiles and the risk of chipping polish or, heaven forbid, breaking a nail, is anyone's guess. Though it has become a great way for players to show off a new ring or bracelet.

How often someone sets up their tiles, just waiting to be the center of attention as they wait to do what is known in Mah Jongg as "the passing." After everyone has the allotted number of tiles on their rack, they begin the passing, where each player gives another player three tiles so they have a better chance of getting the needed tiles for a particular hand before the game begins. With each pass you can keep the three tiles you think you will want, and pass on the three tiles you think you won't need. Since you pass to the player on the right, then over, then to the left, then again to the left, then over, and finally back to the right, the passing has been named "The Charleston." So the person who is trying to show off a new piece of jewelry has ample time for people to notice. She will often pause at a certain point in the passing to take a while organizing her tiles in different combinations, or drum her fingers on the table. At some point someone in the group sees her hands moving, her polished nails tapping on a tile in indecision. Then it happens.

"My goodness!" someone will declare. "Look at that bracelet! When did you get that?"

Someone else will grab the person's wrist. "I haven't seen that on you before. Is that new?" they'll demand.

"It's gorgeous! Fabulous!" someone else will chime in. The woman who is wearing the new, thankfully noticed jewel is now exactly where she wants to be, the subject of everyone's envy. She'll tell her friends where she got it and when. She'll move her hand this way and that, admiring the way it adorns her wrist. Or the way it glistens in the right stream of light. There will be requests from others to try it on, and she'll happily oblige. By the time everyone has discussed the new bracelet, no one can remember where they are in the passing, some swearing they are on the second left, while others are sure they are on their last right.

"You know," Donna begins as we set up our racks for the next game, "I love this game, but I swear it's making me gain weight. Why do we eat so much when we play?"

"Because that's the rule," Jodi answers. "It's the Mah Jongg culture."

"Exactly," Margot says as she refills the bowl of chocolate pretzels. "We diet all week, and then we break our diets when we play. We've been doing this for years."

"For generations," I say, thinking about my mother.

"Well, it must be a Jewish thing. I'm telling you, my mother played cards with the girls every week, and I don't ever recall food being served. Though I do know that while they played gin they did drink a lot of vodka," Donna shares.

"Eight dot," I say, throwing out my first tile.

"West," Donna says. Then she adds, "I propose that next week we start a new food policy. No more fattening snacks. All we do is eat them, and then complain that we ate them. Let's just put out some carrots and be done with it."

"Flower," Margot says with her Boston accent. Margot moved here over 15 years ago, but from the way she drops her "Rs" from words that have an "R" and adds an "R" to words that don't have an "R" to begin with, (car becomes cah while idea becomes idear), you'd think she just stepped off the swan boats in the Boston Public Gardens. So when she throws in her flower tile, it sounds more like "floweh." Then she says, "Oh! My! God! Speaking of carrots, have you see Evelyn's new diamond ring? I swear it has to be at least four karats!"

"We were talking veggies," Jodi interrupts.

"Yeah, yeah—so anyway, it's pear shaped and huge and fabulous! What do you think you have to do to get a ring like that?" Margot asks.

"Find out that your husband is sleeping with his secretary?" Donna ventures as she throws out a nine crak.

Jodi throws out a two dot. " Get out of here!" she says. "Jed is sleeping with his secretary? How do you know?"

"Well, I don't want to gossip," Donna begins as she discards a green dragon.

"You? Who are you kidding! You're the queen of gossip. That's one of the reasons we love you," I say.

"Okay, pass me the bowl of chocolate pretzels," Donna demands.

Jodi gets up and sets the bowl of pretzels back near Donna and then gets the coffee pot and pours cups of coffee. She places a bowl of Sweet'N Low in the corner of the table. It doesn't matter that we spend the evening bingeing; none of us would consider adding sugar to our coffee. Even Donna, who, despite complaining that she eats too much, is still thin as a rail. Sometimes we hate her for this, but we still pass her the Sweet'N Low and listen to her complain with the rest of us about the size of our stomachs and thighs. It seems like the polite thing to do.

"Well, I just know my brother-in-law, who uses Jed as his accountant, has seen him with his secretary in ways that don't add up," Donna says as she nibbles on her pretzels. Donna loves to talk in puns.

"It's been going on for awhile and eventually Evelyn found out. I heard through the grapevine there were ultimatums. My brother-in-law said the last time he was at Jed's office there was a new secretary, elderly with swollen ankles, I recall him saying, and all of a sudden Evelyn is sprouting a rock, so there you go," Donna finishes.

"What would you do?" I ask my friends. "What if you found out your husband was having an affair?"

"I'd go for earrings instead, and a trip to Paris," Jodi ventures.

"No, I agree with Evelyn. I'd go for the ring," Margot chimes in.

"You guys are crazy," I say, stirring the Sweet'N Low in my coffee to wash down my second oatmeal raisin cookie.

"Enough! None of our husbands are cheating. Let's stop yapping and start playing," Donna says. "Does anyone even remember whose turn it is?" she asks.

"Speaking of jewelry, did I tell you that I lost my tennis bracelet on the golf course last week?" Margot asks.

"*Oy vey,*" Donna answers.

Jodi and I look at each other and then at Donna and start laughing.

"What?" Donna asks. We keep laughing. "C'mon, you guys—why are you laughing at me?"

"Oh, Donna, we're not laughing at you. It's just that *Oy vey* rolls so easily off your tongue, I don't think we can call you a 'New Jew' anymore. I think you are truly part of the Tribe now," Jodi says as she presses her fingertips on the table to pick up some spilt Sweet'N Low.

"Well, mazel tov to me, then," Donna says. "But honestly, growing up Catholic and then converting to Judaism is not very different. There's enough guilt in both religions to keep you feeling lousy about yourself. Though it is much easier being Jewish and only having to ask for forgiveness once a year at Yom Kippur rather than weekly at confession."

"Yeah, what's that like?" Margot asks. "Is it weird to go into that confession box and tell the priest your sins?"

"Wait, wait!" I say. "That reminds me of a funny joke I heard the other day."

Everyone waves me off. "What?" I ask.

"Syd, as your best friend for more than 30 years, I can tell you that you are the worst joke teller in the world," Jodi ventures. Donna and Margot are nodding in agreement.

"That's not true," I protest. "I'm sure there's an equally bad joke teller out there. Okay, so anyway, this middle-aged guy goes to confession. The priest asks him, 'What is your sin?' And the guy says, 'Father, I went to this dance club and there was this beautiful, hot girl who was younger than my own daughter. She was so gorgeous and we danced together all night and then I took her home and we had the most amazing sex I've ever had, over and over, all night long.'

"The priest asked, 'And how long has it been since your last confession?'

"'Oh, I've never been to confession before. I'm Jewish,' the man replied.

"'If you're Jewish, why are you in confession telling me this?'

"The guy replied, 'Telling you? Hell, I'm telling everyone!'"

I hear a few snorts.

"Syd, if you had a day job, I'd tell you not to quit it to become a comedian," Jodi says.

"No, wait, I think it was kinda funny," Margot offers charitably.

"I just hope the guy wasn't Evelyn's husband," Donna adds.

"Okay, can I just say that I have no idea whose turn it is and I think I'm getting too slap happy to play?" I say.

We all agree, throw in our tiles, and begin cleaning up.

"Next time we have to focus more on playing," Margot says. "We should be able to talk and play at the same time. We've been playing together for the past ten years and we seem to be getting slower and slower. I think we've managed to play all of five games tonight. We used to play double that."

"We're getting old," I say.

"Speak for yourself. I feel young," Donna says.

"Yeah, well, you're still in your thirties. Wait till you hit your forties and you come down with CRS," Jodi says, and Margot and I nod in agreement.

"Oh my God, you all have CRS? What's that?"

"Can't Remember Shit," we say in unison.

Donna sighs. "Well, don't bring me down, you guys. I still feel young and hot."

"Oh, honey, we're hot, too. It's just that ours comes from perimenopausal hot flashes," I tell Donna.

"Oh, the good ol' days of perimenopause," Margot says. "Just wait until you hit menopause in all its glory!"

Donna stands up, puts on a serious face, and says, "Okay, guys, next week we're playing at my house and these are the new rules: We'll serve low calorie snacks, play more quickly with less talking, and you guys are not to bring me down about the aging process. You should each come ready to talk about something fabulous about being in your forties—"

Margot interrupts Donna. "Hey, I'm already in my fifties, and I complain a whole lot less than Syd and Jodi."

"You do realize we have this conversation every week?" I ask. "Now it's time to promise each other that we're all going to stay on our diets this week and finally lose weight once and for all and blah blah blah."

Jodi pulls us all together for a group hug.

"That's the beauty of true friendship," she says. "We're like watching an old sitcom over and over. Will this be the week that Gilligan and the Skipper, Ginger and Maryanne, the Professor and the Howells finally get off the island?' We know they won't, but we cheer them on anyway."

"Okay, and you know what I always wondered about? If they were just going on a three-hour cruise, why did they have suitcases and entire wardrobes packed?" Margot asks.

"Okay, off point," I say. "First, we're not trying to get off an island, we're trying to stay on a diet. But granted, we do fail as often as Gilligan. Anyway, I really am going to start my diet tomorrow. I've run out of excuses and I know if I just lose these pounds, I will be so happy."

My friends are all agreeing with me, and so I say with encouragement to myself and to them, "Let's really do it. Let's each vow to stick to our diets. We all have so much going for us in our lives; we have everything! All of us could be so blissfully happy if we just lost the weight once and for all."

"I'm in," Jodi says.

"Me too," Donna says, though all of us know she doesn't even need to lose an ounce.

"Me three," Margot says.

I want so badly to believe in this religion of thinness that my friends and I grew up with, the belief that being thin is the salvation and path to true happiness. But as I say good-bye to Jodi, Margot and Donna, with promises to once again stay on our diets, I begin to wonder if perhaps we seem more like the joker tiles in the Mah Jongg set.

Chapter Five

For nearly a month I was good, really good. I had returned to Weight Watchers and counted my points like every other time. And like every other time, I rebelled and stopped counting. And that was what hit me—*like every other time*. I mean, really, if it were possible to just lose weight and keep it off, why would you need a lifetime membership at Weight Watchers? Let's face it, my friends and I are always back on a diet, implying that the latest diet resulted in only time-limited weight loss. I guess my time limit has expired once again.

So here I am, just about to sit down with my morning cup of coffee, a strawberry cheese Danish, and a shopping list when the phone rings. I look at my caller ID to see who it is and if I want to pick up. What did we do before caller ID? This has to be one of the greatest inventions.

"Hey Jodi," I say.

"Hi Syd, what's up?' she asks.

"My weight," I reply, taking another bite of my Danish and stirring my Sweet'N Low into my coffee.

"It sucks, doesn't it? I mean, we can put a man on the moon, but no one can figure out how to lose weight and keep it off," Jodi says.

I wait to answer while I savor the bite of Danish; it's like a party going on in my mouth. "I think we have to pick a new diet. This Weight Watchers thing isn't working for me anymore. And I'm sick of figuring out the whole point thing. I never liked math."

"As I recall," Jodi begins, "you did like something about math. Remember the crush you had on our algebra teacher freshman year of high school?"

"Oh my God! Do you remember how cute he was? Mr. Bowman. It was his first year teaching and he was like only ten years older than we were," I say, taking another bite of my Danish.

"Do you remember how often you used to go in for help?"

I swallow before answering. "Yeah, I used to just like to smell his cologne, and look at his chest. It used to ripple under his shirt. But the only thing I remember from that class is to multiply what's in the parentheses first." I lift the Danish to my lips to finish it off, but then I think of the calories and I look over to Levi, who has been watching me intently for the last ten minutes. Breaking it into smaller pieces, I put it in front of Levi, who gobbles it up in a minute with satisfied smacking sounds.

"I've been tired of Weight Watchers, too, and my weight has sort of hit a plateau," Jodi says. "We only have a few weeks until Thanksgiving, and we know we're going to splurge then, so I think we have to prepare and do some damage control now. Agreed?"

"Agreed," I say, using the tip of my index finger to pick up the few remaining crumbs on my plate and lick them off. "So what diet should we try?" I ask as I put my plate in the dishwasher.

"Uck, I don't know. We've done them all," Jodi whines.

"You know, the year we had Mr. Bowman was the year all the girls we knew were on the grapefruit diet. Remember that?"

"Oh yeah, I do." Jodi says. You had to eat a half a grapefruit before every meal. But I can't do that one now."

"How come?" I ask, as I spray Windex on the outside of the dishwasher, cleaning off the fingerprints.

"Because of my blood pressure medication. You're not supposed to have grapefruit within a few hours of taking the medicine. It weakens its effect, and lately Melanie and Rebecca have been driving me so crazy that I can't afford a weakening effect," Jodi declares. Melanie is a junior in high school with a Type A personality, and Rebecca is a high school freshman who aspires to hang out with the older boys.

"Okay, then let's think. What haven't we tried in awhile?" I ask.

"I don't know—we've tried everything. Oh wait! You know what we haven't tried in ages? The Cabbage Soup Diet. Remember that?"

"God, I forgot about that. But I can't do that one again. I was on it after Gary and I were married and it drove him crazy. He couldn't stand the smell in the house from the soup I had to keep making, and he kept spraying air freshener everywhere. Between the cabbage soup and the spray, our house ended up smelling like dead roses.

Silence.

"Well, there has to be something," Jodi says. "Should we just try for the generic 'cut calories and exercise more'?"

"Why not? Let's just see if we can lose a few pounds cutting calories so that when we gain weight over the holiday, maybe we'll end up even on the scale."

"Okay," Jodi agrees. "But let's at least figure out how many calories we're going to stick to. How about 1500 calories a day?"

"Fine," I say. "But do you know that I read an article that said that eating 1300 calories a day met the criteria for starvation?"

"Honey, neither of us look like we're starving," Jodi says. "Oh wait, that's Dave calling in. I'll call you back later."

I pour myself another cup of coffee and top it off with another Sweet'N Low. I really hope they're wrong about artificial sweetener causing cancer. I start making a grocery list of the low calorie food I need, and get ready to run to Super Shop. When I go to get my jacket from the closet, Levi is standing by his leash willing me to take him out for yet another walk. I am sick and tired of being the only one home to walk a dog that can't get enough of going outside. I put down my jacket, stuff the grocery list in my pocket, and make a call that I should have made years ago.

I dial the 800 number and wait for someone to pick up. After following the prompts a perky female voice says, "Hello, Invisible Fence. How can I help you?"

I almost want to cry. Happy tears.

"I need to install an Invisible Fence," I tell the perky voice.

"Well, you've come to the right place," she says in an even perkier voice. I wonder if she really loves her job this much, or if she knows that the initial recording informed me that "calls may be monitored for quality assurance."

She takes down some information. The basics: address, telephone number, type of dog, size of yard. She explains that someone will come out to install the wire around the perimeter of the yard. Then they'll put up green Invisible Fence flags to teach Levi where it is safe for him to roam, and where he cannot go past. As in, if he ventures beyond the Invisible Fence, he'll get a shock, which is a horrible thing, but it will teach him to stay within the confines of his yard and have a measure of freedom. The dog just has to wear the special collar with the battery that makes the fence work. Eventually, as the dog learns where it's unsafe to go, he remains blissfully content to stay within his designated area. "A microcosm of suburbia," I think to myself.

"What we need to do this week is send out a technician to set up the wiring, and then we'll schedule a trainer to begin working with your dog on how to negotiate the fence." She still sounds perky.

"You mean you actually have to train him to use the fence? We can't just put him in the yard with the collar on and let him figure it out on his own?" I ask.

The voice on the other end giggles. "Oh, no. The dog must be trained over a period of weeks to learn the rules of the fence."

This is news to me. All I wanted was an easier way of getting him outside to do his business without having to walk him all the time.

"You see, the thing is," I begin," Levi doesn't train very well. We were kicked out of doggie obedience school," I confide.

"I'm sure he'll learn just fine," she says.

"The jury's out on that."

I can feel her using all her energy to maintain her perkiness. I hear her breathe deeply and exhale into the receiver.

"Ms. Arthur, don't you worry. Leave it to us. I can have a technician out to you on Wednesday to install the wire, and I can have one of our trainers come out on Friday at 1:00."

"That'll be fine," I say, penciling it in my calendar.

"Okay, and then next week we have someone available on Tuesday, and on Thursday," she says.

"No, no," I say. "Friday afternoon is fine."

"Yes, I have you down for Friday afternoon at 1:00. But you'll need at least two other training times, and I can send someone over the following Tuesday and Thursday," Ms. Perky explains.

"You mean it takes more than one training?" I ask.

"Oh, yes. It's a lot to learn, and the trainer will work with you and your dog—"

I interrupt her. "You mean I have to be outside with the trainer, too?"

"Of course. The trainer will first put your dog on a leash in the yard and walk him around. Then he'll start pulling him to each flag, which will have been placed just a little before where the wire is buried. The dog will be able to hear a high pitched tone that signals that if he goes past that point, he'll get a shock."

"How will he know he gets a shock?" I ask.

"Because at some point he will venture past it, and once he gets the shock he'll know to pay attention to the tone as a signal. Eventually the flags will be gone, but the dog knows where to stay away from, and happily plays in the yard with room for him to run and enjoy his freedom," she explains.

"It sounds like a lot of work," I offer.

"It means that your dog can be outside at anytime without you having to be out with him, or walking him, especially during the winter, which is just around the corner." She knows that she now has me wrapped around her finger.

"Right," I say. "Okay, what time on Tuesday and Thursday?"

"We can schedule a trainer between 10:00 and 12:00 on both days. Will that work for you?"

It means I have to miss my kickboxing class on Tuesday, but I figure I can take an afternoon spinning class to make up for it.

"That'll be fine," I say.

"Excellent!" her perkiness declares. "That should give you some time on Wednesday to practice."

"Practice what?"

"You'll have to be working with your dog every day for a while with the homework the trainer will be giving you."

"Homework?" I venture.

"Of course. Your dog will need to be reassured when he gets a shock, and you'll learn how to assure him that being in the yard is safe and fun. Then you'll need to work on distractions."

"What are distractions?" I ask.

"Oh, all of the things that make a dog want to run out of his yard and chase. Like a kid on a bike, another dog, a big truck. The dog needs to practice seeing all these things outside of his yard, and not running after them. He has to be convinced that staying put safely in his yard is the only choice. The best way to do this is to ask kids to play outside of the yard, to play with someone else's dog, to ride their bikes, that sort of thing, as a practice for your dog not to follow and break through the Invisible Fence and go out beyond the perimeter. Do you have children?"

"A daughter."

"Wonderful, she'll be a big help!" she exclaims.

"She's away at college. That's why I need to put in the Invisible Fence. She's not home, so I can't bribe her to walk the dog anymore," I tell her. Then I continue, "I knew this would happen. She couldn't have gotten a different Torah portion, huh? She couldn't have gotten Moses receiving the Ten Commandments at Mount Sinai?"

"I'm sorry?" Ms. Perky says, more confused than perky.

"Never mind. Fine, fine. I'll work with the trainer. I mean, this works, right? I'll be able to just let him out in the yard?"

"Absolutely. Just a little bit of training, and you and your dog will be all set. It's truly a remarkable system," she gushes.

We finish up on the phone, confirming dates and times, and I give her my credit card number. I hang up the phone and look at Levi. Yes, he'll enjoy running and playing in his yard, but the learning curve will come with a price.

I feel a twinge of guilt. Levi cocks his head in that really cute way. The twinge grows bigger. I open the cabinet and give Levi a handful of Cheerios, and grab a handful for myself. The commercial says it lowers cholesterol, so

I figure it's more medicine than food and therefore the calories don't count. I look on my kitchen desk for my health club's class schedule and find a Tai Bo class this afternoon that I promise myself I will go to after I've finished my errands. I leave a note and a check for Marina. It occurs to me that I probably don't need our housekeeper three times a week anymore, what with Rachel gone and all, but it's been part of my routine for so many years that I can't imagine reducing her hours. Funny, though, it was easy enough for me to reduce my personal trainer from twice a week to once a week to sometimes not at all a week.

Now I feel guilty.

I put down my purse and coat once again, pick up the phone and dial my health club, punching in Claude, my personal trainer's, extension. I leave him a message apologizing for being out of touch and saying I need to set up weekly sessions.

I mean, hell. If Levi is going to have a trainer, I should have my trainer, too, right? After all, I don't want to get on the scale and get a shock.

Chapter Six

I'm running through a fertile field that is green and expansive, running, running, until suddenly I come face to face with a huge white fence. I stop and ponder how to get through. It doesn't make sense, because the fence is really a freestanding door with a black-hinged lock. There is nothing on either side of the door, but somehow it doesn't occur to me that I can just continue running through this field, moving either to the left or the right. I just keep standing at the door, trying to figure out how to break through.

The warm spring air swirls around me and I smell the scent of lilacs on the soft breeze. The sun heats my face, bathing my skin in warmth. I look up and see the blue cloudless sky and I want to fly. I don't want to stand still. I want to move forward, but the door holds me back.

While I stand in front of the fence door, there is another part of me flying above the pasture and watching how this will all unfold. I watch this me/not me woman standing in a white sundress, barefoot, sinking into the grassy field trying to figure out how to find her freedom. The me floating above wonders, "Doesn't she see that the fence door is just an illusion?

"You are only trapped by your mind," I yell to her, but she doesn't hear me. I watch her study the fence door and then turn away, moving slowly back in the direction whence she came; this time, walking, not running, her head hung low.

"Don't go back!" I call to her. "Run again. Run towards something more!" But she doesn't hear, doesn't see. It's as if she is sleepwalking.

I float above weightless, merging with the sky, ethereal. I breathe in and then, like a gust of wind, I breathe out, exhaling my deepest wish for her to find her purpose and freedom, and in that moment she stops. She turns once again to face this fence door and then begins to walk towards it, surveying its details. Inhaling deeply, she raises her right arm to the door and when her hand touches the lock the door simply falls away.

And this me/not me woman begins running free through the great pasture. She is laughing, calling out with pure joy, and the sound is like no sound she's ever made, high pitched and stretching out beyond where she stands, until the sound overtakes everything, takes on an immediacy that jolts her—

I wake up with a jolt to the sound of a siren piercing the night. I squint through the darkness of my bedroom towards the glow of my alarm clock telling me that it's 1:16 a.m. Images of a big grassy field and a fence float in my mind, and I try to catch them to make some sense out of them, but I can't hold on enough to the snippets to recreate the dream. As I pull the blanket over me, feeling lulled back into sleep, I hear another siren mimicking the high-pitched sound I remember hearing in my dream. Seconds later I hear another siren, their screams stabbing the night.

"Gary, are you awake?" I whisper while nudging him a little on the shoulder.

"Mmm," he mutters without waking. I nudge Gary harder on the shoulder.

"Gary, Gary," I say out loud, no longer whispering. He rolls over and nuzzles me. "Gary, can't you hear all of those sirens?" He opens his eyes just as another siren blares through the streets.

"What's going on?" he asks, rubbing the sleep from of his eyes. "What's happening?"

"I don't know," I say to him. "But it's something bad. I've heard a whole bunch of sirens, and I think they're stopping somewhere close." Gary sits up for another minute and then lies back down.

"Go back to sleep, Syd," he tells me. "I'm sure whatever it is, it's under control." He turns his head, and in a second he is back sleeping, his breathing slow and even.

I try to match his breath, and soon I am close to falling asleep again, the background noises punctuated with sirens and the muffled voice of someone speaking through a megaphone. Just as I doze off, the image of the woman in my dream flying high above reappears. This time, after breathing in, I see her exhale a clear mist of breath falling over where I am standing in my white sundress, bare feet squishing in the dewy grass. I hear her voice as if through a megaphone pleading, "Wake up."

Chapter Seven

Ibarely hear Gary leave for his Saturday golf game, so tired am I from a restless night of sleep. In the shower I try to catch snippets of my dream, but they are like soap bubbles, bursting just as soon as you get close to catching one. After drying my hair and dressing for the day, I decide to give up trying to follow this montage of dream snapshots. Instead I focus on my day at the mall, and the new sweaters and boots I am planning on buying. Real things that don't disappear when you get close.

Stepping into the kitchen, I see that Gary has made a pot of coffee before leaving, but there is no newspaper on the kitchen table. I open the front door to retrieve the *Tribune*, and when I look up I see a group of my neighbors standing in the middle of the street in a huddle. It's not a nice day out. The wind is picking up, and the gray November clouds cling to the sky, blocking any possible warmth from the sun that must be hiding there somewhere. The picture of my neighbors standing outside together on a cold bleak Saturday morning doesn't make any more sense than the bits and pieces of my dream that still hover about me. I wonder if Gary will just play the first nine and then call it quits? I hold the paper close to my chest and watch this huddle of women for a second when Monica Jenson calls to me.

"Oh Syd, isn't it terrible?" she asks me, a statement posing as a question.

I feel a gust of wind whip through me, and pull my sweater tighter across my body. I begin to walk toward my neighbors, wondering what the fuss is about. Probably Jill Campbell's husband left again. They are always separating then getting back together, taking off on a Caribbean cruise, then returning home and threatening divorce once again. *If I liked Jill or her husband, Bill, even a little, then maybe I could be more empathic,* I think to myself as I head over to the group. Gary and I both agree that Jill and Bill are as mismatched as a couple can be. The most they share in common are the last three letters

39

of their first names. Crossing over to the neighbors, I put on my concerned look, readying myself to pretend that I care about the next installment of the Jill and Bill show. Frankly, I'd prefer a juicy segment of *Desperate Housewives*.

I look over first to Jill, as I prepare to share the words of support I have offered her over the past years whenever she and Bill were ready to call it quits. There is a bigger turnout than usual, though. Monica is there, along with Doris, Marilyn, Cathy, Amy and Phyllis. Leslie is there, too, who typically never enters into the Jill and Bill drama.

Monica moves through the group and holds me tightly. "It's just so terrible," she says in a shaky voice. Her eyes are red and swollen, and as I look into the faces of the other women on my street, I can see that they, too, have been crying.

"Oh Syd, how could this happen, how could this happen?" she asks me. I just stand there, clueless. I'm still holding the newspaper against my chest, and I find myself wondering if the facts I need to fill in the missing pieces are somewhere in this newsprint.

"Those poor families," Doris says, clasping her hands together. "How do you get through something like this?" Everyone is nodding their heads in agreement, and I feel my stomach lurch, as if my physical body is preparing for the information that my mind has yet to learn. I look into the shattered faces of my neighbors.

"What is it?" I ask. "What's happened?"

Jill takes my hand. "You haven't heard?" she asks.

I shake my head no.

"About the horrible accident? The car accident last night?"

As she asks me this, I suddenly remember waking up from my dream, where I was listening to a strange, high-pitched sound, to the reality of my bed and the screaming sirens somewhere outside. I had gone back to sleep. I shake my head no, and feel my legs weaken, dreading the news I am about to receive.

Monica takes my hand. "There was a horrific accident last night, on the corner of Sycamore and Main. Two seniors from Deer Creek were driving home from a Highland Ridge party. They crashed into a tree. It's horrible, just horrible."

I am listening to Monica's words, trying to focus on what she is saying. Deer Creek, the next town over and Highland Ridge's biggest rivalry.

"There was a big party. Same old story, parents are out of town and word gets out. Since my Stewart started high school this year, I keep telling him to stay away from those parties. You hope they listen, but I don't know. Nothing seems to get through to these kids."

"You hear these stories on TV, you read about them in the news, but you keep thinking, *it can't happen here*," Doris says as she breaks into sobs.

Leslie looks at me, at my blank face that doesn't know what to do, and she begins to fill me in.

"It was a horror. Jack and I couldn't fall back asleep with all of the sirens. We got in the car and drove down to Main Street where the sirens were blaring. It was easy to find where the commotion was coming from, what with the flashing lights of the police cars and the ambulances. There was a small crowd watching, screaming—" Leslie's voice breaks off, and Monica picks up where Leslie left off.

"Brad Jackson, the driver, was pronounced dead on the scene. Just 17 years old. The passenger, Kevin Mann, was rushed to North Shore Hospital, but we haven't learned much about his condition. I know it was critical, very critical."

"He wasn't moving. When he was taken away in the ambulance, you could see he wasn't moving," Leslie says, pain catching in her voice.

"This is horrible," I say, knowing that my words fall thin in the air. Of course it's horrible, but how do you convey the horror? My God, what if this were Rachel? How many times in high school had Rachel been at a big party? I would tell her over and over not to drink, not to get in a car with someone who was drinking. To call Gary and me, no questions asked, if she needed a ride home. And she always came home. Thank God, she always came back safe, alive. But how does a mother live through this? How can a young life be so violently cut short?

"I know the Jacksons," Phyllis tells us. "They're good people. Brad is their youngest, *was* their youngest—we belong to the Unitarian Church with them. I'm going to go over there soon. Reverend Anne is going to hold a special meeting—" Phyllis stops talking as the tears threaten to overtake her. Then she begins again, "Brad was just applying to college. Had his heart set on Duke. Had his whole life ahead of him."

Phyllis says she is going to go home so she can get ready to go to her church and see what needs to be done for the family, and to pray. The rest of us stand around, not knowing what to do with the enormity of the situation. Some of the women are busy making connections to the boys in the accident; how they know of the family through this or that, as if solidifying their ties to this tragedy gives them permission to cry, to feel connected to the mourners, to be part of a whole that is crumbling, so that in the end it might be possible to regenerate.

"Do you know Kevin Mann?" I ask Monica as I watch Phyllis walk towards her driveway.

Monica shakes her head no, but Cathy says that her daughter, a senior at Highland Ridge, knows him. "She said he plays lacrosse, and that her boyfriend, Matt, knows him from the lacrosse clinics they used to take together when they were younger. She told me she's met him a few times, and that he's a real nice kid. She's really broken up about this. She wasn't at the party last night, but she knows people who were there. One minute Brad and Kevin are just two more kids at a big Friday night party, and the next minute one is dead and the other—well who knows if he'll even survive."

Amy tells us that she knows the Manns; they belong to the same tennis club. "Salt of the earth people, that's what they are. Kevin is the oldest. He has a younger sister, Molly, who's in eighth grade." Her voice catches and she stops for a moment. "Kevin used to go out on the courts and hit balls with his sister, give her a few pointers. Poor Maryanne and Jim—how are they going to get through this?"

"It just makes you want to go home and hug your kids," Doris says.

We are all silent, and then Cathy tells us that early this morning her daughter, Megan, drove up to the scene of the accident where a makeshift memorial was already being erected. "Kids hear about things so quickly, what with Facebook and text messaging. News spreads so fast."

As we stand in the middle of the street, waiting for some sign to appear to tell us what to do or what to say, a ray of sunshine struggles to release itself from the cloud-laden sky. We all look up at the same moment, looking, I suppose, for some direction, some hope.

I don't know either of the families, so the broken-heartedness I am experiencing feels as though I'm not entitled to it. The immeasurable sorrow belongs to the boys' families and friends and acquaintances. I am none of these, so I don't know what to do with the tears welling up in my eyes. Eventually our huddle splits apart, the way our hearts have, the way the car must have split upon impact with the tree.

Back in the house, I google Brad Jackson and Kevin Mann, combining my search with words like "Deer Creek," "tennis," "lacrosse." I feel like I need to learn all I can about these boys. My grief needs to have a focus. I feel the need to connect with these boys, to know them in death, if not in life. Midway through my search the phone rings. I answer and hear Jodi's voice on the other end.

"Can you believe what's happened?" she asks.

"I know, it's so terrible," I agree.

"Melanie is a mess. Turns out that a few of the senior boys she sometimes hangs out with are friends with both Brad and Kevin. She said she met them at the Highland Ridge/Deer Creek football game last month. She's on the phone with her friends crying. I don't even know what to say to her. It's just so tragic."

"I know," I say, wondering what Melanie knew of the boys. Were they nice when she met them? Were they good kids?

"And I know alcohol was involved. Thank God Melanie wasn't there. I keep telling her to say away from those parties, but who knows where the kids go. With cell phones, they're at one place, and before you know it they hear about parents out of town and a party going on, and groups of kids start showing up."

I pour myself another cup of coffee, fighting off the fatigue. "You know, Jodi, in some ways it's better with Rachel at Madison. Neither she nor her friends have cars at school. It just makes me feel she's safer there than here, you know? And for some reason, I worry less when she's at school. I have no idea what time she gets home at night, but I don't stress about it like I did when she was here in Highland Ridge."

"So what are you doing today?" Jodie asks.

I tell her that I had been planning on going shopping, but wasn't sure what I was going to do now.

"Why, because of the accident?"

I take a sip of coffee and tell her yes. "It just feels funny to be looking at sweaters and boots on a day like today."

"Syd, it's not like you know them. You can't show up at their door with a noodle kugel. You can't dwell on this. It's awful, jut awful. But our kids are fine. We use this as a lesson to teach our kids to be safe. What else can we do? Now, how about we go on a shopping spree together and then to lunch, my treat," Jodi offers.

I hesitate for a moment. "Do you know anything about Kevin Mann's condition? Has Melanie heard anything?" I ask.

"I think he's in a coma. Syd, you're not a doctor and you're not a reporter. You can't sit home and monitor the condition of someone you don't even know. I'm sure when there's more information to report, we'll hear. It'll be all over town. But there really isn't anything we can do, so we might as well go shopping," Jodi says. "I'll come pick you up in half an hour."

I hang up the phone and sit back down at the computer, resuming my Google search of Brad and Kevin. I say only their first names to myself, as if now we are old friends. As if I've known them for years, instead of only hearing about them just this morning, one of them dead before I even knew his name. Both honor students, both athletes; Brad a lacrosse star and Kevin the captain of the tennis team.

JODI AND I SPEND THE DAY at the mall. A creature of habit, I lose myself in the merchandise and find an incredible pair of brown leather boots, and beautiful cardigan and cashmere sweaters. Jodi finds a great pair of jeans and a black suede blazer that looks fabulous on her. We have lunch, splurge on dessert. "We can make up for the calories by eating just salad for dinner," Jodi assures me.

As we step outside, the sun has broken through and it has become a brilliant, crisp fall day. But walking toward Jodi's car, shopping bags in hand, the brilliant day mocks the tragedy. How are the Jackson and Mann families bearing their pain?

After Jodi drops me off at home, I see that Gary has left me a note: *Went to the gym for a workout. How about dinner at Café Louis tonight?* I schlep my shopping bags upstairs and begin to hang up my new clothes. I rub the fabric against my skin, willing the softness of the cashmere to envelope me in a cocoon, keeping me safe from a world where bad things happen. Then I run down the stairs, grab my keys, and head to my car.

I drive slowly down my street, letting the car direct me to where I know I need to go. Soon I am traveling down Sycamore, where I can see a crowd gathered on the intersection at Main Street. As I inch closer, I see teenagers and parents hugging and crying.

Around the tree is a huge yellow ribbon, and tacked to the tree are dozens of bouquets, water bottles, and poster boards covered with messages from friends in different colored markers. Teddy bears surround the tree along with pictures of the boys, Deer Creek High School flags, and lit candles. Lying at the edge of the tree are a lacrosse stick and a tennis racket.

I drive past slowly, trying to take in everything, knowing that I don't belong here but feeling such a pull to be here. I turn right on Main Street, and I feel the tears streaming down my face. I drive another block up Main Street, turn right, then turn right again so that I'm back on Sycamore, inching my way back toward the makeshift memorial, back to the tree adorned with the yellow ribbon. I drive past it again, this time quicker, trying to take it all in at once, like I did as a kid when I gasped for a big breath before going under in Lake Michigan.

As I pull into my driveway crying, I try to calm myself by breathing in and slowly exhaling. For a moment, an image from my dream appears, a woman hovering overhead, but I can't catch it. What I'm left with, though, is the feeling that there is something just out of reach, something that I should know, but I don't know, or something that maybe I once knew but forgot. Almost like my heart understands something, but my mind doesn't yet have the words to give it form.

I get out of my car and head into the house. I pick up the phone and call Rachel. She doesn't answer, so I leave her a message: "Hi, it's me. Just wanted to tell you that I love you." Instead of hanging up the phone right away, I hold it first, over my heart.

Chapter Eight

FATAL CAR CRASH LEAVES ONE DEAD, ONE IN COMA

A deadly car crash in Highland Ridge involving two seniors from Deer Creek High School occurred early yesterday morning. Brad Jackson, 17, was killed on impact. The passenger, 17-year-old Kevin Mann, is at North Shore Hospital. According to a hospital spokesperson, Mann suffered an isolated head injury and is in a coma.

Police are investigating the crash, and at this point have not said whether excessive speed and/or alcohol were involved.

Bernard Atkins, Superintendent of Deer Creek Public Schools, stated, "Our hearts go out to the Jackson and Mann families, and the entire community, at this tragic loss."

Deer Creek High School will be open today, and grief counselors will be available at the school throughout the week.

I FINISH reading the news clip in the Metro section of the Sunday *Tribune*. "There's so much more to say, isn't there?" I ask.

Gary is changing a light bulb in the kitchen recessed lighting. "Here, take this," he says as he hands me the old bulb.

"So much grief in so few paragraphs," I say. I watch Gary finish screwing in the bulb as I throw the old one out.

"It's the Chicago paper. I'm sure the *North Shore Weekly* on Thursday will have a big piece on it." I watch him toast a bagel. "Want one?" he asks.

I shake my head no. For once, I don't have an appetite.

Gary spreads veggie cream cheese on his bagel and takes a bite. Through his chewing he tells me that he saw his friend Craig on his morning run. Craig's an ER doctor at Chicago Central. *He's no George Clooney*, I had thought when

I first met him, *but if I had to have someone checking my vitals he'd still make my pulse race.* Gary sucks a bit of cream cheese off his finger. "He told me that typically, if a kid doesn't wake up from a coma within the first few days, it's really dire; could end up with brain damage, or not make it out of the coma at all."

Wake up, Kevin, wake up, Kevin, wake up, Kevin. Every part of my mind and body is pulsating with this longing. Wake up, wake up, wake up!

"So Rachel didn't know them?" Gary asks me.

I'm watching Levi pining away for a bite of Gary's bagel. I wish Levi could read my nonverbal expressions, that somehow Levi would understand that he isn't being withheld some bagel and cream cheese because he's done something wrong, but because Gary thinks that dogs should only eat dog food. Levi doesn't get the whole *it's our secret* thing.

"No," I say as I pat Levi's head, hoping that love and affection will feed his hungry heart. "But I know she's been on Facebook talking with a lot of friends about what's happened. She said there was an RIP Brad Jackson Facebook group that people had joined and were writing on, and a Facebook prayer page for Kevin."

After Gary finishes eating, he asks me what I'm up to.

"I'm not sure," I answer, feeling that for the past 24 hours I haven't known what to do with myself. "Did you want to do something together?"

He tells me that he has some work to do for Monday, a big merger in the works. "Maybe a movie tonight?" he asks.

"Maybe," I say.

While Gary settles himself with his work I find myself pacing, unable to settle down. "I'm going out for a walk," I yell to Gary as I grab my fleece jacket.

Levi looks at me with such longing in his face. "Take me with you," he must be saying. I go back to the kitchen, grab a small piece of muffin, and offer it to Levi. He eats it, but he still looks pissed. I refuse to look back at his longing face as I step outside and begin to walk.

I don't see any of my neighbors outside, and I wonder what they are doing with the grief. Where are they finding comfort? The crunch of the leaves underfoot feels reassuring to me. Crunch, *I am still here,* crunch, *I can make sound,* crunch, *I can be crumbled to nothing*—okay, that thought doesn't reassure me at all. That thought makes me think about life and its fragility. Of Brad and Kevin.

"*Wake up, Kevin,*" I pray in a whisper as I continue walking with no plan or destination in sight. *Wake up, wake up, wake up.* I feel my heart pound with each step as I kick through the leaves, spreading them off course as if trying to alter their destiny.

Last night Jodi and her husband, Dave, had joined us at Café Louis. Jodi told us that Melanie had joined a group of kids who headed over to Deer Creek High School, where a candlelight vigil was held in memory of Brad Jackson, and prayers for Kevin Mann. My eyes had welled up then, and I found myself wishing that I were there, too, that I was holding that grief in community. Gary and Dave had ordered another bottle of wine, and not having any other thoughts about what to do with profound sorrow, when the bottle came I let Gary pour me another glass.

After a few blocks I find myself at Lincoln, Rachel's old elementary school. I stop and look at the solid brick building that now looks so small. I can remember when Rachel first started kindergarten. "It's so big, Mommy," she had said when I brought her here a few days before school started to meet her teacher and to show her around.

And it *had* seemed so big then, so big for my little girl, who now would have part of her world away from me. I can see her skipping out of school carrying her Sesame Street lunch box. It was a second ago, wasn't it? Walking her up those steps every morning? Standing on the grassy little hill each afternoon waiting to see her face as she walked out the door?

I blink back the tears as I walk up to the place against the tree where I used to wait for her. I close my eyes, and for a moment I allow myself to move back in time.

I see a younger version of myself, and I see Rachel at six years old. I follow her growing through the years as she moves on from Lincoln to Fernwood Middle School. I can see Gary and me sitting at her high school graduation, Rachel holding up her diploma and flashing us her beautiful smile, and then there she is, waving goodbye to us in front of her college dorm.

I slide down against the tree and I start to cry. I cry for the miracle of the very existence of Rachel, for the very fact of her being. I cry for the memories I hold of her when she was a little girl at this school, and I cry for the reality that as much as you love someone, you can't always keep them safe. I cry for Brad and Kevin, for a life cut short and a life hanging in the balance, and with tears flowing I pray that Kevin wakes up.

And then I can't stop. It's like a dam has burst. My crying has become violent and rendered almost silent, my body heaving and caving into itself, my shoulders collapsing and shaking as my chest takes in the convulsing sobs. I try to catch my breath, but the choking gasps have taken on a life of their own. My nose is running and the snot is mixing with the tears and I wish I had a tissue but I don't, so I use the sleeve of my fleece and I cry into its warmth.

Where are all these tears coming from?

Images of Rachel flash before me, along with thoughts of the tree draped with remembrances and prayers for Brad and Kevin, and I shut my eyes tight because I don't want to see anymore, can't let myself see anymore. But my eyes see inward and then I know. I know these tears are about more than Rachel, more than Brad and Kevin.

And then her little face is before me, and I breathe in deeply, shakily, and let out a deep wail as I hug my arms around my knees and rock back and forth. All those years ago and here she is and I know that the long buried pain has been picked at and gnawed at and has now been exhumed. I know that I am finally crying for my little sister, baby Rae, who at six weeks old one day simply didn't wake up.

I REMEMBER her face, her smile that dad said was really from gas, but I knew, even at the age of three, that she was smiling at me. One morning I heard my mother scream and I remember my dad rushing to the nursery, and then it's all a blur.

The next memory I have is awakening at night to the sound of my parents' voices. I walk to their room and sit down outside of their closed bedroom door. Mommy is crying out to Daddy, "Rae's gone, she's gone! I can't bear it, how can I bear it?" And I hear Daddy, but instead of his strong, steady voice, he's sobbing and they are both wailing and moaning and begging God to bring baby Rae back. I go to my room, get in bed, and hold on to Mr. Bear. I am scared and I cry myself back to sleep.

A little while after the night I heard my parents crying in their room I remember asking mommy, "Where's baby Rae?"

Mommy scoops me in her arms, puts me in the car, and takes me to the bakery. She lets me pick out anything I want. I choose a chocolate cupcake with vanilla frosting and sprinkles. I want my Mommy to smile again. I hold the cupcake up to her mouth and she takes a bite.

I FLASH on a memory from when I was ten years old.

"Mom, Rae would have been seven years old now. I wish I had my baby sister."

My mother looks at me and I see tears well up in her eyes that she quickly blinks away. "Let's go to the mall, Syd. We'll have a special mother and daughter day. We'll buy some nice new clothes and then we'll splurge on cheeseburgers and shakes and I'll start my diet again tomorrow!"

I love my Mom. We shop, we lunch, and she tells me about calories.

I HUG my knees into my chest and think about the unspoken grief of baby Rae's death. I followed my parents' lead; the rare occasions when I mentioned my dead sister turned into no occasions at all.

For a while when I was 10, 11, 12 years old, I would lock my bedroom door and write poems about love and loss, pose questions about life and death and God and the meaning of it all. I never told anyone I wrote like this, never showed them to a soul. I stuffed all of those writings in a shoebox and hid them in the back of my closet, in the same way, I think to myself now, that maybe I've used food to stuff away my feelings. By the time I was in middle school I stopped writing and began dieting. My friends and I turned our attention to our looks, clothes and boys. I followed the path of my parents; suffering was something you either buried or took refuge from in the world of material offerings. Isn't that what Jodi and I had done only yesterday by going to the mall?

I look up again at Rachel's old school, and I flash on the moments after her birth.

"We named her Rachel," I say to my parents as they hold their newborn granddaughter.

They look at me, and repeat her name. "Rae-chel," I hear them say, the first syllable of her name a quick catch in their voices.

Was this my attempt at *Tikkum Olam*, at mending the world?

I sit like this for a while, lost in the mosaic of memories that make up my baby sister's brief life. When I finally get up and brush the dirt off from my jeans, feeling empty and spent, I walk to the playground in the back of the school.

There are a few kids playing on new equipment; bright, colorful configurations of mazes, winding slides and the requisite swings. I watch them squealing with delight, the familiar sounds of children at play. I look over to the bench and see two young mothers talking, one of them pregnant. I hear the beginning of a long forgotten song playing in my head:

I was swinging on the swings when I was a little girl,
Trying to get a handle on this big, wide world.
When I noticed all the grass in the cracks of the concrete,
I said, "Where there's a will, there's a way around anything."
Life holds on
Given the slightest chance.

I head home thinking of that old game *Don't step on a crack or it will break your mother's back,* and I find myself trying to avoid the cracks. But can you really avoid those inner cracks forever? As I turn down our street I purposely step on a crack, negating my careful avoidance on the previous blocks.

I'm looking down into the sidewalk and I hear Gary before I see him.

"Syd! I was just looking for you," he says, jogging up to me. Gary grabs my hand. "Jodi called to tell you that she just heard that Kevin is out of the coma. He just woke up."

I inhale and exhale deeply. "He's going to be okay, then?"

"Sounds like it," Gary says. "She said to call her as soon as you can."

I stop in front of the potted mum on my neighbor's walkway, deep purple and still flowering with an unlikely new bloom clinging to the stem, so close to winter's chill.

Life holds on.

Given the slightest chance.

Chapter Nine

Sometimes I think I try to avoid the cracks by clinging to the familiar. The emptiness of Rachel leaving, the accident, the unspoken grief of baby Rae—I don't know how to touch that heartache, how to give it voice, or where to reach out. So I turn away from that pain, seek comfort in the familiar routines and rituals.

"There's no time like the present," we all agreed at Mah Jongg the other week. "We can't keep putting off our goals. We have to start today." And for us, that meant staying on our diets.

I've been working out at the health club, both with and without Claude, staying at about 1500 calories a day, and losing weight. With Thanksgiving tomorrow, I will harness all of my willpower to stay on my diet.

The water is boiling and I drop the lasagna noodles in the pot. I wonder if other families have three different entrees on Thanksgiving. I think it was my mother who started it years ago when she would host Thanksgiving. In fact, I can't remember a Thanksgiving where the menu ever varied, so she probably was doing this before I was even born. Now that I have taken over Thanksgiving, who am I to try something new?

I just follow the plan and cook the spinach lasagna (I think that tradition started because of my great-uncle Nathan, who was a vegetarian. He died when I was like eight, but every year mom continued to bake the lasagna as part of our Thanksgiving, so who am I to question?), make the brisket (yes, you heard me, brisket), and of course, roast the turkey.

The lasagna and brisket I can make today so that all I'll have to focus on tomorrow is the turkey, and that's pretty much Gary's domain. Somehow I could never get the hang of putting my hand up the turkey and stuffing it, or tying the legs. It all looks so raw and naked. I prefer my food to look as removed from the source as possible.

My parents flew in from their home in Boca Raton on Monday to spend Thanksgiving with us, and Mom insists that they are settled in enough in their Highland Ridge condo that she can make her green bean casserole and her mashed potatoes, so all I have to do tomorrow is make the cranberry sauce and bake the sweet potatoes. Gary's parents are flying in from Florida this evening and will be staying with my parents. Then they'll all fly back to Florida on Saturday to avoid spending a Sunday at O'Hare with the delays and cancellations that inevitably occur.

Fred and Arlene Kaufman, Gary's parents, sold their home in Scarsdale three years ago to live on the West Coast of Florida, in Longboat Key, full time. Gary's older sister, Nancy, and her husband, Evan, moved to Palm Beach soon after Evan made a fortune when his company went public. My brother in-law and sister-in-law took up the activities of the prematurely retired. They played golf together, traveled to the Caribbean at the drop of a hat, and went skiing in Aspen for their version of winter getaways. Sometimes they waited in line for their coffee behind Donald Trump.

Their children, Jenny and Joshua, are fraternal twins who are graduating from college this year. They had talked this past summer about spending Thanksgiving with us, but then they were invited to spend the holiday with close family friends who have children that Jenny and Joshua grew up with. The fact that the family had invited them to celebrate Thanksgiving at their timeshare in St. Martin didn't make the decision very hard for them, I imagine. It's a dreary and drizzly 38 degrees in Highland Ridge today. Plus, Nancy sees her parents in Florida frequently enough, and though Gary gets along with Nancy, the two have never spent a ton of time together. By the time Gary started high school Nancy was already in her second year of college.

When the children were younger, we established a nice pattern of visiting them once a year during the winter. Rachel always loved visiting her Aunt Nancy and Uncle Evan, and was fully enthralled with the idea of having two big cousins; the fact that they were twins only intrigued her all the more. But just like the age difference between Gary and Nancy, the cousins spent less time together as the years went by. When Jenny and Joshua began college, our visits to Palm Beach dwindled. And now that Gary's parents have moved to the West Coast of Florida, a whole new dynamic is set up where each set of grandparents, we suspect, are measuring any differential in our love by which coast we are buying airline tickets to.

I finish spreading the last two cups of cheese over the lasagna and put it in the oven when I hear footsteps coming down the stairs. My heart quickens. God, I've missed her.

"Good morning, did you sleep well?" I ask. There was a terrible traffic jam on Interstate 94 last night, and Rachel's bus didn't pull in until about 10:30, an hour and a half later than it had been due to arrive. On the 20-minute drive to our house she had told us about her friends and her classes, about her decision over whether she should be a political science major or go into communications. When we got home I suggested we make some hot chocolate and spend more time talking and catching up. She had walked into the house and Levi received a greeting that makes a mother wish, for a moment, that she were her child's pet. Gary followed Levi and Rachel up the stairs carrying her suitcase, while I trailed behind. She flopped on her bed and, lying on her back, smiled at us, saying how good it was to be home.

"I'll get the hot chocolate started," I had said, smiling at this perfect reunion. My heart felt full.

"Oh, I can't sit and have hot chocolate. I'm already late. I'm leaving in a second," Rachel said.

I looked at Gary, who tells me he'd be happy to have hot chocolate with me. "When did you make plans? Where are you going?" I asked her.

"I was texting while we were driving home, and I'm going to Keith's house. Everyone is just getting in from school, and I can't wait to see them," she said, smiling.

She's happy and healthy, I said to myself. *No need for your heart to deflate, no need at all.*

"And Tammy got home like a half an hour ago, so I'm just meeting her there," she added. Tammy and Rachel have been best friends since kindergarten. Rachel got up from her bed and began brushing her hair, and spraying on her Burberry perfume.

"What time do you think you'll be home?" I had asked.

"I had forgotten about this," Rachel had said.

"About what?" I asked.

"About this 'when will I be home' business. I'm in college now. You don't have to worry."

I gave Gary a look.

"Okay, Rachel, your Mom and I are your parents. We're always going to worry. But just give us a time so Mom won't stay up ringing her hands and will let me get some sleep," Gary said.

"How about I'll be home or call by 2:00?" Rachel answered.

My face fell. The image of a car crashing into a tree was still fresh in my mind. The makeshift memorial on the intersection of Sycamore and Main had only gotten bigger over the past few weeks.

"I hate when you go out that late. I worry about you. I worry because I love you so much," I said, hugging her.

"Maybe you can love me a little less?" she had asked, smiling.

We've said those lines to each other since she was little. I'll never forget the first time she said this to me. It was when she started kindergarten, and I thought the equipment on the school playground seemed unsafe. Rachel had asked me why I worried so much, and I told her it was because I loved her so much. She had taken my hand in hers and brought it up to her cheek, saying, "then maybe you should love me a little less." I remember that moment like it was yesterday. Yet here she was, home from college, and somehow the years have gone by. *Love her a little less?* I thought to myself. *Impossible.*

"I promise we'll have time to see each other. I'm home all weekend," she had said, offering me a hug in lieu of a curfew.

I heard the garage door open a little after 2:00, and only then did I fully allow myself to drift off soundly.

SHE PULLS out a carton of orange juice from the refrigerator and reaches for a glass from the cabinet, then gets out a bowl for her Cheerios. Rachel and Gary have always been big Cheerios fans. Even when she was little, she liked Cheerios more than Fruit Loops or Frosted Flakes. I still like Fruit Loops and Frosted Flakes better. I'm like the Peter Pan consumer of cereal.

"So what are your plans today?" I ask, hoping that I can take her shopping and out to lunch.

"Me and Tammy are going—"

I interrupt her. "Tammy and I are going—'"

" Ugh, Mom. I hate when you do this."

"I'm telling you, that's the surest way to blow a job interview."

"So you've told me. Do you want to know my plans, or do you want to talk grammar?"

"Is this a trick question?" I ask.

"Okay, Mom, this is what I don't miss. So, Tammy and *I* are going to pick up Andrea and go to the high school to visit, and then we're going to go out for lunch, and then we're going to just hang."

"Sounds fun. Will I get to see you later this afternoon?" I venture.

"Sure, if you want me to be around, just tell me."

"Well, I thought it would be fun to go to Starbucks or something and have a fun coffee drink and talk. I want to hear all about college," I tell her, willing to settle for a Cliffs Notes version of the day I had wished to spend with her.

"Yeah, that sounds good. Then can we stop at the Shoe Boutique? I need a new pair of Uggs."

"You got it!" I tell her as I check on the lasagna.

While Rachel runs upstairs to finish getting ready, the phone rings.

It's Gary.

"Hi, Syd. I thought I'd head home early from work, so you and I could take Rachel to lunch," he says happily.

I laugh.

"What?" he asks.

"You know at the deli counter, how you have to stand in line and take a number?"

"Yeah."

"So, hon, take a number and get in line."

Chapter Ten

I wake up early, but apparently Gary woke up even earlier. The warm morning light shining through the skylights is deceiving; the clear blue sky could easily pass for July. I sit up and roll my neck, and then stretch it from side to side.

The clicking of my joints is relatively new. It started last spring. Initially, it felt good. I felt like I was realigning myself. Then it became an addictive habit. Now I worry I have arthritis, which I figure I'm making worse by my morning ritual of cracking.

I get out of bed, go the bathroom, pull on my bathrobe and head downstairs. Mmmm, I smell coffee. I pull out a mug decorated with polka dots, shoes and handbags that reads *Whoever said money can't buy happiness doesn't know where to shop,* which my mom bought for me years ago. As I take my first sip I hear the door open and Gary walks in, cheeks red and sweat on his brow.

"We've lucked out; it's beautiful today," he says as he walks in and closes the front door. Levi comes rushing up to him, sniffing his running pants.

"Did you bring in the paper yet?" I ask.

"No, I'll go get it."

As Gary opens the door Levi runs out, and I yell to Gary to get the dog. He starts to run after him, and then turns around to face me in the doorway. "Wait, we put in the Invisible Fence."

"Yeah, but I don't always trust it yet. When I let Levi out, I usually go with him."

"Doesn't that defeat the purpose?" he asks.

I push past him and run out in the yard to make sure Levi hasn't escaped or gotten a shock. At first I don't see him, but then I hear the crunch of leaves and trace the sound to the side of the house.

"Levi, come inside for a treat," I yell to him, and he comes running. Gary is watching us and shaking his head.

"What?" I ask, as Levi follows me inside.

"You're going to make him fat with all the Milk-Bones you give him," Gary says as he pulls off his running shoes.

He should only know what Levi and I eat together. The other day I discovered that Levi shares my affinity for hummus.

After a quick cup of coffee and a quicker glance at the paper, I head up for my shower. I let the warm water pulsate on my head and neck, hopefully easing the arthritis I have diagnosed myself as now having. I pick up the first of many products containing promises: shampoos offering glossy, lustrous hair, shaving gel guaranteeing silky smooth legs, shower gels that offer scented, soft skin. I admit that I do feel guilty sometimes when I hear about droughts and water shortages when I'm taking my really long showers. But frankly, my dear, while I do give a damn, I can't let my routine go, and my conditioner needs time to set in.

I follow up my shower with more promising products: scented lotions and moisturizers, spritzes of perfume.

I apply my make up, blow-dry my hair, and follow up with a hair straightener for insurance against any chance of humidity. Flipping through the hangers in my closet, I choose a pair of Seven jeans, a pale blue cotton camisole under a brown V-neck cashmere, and my brown suede boots. I add a pair of turquoise earrings and a large silver turquoise necklace that sets off the line of my sweater. I feel that adding the turquoise accessories to my outfit today fits in nicely with the whole Thanksgiving mood, what with the Native Americans and all.

I hear Gary calling me from downstairs. "Syd, you're missing the Macy's Thanksgiving Day Parade."

"Shh," I call out in a whisper from the landing. "You'll wake Rachel." I go downstairs and find Gary in the family room stoking a fire. It smells warm and cozy. I give him a hug and ask him if I missed the Snoopy float.

He ruffles my hair and says, "No, I haven't seen Snoopy yet, but you did miss Tigger and Eeyore."

"Oh, shoot," I say, pulling away from him and smoothing my hair. "I love those guys. I just wish Disney would try Eeyore on Prozac or something. You know, depression can be treated."

I look over to the kitchen, where I can see Gary has been preparing. "Thanks for doing the turkey. I'd say it looks great, but the whole thing kind of grosses me out," I tell him.

"You love turkey sandwiches," Gary says. "I still don't get it."

"I've told you this a thousand times. When I eat turkey on a sandwich, it feels very removed from being a real turkey. It's just thin meat between slices of Swiss cheese and lettuce. Not a leg or wing to be seen."

Gary walks into the kitchen and gets ready to put the bird, as he calls it, in the preheated oven. "But you do know that the slices of turkey you use on your sandwich come from this," he says, waving his hand as if presenting the turkey before he puts it in the oven.

"I'm aware of this fact intellectually. I just refuse to take it in emotionally." I grab a cereal bar with another cup of coffee and move into the family room to enjoy the parade while sitting by the fire.

I figure if I eat a cereal bar for breakfast, and have a Slim-Fast shake for lunch, I can relax and enjoy Thanksgiving dinner. I've been having what I call my "thinner week," and I'd like to do whatever I can to keep it that way, despite the four different pies I have in the extra fridge downstairs. Jodi, Dave and the kids are joining us for dessert later.

I notice that something feels different in our house. Quieter. I don't hear paws on the hardwood floors. I don't hear any barking.

"Where's Levi?" I ask Gary as I get up to look for him. Maybe he's in the basement. He loves lying on the old leather couch.

Gary smiles. "I'll have you know," he begins, "that Levi has been outside in the yard by himself for the past hour. Ever since you went up to shower."

"Really?" I ask. "Have you checked on him?"

"Syd, he's fine. You've just got to learn to let go," he says, a bit too patronizing.

"Isn't that what I've been doing ever since we dropped Rachel off at college? Learning to let go?" I ask.

I open the front door and see Levi sunning himself in the yard, lying so flat in the grass that he looks like a feather, his fur all spread out. When a kid walks his collie in front of our house, Levi gets up and begins running and barking, but only along the perimeter of the yard. He doesn't run out in the street, or even attempt to go past where he knows he must stay to avoid any shock. Our training and homework has paid off. He's mastered Distractions.

"Wow, we've come a long way. We might have gotten kicked out of obedience school, but Levi has figured this thing out," I say excitedly.

"Yep, he's got his freedom," Gary says.

"Levi, do you want to come inside for a treat?" I yell to him. He picks his head up, looks at me, walks around in a circle, and then settles back to his spot in the sun and plops himself down. I shrug my shoulders, close the front door and then busy myself with Thanksgiving preparations.

I set the table using a gold threaded tablecloth, forest green sheer table runner and festive autumn dishes from Pottery Barn. First I put out the metallic forest green dinner plates, and then lay the gold metallic salad plates on top. To the side I place the bread dishes that are in the shape of a leaf and alternate in colors: gold, green and a reddish maple. The wide-rimmed water glasses are crystal with gold rims, and the wine glasses have a gold stem. I fold each gold cloth napkin with silverware and a gold leaf napkin ring and place it atop each place setting.

I stand back and observe the table for color and balance. Then I go into the kitchen to get the centerpiece, a large glass vase filled with cranberries and white roses, and a small beaded wreath, and walk back into the dining room. I place the wreath in the middle of the table, and fit the cranberry/rose filled vase in its middle.

Perfect.

"The table looks great," Gary says as he walks over and puts his arm around me. "Nothing like having a nice, small gathering, without having to put a leaf in the table."

We both look as Rachel comes bounding down the stairs.

"Morning," she says.

"Happy Thanksgiving," Gary and I say in unison.

"The Macy's Day Parade is almost over, you wanna watch?" I ask.

"Can't," she says. "Me and Tammy are going to meet some friends for coffee."

"You mean 'Tammy and I,'" Gary begins before I interrupt him.

I shake my head and laugh, but it comes out more like a snort. "I've tried, but I only get short-term results," I offer. "Like my diets," I add.

"Why don't you have coffee here? I've made a whole pot," Gary says to Rachel with a glimmer of hope in his voice.

"We're going to Dunkin' Donuts. Their Dunkaccinos are really good, and they always have those holiday frosted donuts," Rachel says as she pulls on her new chestnut-colored Uggs.

"Well, be careful with the donuts. Empty calories. Maybe tomorrow we can go for a run together?" Gary ventures.

Rachel gives him a smile. "Sure, maybe," she says. "Oh, and Tammy wants to come over for dessert tonight, around 5:00, is that okay?"

"Oh, honey, we'd love it," I say. "It's so strange without you home, and getting used to your friends not being around either. I've missed Tammy a lot." I don't tell her that I've also missed the pizza bagels, Pop Tarts and cookie dough ice cream.

"Great! I'll be home before everyone gets here," she says as she heads out the door.

"Wait," I say, and hand her a coat. She puts it on and grabs her keys from the hook by the door and heads out.

"It's so good to have her home," I say to Gary. *Even though she's hardly here for more than twenty minutes at a time,* I think to myself.

Gary tells me that Rachel seems like she's really happy, and that he's so pleased that she looks as though she hasn't gained a single pound.

Chapter Eleven

"Oh my God, the dog is running loose in the yard," my mother says as she walks into my house. "You look wonderful, Syd. You even look thinner than the other day."

"Levi, Levi, come here," my dad is yelling as he balances two casserole dishes in his arms.

Rachel runs to the door. "Hi Nana, hi Papa," she says as she takes a casserole dish out of my father's hands. "Don't worry about Levi, he's fine. Mom put in an Invisible Fence."

"Well, she must have, because I don't see it," my dad says. To me he adds, "Fred and Arlene wanted to drive separately. Arlene had one of her headaches and she didn't want to make anyone leave early on her account if she didn't feel well later."

I see my in-laws coming down the street driving my father's BMW and I give a wave.

"Max, doesn't Syd look like she's lost weight?" my mom asks.

"She looks wonderful, like the princess she is, and so does Rachel," my father says.

"Rachel, why don't you and Papa go inside and put the vegetables and potatoes in the kitchen," I say. My dad puts his arm around Rachel and says, "It was so good seeing you yesterday when you stopped over, but you were in and out so fast I almost got whiplash following you in and out the door."

Rachel kisses my dad's cheek and he puts his arm around her, giving her a squeeze, holding the casserole dish with one hand.

"Be careful," I yell to him as he heads inside. "Use both hands."

"So what diet are you on?" my mom asks. "It's obviously working. I need to go back on my diet as soon as the holidays are over."

Before I can answer, the BMW pulls in front of the house, and my mom runs out to greet them. I yell for Gary, telling him his parents are here. He stops to give my father a hug in the hallway and comes outside, where he joins my mom with more welcome hugs. Then it's my turn, and I hug and kiss my father-in-law and mother-in-law. Well, I don't actually kiss my mother-in-law—I kiss the air next to her cheek, and she kisses the air next to my cheek, and we call it an intimate gesture.

"Where is she?" my father-in-law and mother-in-law call out.

Rachel comes running out of the kitchen. "Grandma, Grandpa, hi!" she says, giving them hugs.

"Will you look at her? A college girl!" my mother-in-law says.

"So grown up!" my father-in-law adds.

"Oh, I wish Jenny and Joshua could have been here. You and your cousins would have so much to talk about. You know, the college years are your best years, but they go by so fast. Just think, this May both Jenny and Joshua will be graduating, both of them Phi Beta Kappa," my mother-in-law says with pride.

Rachel and my father-in-law join my dad and Gary in the family room, a football game blaring from the TV. My mother is pulling Arlene into the living room to show her the new sofa and hutch. My mother's voice trails behind her. "Isn't this something?' I hear her say, as my mother-in-law murmurs appreciative sounds. "I've always said she could be an interior decorator. She has such a knack for it, doesn't she?"

My mother-in-law nods as she runs her finger across the smooth finish of the hutch. "You should see what Nancy and Evan have done to their home. They added on a home theatre with actual stadium seating. And their new living room is simply magnificent—Nancy's decorator just told her that *Coastal Living* wants to feature their home in the summer issue!"

I see my mother grimace as my father-in-law calls out, "Arlene, come here." She walks back through the dining room, past the kitchen and on into the family room, stopping to smell the mixture of roasting turkey and brisket in the oven. I can't tell if she approves of the aroma or not.

"Arlene, listen, Gary's explaining to me all about that TiVo contraption we keep hearing about."

Arlene sits down in the oversized chair, saying, "I don't understand that whole thing, not the contraption and not the grammar of it. In my Mah Jongg group, Sarah Goldenberg talks about all of the shows she's TiVoing, like it's a verb."

We all make ourselves comfortable, my mother sitting beside my dad and Gary on the couch while I sit down on the arm of the loveseat by my father-in-law and Rachel relaxes on the chaise lounge. Levi plops himself on the floor beside Rachel, content to have Rachel petting him.

"I'm telling you guys, it's so easy to use, and when Evan and Nancy visit, Evan can set it up for you. That way you can record your shows and watch anytime you want," Gary explains. "Or you can watch a show live through the TiVo, pause it whenever you want to get a nosh, answer the phone, or use the bathroom, then press play and the show is exactly where you left off."

I wonder if Gary is recommending their stock; he sure knows how to pitch it to the senior set.

"You know, Rachel pipes in, "Me and my roommate couldn't survive without TiVo."

"'My roommate and I,'" both sets of grandparents say in unison.

I get up and go to the kitchen, returning with a tray of appetizers: mini quiches, a sliced baguette and brie, grapes and olives. I set it down on the coffee table, along with plates and cocktail napkins.

"Enough of this technology talk. Tell us, Rachel, how is school? We want to hear everything!" my mother exclaims as she reaches for a quiche and takes a bite. "Delicious," she pronounces.

Everyone else reaches for the food, and I feel virtuous, because I don't.

Rachel spreads some brie on a slice of bread and then proceeds to tell us all about her roommate (Melissa from San Diego), her sorority (Alpha Epsilon Phi), and her classes. About the guys next door (what are their last names, my mother and mother-in-law ask in unison, which is code, of course, for "are they Jewish?"), the parties and the food. It seems that she and her friends prefer eating out rather than eating in the dorm, which explains the many restaurant charges Gary receives on his Visa bill. Apparently at college Rachel has developed a love of sushi, and frequents Italian and Mediterranean eateries.

"In my day," my father begins, "we ate the rubbery Salisbury steak served at the dorm, and on occasion, we splurged on pizzas."

"Oh, we splurge on pizza, too, but that's not really a meal thing. It's more an after-bar thing."

Gary and I exchange a look, hoping to move on to the next subject. "Whoa! Look at that fumble!" Gary says, turning toward the game.

None of her grandparents look at the TV. I shoot Gary a look that says, "Hey, you gave it a good shot."

"Bars?" Gary's mother says. "Isn't the drinking age 21 years old? You can't go into bars."

"Oh no, Grandma, it's fine. Everyone goes to the bars," Rachel explains.

"If everyone was jumping off a cliff, would you jump too?" she asks.

"No, I'm afraid of heights," Rachel says.

"I see she has your sense of humor, Syd," my mother-in-law says.

"Is that good or bad?" I ask.

"Okay, okay, listen. Grandma, everyone has a fake ID to get into the bars, but it's more so we can dance than drink. I mean, I might have a beer, but that's all. Really, I'm fine."

"I'm sure that Evan and Nancy didn't condone Jenny and Joshua drinking before they were of legal age."

Rachel looks briefly in my direction and rolls her eyes. I follow suit by giving a look to Gary, who then stands up and asks, "Who of legal age would like a drink?"

My mother-in-law asks for a glass of Chardonnay, and my mother says she'll have the same. Then she starts giggling.

"What's so funny?" Rachel asks.

"It's just this commercial I heard the other day. They were advertising a wine called Fat Bastard. A woman announces that she loves to climb into a tub with a little Fat Bastard. I'm intrigued. I'd like to see what a Fat Bastard's like."

"Hey, you've already got one!" my father says, pulling her up from the couch and dancing her around.

My mother-in-law clenches her jaw.

"And you're all worried about me?" Rachel laughs.

I notice my mother-in-law give my father-in-law a look. He, in return, refuses to acknowledge the look, and instead turns his attention to the football game. Gary finishes taking drink orders and heads over to the bar to prepare the drinks. Rachel's cell phone rings, and she heads into the dining room, where the reception is better, to take her call.

I get up and go into the kitchen to make sure that everything is cooking and reheating in unison. My mother comes in behind me and whispers, "Arlene is acting so smug again. You've noticed, haven't you?"

Before I can answer my mother-in-law walks into the kitchen, and right on cue my mother grabs her hand and says, "Isn't this so wonderful, all of us being together like this?"

Arlene smiles and nods as she inspects the brisket and asks me if I think that maybe I've overcooked it.

"You know what, Gary?" I call into the family room, "I'll take that glass of wine after all."

I was trying to save calories, but I figure that walking the thin tightrope I find myself on has to burn some calories.

THE REST of the afternoon proceeds smoothly enough. When Gary carves the turkey, my mother-in-law announces that with the skill he shows, he could have been a surgeon.

We all seat ourselves in the dining room, and I propose a toast to family.

"Here, here," everyone says, clinking glasses.

"You know, I read somewhere that clinking glasses is now passé," my mother says, after she has made sure she has clinked with every glass. "They say you should just hold your glass up to toast."

"Who makes up these rules?" Gary asks as he butters his sweet potato.

It turns out that my brisket is not overcooked. It is delicious, and I notice that everyone, including my mother-in-law, is thoroughly enjoying it.

At the table, my father and father-in-law discuss the beauty of retirement.

"Boxes were very good to me," my father says, taking a turkey leg from the platter and biting into it with gusto. I obviously didn't inherit my disgust of meat on a bone from him. My father was the president of Corrugated Boxes Inc., a company that made boxes for storing and packing.

As the food is being passed around I'm careful to take only small helpings, and am aware that my jeans continue to feel loose in the stomach. I remember the old saying, "nothing tastes as good as thin feels," and I have to agree.

"Yep, there's nothing like waking up to another sunny, warm Florida morning and playing 18 holes," my father continues. "The key is to retire early, so you're young enough to enjoy it."

"Amen to that," my father-in-law says. He was CFO of a men's clothing chain. He still dresses impeccably.

"Gary, when do you think you'll retire? I have a foursome with your name on it," my father says.

"When Gary retires, we want him with us in Longboat, not in Boca," Arlene says.

"Well, I'm having too much fun at Global Investments right now, so I'm in no hurry to retire. I've got some really interesting companies that I'm helping to go public, and getting ready to watch their stocks soar."

"What companies?" my mother asks.

"If I tell you, I'll have to kill you," Gary jokes.

"Don't worry yourself with investments, Estelle. You keep to your scratch tickets." My dad explains that my mother has become quite fond of buying scratch tickets at the Seven-Eleven.

"Last week I won $100 dollars on a $2 card," she says proudly, as if it were due to skill.

"So, political science," my mother says to Rachel, changing the subject when she realizes no one was as impressed as she thought they should be. "There must be some smart boys in your class. A lot of pre-law students?"

"I guess," she says. "I think I might want to teach," Rachel explains as she takes another piece of lasagna. "It would be cool to teach in a high school," she adds.

"That's a very good idea," my mother agrees. "Then after you get married and have kids, if you decide to keep working, you'll be on the same schedule as your children."

"*If* I get married and have kids," Rachel says. "The lasagna is great, Mom," she tells me.

All four grandparents put down their silverware at the same time, making a clattering noise.

"What 'if?'" my father asks. "Of course you'll get married and have children."

"A beauty like you? They'll be knocking down your door," my mother-in-law tells her.

Gary informs Rachel that anyone she is dating must pass his test.

"What's the test?" Rachel asks him.

"I haven't made it yet, but trust me, it won't be a walk in the park."

I begin passing the green bean casserole around the table, asking everyone to help themselves and take more.

"I'm not saying I won't get married," Rachel explains, "I'm just saying that there are lots of things to consider. Do you know that Sierra, a girl in my dorm who's an art major, is planning on joining the Peace Corps when she graduates?"

"Well, with a name like Sierra, I'm not surprised," my father says. "She sounds like a hippie. Don't go getting any ideas in your head," he adds as he finishes the bone he's been gnawing on.

"Do you know the diseases you can get traveling in those third world countries?" my mother-in-law asks.

"Well, I think it's cool. I'm not saying that I could see myself doing it, but I think it's neat. Don't you, Mom?"

I flash back to my freshman year at Madison. I was a marketing major; my parents had already talked with me about how that degree would be nice to have should I want to work at my father's company. I signed up for the requisite business classes, but I found myself filling my electives with courses that intrigued me and scared me a little at the same time, courses like Comparative Religion, and *I Ching*.

I remember on one of our first dates Gary giving me a hard time about taking the religion course, saying, "What's the point, Syd? You'll end up defending your Judaism in a class of people who'll probably be trying to convert you."

When my parents learned I had signed up for *I Ching*, my father said,

"Isn't that the Chinese philosophy of tossing coins to read the future? I didn't send you to college so you could learn to play a variation of *heads* or *tails*."

My mother added, "If you're looking for an elective, take a nice English literature class. That way you'll impress people at cocktail parties by being well-read."

By my sophomore year I had heeded their advice.

I look over to Rachel. "You know, I met Dad that first week of school, and we dated all four years, got married, had you," I say to her, smiling.

"Like a fairy tale," my mother says.

I look at Rachel and continue. "Then I stayed home taking care of you, dad and the house full time. Which was a much easier job before the dog," I add, as I see Levi sitting again in front of the door. A little taste of freedom, and now he can't get enough. "Gary, can you let the dog out?"

"I'm not saying that I don't ever want to get married and have kids, I'm just saying that I want to keep my options open," Rachel says. "You know, see what's out there and explore, like Sierra talks about."

I'm not hungry and I'm not full, but all of a sudden I feel a strange sensation in my gut. I take a sip of wine to try to ease it.

My mother-in-law sighs and says, "Well, don't explore too long or you'll find yourself like my friend Gertrude's daughter. Forty-five years old, and still not married. Never thought anyone was good enough for her, and now she's alone. And she doesn't look like any spring chicken, I'll tell you that. Now your mother," she continues to Rachel, "she keeps herself up."

To me she says, "Syd, you look wonderful. Doesn't she, Gary? And it's a fulltime job, isn't it? Hair, nails, waxing, working out. It might take a village to raise a child, but I'll tell you it takes a team of spa professionals to keep us looking young and fresh. That, and a little help from plastics," she says, touching her face.

My father-in-law pushes his plate away with a flourish and announces that he's now officially stuffed.

"Now, men," my mother-in-law continues, "they grow more distinguished with age. Just look at Paul Newman."

"Who's that? A neighbor of yours in Florida?" Rachel asks as she takes her napkin off her lap and puts it on her plate. "Oh no, wait. He's the guy who makes that brand of salad dressing and popcorn, right?"

"*Oy vey,*" my father says.

"Can I get anyone anything else?" I ask.

Everyone tells me that they can't eat another bite, so I begin to clear the table. Gary heads into the family room to check the score of the game. My father and father-in-law put on their winter coats and head outside to smoke their yearly Cuban cigars, encouraging Gary to come and join them. My mom, mother-in-law and Rachel join me in cleaning up the table.

"Just delicious," my mother tells me. "Everything was just delicious, wasn't it, Arlene?"

"Mmmm, superb," she tells me. "Rachel, you let your mother teach you to cook. You know what they say, the way to a man's heart is through his stomach."

"Really, Grandma? Who says that?" Rachel asks.

"Why everyone, honey. It's an old saying."

"It seems pretty sexist," Rachel says.

My mother-in-law sighs. "According to who? Sierra?"

"Okay, okay, let's not argue," my mother says. "Come here, honey," she says to Rachel. Rachel puts down the stack of dishes she is carrying and walks over to my mother, who gives her a big hug. "Isn't this just perfect," she says to all of us and to no one in particular. "All of us together like this? Just perfect."

After we finish cleaning up I put on the coffee and begin organizing dessert. The doorbell rings, and Rachel runs to the door. I hear Tammy's voice and I come running out of the kitchen. "Tammy!" I say, with my arms open. She gives me a hug, and I tell her how much I've missed her.

"Hey, Tammy," Gary says. "Long time no see."

"Hi, Gary," Tammy says, walking over and giving him a hug.

I hear my mother-in-law whisper to Fred, "Did you hear that, she calls him by his first name." I see her scowl.

My parents get up and hug Tammy. "How are those Michigan Wolverines?" my dad asks.

"Having a better season than the Wisconsin Badgers," Tammy answers.

"You look wonderful," my mother tells Tammy. With Rachel and Tammy being best friends since kindergarten, Tammy has gotten to know my parents well.

"Thanks, Mrs. Arthur." I see a slight smile of approval form on Arlene's lips. Then Tammy turns to my in-laws and says, "Hi, Mr. Kaufman, Mrs. Kaufman," and I see a definite smile on Arlene's face.

Just then the doorbell rings again, and Gary opens it to let Jodi, Dave and the girls in.

With greetings flowing every which way, I excuse myself to the kitchen, where I get everything ready for dessert. I hear the girls run upstairs to Rachel's room, and Jodi's footsteps in the kitchen.

"Need some help?" she asks.

"Just the emotional type," I say. "How was dinner at your cousins'?"

"There were thirty-two of us," she says.

"Wow, and how'd that go?" I ask as I pour the coffee in a carafe, and set out the pies.

"Let's put it this way. We put the 'fun' in dys*fun*ctional," Jodi says as she gets out the milk and sugar and Sweet'N Low for me. "My only coping strategy was to eat. I need to go to the gym for like ten hours tomorrow."

We put the coffee and pies out buffet style, and announce that dessert is ready. There is apple, pumpkin, pecan and French silk. Gary makes another fire, and instead of eating dessert I decide to pour myself another glass of wine.

Rachel, Tammy, Melanie and Rebecca bound down the stairs and help themselves to dessert, happily eating and talking. My mother and Arlene each take a slice of pie, all the while saying that they shouldn't be eating this and that tomorrow they'll have to go right back on their diets. Jodi tells me that she's so blown her diet today that she might as well go to town with the pies, so I offer her some vanilla ice cream to make hers *a la mode*.

My mother-in-law fears her headache is coming back, so she and Fred say their good-byes and get ready to leave. Gary promises them he'll come visit tomorrow and spend the afternoon with them. I insist that I don't need any more help cleaning up, so my parents decide they'll go home and keep Fred and Arlene company.

After everyone says their good-byes, Rachel and the girls decide to watch a DVD of the final season of *The OC*. Jodi, Dave, Gary and I move into the living room, and wonder together how our kids will experience us when we're older and they're hosting us for the holidays.

"Thank God for booze," Dave says, swirling his scotch in his glass.

"Thank God for chocolate," Jodi says, as she takes a Hershey's Kiss from the crystal bowl to her right.

"Thank God for sex," Gary says, as he puts his arm around me.

"Please tell me you're joking," I say to Gary. "I'm way too tired. Thank God for sleep."

By 10:00 we all agree that we're exhausted, and decide to call it a night. We make plans to go to Bar 23 soon, a great new restaurant that recently opened in the city that everyone has been raving about. We figure that if we have enough notice we can pace ourselves so that we can actually make it up past midnight, when the bar is supposed to be in full swing.

We head back into the family room, where the girls are still watching *The OC*, and none of them claim they are tired.

"Oh, to be young again," Dave says.

"We're not that old," Jodi says, slapping his shoulder.

"Shhh," the girls say in unison.

Rachel promises she will drive Melanie and Rebecca home by 12:30, so Jodi and Dave leave.

With Gary's help I do a final clean up and we turn in to bed. After getting my pajamas on and getting washed up, I decide to weigh myself, a scary prospect on any night, an even scarier one on the night of a holiday dinner. I am pleased. Tonight, the scale is my friend. I can't remember the last time I was able to control my eating so much during a holiday celebration. If I keep up with the gym, and stick to my salads and Lean Cuisines, I can probably lose another five pounds before the New Year.

I get in bed and Gary rolls over, snuggling me.

"Gary, I told you, I'm really tired. Can't we just be together tomorrow night?"

"Yeah, of course. But think how many calories you can burn up with a quickie," he teases.

I roll over on my side, and he rubs my neck. It feels nice. I could fall asleep to that. Then he moves his hand down my back and around onto my stomach. "Getting nice and flat," he says.

"Okay, that's really scary that those words are a turn on," I say.

That's all the encouragement he needs. He begins stroking my breasts, and when I don't resist, he allows his hand to travel down my stomach again, pushing down my pajama bottoms. He rubs his fingers over my panties in a teasing way, and I feel myself getting wet. I roll over and realize that Gary is already naked. He pulls off my tank top and begins licking my nipples and moving toward my belly. Then he pulls off my panties and tells me he's ready for more dessert. Who am I to argue?

When we make love I need to start out slowly, being so sensitive from the phenomenal orgasm Gary has just given me. It all feels so wonderful, I don't care if it burns a calorie or not. Why is it that sometimes the prospect of having sex can feel so overwhelming when you're tired from the day? And then the minute you start, you can't for the life of you figure out why you ever resisted?

Gary begins thrusting harder and moaning, and I suddenly remember that we are not alone in the house. "Gary, shhh, be quiet," I say into his shoulder as he pushes deep inside of me. He starts to moan and I tell him again, "C'mon, really, you can't let the girls hear you."

He listens to me and comes forcefully, but silently.

We fall asleep, and at about 1:00 in the morning I hear Rachel come in from driving the girls home. I hear her get washed up in the bathroom, and then I hear her bedroom door close. I'm happy with how the day went. I think it was a lovely Thanksgiving dinner.

I sound like my mother.

I can't fall asleep.

I think everyone had a good time, and I know the food was wonderful. I love the way my house looked.

I still can't fall asleep. I look at the clock; it's 1:53.

I think about some of the things that Rachel talked about at dinner. I wonder about her friend, Sierra, who wants to join the Peace Corps.

I picture an earthy woman with long, blonde hair and no makeup. Someone who doesn't get manicures; who keeps her nails short and her hands functional because she loves pottery and uses her hands for her art, and for working in her vegetable garden, where she grows arugula and heirloom tomatoes. I picture her walking along Big Sur with her jeans rolled up and her silver toe ring glimmering in the sun as the waves hit the shore and her feet get wet. Unpolished toes. She would be wearing a thin white cotton blouse, made in India, with a turquoise necklace against her smooth, tanned skin (*at least we have the necklace in common,* I think to myself). She answers to no one but herself and marches to the beat of her own heart.

Would she work in an orphanage in Calcutta, a medical clinic in Guatemala? What would it be like to be a Sierra?

For some reason this question scares me, but I don't know what I'm scared of. I could never be a Sierra. I get weekly manicures, monthly pedicures—biweekly, in the summer. I get waxed and plucked. I pay well for my hairdresser to hide any grey. I shop. I diet.

I'm all for peace, but the Peace Corps?

I have that funny feeling in my stomach again. I know it's not hunger, but all I can think to do is to slip downstairs and have a slice of pecan pie, and so that's what I do.

As I sit in the dark eating the pecan pie, I yell at myself for breaking my diet, and determine what I can do to rectify it. Even as I'm eating the pie I'm figuring out how long it will take me on the elliptical to burn the calories. How I should just skip breakfast tomorrow, and try to cut an extra few hundred calories from my intake for the next few days. How I can still lose the last five pounds before the New Year, if this is my only transgression.

And an interesting thing happens.

I'm so busy obsessing about my weight, I realize in an instant that comes as quickly as it goes that I am no longer thinking about girls like Sierra, who have strong hands and join the Peace Corps to bring aid to the trouble spots of the world.

No, I'm back in my own head in suburbia, tackling trouble spots of my own—my stomach, hips and thighs. And just to be certain that my focus is where it needs to be, I cut another sliver of pie to eat, and yell at myself for eating it, before I head back upstairs to the safety of my husband and my room, and the box I built for myself.

Chapter Twelve

The holidays are over and my weight is stable. Well, stable enough. Hovering up and down a pound or two here and there, but all things considered, not a bad beginning to the New Year. Rachel is spending the last week of her winter break visiting her roommate in San Diego, and they will fly straight back to Madison at the end of the week. So my house is nice and quiet again.

It was wonderful to have her home, and I miss her, don't get me wrong. But it's different than when she left for college in August. I know how happy she is now at school, so that's reassuring. And I hope I'm not a bad mother admitting this, but you spend so much time missing them when they first leave and counting the days until they come home to visit, and then all of a sudden, they're a little in your space.

I miss Rachel, don't get me wrong.

It's just that now I miss her more in theory.

I turn to face Jodi and smile. "Okay, when was the last time we rode the train into Chicago?" I ask her as I take the window seat.

"Oh God, I can't even remember," Jodi says as she plops down on the aisle.

"I feel old," I say.

"Why? You look great."

"Thanks, no, it's just so weird, isn't it? I mean, we have old kids. Look, Rachel is already away at college, and we just asked Melanie to drive us to the train station so we could meet Gary and Dave for dinner, and *she* was the one who asked *us* what time we'd be home."

"You missing Rachel?" Jodi asks.

"Maybe, I don't know. I'm missing something, but I don't know what," I say as I look out the window and watch the shops roll by: North Shore Fitness Center, Pancake Oasis, James Square Liquor store. "I mean I like the quietness in the house, but sometimes, with Rachel gone now, I feel a little useless." I watch the train dip into the tunnel.

"See, it's that Invisible Fence. Now that you're time is freed up by not having to walk Levi, you don't know what to do with yourself. It's like the empty nest and empty leash all at once," Jodi tells me.

"You know what? Just ignore me. I think I'm just premenstrual."

"I thought you had your period last week," Jodi says.

"Yeah, you're right. I'm postmenstrual."

"Oh. And what is that?" Jodi asks me.

"It's the same symptoms you get before your period, only you experience them after your period," I explain.

"Okay, let me get this straight. You have a week of PMS, then you have the symptoms that go with your period, and then you have this postmenstrual week which is pretty much like the last two weeks, is that right?"

"Yep."

Jodi looks at me and says, "I think that's just called 'life,' Syd. I don't think you can chalk that up to your menstrual cycle."

I look at Jodi and decide she's right. "This must be menopausal, then," I tell her. "Anyway, I'm not depressed. I just feel a little at loose ends. Like I have a million little things to do all the time, but then when I look back at my day, at my week, I think, 'What have I really done?'" I'd forgotten how soothing the rhythm of a train can be, how lulling. I watch the rush of the train glide back out of the tunnel and into the darkened night.

"Well, if I were you I'd keep that to myself. If word gets out to Cynthia Goldberg that you're looking for something to do, you'll be on the top of every volunteer list at the club. They're working on at least three more events for next year, and you'll never have a moment to yourself if you get roped into helping with another member luncheon or fashion show or whatever it is they're planning," Jodi advises.

"Yeah, you're right. Mum's the word. Hey, thank Melanie again for driving us to the train."

"Oh, she was happy to. Now that she has her license, she's always looking for an excuse to drive. But tell me again why we're taking the train instead of driving. You were talking so fast on the phone, all I really picked up was 'Al' and 'drinking,'" Jodi tells me.

"I was just saying that with Gary's and Dave's cars downtown already, it seemed silly to have another car in the city. I was thinking about Al Gore and *An Inconvenient Truth*, the movie that Rachel's friend, Sierra, told her to watch. We saw it when she was home and it made me think how it's no wonder that we cause so many problems for the environment when we do things like drive three cars in the city for four people going to the same place,"

I explain.

"I haven't seen the movie yet, but I'll be sure to take a train to the theatre so as not to offend anyone," Jodi tells me.

"Okay, sarcastic one. But before you think I'm some Sierra type—"

Jodi interrupts me. "I'm sorry, did I miss something about Rachel's friend? What's a 'Sierra type'?"

My mind flashes back to the image I've created for Sierra based on the few things Rachel has mentioned about her artsy, activist friend. "Never mind. It doesn't matter. The other issue is that if we drove a third car in, one of us would have to be the designated driver. I hear that Bar 23 has an incredible martini menu, and I don't think either one of us wants to order sparkling water tonight."

"Amen to that. I can almost taste my appletini even as we speak," Jodi says.

"My point," I say.

"Point taken," Jodi says.

"Next stop, Union Station," the conductor announces.

"Amazing. Do you realize how quickly we got to the city? If we were driving, we'd still be sitting in traffic," Jodi marvels

"I'm telling you that Al Gore, he's a winner," I say.

"Except in Florida," Jodi offers.

"Except in Florida," I agree.

"And after he lost the election, he gained a lot of weight."

"And grew a beard," I add.

"God, if he were a woman, he would have gotten a lot of shit for that," Jodi says.

"For the weight gain or the beard?' I ask her as we start walking toward the opening train doors.

"For both," she says without hesitation. "For both."

After we get off the train we hail a taxi and take it to Water Tower Place to meet Gary and Dave. I consult my watch and see that it's 8:00 and we are right on time.

"Yo, Jodi," Dave calls, and we look up to see Dave and Gary waving at us. After hello hugs we walk the few blocks towards Bar 23, the guys chatting about the exciting season the Bears are having. There are lots of people milling about, the restaurants and bars are getting full, and the evening is heating up, though of course not in the weather department. It's really cold, and I have to give Nancy and Evan kudos for moving to Florida. Plus, if global warming is real, it hasn't hit Chicago yet. It's absolutely freezing.

"You're so lucky you have on your fur coat, Syd," Jodi says as she holds the collar of her long wool coat together, fighting her own battle with the wind.

"Dave, I need to buy a new fur soon." To me she says, "I never got the lining fixed on my old fur, and I really think I'd prefer a different style now. God, I've had that fur since Dave and I first got married."

"They say it's supposed to get even colder over the weekend. I think they're predicting a high of, like, 2 degrees with a wind-chill of minus 20," Dave says.

"Fine, that's it. Sunday you're going with me to Saks, Dave. I really need a new fur."

"The Bears are playing Sunday. Why don't you have Syd go with you?" Dave suggests.

"Yeah, let's do that. I have to go to Saks and Neiman's anyway. I really need some new pants, and I have to buy some makeup," I tell Jodi.

"Oh, and let's stop at Jimmy Choo too. I need another pair of shoes," Jodi adds.

"Who doesn't?" I ask.

"Great, we'll enjoy another shopping extravaganza," Jodi says happily.

"Don't you two enjoy a shopping extravaganza like on a weekly basis?" Gary asks, giving Dave a smirk.

"You know it takes time and money to look as good as Syd and I look," Jodi says.

"We do look good, don't we?" I concur with Jodi, putting an exaggerated swagger in my walk.

"We look more than good, we look fabulous!" Jodi declares, joining me in my swagger and then holding her arms out and twirling around, her shoulder length light brown hair flying around her face like a shampoo commercial.

"Well, Gary, it looks like at least we won't have to spend money for Jodi and Syd to go into therapy. Our wives are not suffering from a low sense of self-esteem," Dave says.

"Shopping is our therapy," I explain to our husbands. I inhale the cold night air and think to myself how much I love the city. The flashing lights of the billboard signs and the enticing fronts of the restaurants and bars. It's like a pilgrimage, seeking out the latest hot spot and being right in the middle of the new trend.

"Well, you two can shop in any season, but this winter is going on too long. I'm itching for a golf game," Gary says. "Hey, Dave. How about, me, you, and maybe Pete heading out to West Palm next weekend. Evan's been trying to get me down for some golf and today he played in the low eighties."

"Whoa, nice score. He's getting to be quite the golfer," Dave says in an appreciative manner.

"No, I meant the temperature hit the low eighties," Gary explains.

"Well, I'm in," Dave says. "The first half of the week is going to be crazy, but I can leave by Thursday afternoon."

"Sounds good. I'll take care of logistics and email you the flights."

"How do they do that?" I ask Jodi. "Have we, or anyone we know of the female persuasion, ever come up with an idea to go away and figure it all out in less than a minute?"

"Well, let's see. Gary and Dave don't have to worry about who will watch the kids, or walk the dog, or wait for the dishwasher repairman—"

Dave interrupts. "What, is our dishwasher broken?" he asks Jodi.

"No, Dave, I'm just creating the scenario. Because men don't think about the details, the things that need to be taken care of. That's why women can't make plans in a minute, Syd," Jodi says.

"It is so cold out," I say as another blast of wind whips through my bones.

"It's just up one more block," Dave says. As we continue walking, I gaze at the lit up skyline, at the Sears Tower and the John Hancock and all of the other buildings that twinkle their lights in the jet-black sky. Suddenly, the electricity from my hairdryer and my environmentally incorrect Range Rover seems pretty insignificant. I think I've been too hard on myself since watching *An Inconvenient Truth,* and that the next movie I see will be a romantic comedy that never mentions global warming.

We continue walking and I'm listening to the clicking of my boot heels when I see an old, gaunt man sitting on the sidewalk curb. He is wearing thin trousers and a worn sweatshirt, and I can't imagine how cold he must be. In his hand is a dirty plastic cup. As we continue walking to Bar 23, there is nothing we can do to avoid passing him.

"He's got to be freezing," I say.

"Just don't look," Gary says.

"Yeah, don't establish eye contact," Dave adds.

Jodi continues to hold the collar of her coat to her neck.

All of a sudden, despite the frigid temperatures, my fur coat feels heavy and enormous.

"Spare some change?" he asks, his voice surprisingly stronger than I would have thought.

We keep on walking.

"Spare some change?" he asks again.

As we walk on by, pretending that he isn't there, I hear him say, "God bless you, you all have a good night."

"It's just up there," Gary tells us, and we see the neon sign boasting Bar 23.

We walk in and the place is happening. Inside the restaurant we are enveloped in warmth and happily hand our coats over to the coat check lady. Our reservation isn't for another forty-five minutes; we wanted to have time to relax over a drink before dinner. We move over to the bar and it's full of energy, with people kicking back and laughing, ushering in the weekend.

As luck would have it, four people get up from the bar and Gary jumps in to get us the seats. The large rectangular bar boasts stools in red, yellow and purple, with scattered high tops that have Indian gauze yellow tablecloths with beaded fringes of purple and yellow on the ends. All along the bar are little tea lights and small lamps with red, yellow, purple and dark green beaded shades. The bartender hands us the black leather bound drink menus. There is an Asian fusion blend of music playing, and I find I like it. Dave signals the bartender, and he comes over.

"What music is playing?" I ask him.

The bartender smiles and tells me it's called *Buddha Bar*. "Great sound, don't you think?" he asks.

I nod my head and order a Cosmo with blueberry vodka while Jodi orders her Appletini. The guys both get their Grey Goose Martinis with olives.

"I'm so hungry," Jodi says. "I can't wait to see the menu."

"Well, is this going to be a point-counting night, or are you in a breaking-your-diet phase of the cycle?" Dave asks Jodi.

"Oh, I stopped counting points weeks ago. I swear you don't listen to me. I told you how I've been doing the diet shake thing. You know, a shake in the morning and for lunch, and then a regular dinner," Jodi says. The drinks arrive, and Jodi makes a toast. "To friends, new menus and no points," she says, and we clink glasses.

I take a sip and enjoy the cool tingling of the liquid on my tongue, sliding down my throat, while I look around at all the animation; hands gesturing, hair flipping over shoulders, bodies leaning forward and then pulling away, quick bursts of laughter. I look past the bar, out the far window, and see that big snowflakes have begun to fall. It looks so beautiful, so festive, and then my mind flashes on the homeless man we passed. The homeless man we pretended didn't exist. I think about what this Sierra person Rachel talks about would do. I don't think she would have looked away.

I shift my gaze from the window back to Jodi, Gary and Dave. "It's snowing," I say. They look towards the window. "That homeless guy we saw must be freezing and hungry," I venture hesitantly. "Maybe we should have given him some money."

"What, Syd, are you like a homeless advocate now?" Jodi says with an edge in her voice.

I swallow hard and look away, and Jodi says, "Wait, Syd, I'm sorry. I didn't mean to make you upset. But you can't just give money to those people."

"Jodi's right, Syd. What are you going to do, give them money that they'll go and spend for alcohol?" Gary says, as he takes another swig of his martini. Drink orders keep coming across the bar and glasses keep clinking. Is the irony lost on him?

"You know, that's what my parents always said; just look away and don't establish eye contact. Don't give them money because God knows how they'll spend it and you can't just give money to everybody. But for the first time, I'm thinking this is crazy. This isn't everybody. This is one guy we saw who has no coat, no food, and here we are, ordering drinks that probably cost the same amount that it would take to feed him for weeks," I say.

"Okay, Syd, you need to take a sip of your Cosmo and chill, " Gary tells me. "You've wanted to come to Bar 23 for the past month. Don't let some homeless guy ruin your evening." Gary strokes my hair.

"Yeah, and you know, Syd, some of those guys aren't even homeless," Dave tells me. "They just pretend they are so people will give them money and they don't have to do an honest day's work. He's probably some actor or something. So let's just forget this guy, and have another drink." He signals the bartender for another round.

Just after our second drinks arrive the hostess tells us our table is ready, and we follow her. Once seated, we look at the menu and we are not disappointed. Everything looks delicious, and without having to calculate points, Jodi is bordering on ecstatic. I had yogurt for breakfast and a salad for lunch, figuring that way I could save my calories for dinner. And I'm glad I did. I'm deciding between the parsley- and garlic-studded beef tenderloin with garlic whipped potatoes, portabella mushrooms, grilled sweet onions and orange béarnaise or the boneless chicken breasts with a walnut mustard crust, mashed potatoes, shredded brussel sprouts, chives and lardons. For an appetizer, I have already committed to the crispy Maine crab cakes with fennel salad and roasted garlic and aioli. Jodi tells me she wants to order the whipped feta and roasted peppers with grilled pita to share, and Gary and Dave want to add an order of smoked bluefish pate to the list. When we finally let the waiter know that we are ready to order, I decide on the beef tenderloin. One by one our appetizers arrive, and then our entrees. We order a bottle of wine to complement our dinner.

The meal is delicious.

The waiter asks us if we care to order dessert. And the truth is, Jodi and I become easy and slutty once we've kicked back a few drinks. Not easy and slutty in the sexual way, but in the dessert way. Our inhibitions are loosened enough that we can imagine licking the fruity juice of a pear tart, or sucking a fork full of creamy raspberry cheesecake clean. Or letting the cool, melting texture of lemon sorbet cool our mouths in a sweet and sour way. Maybe biting into a chocolate covered cherry sitting atop a mound of whipped cream on a fudge brownie and feeling the sweet liquid fruit explode in our mouths. Dessert sluts.

So Jodi and I move from imagining to bringing our fantasies alive.

We are both in the mood for a smooth, velvety dessert, but we each want our own. After all, if you're breaking your diet and throwing caution to the wind, there really is no good reason to split a dessert. We want to indulge 100 percent. So I order the warm bittersweet chocolate pudding with espresso Chantilly and Jodi gets the warm sticky toffee pudding with date-rum ice cream. We eat our dessert and fall in love with all of its decadence.

Gary and Dave order only coffee. They've gone Evangelical on us.

Jodi and I join the guys with a coffee. We each stir in Sweet'N Low. It's our last hold out to our commitment to lose weight.

We get the check. I believe it rivals the gross national product of a third world country.

"I can't believe we have to go back out in the cold," Jodi says. "And oh my God, I'm so full," she adds.

"Me too," I say as we walk out of the restaurant and back through the bar. I look at my Omega and see that it's well after midnight and Bar 23 is living up to its reputation; it's in full swing. My eyes settle on a large group of gorgeous women standing with a group of equally handsome guys at one end of the bar. The women look like they haven't touched a dessert in years. They are all so thin, so buff, and I vow tomorrow I will get my diet back on track. I realize that it's one thing to eat a small breakfast and lunch so that you can save the calories for dinner, but even I realize that the drinks and appetizers alone already exceeded any left over caloric allotment. Add the dinner and dessert and you have a diet disaster.

"I don't want to even think about how many calories we just ate," Jodi continues.

"I think it's best that we don't," I agree.

"Want to meet me tomorrow morning for the 10:00 spinning class?" Jodi asks as Dave helps her on with her coat, and Gary brings over mine.

"I'll be there," I say, feeling my jeans getting tighter already. We bundle up in our coats, dreading stepping out into the night, and jealous of the people who used valet parking.

Gary pushes open the restaurant door, and the cold air blasts us like a bomb.

"Why do we live in the Midwest?" Jodi asks. "This is insane!"

A dusting of snow has settled on the sidewalks, and tiny, intermittent flakes continue to fall.

"It's not so bad," Dave says, pulling Jodi close to him.

"This from the man who just decided he's going to Florida Thursday," Jodi says.

As we continue walking, I see that the old man is still sitting on the same sidewalk curb, holding the same plastic cup.

"Spare some change?" he asks. Jodi, Gary and Dave pick up the pace, keeping their heads focused on the ground, and I follow along, my eyes cast downward, my boots clicking along the pavement leaving footprints in the newly fallen snow.

"God Bless," I hear him call out.

And I use whatever willpower I didn't use back at Bar 23, when I dove into my dessert, to not look back.

Chapter Thirteen

The heart-shaped box still sits on my counter, though Valentine's Day was over more than a week ago. Most of the box consists of empty black ribbed candy wrappers, and a few poked and rejected jelly centers. Only the occasional wrapper still holds the anticipation of a delectable candy waiting to get picked.

I stick my fingers into the few remaining chocolates and on my third try I find a raspberry cream.

"How have you escaped notice all week?" I ask this sweet little chocolate. I take a bite, and my mouth is filled with the wonderful combination of milk chocolate and creamy, lush raspberry. As I go to finish this gem of a candy, Levi looks at me with his earnest face, willing me to share.

I don't.

It tastes too good. I offer him a Milk-Bone instead, and he looks at me with disgust and walks away. I guess it would be the same reaction I would give someone who refused to give me a bite of his or her flatbread pizza and instead gave me a bite of Melba toast. I open the fridge and take out a slice of cheddar cheese. I break it into bite-sized pieces, place it on a dish, and bring it over to Levi.

"Here you go Levi, yummy cheese." He walks over to the plate, smells it, and walks away.

"C'mon Levi, you love cheese," I say, coaxing him and trying to ease my guilt of not sharing. He looks at me and walks away, his cheese untouched. I know what he's saying to me. He's saying, "Hey, I want chocolate, and you're offering me protein. That's not going to cut it."

And he's right. You can't say that cheese is the new chocolate. Cheese is cheese and chocolate is chocolate, and if you want that sweet, melting cocoa, nothing else will suffice. That's the whole problem with diets, isn't it? Everything in you is craving something specific, and you're supposed to resist that urge and satisfy it instead with a celery stick, a tablespoon of cottage cheese, an apple.

Well, it doesn't work for Levi, and as you can see, it doesn't work for me. A substitute for what you really want, for what you really hunger for, can't be silenced so easily.

Oh, and I should tell you. Gary didn't buy me this big heart-shaped box of chocolates for Valentine's Day. He knew I was trying to stay on my diet.

I bought it for myself.

I was sick of my diet.

Okay, so it's moving toward the end of February and I've regained most of what I lost over the past few months. What can I say? I'm trying.

But I'm hungry.

I'm still meeting weekly with the trainer and exercising. Still fighting with myself to get out of bed early to hop on the elliptical or jump on the treadmill. I do my best.

But I love going out with my friends for lunch and ordering something other than a salad with dressing on the side, love making a bowl of popcorn and watching *Grey's Anatomy*. Love ordering a pepperoni pizza when Gary's away on a business trip.

And then, when I know I'm about to go over the edge of no return, I regroup. I order the salad with dressing on the side, heat up the Lean Cuisine for dinner when Gary is away on business, eat the celery sticks while I'm watching *American Idol*.

And anyway, this evening Jodi and I are going to hear the new diet guru, Dr. Samuels, speak at the community college. He has a new book out called *The Combo Diet*, and has been on the TV circuit. When I first heard of the book I thought it sounded too good to be true. I mean when I hear words like "combo" I'm thinking, "I'll have the #4 combo." As in double cheeseburger, large fries and Diet Coke. One can dream, can't one?

But then I caught a little of him on TV. Apparently he meant "combo" as in pairing certain proteins with certain carbohydrates to induce weight loss, certain vegetables to eat with certain fruits.

Today I figured that as long as I was about to start another diet, I might as well finish what was left of the Valentine chocolates, and the slice of cold pizza in the fridge as well. You know, eat it now while I can, cause who knows what's allowed on The Combo Diet.

I see Levi at the door and let him out. I can't imagine how I lived without the Invisible Fence. It's like indoor plumbing. Once you have it, there's no turning back.

I glance at the clock and see it's almost 7:00, so I run upstairs to brush my teeth again, spritz on some Allure, and reapply my lipstick. I head back downstairs, let Levi in, and look down the street for Jodi's car, which is nowhere in sight.

By 7:15 I'm frustrated. The community college is at least twenty-five minutes away, so we're going to be late. I don't want to be late. I don't want to miss any combinations. I want Dr. Samuels to tell me what to eat. I want him to give me the key to the combination of the combo diet. I want Dr. Samuels to make me thin. I open the door again and wait.

Finally at 7:25 I see her car, and closing the door behind me, I step outside and wait for her to stop in front of my house. She pulls over and I jump in.

"Before you yell at me for being late, I'm so sorry," she says as I close the car door and buckle my seat belt.

"I'm not saying anything," I say as I take an exaggerated look at my watch.

"Okay, just listen," she says as she speeds down my block. "I was all set and running on time. It was all because of Rebecca. I call to her that we're leaving, that it was time to go to her dance rehearsal. She runs downstairs, ready to go, puts on her coat, checks her dance bag, and realizes her tap shoes aren't in there," Jodi's explaining.

"Stop!" I yell. Jodi slams on her brakes. "Did you not see that Stop sign?" I ask her, breathless.

"Oh God, Syd. I'm sorry. I just feel so badly that I'm late. I know how you hate being late."

"Yeah, but I think I hate dead more," I say.

"Right," Jodi agrees.

"Just slow down," I advise. Though now, as Jodi continues with her story, I feel like I did when Rachel had just gotten her driver's permit. I am watching every sign and looking over at the other lanes to make sure Jodi is being careful when she is merging. We stop at a red light and Jodi pulls down the visor in order to use the vanity mirror to put on her lipstick. The light turns as Jodi is blotting her lips together.

"Green," I say as Jodi closes the mirror, flips up the visor, and puts her lipstick in the cup holder as she accelerates through the intersection.

"Anyway, so we're looking everywhere for her tap shoes and finally I sit her down and we retrace her dance rehearsal from last week and by the time she remembers that she let her friend Jessica from dance class borrow them, and calls Jessica to confirm that she has her shoes and is going to be at rehearsal tonight, it was late. Then I still had to drop her off at the dance studio and—"

I interrupt Jodi. "Take a breath," I tell her. "I don't think you've breathed through that whole explanation."

"I don't have time to breathe, we're too late," Jodi declares solemnly.

I glance at the clock and see that it is now 7:50. "Maybe Dr. Samuels will start late."

"Maybe," Jodi says. "Okay, there's the parking lot," she says as she turns left. The front of the lot is full, so we head around towards the back. We find a spot, pull in, and make our way to the building, using the back entrance.

"What's the room number again?" I ask as I step into the school corridor. The school has that familiar school smell, like sneakers and books.

"I left the flyer at home, but I think it's room 232," Jodi says as she locates the stairs. We walk up the flight and head into the hallway, searching for room numbers.

"Wait, I think it's this way," Jodi says, turning left and heading down the corridor. "228, 230, here it is, Syd, 232," she says, pointing.

I look at my watch and see that we are twenty-five minutes late. We slip into the crowded room and find seats in the second-to-last row. I open my leather Gucci bag and pull out two small notepads and pens. I hand one over to Jodi and keep the other for myself, writing The Combo Diet on the top of the page.

"Thanks, it's amazing how prepared you always are," Jodi whispers.

I smile back at her.

I look around at the full room and at the man standing in front. Dr. Samuels looks different than I remember him looking on the talk show where I caught the last few minutes of his interview the other week. He looks younger and hipper now. And I think the bit of scruffy beard is new, too.

I look up at the blackboard to see what he has written so far, what we have missed, and this is what it says:

There is suffering.
Suffering is caused by craving and desire.

"Do I have lipstick on my teeth?" Jodi asks me as she is sliding her tongue over her pearly whites. She looks toward me giving me a big smile so I can check. I give her a quick glance and assure her she has no lipstick on her teeth.

"Okay," she says, looking back toward Dr. Samuels, though she is still running her tongue over her teeth. After all these years, I swear I can't believe she doesn't trust me. Then I realize that maybe that's her way of telling me that I have lipstick on my teeth. I nudge Jodi and ask her if I have lipstick on my teeth, and I smile at her so that she can check.

"No, you're fine," she whispers back. Then she adds in a hushed tone, "But look around, most of the women in here could use a little lipstick."

I look at the women sitting around us.

And a fashion makeover, I think to myself. I can't remember ever seeing so much flannel. Where do these women buy such things? And why? I relish the feel of my soft green cashmere against my skin.

"And what's with all the men?" Jodi whispers.

She's right. There are quite a few men in the room, I now notice. You usually don't see as many men as women in diet groups.

"Well, I think that's probably a good sign," I whisper back to Jodi. "This Combo Diet must use science to actually let you pair lots of good foods together and still lose weight. That's probably why so many men are using it."

I hear Dr. Samuels' voice booming, and return my focus to him.

"So you see, we have a problem. And the problem is that life is full of suffering. We are all suffering in so many ways."

Jodi kicks me under the desk. "Well, this is a bummer," she whispers. "I'm not suffering in so many ways. I just want to lose some weight."

"Shhh," I whisper back. I look again to the front of the room at Dr. Samuels, who, incidentally, looks really good in flannel.

"And when we look at the causes of suffering, we find that what drives that suffering, that pain, is craving and desire," he explains, underlining those key words he has already written on the board. "It is the pushing away of things we don't want, and the coveting of things we do want, that brings about the constant struggle that leads to so much suffering."

He continues discussing this topic, using different examples to show how people create suffering beyond what suffering that we all, having a human body, must inevitably endure.

"Syd," Jodi whispers.

I shake my head slightly, and then put a finger over my lips. I worry that we are disturbing the people sitting around us. I'm listening to Dr. Samuels talk about the ways we, as humans, suffer, when I notice that Jodi is busily writing something down. I figure she is just taking notes, but then she passes her notepad over to me, and I feel like we're back in 6th grade with our teacher, Mrs. Larson. Jodi and I spent the majority of that year writing notes to each other during class, mostly about Jonathan, on whom we both had a not-so-secret crush.

I read her note. It says: *Syd, what the hell is this Dr. Samuels talking about? We've already been here for 15 minutes and all he talks about is suffering and desire. When the hell is he going to talk about what to eat with what so I can lose weight??????????*

I pass her notepad back to her and shake my head just slightly, attempting to refocus her attention. She gives me a pout.

I continue listening to Dr. Samuels while I write back to Jodi: *You're being a lousy student. Anyway, I think it makes sense and I'm sure he'll get to the food after he explains his theory. Besides, he's right. Craving and desire are my downfall—I finished an entire box of Valentine's candy this week. Now can we stop writing notes to each other and pay attention to the lecture???????* I move my notepad to the side of my desk and angle it so that Jodi can read it.

"And so, we are left with a problem, but now we know what that problem is. Now we can bring our dilemma to our consciousness. Once we can understand that we suffer because we crave and desire, that we suffer because we want things the way we want things, we are in a position to do something about it. And that leads us to the third Noble Truth."

He turns to the board and writes the following: *There is a way to end suffering.*

Jodi kicks me again and I turn towards her. "Finally," she says, getting ready to take notes. I get my pen ready too, waiting for the magic combinations of food to melt the pounds away.

"And that takes us right to the fourth Noble Truth, which says the following—" and he turns again to write on the blackboard: *The way out of suffering is through finding the Middle Way by following the Eightfold Path.*

Okay. I'm ready. Tell me the eight magic foods. Tell me the middle way. C'mon, Dr. Samuels, make me svelte!

"And what is the Eightfold Path? What is the Middle Way? Let's list the steps on this path. First, we have *Right Understanding.*" He writes that on the board.

Okay, well, you have to understand the basics underlying the diet to make the diet work, I figure. I'm with you, Dr. Samuels, I'm with you.

"And next, we have *Right Thought.*" And he writes the next step on the board.

Jodi leans over to me and whispers, "I'm going to the bathroom. If he finally mentions a protein or carbohydrate, take notes for me."

I nod to her as she gets up and makes her way to the door. I look back to the board and I'm thinking that "right understanding" and "right thought" are not all that different, and really, I'm trying to be patient, but I wouldn't mind him telling me what I should eat for breakfast tomorrow.

But then, when I think about it again, it's true. It's not enough to understand the principles of the diet you're on; you have to have the right thoughts about the diet. You have to think positively, you have to think willpower and self-discipline; you have to think yourself thin.

My pen is poised. I'm ready for more.

"The third step on the Eightfold Path is *Right Speech,*" he explains as he turns once again to the board to write that down.

Okay, I'm thinking about "right speech," and imagining it has to do with how you talk about your diet. I mean, let's be honest. Most of us dieters complain a lot about what we can't eat. And that's a downer. If you're like me, you complain for days how you can't eat things like pizza and before you know it, you're checking your watch to see if Domino's is really going to be able to deliver the pizza you just ordered in the promised time. So maybe part of the key in the Combo Diet is to be able to speak well of the foods you can eat in the combination you are allowed to eat them.

As I ponder this I see Jodi walk back into the lecture and she looks agitated. She hurriedly returns to her seat and starts gathering her things.

"Syd, c'mon, get your stuff," she says, trying to be discreet and trying to make a dash.

I grab her arm and ask her what's going on. When she sees that I haven't moved she coaxes again, "C'mon, Syd, let's go."

"What are you doing?" I ask, while still not budging.

"We're in the wrong lecture!" Jodi tells me. She leans in closer and whispers, "When I went to the bathroom, I had to walk all around to the other side of the floor, and I passed a big sign at the hallway near the front stairs; remember how we came up through the back door and the back stairs? Well, the Combo Diet lecture is in room 223! We're in room 232. We're in the wrong room! This lecture is an 'Introduction to Buddhism,' with Scott someone or other." She looks around the room and then at me. "No wonder there's so much flannel and no lipstick! C'mon, let's get out of here."

Jodi moves to leave the room, but I don't follow. For some reason, I can't leave my seat.

"You go," I whisper to Jodi. "I'll meet you afterwards. I want to stay."

"Why would you want to stay, Syd? C'mon, we've already wasted time here. I peeked in the Combo Diet lecture, and I saw Carol and Diana. We'll go and sit by them, see what we've missed."

"You go ahead. I'll meet you at the top of the stairs after," I tell her.

Jodi is about to argue with me, but we are starting to get a few looks, and even the attention of Dr. Samuels—or, I mean this Scott Someone-or-other, who says in a kind voice, "Everything okay back there?"

Jodi takes this as her cue to leave, which she does as she gives me an exasperated look. I nod slightly to Scott whoever-he-is, and realize to myself that everything *is* okay back here. For some reason I want to stay, even though I really wouldn't mind if he included a list of what to eat.

This Scott Someone continues to write on the board the remaining steps in the Eightfold Path. He writes: *Right Action, Right Livelihood, Right Effort,*

Right Mindfulness, Right Concentration.

"Now these are not steps that you take one at a time, but are to be practiced everyday. They are rather like a road map that you live by, that you practice, and in that way, the road you are traveling becomes the road to your own enlightenment. In fact, once you have attained enlightenment, you will realize that enlightenment and the road you have been traveling is one and the same. But now you understand."

Okay, only I don't. Not really.

"Does anyone have any questions?" Scott Someone asks.

I am willing somebody to ask a question about what he just said; I feel too self-conscious to raise my hand.

He looks around the room, and thankfully, someone has her hand raised.

"Yes," Scott Someone says.

"Well, I wonder if you could explain more about enlightenment. I mean, what really happens? How do you know when you've reached enlightenment and how does your life change?"

I notice a lot of heads nodding in agreement and eagerness to learn. I'm feeling just a tad shallow, as my impetus in coming here was to find the heavenly secret to losing weight, while apparently the rest of the people came here to find the secret to reaching enlightenment. Still, I'm intrigued.

"Let me tell you a story," this Scott Someone says. "A novice monk once spoke to a Zen Master, asking, 'Master, tell me. What is it you did before you reached enlightenment?' The Zen Master replied, 'I carried water and chopped wood.'

"'And tell me, Master,' the young monk continued, 'What did you do after you attained enlightenment?' The Zen Master replied, 'I carried water and chopped wood.'

"So you see, when you attain enlightenment, nothing changes, yet everything changes. Do you understand?"

I see a lot of heads nod yes, though I hold mine steady. I understand, but less in my head than somehow in my heart. Something makes sense, but I don't understand it enough to say what it is.

"It's like your meditation practice. At first, as you begin to learn to meditate, you think that you are trying to get somewhere by meditating. But as you reap the fruits of your practice, you realize that there is nowhere to go and nothing to attain. Everything you ever hoped to reach is in each breath; every truth is in the inhalation and the exhalation, but you have to discover that truth for yourself. The Eightfold Path, the Middle Way, can help guide you to that understanding."

He continues, "This path, the Middle Way, is about living a life of fullness in balance and harmony. It is not about extremes. It's not about overindulgence or self-denial. For what good can come from either of those situations?"

Actually, I think to myself, *this Scott Someone sounds pretty much like a wise diet guru.* I mean, he basically just explained the problem of dieting in a few simple words: Overindulgence (read: breaking the diet) and self-denial (read: following the diet rules)—what good comes from it? Certainly not balance, as the scale moves down, then up, then back down and up again, just like a yo-yo.

This time a guy raises his hand. Scott Someone points and nods to him, encouraging him to ask his question.

"I meditate everyday, 20 minutes each morning and 20 minutes each night. And I do feel a sense of calmness in my life now. But what else should I be practicing?"

Scott Someone smiles and begins to answer. "Good question," he says. "What you are practicing in meditation is mindfulness. So what you want to do is bring that mindfulness, that attention, to what is right before you in every situation you encounter. We've all had numerous situations where our physical body is somewhere but our mind, our spirit, is somewhere else entirely."

As he is talking about this I can't help but picture the scene in the movie *Annie Hall* where Woody Allen and Diane Keaton are having sex, but she has left her body and moved to a chair where she is wanting both a joint and her drawing pad.

He continues, "When you move through the world with mindfulness, a hallmark of the Buddha's teaching, you will act in accordance with the Eightfold Path and the four Noble Truths. How can you not? When you walk through the world without that mindfulness, the consequences of your actions are sure to follow.

"Let me give you an example. Let's say you're walking down a street and a homeless person asks you for money. You can refuse to see what is right in front of you, and keep on walking, ignoring the suffering of another person. In that instance, you have separated yourself not only from another human being, not only from the reality of what is right before you, but from your own humanity and interconnectedness with every other living creature.

"But if you are acting mindfully, you see this other person as no different than yourself. Another human being who, like you, wants to be safe, warm and fed. When you can see this, when you are mindful of this, there is only one thing to do, and that is to help this person by offering what you can. And in this way, you offer something of value to this other being in need, and to yourself.

"For if you act mindfully, you will automatically act in accordance with the principles of the Eightfold Path. It is when we live with our own delusions, and when we let our own desires take us away from seeing things as they truly are, that we suffer."

How did he know?

How did he know that I have carried that homeless man I saw on the way to and from Bar 23, who I didn't help, every day?

"Practice," Scott Someone is now saying. "Practice meditation, practice yoga, and practice going through your day with mindfulness and open-heartedness.

"You know, so many people right now in this world want someone to tell them what to do and how to do it. Buddhism can point you in the direction of truth, but don't mistake the finger that points for the truth itself.

"While the Buddha was dying, his last teaching was to be a lamp unto yourself. What the Buddha taught was that it is ultimately up to each person to experience things for themselves, and then decide whether something holds true for him or her. Don't just listen to a teacher and take his or her experience as the truth. Try it out for yourself. Trust yourself. Learn the truth for yourself.

"Our job is simply to wake up, like the Buddha taught, to our own Buddhahood, our own Buddha nature. To shed our dreamlike trance of illusions and see things as they truly are, see things clearly. By doing this, we attain freedom and peace.

"We all have the potential to awaken, every single one of us."

Kevin Mann waking up from his coma? That kind of waking up I understand. But what about me? Do I need to wake up, and if so, how would I do that? I'm guessing it entails more than the caffeine buzz I seek from my morning coffee.

I look around me and people are nodding in agreement. I sit for a moment with my own thoughts as I hear a woman ask Scott Someone another question. I let it fall into the distance, and what I think about instead is how I came here for Dr. Samuels and the Combo Diet. I came here for someone to tell me what to eat, and how to eat it so that I can reach the ultimate goal: weight loss. And what I think I heard instead was something much bigger. Something huge.

"So up here, there are some pamphlets for various mediation centers in the area, and schedules for yoga classes at different studios. I also have a few copies of *Tricycle: The Buddhist Review,* which is a quarterly magazine, if anyone would like to take a look. Feel free to come up afterwards, and I'll be happy to stay for some individual questions. But if we can, I like to end my talks with just a few minutes of meditation so we can honor this sacred time we have spent together this evening.

"So if everyone can just please get comfortable with your feet on the floor, and your eyes gently closed. Give yourself this moment to reconnect with yourself, and with the others in this room, to just be thankful for this time, for this moment. And becoming mindful of your inhalation and your exhalation, let's just breathe."

I'm sitting here in this room full of strangers breathing, and wondering if I'm breathing right, if I'm actually meditating. But despite my self-consciousness, I'm still glad to be doing it, still glad to be sitting here.

After a few minutes, Scott Someone has us open our eyes. He presses his hands together as if in prayer and says, *"Namaste."*

The rest of the audience puts their hands together as well, and answers with, *"Namaste."*

I had heard that word before, but was curious what it meant, and thought that maybe I would muster the courage to ask the person in front of me. As if reading my mind, Scott Someone says, *"Namaste* is a greeting we use which translates as: 'The divine within me honors the divine within you.'"

Okay, that's really nice. I mean, I don't put bumper stickers on my car, but if I did, that one would be on it. I like it better than the one I keep seeing all over town: *My hockey player can beat up your honor student.*

As people begin getting ready to leave, I join a group up front picking up various brochures. I grab a bundle and smile at Scott whatever his last name is, who returns the smile. And there, standing in my cashmere in a sea of flannel, I feel like I might just belong.

I go out in the corridor and walk toward the staircase, where I find Jodi standing and talking with Carol and Diana, who turn to give me hugs.

"Hey, Syd, it's good to see you," Carol says.

"You too," I reply.

"Yeah, we missed you! How come you didn't come in with Jodi?" Diana asks.

Jodi has her hands on her hips and is waiting for me to answer.

"I can't explain it," I say as we begin walking down the stairs. "It was just interesting. I don't know, it's hard to put it in words," I venture.

"She's been having weird PMS and postmenstrual symptoms. Maybe it has to do with that," Jodi teases me. "Anyway, not to worry. While you were getting sucked into a cult, I took copious notes and I'll make copies for you. Oh, and I bought you a copy of his book too. And it's autographed."

"Thanks," I say as I take the hardcover book with its glossy cover from her hands.

Jodi smiles at me, saying," I know you'll start reading it when you get home, but let me just say three words: ham and cheese."

"Ham and cheese?" I ask.

"Ham and cheese!" Diana, Carol and Jodi say, giggling happily and in unison. They give me a thumbs up, which I return. But I realize what I am thumbs-upping about goes way beyond the combo of ham and cheese.

I think, quite possibly, I may just have stumbled upon the whole enchilada.

Chapter Fourteen

Yogi Berra, the great baseball player known for his zany pearls of wisdom, once said, "When you come to a fork in the road, take it." A little vague, perhaps, but after Scott Someone's lecture, I felt the point as sharp as a knife. I figured that if I kept traveling west, the way I've been heading, I'd likely pass more diet centers and shopping malls. But if I headed east, maybe I'd be able to fill the hole in my heart I've been feeling. Just maybe, if I switched course, I'd run smack dab into enlightenment.

When I looked over the pamphlets I had picked up from Scott Someone's lecture, trying a yoga class seemed less intimidating than trying a meditation class. I know more about exercising the body than quieting the mind, and decided that this would be a good first step.

So here I am driving to the Prana Yoga Center. Granted, beginning this journey guided by quotes from Yogi Berra may not be the most illustrious way to start a spiritual quest, but the fact that I'm thinking about his sage advice now might be an omen of sorts. After all, he was called Yogi. Maybe he'll keep pointing me toward the mystical east.

Feeling more confident in trying this new direction (and feeling the need to prove that I can quote a more literary figure), the last verse of Robert Frost's poem rises up within me:

I shall be telling this with a sigh
Somewhere ages and ages hence:
Two roads diverged in a wood, and I—
I took the one less traveled by,
And that has made all the difference.

So I take that road, turn into the parking lot of the Prana Yoga Center, and realize that a lot of people seem to have chosen the road less traveled. There is a crowd of mostly women walking out the door as I maneuver my car into one of the few empty parking spots. A class must have just gotten out. I watch them laughing and talking as they head to their respective cars, a fair amount of them hybrids. I feel my Range Rover blush with shame.

I never even knew this place existed. It's about a 20-minute drive from my house, and it's located in a strip mall with nothing of note: a bank, convenience store, questionable Thai restaurant, and a children's indoor play gym. But as I walk into the yoga center I am transported. It's like I left behind suburbia and strip malls and the hustle and bustle of the world with a million little things to do.

Standing here in the lobby of the Prana Yoga Center, a few people still milling about, I admit I feel a bit out of my element. It's a totally different scene from the familiar frenzy of my health club, but I'm smitten with the décor.

What hits me most when I enter this yoga studio is an irresistible sense of a welcoming stillness that entices you almost immediately to turn your life down a notch. The smell of incense makes me feel both exotic and relaxed, and I hungrily breathe it in. The floors are a beautiful hardwood, glossy and shiny, and somehow, despite the traffic of people coming in and out, perfectly clean. The receptionist's desk in the front is made of rattan, and the couch and chairs to the right are made from bamboo. The walls are painted a soft spa green, and pictures of the Buddha, and a bunch of gods or deities, are hanging on the walls. All through the entranceway there are lit candles. They grace the bamboo table in the corner holding brochures, magazines, and schedules, and they are along the staircase leading up to the studio. At first I think this is a fire hazard. I mean, c'mon, would you feel comfortable putting candles all along the stairs in your house? But then I realize they are faux candles, made to look real but battery operated. I saw them in Brookstone's the other month.

Note to self: Stop at the mall this week and pick up faux candles for home.

No shoes are allowed in the yoga studio, so I take off my Coach sneakers and put them in the cubbies, which I notice are full of Birkenstocks.

Note to self: DO NOT stop at mall to buy Birkenstocks. Walking toward the east is one thing, but I'll do it in designer footwear, thank you very much.

In the back of the room there is a rack of yoga clothes. Above the rack I see some really cute shirts on display with the yin/yang sign, and other pretty long-sleeved shirts with some symbols that I don't know, but I like the colors and designs.

The cool-looking receptionist with a pierced nose sees me gazing around and asks me if I'm new to the studio. I tell her yes, that I am both new to the studio and to yoga. She looks sort of familiar to me, but I can't figure out from where I would know her. Her pretty lips spread into a smile and she says, "Welcome, *Namaste,*" with her palms together.

My heart jumps a little. "I know this one!" I want to yell, but instead I just put my hands together and say, *"Namaste."*

She tells me her name is Laura, and then shows me where to sign in on the class participation book. I notice that she has amazing hands and arms, graceful, yet really strong. I see that she doesn't have her nails polished, but they look beautiful, functional.

"Glad to have you here, Syd."

At first I'm surprised she knows my name, and I think that maybe she has psychic abilities, maybe as a result from an intense yoga practice or something. But then, with a hint of disappointment, I realize that she just read it in the sign-in book.

"So you're going to take the Power One Yoga class?"

"That's the plan. Do you think I'll be okay?" I ask.

"Oh, absolutely!" Laura tells me. "Power One Yoga is a great workout for beginners and seasoned practitioners alike. Just let Kali, the instructor, know that you're new. She usually asks if anyone's new to the class anyway, so you'll be fine."

"Okay, great," I say. Then, remembering a TV show I once watched about yoga where the person was able to put her legs around her neck like a pretzel, I ask Laura, "If it's too hard for me to follow, is there another class you can suggest?"

She smiles kindly and says, "There's a beginner's yoga class tomorrow morning at 8:00 that you could try."

I smile and nod as she opens the drawer and pulls out a schedule, using a black marker to cross out two classes.

"The 5:30 a.m. sunrise yoga class on Tuesday and Thursday mornings didn't go over too well during the winter months," she explains. "But here's a class schedule and on the back," she says as she flips the schedule over, "is a description of each class."

I glance at it briefly and nod, saying thanks. Then I do a double take. "Wait, I don't get this. Why does each class have a temperature after it?"

Laura smiles at me again and explains. "The temperatures tell you how hot the yoga class is."

"How hot?" I ask, confused.

"Yep," she says. "How hot we keep the room. Have you heard the term 'Bikram yoga' or 'hot yoga' before?"

I'm thinking maybe I should have taken the other road heading west. I think there's a one-day sale at Nordstrom's today.

"No," I tell her. Though now I'm thinking I'd like to be as hot as Laura is, hot in a very cool way.

This Laura is something special. She has shoulder length blonde hair and sparkling blue eyes, and her beauty is so simple and natural, which, I think, only makes her that much more attractive. I notice she's wearing a silver peace ring, and when she reaches across the desk to answer the ringing telephone her shirt falls lower, accentuating her to-die-for collarbone and revealing a small butterfly tattoo on the top of her breast.

I imagine her deciding to get a butterfly tattoo because she has made a promise to herself to continually evolve, to grow and change just as the caterpillar becomes a butterfly. Laura, who probably is no more than 23 years old, could fly with the beauty and grace of a butterfly, landing only briefly on the top of a tulip, or the ear of a kitten, before taking flight again to explore the wonders of the world in an open and flexible manner (flexible because, after all, she practices yoga) and enjoys an inner peace that radiates so much from the inside out that she can get away without wearing a smidgeon of makeup and still look fabulous.

I hear Laura winding down the conversation, and then it hits me. Laura looks like how I have imagined Sierra from the bits and pieces Rachel has told me about her and her ideas. My thoughts are interrupted as Laura hangs up and then proceeds to pick up where we left off.

"Okay, sorry about that. So, I was telling you about hot yoga. It's basically a system of yoga where the class is taught in a studio with the heat turned up. Some classes, mostly the more advanced classes, have the heat turned up to about 95 degrees," she explains.

"Holy shit," I respond, realizing only after the words are out of my mouth how un-yogalike I sound.

Laura laughs. "No worries. Trust me, you'll get used to it and your body will thank you for it. Practicing yoga in the heat helps you burn up toxins," she explains.

And probably burns a lot of calories, I think to myself but don't say aloud. Old habits die hard.

"It also keeps your muscles warm and allows for them to become increasingly more flexible," she adds.

This heat business is all news to me, and I'm worrying that I'm going to feel claustrophobic in a crowded, hot studio. Laura must sense my concern, because she hurries to say, "Believe me, after taking a few classes you're going to love it, especially on a cold morning. Just make sure you have a bottle of water with you."

Again she reads my face. Maybe she does have some psychic powers after all. "No worries, we sell bottled water right here," she says breezily, reaching into a box behind her and pulling out a Fiji bottled water.

I reach into my purse to get my wallet, but she tells me," No worries, for your first class, the water's on the house. And the recycling bin is right over there." She points to the left of the cubbies.

"Thanks," I say. Then she explains how much each class costs if I pay for them individually, or I can pay a monthly fee that gives me unlimited classes for a set price. As I think about it, she tells me I can decide after class how I'd like to proceed, and pay then.

"It's very chill here," she tells me.

"Except for the thermostat," I say.

"Sorry?" Laura says.

"No, nothing, never mind. Thanks again for all of your help."

Then she asks, "And do you have your own yoga mat?" I shake my head no. "No worries. Right up the stairs in the yoga studio you'll see a big closet with yoga mats, blocks, and straps, so you're all set. Some people just like to use their own mats, but you're welcome to use the studio's."

"Great," I say.

"But if you change your mind as you move forward in your yoga practice, we sell a nice variety of yoga mats here."

I look over toward the rack of yoga clothes and see another shelf filled with colorful mats in spring green and sky blue colors rolled up into black-netted carrying bags, and notice that they also sell the faux candles. I really like the bamboo coffee table, and I'm wondering if maybe that's for sale too.

I feel a draft, and turn to see a group of women walk in, their rolled yoga mats slung over their shoulders in the carrying bags, and Laura welcomes them by name. I notice that two of the women are wearing the yoga pants and shirts that are sold in the studio, and they look really good in them. I realize that while the workout clothes that I'm wearing are fine, I would probably feel more yoga-ish if I buy some clothes specifically designed for yoga. I decide that after class I'll take a few minutes to try on some yoga pants and shirts.

I thank Laura again for her help, and she responds with a warm smile and another *"Namaste."* Then she adds, "May your yoga practice bring you merit and peace."

I'm not sure of the appropriate response, so I just flash her a nice smile because saying, "yeah, you too," seems weird.

Looking across the room, I see a shelf holding a Zen triangular clock, and ⟩

determine (with some difficulty because the face of the clock is a picture of sand and there are no numbers) that class starts in ten minutes and I have time to use the bathroom. I have just finished a grande cappuccino from Starbucks, and fear that my bladder won't make it through class, even if I do.

When I head up to the yoga studio and reach the top of the stairs I want to scream out, "Are you kidding me?" It's like hell up here, it's so hot. I breathe in, and I feel as though I'm suffocating. A woman walking past me carrying two big blocks sees me and smiles.

"You're new here, aren't you?"

I nod my head yes.

"Don't worry," she continues, "you'll get used to the heat. And trust me, you'll love it. Sweat everything out, all the toxins, and all the negative energy that can accumulate. You'll feel great." She walks over to her mat and places the blocks to her side. She looks like she's in her mid-thirties, with long auburn hair that falls to the thick of her back in soft, tight curls.

"It's like Florida in August," I say to her.

"Here, I'll save you a spot next to me, cause the class is going to fill up quickly," she offers.

"It'll get even hotter with all those bodies," I say nervously, "and I think I might already be getting dehydrated. Do they offer a yoga class here that comes with an IV drip?" I wonder aloud.

She laughs. "My name is Montana," she offers.

"I'm sorry, what? You're from Montana?" I ask her.

She laughs again, and says, "You really are funny."

"No really, the heat, I think, is getting to me. Didn't you just say you're from Montana?"

There is a moment of awkward silence. I think I've offended her. Then it passes as she waves her hands in front of her face like she's erasing something, maybe accumulated negative energy, and explains, "No, my name is Montana."

"Oh! I'm sorry," I say. "I mean, I'm not sorry that you're name is Montana, that's a great name. I just got confused. Really, it's the heat," I explain. "I'm Sydney," I introduce myself. "But everyone calls me Syd."

"Pleasure to meet you Syd."

Then Montana tells me to go and get a mat, a strap and two blocks from the closet. I do as Montana says, and feel like I'm in kindergarten getting toys for recess. I retrieve my yoga equipment and return to where Montana is saving me a spot. And a good thing she is, because the studio has totally filled up in just a few minutes. I smile at her and tell her thanks.

"No prob," she says as she rolls back on her mat, stretching her legs over her head, her arms reaching in the opposite direction.

"Wow," I say. "You're really flexible.

"Thisposeiscalledtheplowandit'sareallygoodstretch,"she mumbles. With her chin pushing into her chest, her speech is hard to decipher. She comes out of her pose and repeats herself so that I can understand her.

"I was saying that the pose is called the plow and it's a really good stretch," she explains.

I smile, and hope I'm not in over my head.

Literally.

I unfold my mat and place the strap and blocks to the side, as everyone else is doing. I set my water down as well, and it beckons me the way chocolate beckons me because of the heat of the room. Maybe it's a good sign that I'm craving something that has no calories. This is a first. Maybe my journey east toward enlightenment will also make me thin. That'd be nice. I look around the room and see a mix of women, and two men. The women are of all different ages and body sizes, everyone stretching and some in poses that I fear they will get stuck in. My mother used to threaten me with that when I was little and would make what I thought was a funny face.

"If you keep doing that, Syd, I'm telling you your face will freeze like that. Do you think any man will marry you with your face stuck like that?"

My eyes zero in on one woman who I swear has the most unbelievable body I have ever seen. She is wearing black yoga pants and a pale blue sports bra. No top, just the bra that I suppose is to combat the heat, but which deep down (okay, not even so deep down) I think she is wearing simply to make the rest of us feel like shit. Of course, she is up in the front row, and I'm telling you there is not one ounce of fat anywhere on her body. She is moving in and out of poses seemingly effortlessly, her body is so tight and strong.

I think I hate her.

I remember Montana's words about the heat helping to burn off negative energy, which I seem to have. I see that Montana is watching me watch the people in the class. I smile at her and try to harness some positive energy. I stretch my legs out straight in front of me and reach for my toes, letting my head hang down toward my knees. The stretch feels good on my neck, which seems to feel progressively more sore and achy each day. I then spread my legs out in a V-shape and stretch over each leg, and then let my body fall into the center, my chest and face pressing against the mat. As I think about how many others have stood on this mat, and stretched and sweated all over it, I realize that after class I must buy my own yoga mat.

I continue to let my legs and head stretch as I rest in this position, and then I hear the low tones of someone singing, "OM," and then something like, "OM Shanti, Shanti, Shanti, OM."

I see that the yoga teacher has entered the studio and is adjusting the volume of the CD she has just put on. She has brown hair that is streaked blonde in the front, looks to be in her late twenties, and is wearing black yoga pants with a cropped army green shirt with a picture of Buddha on it. As I watch her walk toward the front of the studio I see that on her lower back she has a tattoo of the yin/yang symbol.

"*Namaste,*" she says with her hands together as she stands in front of us surveying the room.

"*Namaste,*" the room answers back.

"As most of you know, my name is Kali."

I see that Kali is wearing an ankle bracelet that looks very trendy. I wonder if I could pull that off this summer?

Montana whispers over to me, "She's one of the best teachers."

I smile and nod. Then Kali asks if there is anyone new to yoga in class today. I raise my hand, as does another woman who looks about my age and who is wearing sweatpants and a sweatshirt. "She must be sweltering," I think.

"Wonderful, welcome. And what is your name?" she asks, looking at the other woman.

"Gina," she answers.

"Welcome, Gina. Now, are there any health problems or physical limitations I should know about before we begin class?" Kali asks.

"Not really. Lately my lower back has been giving me some trouble," she says.

"Okay, Gina. Thanks for letting me know that. I'll make sure we work on some poses that can help strengthen your back. But some of the poses may feel too much on your lower back at first, and then I'll show you some modifications of the pose to avoid injury. Remember yoga is about being where you are. There are no judgments, no good—no bad. And there is no competition between others or within you. Wherever you are today in your yoga practice is exactly where you need to be today. Thanks for being here, Gina, and *Namaste.*"

"*Namaste,*" Gina answers.

Then Kali looks at me. "And your name?" she asks with a smile.

"Syd," I answer.

"Welcome Syd, *Namaste,*" Kali says.

"*Namaste,*" I answer.

"And you are new to yoga as well?" Kali asks.

"Yes," I say, smiling.

"And do you have any health problems, or any physical limitations?" Kali asks.

"No, just some arthritis in my neck," I tell her.

Kali nods her head in sympathy. "And what are you doing for it?" she asks.

"Mostly complaining," I answer.

I hear a few chuckles. Then Kali gives a yelp of laughter. "C'mon, everyone, laugh with me, even if you have to fake it."

Okay, I've heard of faking an orgasm, but laughter? The room has become full of hilarity. I feel like I'm in the movie *Mary Poppins* during the "I Love to Laugh" scene and song.

Then Kali explains that laughter is one of the healthiest things you can do for yourself. "It helps you take deep, rich, cleansing breaths, it boosts your immune system, and it makes your skin radiant." After everyone is once again quiet, she says, "Laughter, like yoga, makes you light and joyful. Remember that during your practice. Thank you Syd, for offering us the gift of laughter. Now, back to your arthritis for a moment. How long ago were you diagnosed?"

"Um," I stammer, "I was never really diagnosed by anyone. I just assumed that I had arthritis when my neck started hurting."

Kali smiles and says that it may be arthritis, it may not be, but that either way, yoga can help by keeping the muscles well-stretched and by relaxing the built-up tension that accumulates in your weak spots, in your trigger points.

"As you go through your practice today, stay mindful of how your neck is feeling, and just as for Gina, I can offer modifications in some of the poses to protect your neck." As an afterthought she says, "And if it continues to bother you, you might want to talk to your health care provider to determine the cause of the pain."

I smile and say thanks.

"Okay, so does anyone else have a body part that they want to focus on today?"

A woman in the middle of the room says she wants to work on some hip openers, and a bunch of people nod in agreement. Kali smiles her encouragement and says, "Great! We'll make sure we incorporate poses to strengthen the back, open the hips and stretch out the neck. Power One Yoga is a 90-minute class, so we have lots of time. Now, just a reminder. I will be walking around the room making subtle adjustments to your body to help you ease more fully into the pose. If you don't want me to touch your body, please let me know so that I can honor that. Also, as most of you know, I like to find the points of tension in your body and massage them out a bit while you're in pose, so again, if you don't want to be massaged, just let me know."

Yay! I think. *Free massage!*

"Let's all come to a comfortable seated position, legs crossed in front of you. Those of you wanting to sit in a half lotus or full lotus position, that's fine."

I see some people, like the sports bra woman, maneuver into a pretzel-like position with their legs crossed, and even though there is, as Kali says, no good and bad, no judgments, already I am thinking that the pretzel position they are sitting in must trump my old Indian-style position.

"Now let's settle ourselves in the room so that we can truly be here now," Kali suggests in a soothing voice. "Let's truly arrive. Let's honor this sacred space we are creating together in this moment in time by chanting the universal sound of 'OM' together three times, with our eyes closed and our hands in *mudra* position."

I have no idea what *mudra* position is, so I keep one eye squinted open so I can hurriedly glance around the room to see what people are doing with their hands. I see that people are sitting with their arms stretched out over their legs; palms are face up, with only their thumbs and index fingers touching each other. I imitate this posture, and then close my eyes fully.

For a second. I open them again to see if everyone else really has their eyes closed. They do. I close my eyes and then take another quick peek. I shut them and realize I just might be a little insecure. Maybe the heat will burn that out along with the toxins and negative energy.

I hear everyone inhale, and then defer to Kali for a quick second to see what note she will be chanting on. Then I hear the sound of mingled voices chanting OM, with some voices fine-tuning their note to match Kali's pitch. The OM goes on until breath has run out, and the last voice heard is Kali's. Then Kali takes another deep breath and begins chanting, and when that OM is finished, she leads us in the final OM.

Then she has us all stand up and watch our breath, encouraging us to breathe in and then breathe out. "Just be here now," Kali advises.

Aren't I already? I think to myself, feeling the humid air of the studio.

Then the yoga begins. I don't know a word of Sanskrit, which is apparently the language of yoga, so I feel as if I'm more than a tad behind in trying to master both the poses themselves and their names as well. Thankfully there are corresponding English terms, though I find them a bit odd. For example, Kali tells us that we will begin in *Adho mukha svanasana,* or Downward Facing Dog. This term does nothing to enhance my fledgling self-esteem as I continue to drool over blue sports bra woman. I look to Kali and see what a Downward Facing Dog pose looks like, and I try to imitate.

"Ah," I hear Kali say. "Nothing like *Adho mukha svanasana* to stretch out the body in the morning. Just feel the spine opening, and press the heels to the ground while your hands are splayed out on the mat in front of you. Just let your neck hang, your eyes focused back toward your heels."

I find this all somewhat difficult to take in, as I can't relax my neck down when I have to keep picking up my head to see if I'm doing the pose right. When I think I look pretty much like everyone else, I find that my body actually likes being a Downward Facing Dog. I wonder if Levi would enjoy stretching with me like this. It'd probably be easy for him, since he's already got the dog thing down pat.

As I follow Kali's suggestion of allowing my body to relax deeper in the pose, I'm startled as I feel a hand on my back.

"Lovely, Syd," Kali says as she rubs my back almost like she's ironing a shirt. Now, I want you to pull your neck down further toward the mat, while you lift your spine up to the sky, and your heels press closer to the mat." She presses on my body this way and that to help me move into the proper position, and oh, my, God, do I feel the difference.

"There you go Syd, beautiful," Kali says. I look up to thank her, but she gently pushes my head back to the desired position. I hear her move to other people in the class, pressing and sculpting bodies into yogic poses.

"Keep breathing," Kali reminds the class. Until she said these words I didn't realize I was holding my breath. "Yoga is all about breathing," her voice soothes. "Breathe into the parts of the body that feel tense, and let your inhalation and exhalation reach deep into those points. Let your breathing guide you into those places, both physical and emotional, where you are holding fear. Dare to go there, dare to breathe there."

Suddenly I'm having the hardest time inhaling and exhaling. For 43 years I've been breathing with no problem, one thing in my life I don't have to think about, don't have to put on my To Do List. Now, five minutes into a yoga class that apparently is all about breathing, and it's become this very conscious, difficult thing to do. Go figure.

"Beautiful, just beautiful," Kali says. "Now let's start opening our hips. Pressing your left heel closer to the ground, lift your right leg high in the air. Ah, can you feel your thigh stretching up to the ceiling? Now, ignore the ceiling and keep lifting your leg past this artificial barrier and lift your leg to the heavens. Offer your leg to the gods and goddesses. Now, bend that right leg at your knee and let your foot point toward the other side of the room."

I glance at Montana to see if my position looks anything close to hers, and it does. I'm waiting for Kali to call this pose Downward Facing Dog Takes a Leak, as that is clearly what we all resemble, but no, she just has us reverse the pose and do it on the left side. My leg trembles a bit in the pose, and Kali reminds us to breathe deeply into the places that tremble, and that shake us awake.

When we are finished with *Adho mukha svanasana,* she has us stand toward the front of our mats and take some deep cleansing breaths. Kali smiles at us and says, "Oh, I can feel such wonderful energy from all of you today. And look at the rays of sun pouring in through the window. Can't you just feel that spring is around the corner? What a perfect day to perform our Surya Namaskar, our Sun Salutation."

Kali begins to call out the many poses that comprise the Sun Salutation. "Listen to your body," Kali keeps repeating. "Your body has an inner wisdom that will guide you into what your body needs now, at this moment. If your body is craving a certain stretch, a certain pose, go with it. There is no right or wrong, there is only this moment, this breath, this sensation, this truth."

Kali's voice, cool and calm, soothes me like a lullaby. Still, I'm sweating like a pig.

From Sun Salutations we move into *Virabhadrasana,* or Warrior Two, and then on into *Trikonasana,* Triangle Pose. I become a snake in *Naga-asana,* the Cobra pose, and feel my inner strength in *Ushtra-asana,* the Powerful posture. Thank goodness we have learned *Balasana,* which is the Child's pose. This is what Kali calls a "resting pose," useful when taking refuge, as she says, from the rigors of demanding poses.

Kali urges us to "retreat" into *Balasana* if a pose becomes too much to hold and our bodies are asking for respite. So, towards the end of the class, when Kali is having people go into *Sirsha-asana,* Headstand posture, and *Parivritta-parshvakona,* Turned Side-Angle, Child's pose becomes my best friend. Like a preschool buddy. All you have to do in Child's pose is curl into a ball, your head face down on the mat, sitting on your knees, which are drawn into your stomach, butt facing the ceiling (or the heavens) and your arms either stretched straight in front of you or relaxed at your sides, facing down toward your feet. It's called Child's pose, after all, so it's best to offer a choice to avoid a tantrum.

Resting in Child's pose, I am very relaxed. As I am melting into the comfort of my spine stretching out, I feel hands on my neck. Kali begins kneading my neck muscles and I think I've died and gone to heaven, or should I say nirvana? It feels so good. She is pressing and rubbing just where my neck is sore.

"That's it, just let go. Let it all go," Kali says. She then moves in front of me and takes my hands and stretches my arms out, pulling until I hear my middle spine and low back crack. "Ah," Kali says. "Consider that a free chiropractic adjustment." She rubs my back gently again, and then I feel her hands leave as she moves on to someone else.

I want to cry, "Don't leave me!" I feel like a jilted lover. I am jealous of whoever she has her hands on now. I want them back. I think I'm becoming spoiled in Child's pose. I think I should be trying to keep up more with the class.

After learning and practicing more poses and postures, Kali's gentle voice winds down the class. "You've just worked your body hard, let it come to a rest while you invite your mind to continue to empty itself of all it doesn't need to hold."

I look up front and see that blue sports bra woman is glistening in sweat. She is actually glowing with it. How can she look so gorgeous with all that sweat? I pull out my ponytail, shake my head loose and then gather my hair with my ponytail holder, fixing it in a messy bun. It feels sweaty, and all I can think about is getting in the shower.

"The mind has a way of chattering on, jumping from one thought to another, distracting us from being who we really are in our inner most essence, our inner most truth. So in yoga, we learn to slow the mind down—" Kali is saying.

A really long shower, I am thinking. But maybe not that long, because when I look up at the clock I see that the morning is slipping away. I still have to get Levi to the dog spa to get groomed and it's my turn to have Mah Jongg tonight and I realize that I haven't bought any snacks for the game and *oh shit! I forgot that I was supposed to drop off Gary's suits at the dry cleaner—*

"Because it is the uncontrolled mind that creates the stories of our lives that we believe to be true. But the ultimate truth is that these thoughts arise and fall away and it is only when we follow them, chasing after them, that we create our own suffering. Practice being in the moment, because really, all we have is this moment—"

Did I cancel my dentist appointment for Monday? I am worrying. I meant to do it last week, and now I can't remember whether I called or not—

"—and if we miss this moment, thinking about the past, wondering or worrying about the future, we miss the moment we are actually living in, and so really, when we are not living in the moment, breathing fully into this space, we are actually missing our life—"

No, I'm sure I called, I think to myself. *I just didn't reschedule the cleaning yet, that was it. When I get home, I'll call and make the appointment—*

"Yoga helps you learn to slow the mind even as it strengthens your body," Kali is saying. "Yoga teaches you to breathe into the beauty of each moment with focus, strength and love. Now we finish with the last and most important pose of our class, *Shava-asana,* the Corpse pose."

With the sound of that pose, my attention is back. I know I've only been a student of yoga for 90 minutes, but I think that sounds like a bad pose to end with. Yoga is supposed to invigorate you, get your endorphins pumping, and make you happy, healthy and strong. Why end with such a downer?

Kali tells us to lie comfortably flat on our backs, letting our feet fall whichever way they do, letting our arms relax by our sides with our palms up and our eyes closed.

I decide not to open my eyes to peek if others have their eyes closed. I'm a quick learner. This group does what Kali requests.

"Resting in this Corpse pose, allow your body to sink fully into the mat, and invite yourself to enter full relaxation. Just watch your breath as you breathe in, and watch your breath as you breathe out. Don't try to control your breathing. Just notice if it is shallow or deep, and wherever it is, know that it is perfect. All is as it should be. There is nothing to change—"

Listening to Kali's voice, following my breathing, I actually am feeling really relaxed.

"There is nowhere to go—there is nothing to do—"

My eyes open at that. Of course there are places to go and things to do. A million little things to do. I let my eyes close again, thinking of the list I need to make before going to the grocery store for Mah Jongg treats. Our old plan of eating just carrots never worked, and we are back to eating sweet foods, salty foods, and then complaining about our sugar and sodium intake.

I realize that Kali is still talking, but I'm not sure what she is talking about.

"—let the kundalini energy uncoil from the lower spine, and be mindful of the chakras it passes through. The Corpse pose will allow your body to absorb all of the work you did on your poses today. This is the most important pose of all—"

I'm thinking that while this is relaxing, it's sort of like taking a nap in the middle of the day, and the class is over anyway, so maybe I should just get up and put my mat away so that I can get started with all of the things I have to do today.

"—That's why we have a rule here at the studio that no one can leave during Shava-asana. If you have to leave early from class, do so before we begin this last pose, so as not to disturb anyone during this very deep, very important pose—"

I stay where I am.

"So very slowly, I want you to imagine all of your body parts, beginning with your toes, and going on up to your head, and invite each muscle to fully let go, to fully relax."

I try doing this and am up to my hipbone when I feel something overtake me. Like I know my hands are there, lying on the mat, but I can't really feel them anymore. Same with my feet. It's almost like I'm floating in air. I like the sensation, and as I give myself over to it I think I fall asleep, because from somewhere far away I hear Kali's gentle voice telling us to slowly begin wiggling our toes and waking our muscles up.

"And when you're ready, allow yourself to roll onto your right side in a ball, resting briefly in a fetal position. Then when you feel ready, birth yourself into a sitting position as newly refreshed."

I birth myself up.

"Now, sitting in either full lotus, half lotus, or comfortable cross-legged position, please join me as we close our sacred space with the chanting of OM."

After we have chanted OM, Kali puts her hands together in prayer and says, *"Namaste."*

The class answers in unison, *"Namaste."*

Then mats are folded, and chatter resumes. I drink hungrily from what remains in my water bottle.

"So, what'd you think?" Montana asks me.

"Great," I say as I'm wiping my mouth. "Do you take a lot of classes here?"

"Yeah, I try to come here at least four times a week. It's addicting. Once you feel your body stretched like this, you can't get enough," she tells me.

"I think I'm going to try to get here tomorrow," I tell her as I gather up the mat, blocks and strap.

"You should. I'm going to take the 8:00 Vinyasa class. It's only an hour, but it feels great. It's more of a slow flow class, where one pose flows into another. Really clears your head."

"Maybe I'll try that one," I tell her. She gathers up her yoga props and we walk together to the closet to put them away. I watch her sling her sky blue mat in its black netting over her shoulder.

"I think I'm going to buy a mat," I tell Montana as we walk down the stairs.

"Oh, you absolutely should. It's good to have at home too, to practice some poses."

"Hi, Montana," Kali says as she follows us down the stairs.

Montana turns to her with a smile, saying, "Thanks for the wonderful class."

"Thanks, but our gratitude is to the yoga masters who have paved the way to bring us such a rich and fruitful practice," she answers.

I'm thinking a simple "you're welcome" would suffice, but what do I know?

"And Syd, beautiful job today. I hope you'll keep coming back and give the gift of establishing a yoga practice to yourself."

We are back in the much colder lobby, and I see blue sports bra woman bending over to tie her shoes. When she bends, her stomach remains flat and muscular, and I say to Kali, "Yes, I'd like that."

"How did it go?" Laura asks, looking up from the reception desk.

"Great, " I say. "I think I'd like to sign up for the monthly fee so I can take unlimited classes."

"No problem. I can sign you up now."

I walk over to the desk and give her my MasterCard.

Laura hands me a blue membership card. "We also offer workshops and special lectures, and we'll always post these events on our calendar over there." She points toward the back right wall. "And you can always check our website for upcoming events and schedule changes."

Montana tells me she's glad that I'll be joining Prana, and that she'll see me tomorrow, if I decide to go to the morning Vinyasa class. I tell her I'm sure I'll be there.

Then I try on some yoga pants and a few shirts that I decide to buy. I pick out a spring green yoga mat, and a few faux candles. I see a Prana yoga towel with a stick figure in the lotus position, and I throw that into my pile of purchases as well.

By the time Laura rings up my yoga "necessities," I have a substantial bill.

Who knew that the road to enlightenment was going to be so expensive?

Chapter Fifteen

"Oh God, Gary, I swear I can't move my neck," I say, rolling over and putting my head on Gary's chest. I take his hand and put it on my sore muscles, willing him to rub the pain away. He starts massaging, but keeps missing the point where it's aching. I keep trying to adjust his hand this way and that, to get to the spot that is screaming for attention but somehow keeps eluding him.

"Gary, right *there*," I say, pressing his fingers into my sore flesh, getting frustrated.

"I'm trying, but I think you'd be better off rubbing it yourself. You know where it is."

"That defeats the whole point," I tell him, pushing the blanket down from my legs and sitting up. The bright sun is already filtering its way through the windows, holding the promise of a warm day. "And anyway, it's your fault that I'm so sore."

Gary pulls his hand from my neck, and moves to sit up. "How is this my fault?" he asks.

"You made me take the middle seat while you took the window. My seat hardly went back and I was so squished in between you and that snoring man in the aisle seat whose head kept flopping near my shoulder, that I couldn't get comfortable. My neck is killing me now," I complain.

Gary spreads the sheet over our feet and looks at me in earnest. "Okay, I've told you for months now to see a doctor about your neck."

"I've been doing yoga stretches for it," I tell him for the millionth time.

"Well, apparently it hasn't cured it," Gary tells me.

"It's a process," I explain, sounding like Kali. "My body needs to be where it is, and I need to honor its wisdom."

"Dr. Maynard's wisdom is better. He fixed my tennis elbow in three visits and two cortisone shots."

"Well, if you really loved me, you'd have taken the middle seat. Now the least you can do is to rub my neck," I beg him.

"I'll tell you what I'll rub," Gary says as he pushes his hand up my tank top and starts massaging my breast.

"Gary, stop that," I hiss as I grab his wrist and pull his hand down. If only he'd rub my neck the way he goes for my boobs.

"I thought you told me that your yoga classes are making you more loving and accepting," Gary tells me as he slips his hand back under my shirt and I again push his hand away. "Yeah," he says, dropping his hand in his lap. "I don't see loving, I don't see accepting."

"You want loving and accepting? Make sure on our return flight home I get the window seat. And if you really want to see loving and accepting," I say as I put my hand on his cock and teasingly begin to rub, "upgrade us to business class."

I kick off the sheets and tell Gary that I'm getting up to take a shower.

"Hold on!" Gary says, jumping out of bed. "Your dad and I have to meet my dad and Evan for our tee time. Let me shower first, I'll be quick." He sprints toward the bathroom, naked and with his erection sticking straight out in front of him.

I stretch out in bed, happy for the few extra minutes to let my body relax, and maybe the tension in my neck ease. I'm looking forward to a few days of Florida sunshine.

My mother and Arlene felt that because the entire family couldn't all be together for Thanksgiving, we should celebrate Passover together. My mom insisted on having the Seder at her house because, as she says, "it fulfills her," but I suspect it has more to do with the fact that she just redid the living room and wants to show it off.

This will be a nice, quick weekend, I think to myself. Tonight Rachel and my niece and nephew will fly in, and then Saturday evening we'll have the Seder. Even if the kids weren't leaving to go back to school on Sunday evening we wouldn't have a Seder on the second night, as the ritual dictates. When I was growing up, my mother used to say to me, "Please, it would be like the 11th plague—it's such an ordeal. One Seder is enough."

I hear the water turn off in the shower and give my body one more big stretch. I love this guest room at my parents' house. The soft blues and creams of the room blend effortlessly with the distressed white wooden furniture. Though I do think my mother may have gone overboard with the shells. They are everywhere in the room. They fill glass jars and little bowls. They stand big and proud as book ends. They are on the bathroom counters in little baskets. Last year when I was here visiting, I asked her how she managed to collect so many shells. She looked at me and said, "Target, $7.95 a bag, and the big shells I bought at Pottery Barn." I had opened my mouth, but before I could say anything she said, "Well, I do supplement. When I take my walks on the beach I pick up the ones I like and add them to the piles. You can't tell them apart," she had said proudly.

I hear a knock on the door.

"Syd, honey, are you awake?" my mom calls.

"I'm just going to get in the shower and then I'll be down," I yell back.

"Okay, but your father wants to make sure Gary is up because they have to leave soon for their golf game."

Gary emerges from the bathroom dressed in his khakis and a polo shirt. "Morning, Estelle, I'll be down in a sec," he says to my mom through the door.

"Okay."

Silence. Then, "Can I come in?" My mother asks.

"Sure, c'mon in," Gary tells her.

My mom comes in carrying a tray of bagels, mini muffins and coffee. "I thought you might be hungry," she says, setting the tray down on the table across from the bed.

"When we're hungry we'll come down to the kitchen," I tell her.

"I know, but you got in so late last night and you didn't have anything to eat when you got here," she explains.

"Mom, we had dinner at the airport. I told you that."

Gary walks over to my mother and gives her a big hug. "You've always loved feeding us," he says as he picks up a blueberry muffin and stuffs it in his mouth.

Then she turns to me and says, "Here, Syd, have a bagel. I'll put on a shmear of cream cheese for you."

I decline the offer.

"What, you're back on Atkins?" she asks me as she hands Gary another muffin.

"No, I'm not on Atkins, I just don't want a bagel right now. I'm going to take a shower and then I'll come down and have breakfast. I'll make some eggs," I say to her, thinking how good that sounds all of a sudden. Maybe I'll add some cheese and green peppers.

"No, you shouldn't have eggs," my mother says to me. "Here, have a bagel." She pushes the tray at me again.

"Mom, I told you I don't want a bagel. What is it with you?"

My mother looks disappointed, and then smiles. "Okay, then here, have a muffin," she says, picking up the tray and holding it in front of me.

I look at her again and roll my eyes at her.

"What? They're good muffins. Gary, aren't the muffins good?"

Gary nods his head.

"Go ahead, tell her, then."

Gary looks at me, holding back the smirk that is struggling for release, and says with a straight face, "Syd, the muffins are very good, have one."

"Enough!" I shout to my mother, getting out of bed.

My mother moves to put the tray back down on the table.

"What is it with you? I'm getting in the shower and then I'll be down for breakfast and you'll keep me company while I make my eggs and we'll call it a morning," I say.

My mother sits down on the chaise lounge, looking defeated.

"Okay, mom. What has gotten into you?"

"I give up," my mother says, "I'll come clean. I'm trying to get rid of the *chametz*. I plead guilty in the name of tradition." She puts her arms up like she's under arrest.

"Oh, good God," I say. Since when do we get rid of *chametz?*"

Chametz, if I remember correctly from Sunday school, is all of the unkosher-for-Passover foods that must be cleaned out of the house, like bread and cookies and cake. Anything made with yeast.

"As you get on in your years, you realize the importance of tradition," she tells us rather smugly. "And I have all these bagels and muffins that have to be out of the house by sunset tomorrow when Passover begins, and it's a waste to just throw them away, and I have no room for them in my freezer."

Gary sits down by my mother and pats her shoulder, saying, "My mom used to always do that. She always prepared the house for Passover by getting rid of all the breads and stuff." He takes a sip of coffee. My mom is eagerly nodding her head yes to him. "When I was younger, we even had a separate set of dishes and silverware we had to use for Passover. Every year it felt like we were getting ready to move with all of the boxes and stuff that had to be packed for the week and then unpacked after the holiday."

And then I get it. My mom is worried what her in-laws will think if she has baked goods in her house when they arrive for the Seder. It's like competitive Judaism.

"I shouldn't have bought so much," she says sadly.

Gary smiles and takes a half a bagel and spreads on some cream cheese.

"You," my mother says, pointing at Gary. "I always loved you, right from the start. But Gary, honey, you need more cream cheese on that bagel. Here." She takes the bagel from his hands and proceeds to spread on more cream cheese.

"You know," she says as she hands him back a cream-cheese-loaded half bagel, "those mini muffins come 12 in a pack and there was a sale, buy two and the third is free, so I thought why not? Such a deal, no?" But I forgot about it being *chametz,* and now I'm stuck with it, so I'm asking you, Syd, to forget the eggs and help me get rid of all this *chametz,*" she implores me.

My mother reminds me of Rachel when she was younger and would learn a new vocabulary word in school and then use it constantly at home, in sentence after sentence. I think my mother has used the word *chametz* more in the past five minutes than in her entire life.

"Gee, mom, when you make it sound so mouthwateringly appetizing like that—hey, that reminds me of a joke," I say.

My mother looks over to Gary and says, "She hasn't given that up, huh?"

Gary shakes his head no, but adds, "On the good side, I'd say she's getting better at being able to remember the punch line more often than not."

"Okay, are you ready?" I ask them.

"Oooh, big set up here," Gary says, looking over at my mom, who gives his shoulder a squeeze and hands him another mini muffin.

"What do you call a Jewish dilemma?" I ask them.

"Pork on sale!" my father says as he barrels into the room.

"Dad, you ruined my joke," I whine to him.

"Couldn't be helped," he says. "That's always been one of my favorites. Did you sell all your baked goods?" he asks my mother. "Any takers? You should have seen her this morning with me. Always on me to watch what I eat, and it's like I've died and gone to heaven. She's like a drug pusher, I'm telling you. More, more, more. I probably should have my blood sugar checked after all of the lemon poppy seed muffins I ate this morning."

"Lemon poppy seed? I love those kind," Gary says.

This is music to my mother's ear. "Gary, dear, come downstairs. I have some lemon poppy seed muffins left, and I'll pour you a nice glass of fresh Florida orange juice and then you and Max can be on your way to the club for your tee time."

"I put your clubs in my car, Gary," my dad says. "We'll drive with the top down today. Pretty nice for March, huh? The weather in Florida is not too shabby," my dad gushes.

My parents and Gary go downstairs, and I get in the shower to get ready for the day. By the time I've finished drying my hair and getting dressed, Gary and my dad have already left and my mother has placed her tray of bagels and muffins in the center of the kitchen table. She is sitting and sipping a cup of coffee, but jumps up and smiles, pulling out a chair at the kitchen table for me, when I walk in.

"Sit, sit," she tells me. "Let me serve you. I miss having my little princess around."

"Forty-three years old ain't so little," I tell her, but she shakes her head no.

"You'll see, Syd. You'll see with Rachel. Your little girl is always your little girl."

And is baby Rae always your little baby? I wonder silently. *She would be forty years old, and still we don't speak of her.*

My mother hugs me and tells me, "To me, you'll always be my little princess, Syd. Now, what can I get you for breakfast? How about I toast you a sesame bagel with cream cheese," she asks hopefully.

I love her, so I decide to make her happy, and I tell her that a toasted bagel sounds great. For her part, she smiles and tells me to have a muffin while the bagel is toasting. This is becoming a bit on the stressful side, so I take a big yoga cleansing breath and think to myself, *I am breathing in light and joy,* and I invite in positive energy.

Then I pour myself a big mug of coffee because I've found that inviting positive energy into any situation is often helped by the addition of caffeine. My mom brings me my bagel, which she has already spread with cream cheese, and sits across from me.

"So tell me. What time does Rachel's flight come in?"

"Around 4:30. Gary and I will pick her up and then come back here. We're supposed to meet everyone for dinner at 8:00."

"You have a little bit of cream cheese on your chin, honey. Here, let me wipe it off," she says, using her napkin.

I feel like I'm five years old.

"So where are we going for dinner? I wanted to make a reservation last week, but Arlene said to wait because she wanted to talk to Nancy and Evan first."

"We're meeting them at P.F Chang's. I guess Joshua and Jenny really love it there, and you know, what Jewish family doesn't spend Friday night at a Chinese restaurant, right?"

My mom looks disappointed.

"What? Is something wrong?" I ask her.

"No, nothing's wrong," she says in that way that means something is absolutely wrong but that she is willing to suffer as a martyr in silence.

"Tell me what's wrong," I ask her.

"Nothing, dear."

Silence.

I take another cleansing yoga breath, willing the caffeine to help that positive energy filter into my veins.

"So everything is fine, then?" I ask her.

She's finishing her last drop of coffee, and clearing the breakfast dishes. "Yes of course, everything is just fine," she insists.

"Okay then," I say as I bring my coffee cup to the sink.

"It's just that—" her voice trails off.

"What?"

"Oh, nothing, just forget it," she insists.

I look at her and then she says, "It's just that I don't understand why Arlene gets to decide dinner on her own," she complains. "It's a unilateral decision with them. She talks to Nancy, and then they make the decision without consulting with me. I find it a little rude, and I like China Gardens much better than P.F. Chang's."

"Well, you're having the Seder here, so really, it's only fair that Arlene gets to choose dinner tonight, " I say tentatively.

My mom looks at me and says, "I suppose that's true. When did you get to be so wise? It wasn't very long ago that Arlene would drive you a little *meshuga.*"

We finish putting the dishes in the dishwasher, and I wipe the table clean.

"I told you, I've been taking yoga and I'm trying to learn to be more accepting and to just be with what is. To see things more clearly," I try to explain.

She gives me a confused look, and then runs over to her kitchen desk and says, "Speaking of seeing clearly, look at these magnifiers. I just love them; I can read everything with them, even the phone book. Look, don't they look great on me?" She puts on the green rimmed reading glasses.

"Yeah," I agree. "They look really good on you."

She takes them off and tries to put them on me.

"Mom, what are you doing?"

"See how they feel. This is seeing clearly. I don't know what they're teaching you in yoga, but no stretch is going to help you see anything more clearly than a good pair of reading glasses," she says, and I suddenly realize that seeing things clearly also means seeing when to give up and change the conversation.

My mom tells me that she wants to take me shopping at a new boutique, followed by a stop at the Town Centre Mall, and then she wants to have lunch at this outdoor café that apparently has the best panini sandwiches my mother has ever tasted. "One bite, and it's like you've died and gone to heaven," she tells me.

So hours later, sitting at the outdoor café, my mom and I have to get a table for four. We need the extra chairs to hold all of our shopping bags. After lunch we have to stop at the grocery store to pick up a few last minute things in preparation for tomorrow's Seder. Just like when I was little, I walk down the Easter aisle to look at all of the pastel candy and Easter chocolates.

"Let's get some prunes," my mother says, throwing two packages in the shopping cart from the Passover side of the aisle.

"Why prunes?" I ask her, passing by the chocolate eggs filled with different cream centers. I don't remember prunes having anything to do with Passover.

"Oh, Syd, honey. That matzo is so constipating. And to eat it all week? We need the prunes to keep the plumbing going," she explains to me.

"Shhh," I say, looking at the people around us. "People will hear you," I tell her.

We pass an Easter basket made with real chocolate and filled with bright pink, blue and yellow marshmallow baby chicks, with a plush Easter bunny in the center. Looking at our shopping cart with matzo, prunes and jars of gefilte fish, I wonder if my mom entertains Easter fantasies the way I always have.

"We need to buy the dessert, and then we're done," she tells me. She finds the Manischewitz kosher-for-Passover desserts and chooses a marble cake mix and a chocolate brownie mix.

By the time we get home Gary and my dad are already back and are lounging at the pool. My dad is once again busily trying to convince Gary to consider retiring early.

"This could be your life, Gary," he says, pulling his baseball cap over his forehead and leaning back in the lounge chair.

"Someday, Max," Gary tells my dad. "I'm still having fun at Global Investments."

"We could play golf all the time, you'd be near your parents, near Evan and Nancy, what's not to love?" my dad continues.

"So how did you play?" I ask Gary, sitting beside him on the chaise lounge.

"Pretty good," Gary tells me.

My father tells us Gary could improve his game in no time if he was playing year round in Florida.

My mother walks closer to my father and says, "Max, you need to put more lotion on. Your nose is burnt."

My father sighs and dutifully puts on more lotion.

"How was lunch at the club?" my mother asks.

"Great," Gary says. "And my mom and Nancy came and met us all for lunch, so that was nice."

"Oh, how wonderful. I'm looking forward to seeing everyone at dinner tonight. And I just love P.F Chang's," my mother gushes. "How wonderful that your mother organized everything for us."

Breathe in, I think to myself, *breathe out.* I look at my mother and smile.

A LITTLE while later, Gary and I get cleaned up and are ready to go to the airport to pick up Rachel. My parents both offer to come with us, but my mom is busy setting the table for tomorrow, and my dad is watching a Bulls game on T.V. We tell them to stay put, we'll be back soon.

As Gary and I are driving to the airport I ask him if he could imagine retiring soon, if this is the life he could see living. He tells me that he's not ready now, but a little while down the road, this is just where he'd like to be. "Beautiful golf course, terrific country club, the ocean, our family, it's really a done deal. And just think about it. No more Chicago winters. No more blizzards," he adds as he adjusts the car visor to lower the glare of the sun.

I'm quiet, and so he says, "Why, what about you?"

I don't answer right away. I don't know how to answer. I begin slowly.

"It's not that I couldn't picture us here," I say. "It's just that lately, I keep wondering what else there is. We've both always assumed that when you retired, we'd move to Florida, continue in our lifestyle. I guess lately I'm wanting to think about other options. I mean, it's all wonderful, but c'mon. Golf, country club, shopping; is this all there is?" I ask.

"Of course not!" he says emphatically. "There's tennis, and sailing and quick weekend flights to the Bahamas. And you should see the new restaurants that are moving in out near the club."

I take a breath and feel it filter into my lungs before exhaling. Then I tell him that that wasn't what I meant when I asked if this was all there was.

"Okay, then, what did you mean?" Gary asks, looking at me.

I tell him to keep his eyes on the road.

"I don't know. I mean, don't you ever want to buy the Easter candy instead of the gefilte fish?" I ask him.

"Syd, I love you, but half the time I don't know what you're talking about," he says.

I want to explain. I want to ask him if he ever wants to experience something different from how we live, if he ever thinks that maybe we're missing the boat, having been living on cruise control for so long. If maybe the things we've always felt were so important, actually weren't the things that, in the end, are really important.

I think of Montana in my yoga class. At age 36 she is single and a free spirit who, she tells me, is searching for the ultimate. When I asked her what kind of guy she was looking for, who would be the ultimate guy for her, she had laughed, saying that the search for the ultimate wasn't about a guy, but her search for the ultimate Truth. I was skeptical, but intrigued. I've spent most of my years searching for the ultimate: the ultimate diet, the ultimate black dress, the ultimate pair of shoes. But Truth? What did I know about the ultimate Truth?

When Montana talks about searching for the ultimate Truth, the meaning of life, the understanding of the sacred, as she says, I think to myself that I have a long way to go to understand what this Truth that she seeks is about. But just like the lecture with that Scott Someone, I am riveted. Could I ever step out of this planned life and try something different?

I think back to those long ago classes on comparative religion and *I Ching* of which both Gary and my parents disapproved. Was I now ready to take a bite of Easter chocolate, metaphorically speaking? Could I study Eastern thought like Kali does, like Montana? What would I learn? Who would I be? What would I wear?

"Look, Syd, I'm open to Florida's West Coast, if you think you'd be happier there. My parents love Longboat Key, or we could look at Naples. If you feel like you need to try someplace new, I'm open," Gary says encouragingly.

Montana told me last week that her dream is to travel to India to see her guru in an ashram. I watch as the sign for the airport comes up and Gary signals right to enter the exit ramp.

"We should try that new Indian restaurant that opened at home, near the mall," I tell Gary. He just looks at me with this confused expression. "I thought we were talking about Florida, the east coast versus the west coast for my retirement. How did you move to Indian food?" he asks me as he pulls into the parking garage.

"Gary, right there!" I yell to him as he misses a perfect parking spot.

"Sorry, I didn't see it," he says. "I'll find another." But he circles and circles and we go up three more levels before he finally finds another spot. "Perfect," he says as he eases the car into the space.

"It's not perfect," I say, unlocking the door and getting out of the car. "You missed the perfect spot three levels ago, and it was right by the elevators."

"Syd, it's Passover. Our people had to wander through the desert for 40 years, and you're complaining about taking an elevator a few extra floors?"

"Dear God, less than 24 hours in Boca and you already sound like my parents," I tell him.

We wait at baggage for Rachel's flight. "There she is," Gary says, and I turn to see Rachel coming down the stairs. We give each other big hugs, and once again my heart is filled with so much love it could burst.

"Where's your bag?" Gary asks her. "You're only here for the weekend, didn't you use a carry-on?"

Rachel takes our hands and moves over to the baggage carousel for her flight. "Couldn't," she tells us, as we hear the beep signaling that the luggage is starting to come out. "You can't bring liquids on the plane, and I had nowhere to put my shampoo, conditioner, hair gel, perfume, lotion. You know, all my stuff," she explains.

It's true, I think to myself. The biggest things and the littlest things changed after 9/11.

"Oh, look! There's my bag already," Rachel says, edging closer to the carousel. Gary starts to pull off a small black carry-on type bag and Rachel pulls his hand back and says, "No, dad, it's that blue duffel."

Gary pulls off the blue duffel, shaking his head and asking Rachel why she would pack such a large duffel for only two days.

She looks at him as if this were obvious. "Dad, once I knew I had to check a bag anyway, cause of the liquids and stuff, I figured I might as well fill a suitcase so I had options."

"Options?" Gary asks.

"Yeah, options. You know, so I have choices about what I want to wear while I'm here," she explains.

"This makes sense to you, doesn't it?" he asks me.

"Perfect sense," I say, hugging Rachel close to me. "Here, let me take your backpack, it looks heavy," I say to her while Gary pulls her duffel toward the elevator.

"No, really, mom. It's fine, I can carry it," she tells me.

I tell her that she's had a long flight and that she should let dad and me take care of her. I hoist her backpack over one shoulder and my neck gives me a silent scream. "What do you have in here?" I ask.

"My laptop, books, and some other stuff," she says. "Here, it's too heavy for you, I'll take it back," she offers.

"No, no, I'm not that old yet, I can carry it," I say, though I don't sound all that convincing.

"You know, mom, it's easier to carry if you use both the straps instead of just putting it over one shoulder. That's how you distribute the weight," she explains.

"Yeah, I know," I say, following Gary onto the elevator and holding the door open for Rachel. "But this was the cool way to hold a backpack. That's how we carried our backpacks all through college," I explain.

"Maybe that's when you started screwing up your neck," she suggests. "Really, mom, use both straps or let me carry it. You're going to hurt yourself."

I take her advice and put my other arm through the strap, and it is so much easier to carry. In my mind I hear Kali's voice saying, "It's all about balance."

"Rachela!" My parents say in unison as we pull into their long, paved driveway. They're like the paparazzi. My dad is escorting her from the car as my mother snaps pictures.

"Hi Nana, hi Papa," she says hugging them. My mother holds her out in front of her to get a full view.

"Just look at you, so grown up," my mother gushes. "Look at her, Max, doesn't she look wonderful?"

My father hugs Rachel and announces that she grows more beautiful every time he sees her, and how is that possible because she has always been so beautiful. Then he sees her duffel bag and beams. Looking at Gary, he says, "See, she's ready to move to Florida for good, look how much she's packed! Now wrap up your business deals in Chicago and join us in the Sunshine State."

We follow my parents into the house, and while Gary carries Rachel's duffel to her bedroom the rest of us settle in the living room.

"You had a good flight?" my father asks her.

"Yeah, it was easy," Rachel answers.

"Did you have a middle seat?" I ask her.

"No, the aisle," she tells me.

"Good girl," I say, rubbing my neck.

"Are you hungry?" my mother asks her.

"No, I ate on the plane," she says, plopping herself down on the new palm printed couch.

"They serve *bupkis,* nothing, on the plane these days. What could you have eaten?" my mother asks as if she is in a detective show. My dad has reclaimed his favorite chair, and I sit next to Rachel on the arm of the couch. Gary returns to the living room and asks my father what the final score of the basketball game was.

"Bulls 97, Celtics 94. Paul Pierce almost tied the game with a three pointer at the buzzer, but he missed," my dad tells Gary.

My mother shoos her hand at them like she's shooing away a fly. She is focused on more important things than basketball.

She is focused on food.

"What could they have given you on the plane? A little bag with three pretzels in it?" my mother persists.

"I had to switch planes in Chicago, and I bought a turkey sandwich for the flight to Ft. Lauderdale," she tells my mom.

"But that had to be hours ago. Here, let me give you a little something. How about a bagel or a muffin?" she asks as she goes into the kitchen and returns with her tray.

"Ooh, that looks good, but I'm not really hungry now," she tells my mother.

"How about a little nosh?" she begs Rachel. "I have some corned beef in the fridge, I could put a few slices on a bagel for you."

"That's a nosh, mom? That's a meal," I tell her.

"Thanks, Nana, but I'm really not hungry right now, and mom says we're meeting everyone at P.F. Chang's at 8:00," Rachel says.

"Well, it's only 6:00 and by the time we order and actually eat something, it could be close to 9:00, so here, have a little something," she coaxes.

Rachel looks at me and I shrug my shoulders. "She's been at it all day," I explain to Rachel.

"Your father loved the lemon poppy seed muffins," my mother says, as if this is a selling point for Rachel.

"Maybe later, Nana," she says.

"What later? There is no later," my mom says, heading back into the kitchen to put the tray down.

I explain to Rachel that Nana is on a *chametz* kick. Rachel wants to know what a *chametz* kick is.

"What did they teach you in Hebrew school all those years?" my father asks, shaking his head.

"Mostly I remember learning the quick version of Jewish history and how we celebrate our people," Rachel says.

"And what is the quick version?" my father asks.

Rachel smiles, flips her hair to one side, and says, "They tried to destroy us, we prevailed, now let's eat."

"Yeah, that about sums it up," Gary agrees.

"Okay, but what did I miss? What's this *chametz* thing?" Rachel asks.

I explain to her that it's when you clean the house out for Passover by getting rid of anything with yeast, anything that's not kosher for Passover. Rachel asks if that's why my mother is trying to get her to eat the bagels and muffins, and I nod my head yes.

My mother sits down on the loveseat.

"Nana, since when do you do this for Passover? I don't remember you getting rid of stuff like this."

"Well, dear, I thought it would be nice to honor our tradition by following more of the rituals," she explains.

"Oh. Dad, did you ever do this when you were growing up?" Rachel asks.

"All the time," Gary tells her. Rachel gives a nod and says that now it all makes sense.

My mother puts on her innocent look. "What do you mean, dear?" she asks.

"No, it's just that you and Grandma do this little thing." Rachel begins.

My mother interrupts her. "*Thing*? I don't know what you mean by 'we do this little *thing*,'" my mother says, straightening a pillow.

"Nana, it's not a bad thing. You and Grandma just get a little competitive with stuff. It's normal."

"Competitive? I'm the most uncompetitive person in the world. You want competitive? I'll give you competitive. You should meet our neighbor down the street, Marsha Bloom. Whatever you say, she tries to one up you, whatever you buy, she has two, whatever—"

"See, kind of like that, mom," I say to her. "It's like that with you and Arlene."

"Syd, I don't know what you are talking about. This has nothing to do with Arlene. This has to do with God," she announces.

And wisely, we leave it at that.

Then Rachel, the ever-dutiful granddaughter, looks up at my mother and says, "Nana, I am a little hungry. Can I have a muffin?"

"Sure, dear, if you're hungry." My mother says, bringing the tray from the kitchen back over to the couch. "But don't fill up too much, we're having dinner soon."

Chapter Sixteen

"Max, I need you to take out the garbage!" I hear my mother call from the kitchen.

"Be there in a minute," I hear him yell back.

I walk into the dining room and see my father on a stepladder changing light bulbs in the recessed lighting overhead.

"Good morning, princess," he says to me as he twists another bulb into the socket. "You know, when God said let there be light, he should have supplied us with a lifetime's worth of light bulbs." He pops out another bulb and hands me the burnt out one to throw in the garbage bag at his side. I watch him as he finishes, and marvel at what great shape he has kept himself in.

As he comes down from the stepladder, he tells me that Gary and Rachel were up early, going out for a run.

"It's their special time together, and I'm happy to give them the space," I say.

My father smiles. "That's code for 'you're too lazy to jog,' right?"

"I'm not lazy," I tell him. "Besides, I'm really into taking these yoga classes. It's really great for your body and your mind."

"Just don't let them brainwash you," he says.

"Brainwash me—what are you talking about? It's an exercise class."

"You sure it's not full of those Hari Krishnas? There are a lot of nuts out there," my dad explains. "You've got to be careful in those kind of classes."

"I think the Florida sun has gotten to you," I tell him as my mother's voice interrupts us and she yells to my dad, "for the zillionth time," to take out the garbage.

My dad puts the stepladder away, and walks into the kitchen stuffing the bag of used light bulbs and cardboard packaging into the large black trash bag my mom has at her side. As he stuffs in his bag he says to my mom, "no takers this morning, huh?" I look at him, and he shows me the remaining bagels and muffins that have been discarded.

I think of the homeless man I passed in Chicago, when Gary and I went with Jodi and Dave to Bar 23, and I say, "We should have given the food to a soup kitchen."

"This is Boca, honey," my mother says, and turns back to chopping the apples. "Now here, while I make the charoset, you can chop up the other apples for the matzo kugel." She hands me me five Red Delicious apples.

My dad leaves to take the trash out, and I begin slicing the apples on the cutting board.

"That was a lovely dinner last night, wasn't it?" my mother asks me as she mixes the chopped apples with honey, cinnamon, red wine and nuts. "It's so wonderful to all be together, isn't it?"

I smile and nod my head.

"I think Arlene has put on some weight, though, don't you think, Syd?" she asks me, as she pokes her finger in the charoset to sample it. "She's lucky she's such a tall woman, because she can get away with it." She says this as if she were paying Arlene a compliment instead of an insult.

As my mom is talking I can't help but think of the charoset she is making that, as part of the Seder, will be eaten with the *moror*, or bitter herbs. As the *Hagaddah*, the Passover service book telling the story of the Jewish Exodus, will explain tonight, the two are eaten together, the sweet and the bitter, to remind us that even in our freedom, we must not forget the bitterness of slavery, and even in times of oppression, we must keep alive the sweet hope of freedom. My mom seems to be telling of both the sweetness and bitterness that tinges in-law relations, and I can understand, as I have had my moments with my mother-in-law as well.

Kali talks about being an objective observer, and of seeing without reacting, so I've been trying to do that more lately. Of noticing the triggers in interactions where habit dictates a response, not always well thought out. So I'm experimenting with these ideas, and I'm realizing that this coming together for Passover might provide the perfect setting to try out these concepts.

Like last night, when Nancy kept taking about her house being featured this summer in *Coastal Living*, I tried to breathe through my resentment. When she brought it up for the fifth time, I tried reminding myself that this magazine piece made her very happy, and that was good, so I continued breathing and smiling. When she brought it up for like the tenth time, I poured myself another glass of Chardonnay and took a heaping helping of the moo shoo pork. And smiled.

Passover is about telling the story of the Jewish Exodus from slavery in

Egypt to freedom and the Promised Land. I am realizing that both Kali and Montana are right. There are a lot of ways that we are oppressed, from within and without, and every day we are offered a chance to move toward greater freedom. Kali says that that is what yoga is about, freeing yourself from your perceived limits, both physical and emotional, and changing habitual responses, confronting your fears, opening yourself to life—

"*Oy vey*, Syd, you're going to cut your finger off like that," my mother says. "Be careful with that knife, and try to chop the pieces a little smaller."

I hear the front door swing open. "Morning," Gary's voice booms, with a red-faced Rachel trailing in behind him.

"*Oy*, you both must be dehydrated," my mother declares as she rushes to get them water.

"You sound just like my mom," Gary tells her as he and Rachel take the glasses she has filled for them. "It must be a Jewish thing. You know, we can't be merely thirsty, we have to be dehydrated."

I stop chopping and turn toward them. "A perfect setup to this joke I heard the other month," I say.

Rachel rolls her eyes to Gary, who says, "Hey, with you away at college, I've had to be an audience of one to her attempted comedic moments."

"Yeah, yeah," I say. "So anyway, this Irish bloke, Italian gentleman, and Jewish man are running a five mile race. Hot and sweaty as they cross the finish line, they go directly to the corner pub.

"The Irish bloke says to the bartender, 'I'm so thirsty, I must have beer.' The Italian gentleman says, 'I'm so thirsty, I must have Chianti.' The Jewish man says, 'I'm so thirsty, I must have diabetes.'"

I get a few chuckles and then my mother tells us that her neighbor, Marsha Bloom's husband, was just diagnosed with diabetes. I go back to chopping the apples.

"So where did you run?"

"Oh, it was beautiful. We ran all along the intercoastal route," Rachel says, sipping her water.

My mother pulls out two chairs and says, "Come sit, and I'll fix you both something to eat."

Gary and Rachel tell my mother that they're not hungry now, and that they'll eat something later, after they've showered. My mother looks disappointed.

"Don't make the water too hot in the shower after exercising like that, you'll get dizzy and faint," she calls out after them as they both head up the stairs.

"Where did you learn that?" I ask as I begin chopping another apple.

"Everyone knows that, honey," she tells me as she puts the charoset in a Tupperware container and places it on a shelf in the fridge. "Here, let me help you chop," she says as she pulls out another cutting board and takes an apple from my pile.

AFTER SPENDING the morning helping my mother in preparation for the Seder, the afternoon lay gloriously ahead. Gary, Rachel and I spend the afternoon at the beach, soaking up the sun. Returning late in the afternoon, we shower and dress for the evening.

My mom is still in the kitchen.

"Have you been in here all day?" I ask her.

She smiles at me and says, "Of course not. Every now and then I had to go to the bathroom. Here, can you put these salted water bowls on the table?"

I put the bowls on either side of the table, and then ask her what else I can do to help.

"I don't think anything. I've got it all under control," she says, and looking around, I see she does.

"Moses could have used you as his assistant," I tell her. "You could have organized everyone when they had to hurry and leave Egypt."

"Please! Assistant? Moses would have been *my* assistant! I would have been the leader and would have anticipated the Exodus. I would have frozen some loaves of baguettes in advance so we wouldn't have had to leave with only unleavened bread. But Moses is a man, and they don't anticipate."

"I don't think they had freezers back then," I say, pouring myself a Diet Coke. "And I don't think they ate baguettes in Egypt," I offer.

My mom is peeling the shell off the hardboiled egg for the Seder plate. "Well, pita bread, then," she says. She doesn't address the freezer problem.

My mother carries the Seder plate and places it in the center of the table. On it she has included all the requisites that tradition dictates: a hard boiled egg, a roasted shank bone, raw horseradish root, charoset, chopped horseradish, sprigs of parsley and lettuce. She adds to the table a plate with three whole matzohs covered with a cloth, an empty wine glass for Elijah, candles and matches and, thankfully, bottles of wine. Each item symbolically represents part of the story of the Exodus, the story of leaving Egypt for the Promised Land. My mother has set each place setting with a *Hagaddah,* the book that is used for the service during the Seder.

"Nana, the table looks so nice," Rachel says, coming in from the deck where she was sitting with Gary and my dad.

"Thank you, honey," my mom says, giving Rachel a hug.

Rachel inspects the Seder plate and then tells my mother that she should put an orange on the Seder plate.

"Rachel, dear, if you're hungry for an orange, just ask. I'm happy to slice you one. Our Florida oranges are delicious," she exclaims proudly, as if she grew them herself.

"No, Nana, I don't want to eat an orange. I just suggested it because, you know, like a lot of people are putting an orange on the Seder plate these days."

This is news to my mother, and news to me.

"An orange?" my mother asks again. "Why an orange?"

Rachel takes a glass from the cupboard, fills it with ice, and pours the rest of my Diet Coke in her glass. She walks into the living room, and we follow her and sit down. "Well, I learned about the orange from some kids at Hillel at school," she begins.

My mom interrupts her, saying, "Oh Rachel, I'm so glad you're spending time at Hillel. That's a great place to meet some nice Jewish boys." Hillel is the Jewish center at colleges that provides social activities for students.

Rachel informs my mother that she doesn't spend that much time there, but they were having a free pizza and pedicure night, so how could you pass that up?

"Anyway, it was the other week, and some girls were talking about what they were going to do for Passover. And we just started talking about how we celebrate, you know, and about traditions."

My mom interrupts with a resounding version of the song "Tradition" from *Fiddler on the Roof*. Just then my dad walks in, and thinking that this must be performance night at the Arthurs', he joins my mother in snapping his fingers and trying to harmonize with her.

"Did I miss something?" Gary asks, sipping a beer and coming in from the deck.

"Rachel is just trying to tell my mother something, and she's gone and broken into song," I explain.

"I'm the next *American Idol*," my mother says, taking a bow. Then she corrects herself and says, "The next Jewish *American Idol*."

Rachel gives up with her story and goes back into the kitchen to put her glass in the sink.

"And that's why nothing ever changes with Jewish traditions," I say. "No one will sit down long enough without interrupting to hear what someone else is trying to say or suggest," I say as if I'm giving a sermon.

"Rachel, come back in here. We want to hear about the orange," my mom pleads.

"Oh, good. Is this a knock knock joke?" My dad asks as he launches into his own: "Knock, knock."

"Who's there?" my mother asks.

"Banana."

"Banana who?"

"Knock knock."

"Who's there?"

"Banana."

"Banana who?"

"Knock knock."

"Who's there?"

"Banana."

"Banana who?"

"Knock knock."

"Who's there?"

"Orange."

"Orange who?"

"Orange you glad I didn't say banana! I always loved that one!" My dad says, chuckling.

"I rest my case," I say, looking at a silent and resigned Rachel.

My mother, who finds my dad amusing, sees me looking at Rachel and says, "Okay, Rachel. Please tell us about the orange on the Seder plate."

My dad looks at us and says, "Since when is there an orange on the Seder plate?"

My mother says, "Max, shhh, be quiet and listen to Rachel."

Rachel explains that some girls were telling the story about why their families put an orange on the Seder plate. "The story goes that one day, years ago, a woman asked her rabbi when there would be female rabbis. The rabbi had looked at her and laughed, waving her off and saying, 'A female rabbi? Why that's as ridiculous as an orange on the Seder plate!'"

"I love it!" my mother declares. "Rachel, get the orange!"

Rachel goes back to the kitchen and gets an orange from the refrigerator. She hands it to my mom, but my mother tells Rachel that she should do the honors, and so Rachel slices the orange and places it in the middle of the Seder plate.

My mother nods her head in satisfaction and says, "Okay, then. The brisket is warming in the oven, the matzo ball soup is simmering on the stove, the apple matzo kugels are in the warmer, the gefilte fish is on the salad plates, and the green beans have been sautéed. I'm just going to spritz on a little more perfume and I'll be all set."

"I bet that's just what the Jewish slaves said before leaving Egypt," I venture.

"Hell," my mother says. "If I knew that I would be wandering in the desert for 40 years, I'd spritz on a lot of perfume and take some antibacterial gel too," she says as she heads up the stairs. "And I don't think I'd wear these shoes," she adds as she gets to the top and models her Fendi sandals.

A FEW minutes later Arlene and Fred arrive, followed by Evan, Nancy, Joshua and Jenny. We all go outside to greet them. Arlene hands my mother a big box of chocolates and a bottle of wine, explaining that they're both kosher for Pesach.

"Thank you," my mom says, kissing the air by Arlene's cheek. "But you didn't have to bring anything!"

"Estelle, darling. You wouldn't let me make anything for the Seder. What? I'm going to come empty-handed after you make the whole dinner?" she exclaims.

"Don't be silly. It's my pleasure. And besides, you took all of us to dinner last night. It's my turn."

"Well, Estelle," Arlene laughs. "It's not like anyone is keeping score," she says, though that's exactly what they've been doing. She follows my mother into the house.

I kiss Arlene and Fred hello, and then go out to see Evan, Nancy and the kids, who are walking up the driveway entrance. We all kiss hello, and Rachel and her cousins follow the grown-ups (silly to say grown-ups as if they are still kids, but it's so hard to realize that they are adults now, too) into the house.

Nancy walks over to my mother and hands her a big tray of macaroons. "I hope you can use these with dessert. There's a mix of chocolate chip, coconut, coffee and almond. I bought them at Samantha's Puff. Her pastry is simply fabulous, and she offers a whole line of kosher-for-Passover treats," she explains.

"I'm telling you, those poor slaves leaving Egypt with just unleavened bread. They'd never figure all these years later we'd be marking their departure with Passover chocolates, cookies and those Manischewitz kosher-for-Passover cake mixes that mom made for dessert," I say to no one in particular.

"It's all about marketing," Gary adds, and Evan is nodding his head in agreement.

"Well, marketing, sure, but it's ultimately about tradition, don't you think?" my mother asks, and I'm hoping that she doesn't break into song again. "Here, let's all sit down, because everything is warming and I don't want anything to get dried out," my mother explains as she invites everyone to be seated. Though my father typically sits at the head of the table, my mother insists that that is where she must sit so it will be easier for her get up and down with the meal, which must be coordinated with the service.

Arlene tells my mother that the table looks beautiful, and my mother is beaming until Arlene's face falls.

"Estelle, why is there an orange on the Seder plate?" my mother-in-law asks as if she is informing the waiter there is a fly in her soup.

Before my mother can answer, Jenny says, "Oh cool. It's from that feminist rabbi story, right? Way to go, Estelle!"

"Well, Jenny, I can't take credit for that. Rachel just shared that story with us, and added this tradition to our Seder," my mother explains, winking at Rachel.

"Could someone please fill me in?" Fred asks. "I don't get it."

Jenny looks over to Rachel to tell the story, but Rachel says, "Go ahead, Jenny. You can tell them."

And so Jenny tells the story and Arlene says, "leave it to college life to rewrite tradition," but Nancy and Evan say they think that's a great story and Fred says the color orange looks nice on the Seder plate and so Arlene smiles and says, "I know of some female rabbis. You have to get used to it, like female pilots, but they seem to do just fine," and that kind of ends the conversation.

"It's almost like a drinking game," Joshua whispers to Rachel and Jenny.

My mother, who claims her hearing is going, doesn't miss a word. "What do you mean 'it's like a drinking game?'" my mother asks Joshua. Rather than looking irritated, she seems excited. Like the orange on the Seder plate has opened her up to new ways of thinking about Passover.

Joshua looks like he feels badly that my mom heard him.

"No, nothing disrespectful," he says to my mother. "It's just that the Seder starts with a glass of wine—"

"The Kiddush," Fred interrupts.

"Right, Grandpa, the Kiddush, and then there's like all these places in the *Hagaddah* that tell you to have like another glass of wine, and another, what are there, like at least four times? That's awesome," Joshua says. "So it's sort of like a drinking game at school," he finishes.

Nancy tells us that he should be hearing from Harvard Med School any day now. I think this is her way of telling us not to get the wrong idea about Joshua. He may be a drunk, but he's a really smart drunk.

"And you know how we leave the extra glass of wine for Elijah? Who one day is supposed to come and drink it and signal the time of the Messiah?" Jenny says to Rachel, who nods her head, "That's kinda like waiting around for the guy you have a crush on to show up, but he never does." Jenny giggles, with Rachel joining her.

Arlene adds, "And Jenny's been dating this nice Benjamin Gellerman," as if to make sure we know that Jenny is not sitting around waiting for a no-show.

"And she's been accepted to a bunch of law schools," Nancy chimes in.

We go through the service taking turns around the table reading from the *Hagaddah*. We perform the washing of the hands, the *karpus,* where the parsley is dipped into the salt water, and the breaking of the matzo. After the retelling of the story of the Exodus, we read the four questions, the ten plagues, sing "Dayenu" and drink the second cup of wine.

At this point my mother, with the help of Arlene, serves the matzo ball soup and gefilte fish. While eating, we take a break from "Passover" and instead talk about college, politics and vacations. We talk about the new nosy neighbors who moved in next to my parents and whom they have privately named Mrs. Kravitz, after the nosy busybody character of the old 1970s hit show *Bewitched.* After we've eaten the soup and the gefilte fish, Nancy and I clear the plates so we can get ready to resume the service. As we're piling the dishes in the kitchen my mother and Arlene join us, checking on the temperature of the brisket and matzo kugel.

Then my mother says, "There should be something on the Seder plate that relates to a story of someone asking the question about when men will help in the kitchen on Passover. And the answer would be something like: Men helping in the kitchen on Passover? Why, that's as ridiculous as a piece of Godiva on the Seder plate."

Even Arlene smiles at this, and I tell my mom, "Good for you. If you're going to dream about fighting patriarchy, you might as well go all out and make it delicious."

Returning to the table, we open more bottles of wine as we go over the symbolism of the foods on the Seder plate, and how they relate to the Jewish struggle to be free.

And then we eat.

And eat.

And eat.

And drink.

And we are so full from eating and drinking that we find returning to the service too taxing. But one look that passes from Arlene to Nancy, and a kick under the table from Gary that follows into a look that I give my mother as I give a slight nod in the direction of Arlene, and my mother perks up, saying, "C'mon, everyone. Our people wandered in Egypt for 40 years to reach the Promised Land. The least we can do is finish the service."

Joshua nods his head in agreement and asks, "Don't we have, like, two more glasses of wine that we need to drink for the service?"

We have already gone through bottles, filling up beyond the dictates of the Seder.

Nancy tells us that she is sure that Joshua will be accepted at Harvard Med. Joshua burps.

Flipping through the *Hagaddah,* my mother says, "We'll continue the service on page 28, where we say grace after the meal."

As Fred is saying grace we drink the third cup of wine, and I notice that Joshua, Jenny and Rachel have gulped their drinks like they're trying to quench the thirst of desert wanderers.

Maybe the wine has gotten to me, because without thinking I blurt out, "This is really too dry."

Arlene takes another sip from her glass and says, "I don't think it's too dry at all."

I realize that my mother-in-law thinks that I'm talking about the bottle of wine she brought that we are now drinking. I correct her. And seeing her expression, I do it quickly.

"No, no, Arlene. The wine is delicious," I say, taking another sip to prove to her my loyalty of her wine choice. "I was talking about the *Hagaddah* we use. It really is dry, isn't it? I mean, there's no real life in it, you know? No spirit, nothing that really connects you to the sacred."

"Yeah, I know what you mean," Jenny says, and Rachel is nodding along.

"We've always used this *Hagaddah,*" my mother says, and Arlene and Fred agree.

"We have the same ones," Arlene says. "Everyone uses them."

"Dude," Joshua says, though I don't know who "dude" refers to. "This *Hagaddah* is put out by Maxwell House Coffee. Of course it's going to be dry. They make coffee, and no one even drinks their coffee anymore. People drink Starbucks, Seattle's Best, maybe Dunkin' Donuts, but not Maxwell House."

"Yeah, why is it that Maxwell House Coffee makes these *Hagaddahs?* That is really weird," I say.

"They're free," my mother says.

"Pork on sale," I respond.

Only Gary and my parents understand my reference. Everyone else looks at me like I'm crazy. I'm tempted to tell Arlene and Nancy my college GPA to redeem myself in their eyes, the way they have been trying to redeem Joshua and Jenny.

"Okay, just because they're free doesn't mean they're good. I've seen tons of different *Hagaddahs.* We should find some new ones for next year," I suggest.

"The people at Maxwell House are good to the Jews. They've been making these *Haggadahs* for over 70 years," Arlene tells us.

"Here's to Maxwell House," Joshua says holding up his wine glass and making a toast.

Rachel and Jenny clink each other's glasses and drink their wine.

"You know," Jenny says, moving her water glass to make room for setting down her wine, "I had to take another history class this semester, and I wanted an easy 'A' so I took this Jewish history class with Professor Rosenberg. Everyone on campus knows that the class is practically all Jewish students, and he treats everyone like young kids in Hebrew school class. You know, coddles them and gives extensions for any excuse you could come up with." She sees her mother give her a look, but continues anyway. "No, really. Like this one guy wanted to see how lenient the professor would be, and so he told Professor Rosenberg that he needed an extension on his paper that was due that day, on Monday, because he had gone to a party Saturday night and drank too much and got really sick, you know, and told him that he was throwing up all day Sunday, and that he had planned to finish his paper that day, but with such a horrible hangover he couldn't move except to make it to the bathroom to, you know, like vomit again."

Arlene and Nancy look mortified. My mother, on the other hand, is as attentive and riveted as I imagine Moses was when God talked to him at Mount Sinai.

"He really said that to the professor?" My mother asked.

Jenny is nodding her head yes. "Yeah, really, I swear that's what he said, I was there. And you know what Professor Rosenberg said? Well wait, before I tell you that, I should tell you that the guy's name is Michael Blumberg, clearly Jewish, right? And so the Professor gets all, like, Jewish grandfather talking to Jewish grandson, having a real heart to heart, you know? The professor first asks Michael if he feels okay now, and tells him that he should eat a banana and drink some orange juice to make sure he gets enough potassium after vomiting so much, right? And then he tells Michael that he needs to be careful about how he treats his body, that his body is a temple, and he is the steward of it, and on and on. He wants to know if this has happened before, and makes sure that Michael knows his office hours if he ever wants to talk about anything bothering him, and that if he can't come during his set office hours, he should just call and make an appointment. Professor Rosenberg doesn't even talk about the paper that's due! So finally Michael asks him about the paper, and you know what Professor Rosenberg does? He asks Michael if he had a bar mitzvah! And when Michael said yes, Professor Rosenberg said to Michael, 'then you've been a man since the age of 13, and know about responsibility.' So Michael looks at him and asks what that means in terms of an extension. And the professor just says, 'you are the best judge of yourself and the keeper of your conscience.'"

"So what happened?" Fred asks.

"And I'm hoping that you turned your paper in on time," Nancy adds.

Jenny shakes her head yes. "But you should have seen Michael. You know, it had started out as a joke because Michael just wanted an extension and heard that you could get away with anything in Rosenberg's course. But after class he went back to his apartment and worked on his paper all afternoon, passed on this really great party that night, and turned in this really long paper, longer than it even needed to be, the next day. So really, it was only a day late, and he ended up working harder than he would have originally. Crazy."

"He sounds like a wonderful professor, " I say, sipping my wine so Arlene will know that I like her choice and wasn't complaining about it.

"Well, I got an 'A' in the class," Jenny says, and I see Nancy's face relax a little. "I remember one class where the professor talked about the Seder, and the meaning of the retelling."

"Wait, honey, hold that thought. Before you tell us, let me clear the table and bring out the dessert," my mother says.

Arlene, Nancy and I start to clear the dishes, and add them to the stacks already sitting on the kitchen counter.

"If we ever reach the time when we can put a Godiva on the Seder plate, can it be a truffle?" I ask. We arrange the macaroons on a serving dish along with the marble cake and brownies from the Manischewitz mix. Arlene carries the tray to the dining room table, and my mother follows behind with a carafe of coffee. I carry the milk, and Nancy brings out the sugar dish filled with white, pink and yellow packets.

"Who wants coffee?" my mother asks. We all put up our hands, and then Joshua asks, "Is it Maxwell House coffee?"

"No honey, it's Starbucks—oh dear," she says to Joshua.

"I think they need a new marketing strategy," Evan offers. "I bet a very small percentage of people using this *Hagaddah* are serving Maxwell House Coffee."

"You've gotta change with the times," Jenny says. "Maybe Starbucks will put out a *Hagaddah.*"

"Maybe Manischewitz will come up with a new cake mix," my dad says, biting into the marble cake. "Estelle, I love you, you know that. But I'm telling you, these Manischewitz cake mixes taste like the cardboard box."

"Well dear, it's kosher for Passover," she explains. "It's more than our people had when they left Egypt."

I take a sip of coffee, savoring the taste. "You know, I've always thought it was kind of ridiculous to have all of these kosher for Passover foods. If you're marking the Exodus, shouldn't you mark it in a way that you give up something the way the Jewish slaves from Egypt had to give up something? I mean, you didn't hear Moses saying, 'Now remember folks, I only want you to chew kosher for Passover bubble gum and drink kosher for Passover Coke. Make sure you only have kosher for Passover cookies.'"

"Marketing," Evan says again, and Gary nods his head in agreement.

I pour myself another cup of coffee from the carafe my mother has refilled. "Maybe the whole Passover thing today is more about us being slaves to the marketers rather than to Pharaoh. You know, wandering around for 40 years, or in my case, 43 years—"

My mother interrupts me. "You know, summer will be here before you know it, and you'll be celebrating another birthday. What do you want this year?" she asks.

I look at her, and my father says, "Estelle, you're interrupting her. Let her finish."

"I'm just saying the Exodus was about leaving Egypt and looking for the Promised Land. You know how when Moses went up Mount Sinai and the people got worried when he didn't come right back down? You know how they built that golden calf as an idol because they needed something to believe in? Maybe that's what we're all doing."

I notice that everyone at the table seems a bit startled by my ramblings. But I can't help thinking about the things that Scott Someone was talking about at the Buddhism lecture, or the things that Kali talks about during yoga class. "I mean, think about it. We all kind of make our own golden calves, don't we?"

My mother looks at me, and I think she is maybe really listening to what I am saying, or what the wine in me is saying, when she asks me, "Speaking of the golden calf, are you more into yellow gold or white gold these days? If I were to get you, say, a bracelet for your birthday, which would you prefer?"

"That's it! That's what I mean!" I say, my hand hitting the table for emphasis.

"Wonderful, dear! A bracelet it is, but yellow gold or white gold?" my mother asks me, reaching over for another macaroon.

"No, that's my point," I try to explain. I look over at Rachel, but I can't read her face. "Sierra would understand what I'm trying to say," I tell her.

Rachel's face registers confusion. "Sierra?" she asks.

"Yeah, your friend at school. The one who wants to join the Peace Corps?"

"Wait, you've never met Sierra," Rachel says.

I realize everyone thinks I've gone a little crazy. I take a sip of my coffee and reach for a brownie, to show that I'm willing to buy into the kosher for Passover idea, to ease them from any worry that I'm going off the deep end and drowning in the Red Sea.

"Well, no, I've never met Sierra, but I think she's sort of like my new friend, Montana," I try to explain.

"Sierra, Montana, what is this, you're new friends are all hippies from out West?" my father asks.

"Actually, I think I'm trying to head East," I say, knowing that I've drunk one too many glasses of wine, and spoken one too many sentences. "I'm just saying that we all seem to make our golden calves and pay homage to them, believing that they are what will bring us happiness. You know for me, I've spent my whole adult life trying to pay homage to diet after diet so I could find redemption on my bathroom scale. But maybe dieting is like a false idol, a golden calf. The gold that glitters isn't really gold, and it keeps us from reaching the true Promised Land."

"So what are you saying, you don't want a gold bracelet after all? You want maybe a silver bangle and a renewed membership at Weight Watchers?" my mother asks, looking befuddled.

Silence.

"Okay, Aunt Syd? This is so totally cool, because this is what I was starting to say before dessert. About Professor Rosenberg and his lecture on understanding the retelling of the Exodus."

Everyone is looking to Jenny, and I am relieved to be off the hook and maybe just floating rather than drowning in the Red Sea.

"Oh, tell us, dear," Arlene says without enthusiasm.

"Yeah, okay. So let me think how he explained this. He was, like, saying that the reason we retell the story every year is partly to remember our history, but also because we are living that history."

She pours herself a little more wine, and I see Nancy grimace. She takes a sip and continues.

"So what I remember him saying was that we are all enslaved by different things, and it is those things that enslave us that need to be brought to consciousness so that we can free ourselves from our own bondage and discover true freedom."

Nancy passes her a macaroon and tells her to try one. I think she wants the dense macaroon to soak up some of the alcohol Jenny has consumed. To me, she sounds wonderfully sober. But then again, I'm not.

Jenny takes a bite of the macaroon and says, "So, like, he was saying that we all have our own Egypt and we all have our own Israel within us."

"Great!" Fred says. "Do I get the free miles for both?"

"Grandpa, let me finish," Jenny says. "I'm trying to remember exactly how he put this. The word Egypt in Hebrew is *Mitzrayim*, which literally means 'the narrow place,' and Israel is described as a land flowing with milk and honey, which really means a land that is both sustaining and sweet. So when you retell this story, year after year, what you are really reminding yourself of are the places within you where you are living as a slave in Egypt, in the narrow place, and how the movement needs to be about finding the Promised Land, you know, like where you find your sweet nourishment to sustain you."

I feel my heart pounding. "This is it!" I want to yell. "This is what I want to be searching for." They have already moved on to another topic, so I keep my thoughts to myself. I don't know how to contain the beating of my heart from this revelation, so I nibble another macaroon.

"I don't think Elijah is coming," Jenny tells Rachel. "His wine glass is still sitting there."

"Yeah, but you're supposed to leave the front door open so Elijah knows to come in," Rachel says, looking at the tightly closed front door.

"*Oy gevault!*" my mother says. "With that Mrs. Kravitz for a neighbor, the last thing I need is to leave the door open. She'll be sitting with a bowl of popcorn across the yard, watching our every move like she's watching a movie."

"Is popcorn kosher for Passover?" Gary wonders aloud.

"What's not to be kosher about it?" my dad asks. "It's just popped corn."

We all start to get up from the table, but Arlene says, "Wait, we need to give the final toast."

This is surprising to me, because Arlene is not one to encourage anyone having more wine.

We all hold up our wine glasses and Arlene says the last words of the Seder: "Next year in Jerusalem!" We all repeat, "Next year in Jerusalem!"

And for a minute, we all seem really united, not just as family, but united in joy and in an understanding of the importance of Israel to the Jewish people, the importance of the Promised Land for everyone.

It's a moment almost suspended in time until Rachel says, "Me and my roommates are talking about going to Israel next summer—" and my mother interrupts her.

"Israel? You don't want to go there now, it's not safe." Arlene nods her head in agreement. "And it's 'my roommates and I,'" my mother adds.

"You can come visit us all in Florida," my dad offers. "It's like little Israel here anyway." And with that, the Seder is over.

SITTING AT the gate the next evening, waiting for our plane to board, I look over to Gary and I take his hand in mine.

"I don't want to be in the narrow place," I tell him, searching his face.

Gary takes the boarding pass from my hand, looks at it, and then gives me his. "Fine," he says, "I'll sit in the middle seat this time."

"Zone one, those seated in zone one are now free to board," the voice booms. Gary and I get up.

"I wasn't talking about the middle seat," I tell Gary as we move up in the line. "I was talking about Egypt. I don't want to live in Egypt, in the narrow place."

"Oh," Gary says with what I take to be warmth and understanding. "That narrow place," and then, he switches back his boarding pass from me and walks on ahead, boarding the plane and claiming his window seat. And the song that I hear in my head is the old song by Stealers Wheel called *Stuck in the Middle with You.*

After we're sitting down in our seats, I take Gary's hand and put it on my neck.

"Rub," I demand.

Chapter Seventeen

"It's too quiet," I tell Montana. "It's so quiet I can hear myself think," I say as we head toward the city in her environmentally correct Prius, my gas guzzling Range Rover hiding safely in my garage.

"Perfect," Montana says. "That's a sign that you're ready to purify yourself by emptying out the clutter in your mind, and waking yourself up to the divine stillness within you."

"Either that, or I should maybe get my engine checked. I never realized how loud my car was," I tell her, still feeling a little nervous about going with her to the Om Guru Meditation Center.

Without the sound of an engine roaring, I feel like I'm riding in a fake car at an amusement park. Montana opens the windows to let in the refreshing May evening air of an unseasonably warm night. I can smell the scent of lilacs riding on the wind. Montana takes a deep breath and sighs contently. She seems so happy and relaxed, I'm worried about asking her to close the window and put on the air conditioning to avert any allergens that might be floating along the breeze. I'm betting that Montana doesn't have allergies. She's too laid back to let something like pollen bother her.

"I love spring," Montana says, her hair flying wildly in the wind. "So much birth and renewal. It's like the season that reminds our own inner self that anything is possible, you know?"

I nod my head in agreement, sneeze, and put my hair in a ponytail.

Montana has been telling me for the past six weeks that I should go with her to the meditation center where she practices. Right after I met her in my first yoga class, we became fast friends. The second week at Prana Yoga I had asked her after class if she wanted to go out for coffee. She had told me no, and I remember feeling a bit rejected until she finished her sentence by saying, "Coffee is the enemy of a healthful lifestyle. How about we go out for a chai?" And so we did. Soon it became our little ritual that twice a week we followed our yoga practice with a trip to Starbucks, where I shunned my dark roast and sipped Montana's soy chai recommendation.

We shared a lot as we sat over our drinks, and got to know one another. Of course, some things I kept private, like how on the way home from our chai dates I often stopped at the Dunkin' Donuts drive thru and ordered a medium hazelnut coffee.

In the weeks following the Passover Seder, I thought a lot about wanting to leave that narrow place and moving into a land that was sweet and sustaining. I didn't know where to look, or where to begin, but here was this really earthy woman on a spiritual quest, and inviting me to come along. I took it as a sign—or, as she likes to say, an auspicious sign.

I had a lot of questions for Montana about Om Guru meditation. Talking on the phone one evening, I told her I thought I was ready to go with her, but I wanted to ask her a few more things.

"Ask away," she had said.

"Well, first, what do you wear to the meditation center?" I began.

Montana had just laughed and said, "I'm telling you, Syd, from day one you cracked me up."

But I wasn't kidding. I need to know these kinds of things. I've spent my life knowing these kinds of things.

"No, seriously. I mean, when I go to temple, I usually wear a suit. Sometimes a pantsuit, but mostly a skirt and a blazer," I explain.

"Okay, you definitely don't need to wear a suit, Syd. Just wear something comfortable. And I promise you Om Guru is not about the clothes. No one cares what you wear. People there are concerned about the inner you, about your journey to realize and meet the Self," she explained.

I thought for a minute and then said, "So let me ask you it this way. When I meet my Self, should I meet her in country club casual or something more dressy?"

All I got out of Montana with that question was more of her giggling. Then she went on to tell me that I should just make sure I'm dressed to sit comfortably on the floor.

"Really? On the floor? Because at our temple, if you come late, they have these seats set up in the foyer for the overflow with a closed-circuit TV," I tell her, thinking of the High Holy days and the need to come extra early to get the good seats.

Montana explained it had nothing to do with coming early or coming late. That at Om Guru, you sit on the floor for the talks and also for the meditations.

"They have cushions on the floor, so it's comfortable," she had told me.

Imagining myself sitting on the floor, I immediately nixed the idea of wearing a short spring skirt. I wanted this to be a search about revealing my inner divinity, not my inner thighs.

I smooth the long gauze skirt that gathers around my ankles as Montana switches the radio station. There's this store at the mall called Earthy Chic, which I'd never set foot in. The mannequins in the window look like someone dressed them back in 1969 and never returned to update their look. They are stuck in the height of the hippie generation, selling fashions that would have been perfect for the summer of love in Haight-Ashbury, or Woodstock. But a few days ago I ventured in because one look in my closet told me I had nothing that would work for a meditation center.

"I love this song!" Montana exclaims, turning up the volume. It's John Lennon singing "Instant Karma." "You know what this means," Montana says, giving me a knowing look. "It's another auspicious sign that the spiritual path is beckoning you," she tells me.

"So tell me again what it's like in there. Tell me what to expect," I say as I look out the window and see an older couple sitting on their front porch, a yellow lab at their feet.

Montana turns down the radio and explains how on Thursday nights at Om Guru, it's Satsang. "Satsang literally means in the company of the Truth. Tonight there will be other devotees who gather to chant, meditate and to listen to a speaker. Either someone who is a teacher in the Om Guru tradition, or a member of the meditation center who will talk about his or her experience as a devotee of this spiritual path and to our guru, Gurujai."

At the end of the street she turns right and drives up a hill on a private way. The road opens up to acres of mossy grass sprinkled with benches surrounded by tulips, and bursts of daffodils. At the top of the hill is a grand brick building that looks like an old boarding school. We drive around to the back where there is a large parking lot, already substantially filled. Montana eases the car into a space, closes the windows, and announces, "We're here."

I get out of the car and take a deep breath. Montana is watching me and smiling.

"Isn't that Pranayama breath just the best?" she gushes. "So cleansing," she adds as I watch her inhale deeply through her nose, letting her lungs fill up completely before slowly exhaling and letting it all out.

"The reason why so many people are saddled with illness is because they don't breathe right—they breathe too shallowly," she tells me as we walk toward the entrance.

Montana works in the billing department of a holistic health practice and often laments on the diseases brought about by a mindless Western culture.

I watch her run her fingers through her tightly curled, long auburn hair, and I remember that my hair is still in a ponytail, so I take out the ponytail holder and shake my long hair loose.

"People breathe too shallowly, and that contributes to so many health conditions," she continues.

We walk into the center, and the smell of incense wafts through the air in greeting. I breathe it in and hope that I am breathing deeply enough to ward off the next medical condition that threatens to afflict my age group. As I follow Montana in the corridor, I see her stop and begin taking off her shoes.

"Is this optional?" I ask her.

"What, taking off your shoes?" she asks me.

"Yeah, do I have to?"

"Of course you have to. You can't walk into a mediation center with shoes, Syd," she tells me as she places her clogs on the shelf next to rows of shoes.

She sees my face fall. "Is something wrong?" she asks me.

I begin taking off my really cute pale pink Prada sandals. "No problem," I tell Montana. "It's just they're perfect with this skirt," I tell her as I place them on the shelf.

I follow Montana into the main foyer, and again, just like with the Prana Yoga Center, I am impressed. To the right is a beautiful slate fountain hanging on the majority of the wall, flanked on either side by trees and foliage. Against the left wall is a long beechwood console table with a large vase filled with fresh cut flowers and a big, sandy pink conch shell on the right. Above the table is a giant framed color photograph of a beautiful young woman draped in a maroon shawl, with a fabulous matching hat covering most of her glossy, short brown hair. Her deep brown eyes are luminous, and though I love Bliss Salon, where I do my waxing, my eyebrows never looked as perfect as this woman's. And it's a good thing that her eyebrows are as perfect as they are, because she has that red dot between her eyes pulling your focus into that spot. Her skin looks like she could do a Dove commercial for naturally creamy skin, and the whole gestalt would be perfect on the cover of *Vogue*.

Montana sees me looking at this enormous photograph and walks over to me, putting her arm around my shoulder and squeezing it.

"She's beautiful," I tell her. "Who is she?"

"That's Gurujai, our guru," she tells me. My jaw drops.

"That's the guru?" I ask, never imagining someone so stunning would hold such a position. "She could be a model," I tell Montana, who laughs.

"More a model of spiritual living," she tells me, and while I feel a bit shallow (not in breathing, just in superficiality), I still can't imagine that this is the guru. I guess I was thinking older Indian woman with wrinkled, weathered skin. And short in stature, with a dreary robe that covers a nondescript body. This woman, on the other hand, looks regal. She could sell anything: a diet plan, a skin regime, a designer handbag.

I turn away from the picture and ask Montana how I missed that her guru was drop dead gorgeous. Before she can answer, a young woman dressed in loose cargo khakis and a tight cotton T-shirt that barely covers her stomach with a picture of some deity with a whole bunch of arms, comes over to say hi to Montana.

"*Namaste,*" she says, and Montana answers her with the same. Then she says, "Candace, I want you to meet my friend Syd. This is her first time at Om Guru. Syd, this is Candace."

"Nice to meet you," I say, holding my hand out, just as she puts her hands together in prayer and says *"Namaste"* to me. I wonder if one of the arms of the deity on her shirt might want to shake hands, but I let my hand drop to what I now know is called my heart center and put my hands together to reciprocate her *Namaste.*

"It's a wonderful night to be here. We have Ajatashatru from the San Francisco Om Guru Center speaking," Candace says.

"Oh, he's fantastic!" Montana concurs. "I did a day long class with him when I was on a month long retreat at the ashram."

From somewhere that I can't see, I hear a loud tone that startles me. I look at Montana and Candace, who begin leading me toward the doors to the left of the fountain that have just been opened. Montana tells me that that is the sound of the conch shell, calling the devotees to the meditation hall.

"I didn't have a chance to show you all around the center, but we can do that after Satsang," she tells me.

I follow her in, and feel like I'm in the grand hall of a museum. There are rows and rows of maroon cushions on the floor, and in the front is a large altar covered with a long maroon silk tablecloth with a smaller yellow cloth covering the top. Small glass bowls with floating lit lotus candles line the perimeter of the table. On the back center of the altar is a spray of pink, orange and yellow lilies, and in the center of the altar is a raised shelf lined in maroon velvet holding a pair of worn, brown leather sandals. I'm tempted to ask Montana if she thinks they have those in a size 7½, but stop myself. I need to focus. I'm here to follow a spiritual path. I'm here to seek enlightenment.

I continue following Montana and Candace to cushions set in the fourth row. As Candace sits, Montana tells me she wants to show me some things in the back of the mediation hall. "Candace will save our seats," Montana tells me.

"You mean our cushions," I correct, following behind her.

She leads me to the back wall where there are dozens of framed photographs, some in black and white, others in color. We move to the far left side of the wall and begin walking its length while Montana explains the pictures.

"This is a history of our sacred tradition," she says. "Photos of our *sadgurus* of the Om Guru lineage."

She says this with such reverence that I make myself take a good, long look at each of the photographs. I proffer the appropriate murmurs of appreciation as I look at various black and white photographs of barely clad old and wrinkled Indian men who look like though they may have found spiritual bliss, they seem to have missed anything resembling a shower and a shave along the way.

"If they've found enlightenment, why are they called sad gurus?" I ask Montana as I make my way down the length of the wall.

Montana corrects me, explaining that the term "sadguru" means "true guru" or "divine master." "Each of these gurus passed down the lineage to the next guru and the next, all the way until the unbroken chain of our own Gurujai."

As we move down the line of photographs, the pictures become less grainy and more recent. She points to an older man wearing only a loincloth, lying on a wooden cot and propped up with a pillow. He looks a little scary to me, with a severe expression on his face. Actually, he looks like he might be in a psychiatric ward.

Montana sees me looking at him, and tells me that is Bhagawan Mulka. "He was such an enlightened master that he lived his life on a different plane enveloped in his own ecstatic bliss," she tells me with veneration. "He lived in the early 1900s, and it's said that he only spoke rarely, and usually if and when he acknowledged the presence of others, did so with a grunt."

She says this as if it were a good thing. I have a friend who just divorced her husband for the same behavior.

"Weren't people offended? Didn't they expect more from their guru?" I ask Montana.

I notice that the room is filling up with people getting comfortable on their meditation cushions. Everyone looks like they shop at Earthy Chic; there is a sea of organic cottons, Chinese silks and crocheted shawls.

"On the contrary," Montana begins. "He was so full of *shakti,* so full of spiritual energy, that conversation wasn't necessary. Just to be in his presence, it is said, was enough to burn people's negative karma and send them into a state of instant bliss."

We move further down, and the black and white photos move into color images.

"And this is Swami Baba," Montana says, putting her hand out like a model presenting a washing machine on a game show. It's a picture of a bearded Indian man maybe in his fifties, in a maroon ski cap and draped in a maroon robe, sitting on a bench surrounded by devotees looking at him in rapture.

"Swami Baba brought the Om Guru lineage from India to the West. It is to him that we owe our supreme gratitude for opening the spiritual path to all who seek." She tells me it is because of him that there are Om Guru meditation centers all over the country, with a huge and beautiful Om Guru Ashram in the Catskills similar to the Om Guru Ashram in India.

"The Catskills?" I ask. "The Borscht Belt where comedians like Jackie Mason kept many a Jew amused through the long, hot summer months? Those Catskills?"

"The very same," she tells me.

She explains that the ashram itself was once an old, grand hotel in the Catskills that was sold to the Om Guru Foundation and renovated. "There are other meditation centers and spiritual centers that have bought and renovated old hotels, too. You've got to come with me one day—it's truly beautiful. The spiritual energy of the place is breathtaking."

The next few pictures show Swami Baba amid bulldozers on a construction site, again in his maroon ski hat and robe, as the building of Om Guru Ashram is completed.

"And this is Swami Baba and Gurujai, when Gurujai was his disciple," Montana tells me, pointing to a younger version of Gurujai sitting beside her Guru. "When Swami Baba died in 1992 he passed the lineage on to Gurujai. Even though she was only 20 at the time, she had been his student since the age of four. They spent many lifetimes together, and it was in this incarnation that Gurujai was destined to head this lineage and fulfill Swami Baba's dream of spreading this spiritual path to the West."

Montana motions for me to follow her back to our cushions. As I sit down, I notice that many people are sitting in the full lotus position that we practice in yoga class. While I haven't yet mastered that, I can fit my legs in a half lotus position, and so I do.

I feel like I fit in, what with my outfit from Earthly Chic and my newly mastered yoga position. Granted, my toes stick out a bit like a sore thumb, given the hot pink polish I'm wearing, but when I look around and see all the triple- and quadruple-pierced ears and the ankle tattoos, I figure I'm entitled to my own self-expression as well.

As people continue to get settled, what looks to be easily over a hundred or so, I look at my watch. Montana sees me looking at the time and explains that the meditation hall opens for Satsang at 7:15 but they don't formally begin until 7:30, so we have another minute or two.

When I look up I see that in the far righthand corner there are three men with musical instruments. One man is wearing what I at first take to be a yarmulke crocheted in a pattern of red, yellow, green and black. But then, looking at his dreadlocks, I realize that it's more a Bob Marley Rasta kind of thing. The other two guys look to be in their 20s, and they are dressed in worn blue jeans and thin cotton T-shirts. They begin playing music that hits me in such a visceral way that the only way I can explain it is that it reverberates in me like the smell of the incense, transporting me to a place that feels calming and otherworldly.

I close my eyes and let the sounds seep into my heart, or rather, my heart center. When I open them again five minutes have passed, and I see Montana looking at me and smiling.

"I knew you were ready to come here," she whispers to me. "You look so serene."

I remember my dad worrying that I was becoming involved with a cult. I'm glad he's not here to hear the words that Montana is whispering to me. I, however, feel surprisingly at ease.

"That music is so beautiful," I whisper to Montana and Candace. "I've never heard anything like that before."

Candace leans over Montana and tells me that it's Indian music and that they are playing the sitar, harpsichord and dulcimer.

All of a sudden I find myself craving naan bread and vegetable curry. As I think about how I have to remind Gary again that I want to try that new Indian restaurant that opened by the mall, I see a tall, very thin bearded man who looks to be about my age move up to the podium in between the musicians and the altar.

"*Namaste,*" he says, with his palms pressed together.

"*Namaste,*" we all reciprocate.

The musicians stop, and the man at the podium moves in front of the altar and bows down in a series of movements that put his palms together at his forehead, then his heart, then by his belly before prostrating himself before, I believe, the worn leather sandals. Then he picks himself up and moves back to the podium, where he blows the conch shell. I hear the entire room explode with the words *Sadgurnath Marharaj Ki Jay!*, with some people pumping their fists in the air as they say the *Ki Jay!* part.

I look over to Montana, my own personal guru tutor, who whispers to me that "Sadgurunath Marharaj Ki Jay" is a Hindi phrase that means "I hail the Master who has revealed the Truth to me."

"Welcome to Satsang," the man says, moving back to the podium. "My name is Ajatashatru and I'm from the San Francisco Om Guru Center. I thank the *shakti* for bringing me here to this sacred space with you, my fellow devotees. This evening, I'd like to take some time to talk about the great mantra of our lineage, and to discuss the transformative power of its recitation."

My foot feels like it's going numb. There is no way I can sit in a half lotus position for the entirety of his talk. I look around and no one is moving; everyone is focused on Ajatashatru. I want to prove to myself that I can sit with focused attention and remain in this yogic position.

"*Om Namah Shivaya* is the great and redeeming mantra. Literally, it means 'I bow to Shiva, I bow to the supreme reality of the inner Self. I bow to the divine within me.' Now as we know, in Hinduism we have three gods who run creation. We have Brahma, who creates the universe, we have Vishnu, who preserves the universe, and we have Shiva, who in the end destroys the universe. I feel especially close to Vishnu, because when Gurujai gave me *shaktipat* back in 1996, when she transmitted her spiritual energy to me and awakened my kundalini, she gave me my Hindu name, Ajatashatru, which is a name for Vishnu. Before that, I was known as Chaim Applebaum, and to this day, the closest my parents will come to accepting my Hindu name is to call me A.J."

There are appreciative chuckles rumbling through the meditation hall.

I can't believe this guy is Jewish—and oh my God (or oh my Shiva), I can't feel my foot at all now. I use this time, while everyone is chuckling, to come out of my half lotus position and sit cross-legged.

"So please, feel free to call me Ajatashatru, or A.J., I'll happily answer to either, but mostly, I answer to my own Truest Self, to the divine within me. Which brings me to the divine within you. Remember always and forever, that God dwells within you, as you."

When I hear these words, I start wondering that if God dwells within me, maybe I can get away with eating for two.

"While Shiva is considered the destroyer, remember that he also symbolizes the inner Self that remains intact even after everything ends. Because in the end there is no end, there is only a merging with Atman, the Divine Consciousness, the Supreme Self that merges with the Absolute.

"We are on the path to our Self-Realization, where we merge with pure Consciousness. And as we travel our path toward enlightenment and to our spiritual bliss, we have at our disposal this powerful mantra. It has the power to grant both worldly fulfillment and spiritual attainment. This mantra is so potent that if you continually recite it in your heart, there is no need to perform austerities, or to meditate or to practice yoga. It has the power to purify you and to guide you in merging your own inner divinity with the Absolute, with the divine Consciousness that is the universe.

"But because we live in a busy world with other things and people pulling at us, moving us away from being constantly focused on the divine rhythm of this mantra, we build into our practice ways of connecting us with the sacred and with the power of *Om Namah Shivaya*. We practice chanting, and meditating, and we perform austerities. We practice *seva,* selfless service that we offer up without attachment. We perform *guruseva* here at the Center, or at the ashram, as a selfless act for the benefit of all. Whether it's making the tea, doing the dishes, or my personal favorite because for so long I resisted it and then pushed through my self-imposed resistance, cleaning the toilets. But when I clean the toilets at the San Francisco Om Guru Center, I feel blessed by the grace of the guru. I feel my most inner divinity as I scrub the toilet. Because here, in this most menial task, I can attain the realization that I am not the doer. I have no attachment to the work. I only can see that divinity is everywhere—in me, in you, in the toilet."

There are more chuckles.

"So now, let us spend the next 20 minutes chanting our sacred mantra," he says as he nods his head to the musicians in the corner. A.J. picks up a drum and joins them.

They play a few beautiful rounds before I hear people chanting the mantra. At first I just listen, and then I figure I should join in, because it's not very hard to follow and I don't want to be left behind while everyone else moves towards enlightenment. So I start to chant along, quietly at first, with the slow rhythm that has been set by the regulars. But then after a few minutes, already comfortable with the melody of the chanting, I hear my voice grow stronger. I feel like all the voices in the mediation hall are rising together as one. I feel my senses heighten, and though I wasn't aware of the incense in the meditation hall during the talk, I now smell it intensely and it fills me with a sense of joy.

I continue chanting and realize that my eyes have closed. When I open them I see the room swaying, with people on their cushions moving their bodies in rhythm with the chant. I give in to the impulse of my body, and let it sway as well. After awhile I don't feel like I'm even on the cushion. I mean, I know I'm on the cushion, but my body feels like it doesn't even exist, like I'm floating or something.

The chanting becomes faster, and all of a sudden we are chanting *Om Namah Shivaya* like there's no tomorrow—which, in a cosmic sense, is maybe true. Like Kali always says in yoga class, "There is no yesterday and no tomorrow. There is only NOW, this moment."

I am really getting into it. Chanting the mantra this quickly, there is really no time to think the words and say them. Instead, it's like the body and the mouth are just filled with this sound and it comes out automatically without any effort. I remember a bumper sticker I once saw that said: *Lose your mind and come to your senses.* Now I get it.

As the music hits the height of its crescendo, they suddenly stop and then there is absolute silence.

Ajatashatru says in a hushed voice, "Now we move into our meditation. I invite you to notice your breath and on the inhalation, breathe in *Om Namah Shivaya,* and on the exhalation breathe out *Om Namah Shivaya.* If your mind wanders, just bring it back to the mantra."

As I ready myself for my first attempt at meditation, I wonder how long we will be sitting for. I want to turn to Montana to ask her, but the room is so quiet I don't dare. And I don't know if I'm supposed to sit with my eyes open or closed.

I need directions.

I look around and see people sitting with their hands in *mudra* position, like the way we do when we chant *Om* in yoga class. I put my hands in position and then take a mental survey to see how many people have their eyes open and how many have them closed. The eyes closed have it, and so I shut my lids.

I inhale and silently say *Om Namah Shivaya.*

I exhale and silently say *Om Namah Shivaya.*

And then, just like the directions on my shampoo, I repeat.

I am in the groove, I think to myself. *I must be a very good meditator, a natural.*

I follow my breath through a few more rounds of mantra, and then I start thinking how I bet it won't take me so long to travel down this spiritual path and meet the true Self. Maybe one day I'll be up there talking to a group of devotees at some Om Guru Center. Maybe in Sedona. I've always thought going to Arizona would be cool, and without the humidity my hair would look great all the time. And it seems like Sedona would have an active Om Guru community, what with all the New Age stuff they have out there; the energy vortexes amidst the towering layers of red rock, the crystals.

My mind wanders on like this until I realize that it's been at least five minutes since I've meditated on the mantra.

Okay, focus, Syd. Breathe in: *Om Namah Shivaya.*

Breathe out: *Om Namah Shivaya.*

Breathe in: *Om Namah Shivaya.*

Breathe out: *Om Namah Shivaya.*

Breathe in: *Om Namah Shiva—shit!* I forgot to pick up Gary's favorite suit at the dry cleaners again and he wanted it for his big meeting tomorrow.

How could I have forgotten that? It was probably because I was so distracted after lunch with Jodi, Donna and Margot, who had been giving me a hard time about canceling our Thursday night Mah Jongg game to come here with Montana. I had felt so guilty that when Margot told us she wanted us all to come over to give our opinion about the paint colors she was deciding between for her family room I went, even though I had a million things to do. After I told her that I voted for desert sand over caramel cream, I excused myself and ran to the drugstore, the grocery store and the gas station and totally forgot to stop at the cleaners.

Well, Gary has a closet full of suits. It'll be fine. I'll put it at the top of my To Do List for tomorrow. Maybe I'll surprise him tomorrow and meet him in the city for lunch. I haven't done that in a long time. Might be a fun way to start the weekend. I'm really ready for the weekend. I hope this streak of warm weather continues at least through Sunday—

And it's then that I realize I haven't inhaled the mantra or exhaled the mantra for quite awhile. Again.

Maybe I'm not such a great meditator after all.

I spend the next few minutes trying to rein in my wandering mind and recite the mantra. It seems like a period of minutes go by when I'm back in the flow, but then my head starts to droop—

I can't believe I fell asleep.

I look around the meditation hall and everyone looks so peaceful and serene. *What's wrong with me?* I think to myself. Can it be that everyone is focused single mindedly on reciting the mantra? Is anyone else thinking of a million little things? Has anyone else fallen asleep?

I settle myself once again, the mantra sailing on the breath. I can do this. I'm on the third inhalation when I hear a chime sound three times. From the shuffling on the cushions, the sounds of the room coming awake, I realize that the chime signals the end of meditation.

I'll get better at this, I tell myself. *I'll figure it out.*

Montana leans over to me and asks me how I'm doing.

"Great," I tell her. "This is really different from anything I've ever done."

"At least in this lifetime," she replies.

Montana has often told me that she believes in reincarnation and has done past life regression, where she has learned about some of her past lives. Apparently at one point she was a Viking.

Just as I'm about to ask her about the whole meditation process, if the mind wandering so much is normal, if she ever falls asleep, I hear Ajatashatru begin talking again at the podium.

"I want to invite all who would like to prostrate before the guru's feet to line up, row by row. For those of you new to Om Guru, let me explain this process. I know many people in the West get nervous with the practice of bowing down to anyone or anything, and tend to hold back. They see it as an act of submission, and they refrain from any such involvement. But that is very much the Western mind. In the Indian scriptures, the guru's feet are revered. They are said to embody both Shiva and Shakti, both knowledge and action. Very powerful spiritual vibrations stream through the guru's feet, and as a devotee, you are offered the guru's grace as the guru's own energy sparks the flame of divinity within you. On the altar, we have the sandals worn by our own Bhagawan Mulka. They symbolize the guru's teachings and the soles of those sandals contain the shakti to pierce our own souls."

"I like his pun," I think to myself. Donna would be impressed.

"And so, starting with the first row, I invite you to come up and prostrate yourself before the guru, and be open to receive the guru's grace."

I watch as the first row gets up and waits in line to bow before the altar. I'm not sure if I want to do this, but I have three more rows after this one to decide. As I think about it, I suppose it's not so different from the reverence Jodi and I show when we go to Jimmy Choo and hold up a fabulous silver high heel like we were holding the crown jewel. Somehow it's easier to bow down to the god of merchandise. We've had so much practice and encouragement doing it.

I look up and see a row of people, one by one, putting their palms together and touching first their foreheads, then their heart centers, then their navels before laying down straight on the floor. They are already on the second row, and I know I'll have to decide what I'm going to do.

I can't help but think about Moses's anger when he returned from Mount Sinai and saw that the people had become fearful that he wouldn't return and had reverted to idol worship and built the golden calf. I know one of the Ten Commandments prohibits idolatry. But why am I invoking this now? If I want to explore the East, don't I have to change directions? Don't I have to be open to new experiences?

The third row is next, and I see people in the fourth row rise from their cushions and begin to form a line. And then I stop thinking and just get up and follow along. What have I got to lose? As I move up closer in line, I watch carefully how to prostrate. Montana and Candace are behind me, and I feel Montana take my hand and squeeze it.

"So much of your karma has led you to this moment," she tells me.

I'm not sure how to respond, so I just squeeze her hand back. When it's my turn I move up closer to the altar, and I put my palms together and I prostrate myself in front of the guru's sandals.

And I think I feel something. I don't know if it has to do with the guru's sandals, per se, or with the entire experience of Satsang, of searching somewhere new for a treasure. As I walk toward the door of the meditation hall and watch Montana and then Candace prostrate before the guru's sandals, I feel like I am venturing into new but welcoming territory.

I have been a seeker all my life, I realize, but a seeker of external perfection: searching for the perfect outfit, praying for the perfect diet, making my house a shrine to contemporary living. But when I die, what will people say about my life?

I can just picture Jodi's eulogy at my funeral:

"Syd was taken from us suddenly, going into cardiac arrest wearing a darling size four Burberry tweed suit and carrying a fabulous Birkan bag. Syd would have been happy to know that she died on one of her 'thin' days, and thus will remain svelte into perpetuity. She maintained a spotless house and, thanks to her wonderful housekeeper Marina, barely had to lift a perfectly polished finger to do so. Syd was my best friend, and she can never be replaced. Though we will need to find a new fourth for our Mah Jongg group. We play on Thursday nights, and if anyone here is interested, please see me after the burial."

Okay, maybe I'm being a little too hard on myself, but I need more in my life. I'm no longer convinced that the magic number on the bathroom scale will bring me bliss. I feel like I've been playing a character in a sitcom about a suburban woman who thinks she is living a full life and moving freely through the world, but, just as with her dog, she is living an illusion. Just like her dog, she is merely running in circles contained by an Invisible Fence.

"So what'd you think?" Candace asks, startling me awake. "Will you come here next week?"

"Yeah, Syd. Will you come with me again next week?" Montana chimes in.

And I tell them both yes, I will come here next week.

As people leave the meditation hall Montana grabs my hand and tells me she wants to show me around the rest of the center. Candace sees a group of friends, so she and I say good-bye and I follow Montana to the right, where, after a quick bathroom stop, she leads me to the center's Nectar Café and buys two cups of green tea and apricot cookies. And, for the first time in a long time, I eat the cookies without worrying about the calories.

Montana and I talk about the chanting and meditation, and she assures me that even though everyone in the hall may look so calm and peaceful during meditation, everyone has this wild mind that jumps from the mantra to any number of topics where it gets lost and then found and brought back for a little while longer to the mantra.

"Over time, your mind will become more able to be in the breath of the moment, and in the sounds and vibration of the mantra. It's just about practice and staying away from judgment," she tells me as she finishes her tea.

"How often do you meditate?" I ask her.

"Twenty minutes every morning and twenty minutes every evening. But you might want to start with just five minutes each morning and night." Montana looks up. "There are some people I want you to meet." She waves over a group of three women and two men who are just about to sit down at a table near us. They put down their mugs and walk over to us, giving Montana hugs while I stand there and smile.

"Everyone, this is my friend, Syd. It's her first time here. Syd, this is Martha, Ruth, Amy, Bill and Kyle."

We all say hello and then Bill asks me what I thought of Satsang.

"It feels good to be here," I begin. "Though it's all very new to me."

Ruth, who is dressed in a brown peasant skirt and a *Save Darfur* T-shirt, says, "New things keep you young at heart and open at heart," and I join everyone nodding in agreement.

"And if you ever want to come to Om Guru in the early morning to chant the *Guru Gita*, I'm usually here and I'd be happy show you the ropes, so to speak," Kyle tells me. "Montana usually doesn't come for the *Guru Gita,* but there's a lot of us regulars for that, and you'd meet them in no time."

We all sit down, and Montana and I move our table closer to their table and continue talking with them while they drink their tea and share some zucchini muffins.

"So what's the *Guru Gita?*" I ask.

Montana explains that it's a sacred text that includes mantras describing the nature of the Guru, the Guru-disciple relationship and techniques for deepening meditation on the Guru. "But they chant it at 5:45 A.M., and so unless I'm on retreat at the Ashram, I can't get myself out of bed for it," she explains.

"I'm a morning person," Kyle tells me. "I love starting the day that way. If you get up early, you should give it a try." I tell him thanks, and then Montana tells them that she is going to finish showing me around. We say goodbye, and I follow Montana out of the café and then to the various meeting rooms, more like oversized living rooms, and the different offices upstairs. Always there are framed photographs of Gurujai and others in the lineage on the walls, or sitting in a picture frame on an end table.

I am amazed by the size of this center and the number of people who come here. It's only about a half hour from Highland Ridge, where I've lived my whole life, but I never even knew this existed. Montana tells me that if this feels like a spiritual tradition I'd like to pursue, I should buy some books that talk about the main beliefs and practices of the Om Guru lineage.

I tell her I'd like to read some. "Are they on Amazon?" I ask.

"C'mon, you can buy them here at the gift shop," she tells me as she heads down the corridor.

Reflexively, my heart jumps. "Shopping? They have a gift shop here?"

Montana nods her head and guides me back toward the large front hallway. I have to confess that even when I go to a museum, no matter how wonderful the paintings are, or the artifacts, or the exhibits, my favorite part is the gift shop.

I follow Montana into the back left of the lobby where there is a doorway leading into a gift shop filled with enticing merchandise from floor to ceiling.

I am dazzled.

"Here, let me show you some of Gurujai's books that would be helpful for you to read," Montana says as she guides me over to a shelf.

I force myself to follow her without stopping to feel the fabrics of the golden silk saris, without stopping to peer at the locked glass cases filled with beautiful jewelry.

Montana surveys the bookshelf and then declares, "Here, this is the one I was looking for. This is a really good introduction to the Om Guru path." She pulls out a glossy oversized paperback and hands it to me. The cover is a picture of Gurujai in her trademark maroon robe and matching hat. She is sitting in a green pasture, a baby lamb at her side, and the sky is the color of dawn, pink/orange and just coming alive. The title of the book is *Finding Yourself, Finding Your Bliss,* and it's written by Gurujai.

"I think you'll really get a lot out of this book," Montana tells me.

"Great, thanks. I'm going to start reading it tomorrow," I tell her, figuring I can always start my new Danielle Steele book later. "Do we have time to look around?" I ask her.

"Absolutely," she says.

I follow Montana's gaze across the gift shop. "I'm just going to say hi to a friend over there. Take your time."

I linger for a moment at the bookshelf, because I don't want to seem shallow by making a beeline to the jewelry case. I read a few titles: *Discovering your Kundalini; Preparing to Meet the Self; Principles of the Guru-Disciple Relationship.* Then I wander slowly over to the rack of saris. The colors are captivating, from gold to deep red to purple. They are accented with sequins and jewels, and the fabric slides sensually through my fingertips as I touch them delicately. Further on there is a rack of silk shirts, and some cotton T-shirts, as well. The T-shirts are emblazed with the mantra *Om Nimah Shivaya*.

I think that I will better remember to recite the mantra during the day, and to meditate, if I own a mantra T-shirt. I choose a cropped T-shirt with an embroidered pink rose above the mantra.

I hold the shirt over the book and continue looking around. In the locked jewelry case there are rows of silver bangle bracelets with the mantra engraved, and thick gold bracelets engraved with the mantra, and charm bracelets with *Om* charms hanging along with what looks like various animal charms which, a helpful saleswoman tells me, are different gods and deities. I ask her how much the silver mantra bracelets are, and she tells me that the single one is $75, but that you can buy three of them for $200. The yellow gold bracelet is $500. There are also silver and gold mantra rings that look like wedding bands, but I decide not to ask her how much they cost.

The saleswoman, who I learn is a devotee doing her *guruseva* work by selling at the gift shop, points me toward the counter where there is a ton of jewelry not in a case. I think she thinks I can't afford the locked jewels. I just think I should wait at least until I read *Finding Yourself, Finding Your Bliss*, or come here a few times, before I buy the jewelry. I also think if I end up doing *guruseva* work at the Om Guru Center I'd like to work in the gift store and not clean bathrooms, despite the fact that A.J. seems to have been able to discover his divinity in the toilet.

On the counter there are strands of beaded bracelets in brown, maroon and yellow. I ask the salesperson/devotee what they are, and she explains that they are mala bracelets.

"They help you to count while you repeat the mantra," she tells me. She explains that the mala bracelet works similarly to a rosary.

I imagine this information would not make Gary or my family or my rabbi very happy. Still, I am intrigued. She tells me that as you finger each of the 108 beads, or a derivative of this number, and recite the mantra, you gain merit for both yourself and for all sentient beings.

I pick up a bracelet and finger the beads.

"That mala bracelet is very special. It is made from the seeds of the lotus plant from India," the saleswoman/devotee tells me.

"Lovely," I say, beginning to hand it back to her, and then fingering the beads and saying a quick *Om Namah Shivaya* to myself so that she doesn't think me un-Om Guruish. She puts the bracelet back, and then my eyes hit upon a beautiful mala bracelet on the wrist of a dressed up hand mannequin.

"Is that rose quartz?" I ask her.

"Good eyes!" she says cheerfully. "Isn't it lovely?"

"It's to die for," I say, and then remembering where I am, say, "Or to be reincarnated for. Can I try it on?"

"Of course," she says as she removes the bracelet from the display and hands it to me. I put in on my wrist, and the smooth coolness of the beads feels almost seductive. I hold my wrist out in front of me, turning my hand this way and that to see how it looks on me.

I love it.

It would look great with jeans, casual and yet interesting. I probably could even get away with dressing it up a bit. It would be perfect with the new summer dress I bought at Bloomingdale's the other day.

The saleswoman/devotee smiles at me. "I can tell by your expression the mala beads are already inviting you to recite the mantra. What a blessing."

"Yes, I could practically hear the rhythm of the mantra in the pulse on my wrist," I tell her, thankful that she is not a psychic mind reader. I console myself by thinking that the fact that the mala bracelet would go with so many of my outfits only means I will be reminded on a regular basis—no, scratch that, I will be blessed on a regular basis—with the gift of reciting the mantra.

"I'm going to take this, but I'm going to look around a bit more," I tell her.

"Here, why don't you let me hold those things up here while you take a look," she says kindly, and I hand over the book and the shirt. I don't hand her the mala bracelet, though. All of a sudden I feel like when I was ten and my mother would buy me a new pair of shoes that I loved so much that I insisted on wearing them home. I remember how the salesperson would put my old shoes in the shoebox as I pranced around in my new footwear. That's how I feel with the mala bracelet. I can't imagine how I've gone 43 years without one.

"Is there anything in particular I can show you?" the saleswoman/devotee asks me. "Would you like to look at some deities?"

Okay, how can you really say 'no' to that without looking—I don't know—shallow?

"Sure," I say with a smile, and I follow her to the end of the jewelry case, where she leads me to a shelf set off toward the back wall. Here there are tons of what I would call figurines, but are, apparently, gods. But they are exquisite; some are set with jewels, others are beautifully painted. Because I have no idea what I am really looking at, all I can manage to say is "wow."

"Yes, it is powerful standing in front of such auspicious deities," she says approvingly.

I feel glad that she translated my "wow" as such.

"But I have to be honest," I tell her, picking up a small statue with more limbs than a person ought to have, "I don't really know anything about who these are or what they represent."

The saleswoman/devotee puts her hands together in prayer at her heart center, and thanks me for offering her the opportunity to share the beauty of the gods with me.

"Pick one up, whichever your heart gravitates to," she instructs me.

For a moment I feel like I'm at a carnival and this is the game where if you pick the plastic duck with a black X on the bottom, you win a stuffed animal.

I pick what in my mind I've named "the elephant boy" in turquoise. The saleswoman/devotee smiles.

"Very auspicious," she tells me.

I look up and see Montana smiling at me from across the room, talking with a small group of people.

"You are holding Lord Ganesha," she says proudly, as though I've just given birth to this statue.

"And who is Lord Ganesha?" I ask her, fingering the inlaid turquoise and what I believe is sterling silver.

"Ah, Lord Ganesha. He represents the power of the Supreme Being who is the remover of obstacles and ensures the success of human endeavors. Are you just beginning your spiritual path?" she asks me.

"Um, yeah. I mean, this is my first time at the Om Guru Center, but I've discovered yoga recently, and my friend, Montana, has been telling me about this path. I feel ready to explore it," I tell her.

"Well, it is all meant to be. Numerous lifetimes have led you here, to this moment, and I am honored to be traveling the path with you. And you must have a Ganesha in your home, because this deity is always embraced at the beginning of any religious, spiritual or worldly activity. He will guide you as you embark upon the journey to your Self and to Brahman, the one god/energy source."

"What is the significance of the elephant head?" I ask her.

"The elephant's head symbolizes the gaining of knowledge by listening with his big ears, and reflecting, through his large head. His two tusks, one whole and the other broken, suggest the existence of perfection and imperfection of the physical world. His big belly reflects his ability to digest whatever life has in store. And his wide mouth represents the natural human desire to enjoy life in the world."

"All that and he removes obstacles and brings good fortune?" I ask, "How can you pass up that? I'll take him," I tell her.

"Wonderful! He will be a guiding force on your spiritual journey, helping to clear the path and leading you to your inner divinity."

After she tells me this, I find that I am unable to turn Lord Ganesha over to determine how much he costs. I mean really, how can you put a price tag on removing obstacles and ensuring success?

"So who are his friends?" I ask instead.

She picks up a female statue with four arms and hands on each side, with a painted red cloth covering her that is lined in gold. She is standing on a pink lotus. "This is the goddess Lakshmi," she tells me. "Her name is derived from the Sanskrit word *Laksme,* which means 'goal.' Lakshmi represents the goal of life, which includes both worldly and spiritual prosperity."

I would think that this would be a good deity to have around, but I don't want to overdo it. It's too bad they don't sell the deities in box sets.

"And this here," she says as she puts down Lakshmi and picks up what I believe is a monkey, "is Hanuman. He is the great monkey hero who symbolizes the traits of an ideal devotee of God. The letters of his name represent those qualities.

H = humility

A = admiration

N = nobility

U = understanding

M = mastery over ego

A = achievements

N = *nishkama-karma.*"

I remember helping Rachel, back in her sixth grade English class, with an acrostic for her name. I feel a pat on my back and turn around to find Montana beaming at me.

"Great, you've met Sarasvati?"

"You know what, Montana? I don't think I've formally introduced myself to your friend. Forgive me," she says, turning back to face me. "I'm Sarasvati, and it has been my good fortune to share with you my knowledge of this great spiritual path."

"And I'm Syd. Syd Arthur. *Namaste,*" I say, pressing my palms together.

"*Namaste,*" she says.

Montana tells me that Sarasvati spent six months last year living at the Om Guru Ashram in India. "It was very auspicious," Sarasvati tells us. "Gurujai was in residence for a large part of that time and I had the good fortune of performing *guruseva* in her midst. The ashram was so full of shakti, it was like we were all on fire. You could just feel the heat of her love permeating the grounds."

"Well, I'd imagine that part of that was the temperature. Isn't it like over 100 degrees in India?" I ask.

Sarasvati smiles and says, "Well, regardless of the source of the heat, my meditation practice blossomed. The ashram is such a fertile place. So much takes root there."

I notice that Montana's face looks enraptured. I watch her take a deep breath, and then she says, "I've been holding this for awhile, but I feel ready to share. By the grace of the Guru, I'm going to go to the Om Guru Ashram in India this fall. Definitely for six months, and possibly for a year," she says, her face beaming. Sarasvati hugs her.

As they embrace, I think to myself how much I'll miss her in yoga class if she really goes. Then I stop myself from my selfish thoughts and try to be more like Ganesha, or Lakshmi or Hanuman. I try to be more like a *mensch*. So after Montana and Sarasvati let go of each other, I give Montana a big hug.

"There is nothing like being in India, Montana. May the grace of the Guru be with you," Sarasvati offers.

"I wonder if I'll ever make it to India," I say.

Sarasvati jumps in. "Oh, but you don't have to travel to India to meet Gurujai. She travels all around the world visiting different Om Guru Centers. And she spends part of the summer in the Catskills at the Om Guru Ashram. That's where Montana has spent time with Gurujai.

"You know what you need?" Montana asks me. Before I can answer, she tells me that I need a picture of Gurujai, "to enhance my practice." Sarasvati invites Montana to show me the many options for sale.

There is a huge framed photograph of Gurujai, just like the one in the foyer of the Om Guru Center. It is lovely, like a work of art, really. But I can't see me spending over a thousand dollars for a picture of the Guru in my house, plus, I can't afford the wall space. There are smaller framed photos: Gurujai sitting on a mountaintop, Gurujai twirling on a beach, her long maroon robe captured in the energy of the wind around her, her hands reaching up to the cloudless, blue sky. Gurujai walking in a field of wild flowers.

I find myself wanting a picture of Gurujai, but feeling like it's too soon, maybe, to be decorating my house with this woman. Then I notice a shoebox filled with laminated wallet size photos of Gurujai. I look through them and pull out one picture that really speaks to me. It is a closeup of Gurujai in her maroon robe and maroon hat, her third eye of wisdom a perfect red circle between her eyes.

Sarasvati tells me that the red dot, or third eye, is called a *bindi*. She explains how during meditation, that spot between the eyebrows is where you are to focus your sight so that it helps with concentration. I also think to myself that it would come in handy if you were subject to premenstrual breakouts in the T-zone. That red dot, or bindi, could cover up an unwanted zit.

I like this photo of Gurujai, and the idea of propping it up on a table if I set up a meditation space at home appeals to me. "I think I'll buy this one,"

I tell Montana, and she smiles in approval.

Sarasvati has moved back to the cash register, and Montana and I make our way over to where she is standing behind the counter. "Are you all set, Syd?" she asks me. I nod, as she pulls the items she has kept up at the register for me. I watch her ring in Gurujai's book, the *Om Namah Shivaya* T-shirt, Lord Ganesha, and the laminated photo of Gurujai. I take off my mala bracelet and hand it over. Sarasvati rings up the total.

"Cash or credit?" she asks me.

I hand her my Visa card.

"You should definitely come back with me for Satsang next week," Montana tells me as I sign the sales slip.

The jury is in. I have spent a small fortune. Sarasvati asks me if I want the receipt in the bag, a powder blue plastic shopping bag with the mantra written across in bold gold lettering.

"Sure, that would be great," I tell her. I thank her for all of her help, and then turn back to Montana.

"I really do want to come back next week, but my friends are going to kill me. This is our Mah Jongg night, and they moved the game to Tuesday for me this week, but told me I'd better be on board for Thursday next week," I explain.

"Why can't they just play on Tuesday again?" she asks as we make our way back into the foyer toward our shoes.

"Because," I tell her as I search for my Prada sandals, which are easy to find in the mix of Birkenstocks and Tevas. "My Mah Jongg group has played on Thursdays for ten years now. It's written in stone. Kind of like the Ten Commandments."

"Well, Syd, there are seven days in the week. Surely you can come up with a new time to play," she says as she slips on her clogs.

"You don't understand. It's not that easy. Like I said, we've been playing on Thursday nights forever."

Montana looks at me while holding the door open. "Maybe it's time for a change," she says.

I follow her out into the still warm night. I look up into the sky and see a few shining stars. I breathe in deeply, and then slowly let it out.

"Maybe it is," I say to her as she unlocks the car door and slides into her seat. As I open the car door I look back at the stars and whisper to myself, "maybe it is."

Chapter Eighteen

"Now that was a great game of doubles," Margot says as she seats herself at our favorite table in the grille room, overlooking the golf course.

I pull out my chair and sit across from Margot feeling fit, fresh and clean after two hours of tennis and a fabulous shower.

"Though we did cause a bit of a racket out there," Donna says. "I thought Cynthia Goldberg was going to report us to the club's president for being too loud on the courts. But is it our fault that we happen to be loads of fun and full of giggles while she and that Paula Kline look as if they have a perpetual stick up their ass?"

"Shhh," Jodi says. "They just walked in for lunch."

I turn and see Cynthia and Paula sit down at a table, and Jodi and I give them a little wave. Claire, our favorite waitress at the club, comes over to take our drink orders.

"I'll tell you, I really needed a day like this. Parker and Brittany got out of school last Friday, and they don't start camp until Monday. That's ten days of having to find things to entertain them," Donna laments.

"Well, you're over the hump. It's already Wednesday," Jodi offers.

"Yeah, and I don't mean to complain. They're great kids, but it's hard to entertain an eight- and six-year-old. By 9:00 in the morning they're already bored and asking me what they can do, and I barely have time to sit and drink my coffee, let alone have time to watch *The View*. Thank goodness for our neighbor, Veronica. She's home from college and has been babysitting so I can find some 'me' time."

"Listen to me, Donna. Before you know it, Parker and Brittany are going to be grown up and off on their own and you're going to be begging them to come home for a visit," Margot says as our drinks arrive.

"Does this mean that Nathan and Scott aren't going to be visiting any time soon?" I ask.

Margot takes a sip of her raspberry sparkling water. "They're so busy, Ralph and I are going to visit them in July." Both of her boys ended up going back to Boston for college. Nathan, her oldest, graduated a couple of years ago from Brandeis and works at Citibank in New York. Scott just finished his senior year at Boston University, and is working for an accounting firm in Newton.

"I know I should be so grateful that they're both happy and doing well, and I am. It's just that this is really my life right now. No more high school soccer games and looking for mouth guards and buying new cleats. No more packing for college and coming home from college and then packing up again. I have two grown children, and to tell you the truth, Donna, I have more 'me' time than I know what to do with. And I'll tell you, it's a little overrated. I mean, c'mon, I have to have been rather desperate to have agreed to co-chair the country club comedy show next year. And by the way, you all have to be there, so don't even try to come up with an excuse. So all I'm trying to say, Donna, is try to enjoy the time you have with Parker and Brittany now."

Before Donna can respond, we hear Karen, Susie, Pam and Mindy calling to us as they walk toward us in their golfing attire.

"What a glorious day!" Pam says, standing beside our table. "Eighteen holes and I shot two under par."

"And we'll never hear the end of it," Susie says.

Pam gives her a pout and then says to us, "Really, I don't know why you four refuse to play golf. It's not too late, you know. The golf pro this year is simply outstanding! I've taken so many private lessons with him because he has such technique!"

"And he's really gorgeous," Karen offers.

"I've heard quite a few rumors about him and a married club member," Jodi says.

Donna interrupts her, saying, "What, like that he's a pro at more than golf? Hey, if you got balls—"

"You know what, Donna?" Margot interrupts. "I think you should participate in the country club comedy night. You can do your whole shtick in puns."

"Wait, what. What have you heard?" Pam asks, visibly agitated.

"Really, I don't know much. I've just heard from a handful of different sources that the new golf pro, Ken, right?" Jodi asks, and Pam nods her head. "Yeah, well, I've just heard through the grapevine that he has a thing going on with some club member, and that's really all I know."

"Who? Who is it?" Pam asks.

"I swear, Pam, I don't know," Jodi repeats.

I can't tell if this bit of gossip upsets Pam because she thinks so highly of the golf pro, or because the golf pro has thought so highly of someone else. Trying to defuse the awkwardness, Jodi tells Pam and her friends that we need to stick to tennis because it burns more calories than golf in half the time. Then Claire comes to take our lunch orders, so we say our goodbyes and watch them stop at Cynthia and Paula's table to say their hellos before seating themselves.

"It's like a soap opera here," Margot says while buttering a roll.

"Always has been, always will be," Jodi says.

"Okay, so who is it?" I ask Jodi. "Who's having an affair with the golf pro, and why didn't I know about this?"

Jodi takes a sip of her lemonade, breaks off half a roll, and spreads it with butter. "First, I have to say, Syd, you're not around as much as you used to be, and so you'll just have to live with the fact that you're not going to always be in the know." She finishes a chunk of roll and then breaks off another piece. "Second," she says as she eyes the butter, but then pushes it away and commits herself to eating the remainder of the roll naked, "You're not around as much as you used to be."

"Wait," I say. "That was first."

"That, my friend, was first, second, third and fourth. We all miss you, Syd, and we all want to talk to you about how you haven't been around enough."

I see everyone looking at Jodi, and then as if on cue they are shaking their heads and looking at me.

"Look, Syd, no one is mad at you. We just miss you," Jodi says gently.

"And we don't understand why you're putting other things first," Donna offers.

"What are you talking about?" I ask.

"Like our Thursday night Mah Jongg that you keep canceling," Margot says, and Jodi and Donna nod their heads in agreement.

My own neck hurts just from looking at all that nodding. I have got to get myself to a chiropractor.

"And our morning walks," Donna adds. "You're always taking your yoga classes instead."

"And when we all went back to Weight Watchers together, you didn't join us," Jodi laments. "We're worried about you. And we're worried about how you've been spending your time."

I look at my dear friends, and all of a sudden I can see that this conversation was planned in advance.

"What is this, an intervention?" I ask, laughing. But no one joins me in the laughter. "C'mon, you guys, we've been friends forever. What's this really about?"

Claire comes with our orders, and we busy ourselves with pouring on the dressing that we've all asked for on the side, while not refusing another basket of rolls.

"Look, Syd," Jodi says, taking a bite of her Greek salad. "The first Thursday that you couldn't play Mah Jongg because you were going to *that place,* we switched to Tuesday. But that was just supposed to be for that week. You know that Tuesday doesn't really work for us. And then you just kept saying that you couldn't play that week if we couldn't switch the day, and we tried to accommodate you at first, but it's been going on for a month. Some weeks we can't play at all because there isn't another night that works for everyone. Thursday night Mah Jongg has always been a priority for us. It's just a given. And now you've just dropped it like it doesn't matter to you anymore, and that feels lousy to us," she says, stabbing at a piece of feta cheese.

"Syd," Margot says. "We all love you and we want to be supportive. But you just kind of changed the rules on us."

"I need my Thursday nights. I count on my Thursday nights with you guys. Remember, my kids are still little. I need girl talk. And now it's like it doesn't matter to you anymore. Instead you're going to some meditation center?" Donna says, clearly upset. She takes a bite of her tuna salad. "And with a woman named Montana, no less!" she adds.

I look down at my Caesar, and push the croutons around. "Gosh, I don't really know what to say. I didn't know you were all so mad," I say quietly.

Jodi puts her fork down. "Look, Syd, we're not mad at you. We just feel that we all need to talk. If you feel the need to join a hippie cult, we'll wave some incense around your head. We'd do anything for you—you know that. But it's really not fair to us when you break up our Thursday nights and expect us to just wait until you grow out of this midlife crisis or whatever it is you're having."

"You know, Syd, when I had my midlife crisis, I made Ralph buy me a Mercedes convertible, remember? And I took all of you out on the town with the top down to the trendiest restaurant in town. Now that's the kind of midlife crisis you should have. One that's fun for your friends, too," Margot says with a smile as she nibbles on the turkey in her chef's salad.

"Why don't you all come with me to the Om Guru Center?" I ask. "It's really amazing. We all have these levels of consciousness and through meditation practice it's possible to enter into realms that we weren't even aware of. It's possible to reach a state of nirvana, a state of true bliss and a merging with the Absolute."

My friends look alarmed.

"Okay, Syd? I'd feel more relieved if you were the one having an affair with the golf pro than what I've just heard you say. Really, what the hell are you talking about? What the hell are you doing—and if you don't want all of those croutons, can I have some?"

I scoop up a spoonful of croutons and put them on Jodi's salad. "A peace offering?" I say, smiling.

"I think it began with your yoga classes, if you ask me," Donna says. "I think those poses you learned really bent you out of shape. There's nothing wrong with yoga, but I think taking yoga classes at that Prana Center is a mistake. Like they get their recruits from the yoga classes for that Om Guru place. It's creepy, Syd, this talk about merging with the Absolute. Absolute what? Absolute craziness, that's what I say. You should come back to kick boxing with me."

"What is it you're looking for, Syd?" Margot asks in a motherly way.

"I guess I'm looking for myself," I say.

"Uh, Syd? You're right here, no need to look any further," Jodi says.

"No, really, you guys. I'm looking for meaning in my life."

Jodi looks at me in disbelief. "What are you talking about? You have everything. Gary is wonderful and Rachel is wonderful and we, your friends, are fabulous. You have a beautiful home and gorgeous clothes and fabulous vacations. What more could you want?"

Everyone is looking at me, and for once, no one is eating.

"I want purpose. I want something I can't put into words. I want to be the kind of person who, if she sees a homeless person asking for money, gives him money. And not only gives him money, but looks him in the eyes, with compassion but also with respect. And maybe the kind of person who isn't scared of the homeless person, but instead sees that we are all interconnected," I explain, looking out onto the expanse of the golf course dotted with swaying trees and men in Polo shirts. I think of Kevin Mann coming out of his coma, getting another chance. *I want to wake up,* I think to myself.

I take a breath and continue. "I want to become a more spiritual person. There has to be something more to life than losing weight. There has to be more to life than buying a new pair of shoes."

"Like what?" Donna asks.

"Like maybe prostrating before the Guru's sandals," I say quietly, almost to myself.

"Look, Syd, "Margot says. "Why don't you take a little break from your Thursday nights at that center? Get away from that for a little bit, you know, to help you gain some perspective."

"Okay, you have to listen to me. I like going to the Om Guru Center.

Thursday night is Satsang. It's important for me to be there. I like spending time with Montana. I like learning to meditate. I like learning about Hinduism, and about the teachings that lead to meeting the True Self. But that doesn't change how I feel about you guys. You're my best friends. I just need for you to understand that this is important to me," I say, wanting so much for them to appreciate how I feel.

Jodi looks at me and says, "Listen, Syd, I can't say we understand what you're doing. Frankly, this talk about meeting the Self is a little out there for me—"

Donna interrupts, saying, "A little out there? I'd say a lot out there."

"Okay, but the point is, we are here for you. We love you," Jodi finishes.

I smile at her and begin to scoop up more croutons for her in thanks, but then I see Margot and Donna give her a look. Jodi returns the look to them and then, as if in resignation, says,

"So Syd, we love you but—"

"Oh boy, here it comes. *But* is never good after 'we love you,'" I say.

Donna can't contain herself any longer. "But we've found someone to take your place for our Thursday night Mah Jongg."

I am so pissed. But I take a deep breath, and conjure up a picture of Gurujai and silently ask for the Guru's grace in helping me to see my friends with love and an open heart.

Still, I'm pissed.

"What Donna means is that this woman, Barbara Cohen, has been looking for a Mah Jongg game and wants to join our group. So instead of trying each week to find a different night to play, which really doesn't work with anyone's schedule, Barbara will play on Thursday nights so that we'll always have a game whether you can play or not. And if you can play on a particular Thursday night, then we'll just play with five. Most games have a fifth anyway, so it will work out fine," Jodi explains.

"Barbara Cohen's son Adam is in Parker's class," Donna says. "She really wants a Mah Jongg group."

"I feel like I've been replaced," I say, no longer hungry.

"You know, Syd, I wish there was a way that your True Self, whoever that is, can go to that meditation center on Thursday nights, while the Syd Self that we've known all these years can come to Mah Jongg," Jodi says, crunching a crouton. "Any chance of that?"

"This is what a divorce must feel like," I say to them.

Jodi leans over and puts her hand on my shoulder. "This isn't a divorce. Whenever you come back, we'll all be so happy. But Syd, we all really love to play and we haven't really been able to get a game together with you running every Thursday to do your Guru thing, okay?"

"You know, if I knew which woman in the club was having the affair with the golf pro, I'd call her husband up to have a drink and commiserate about being replaced," I say.

"Okay, just to show you how much I love you and would do anything for all of you, I'll tell you who I heard was sleeping with the golf pro. I'm almost 99% sure that the rumors are true."

We are all looking with anticipation at Jodi. For a moment I think of Gurujai, and it hits me that this isn't the way a devotee should act, hungry for gossip at someone's expense. This isn't going to help me in any way to merge with the Absolute. But already hurt about being replaced, I am hungry for scandal.

"Connie Silverman," Jodi says.

"NO!" the rest of us say in unison. Connie is so prim and proper, it's hard to imagine her having sex with her husband, let alone an affair with the really hot golf pro.

"She lives in her Lilly Pulitzer pastels, and the hardest drink I've ever seen her order is a white Zinfandel," Margot shares.

"Did a little birdie tell you this, Jodi?" Donna asks.

"Quite a few little birdies told me this," Jodi answers.

"I guess you never know," I say.

"It's kind of how we feel about you, " Jodi says.

"What do you mean?" I ask.

"Well, we never figured you for some dazed-out meditating hippie talking about her guru helping her to discover her True Self and her bliss," Jodi says.

"I swear you guys sound like my parents," I say.

"Well, what does Gary say? What does Rachel think?" Jodi asks.

"Rachel's decided to take two summer courses and hang out with some friends in Madison for a good part of the summer, so she's pretty focused on what she's doing. All she wanted to know was if meditating has made me less nervous and calmer about her going out and stuff and if so, does that mean when she comes home towards the end of the summer she doesn't have a curfew. And you know Gary, he's happy when I'm happy."

Claire comes to clear our plates, and then pours us all coffee.

"Is this a breaking your diet week? Would you like to look at a dessert menu?" Claire asks.

"I think, given how I've been jilted by my friends, that we need something sweet to take the edge off," I propose.

Always looking for a reason to break our diets, everyone agrees. We each order our favorite, the lava cake that oozes chocolate fudge in its center. We console ourselves that there are fresh raspberries on the top, so that it's a little bit like having fruit for dessert.

"So are we all good now?" Jodi asks as Claire pours us more coffee.

"The cake helped," I begin, "but seriously, I feel really badly about this. Thursday nights with you guys are like my anchor. For years, it's been my anchor."

Donna looks at me with her wide eyes and says, "But the anchor is still here. You're the one who's choosing to sail away."

It's silent then, and in that silence I know she's right. I'm choosing to sail away from safety, from what I've known my whole life. But I also know that in choosing to sail away I am also venturing toward—to a new way of living, a new way of being. But I don't say this out loud. Because if I did, it would be like I was putting them down for staying anchored, for staying sheltered in the harbor. And I also know that, as Kali says, it's a process. I still crave the anchor, the safety of our Thursday night Mah Jongg games, of our shared history, our shared goals, the comfort of familiarity. But I'm no longer so sure that weighing less and buying more can offer true happiness, can mend the inner cracks.

"Syd, where are you?" Margot asks. "You look like you're miles away."

I shake my head awake and apologize.

"Were you meditating?" Donna asks me, giggling.

"Oh! My! God! Don't look now, but Connie just walked in," Jodi says, taking a sip of her coffee.

Of course, telling someone not to look now is just like the rules of a diet. Once you know you can't, you absolutely must. So Donna, Margot and I look up, trying to be casual, and see Connie in her short pink and green plaid golf skirt, her pink Lilly polo and her shoulder length blonde hair pulled into a pony tail.

"I bet when she comes she makes little birdie moans," Donna says.

"You already played the birdie pun, " I tell her.

"I can't believe she's having an affair with the pro. Really, she is the last person I'd imagine having an affair in this club," Margot says.

"That's always the way, they surprise you," Jodi says, looking at me.

I don't want Jodi to start in about the Om Guru Center again, so I tell them that this whole Connie thing reminds me of a joke about how you can tell when you're getting old.

"Oh. Are you still allowed to tell jokes? Is the jokester a part of your True Self?" Jodi asks.

"Hey, in my first yoga class, my teacher, Kali, told me I offered others the gift of laughter," I tell them.

"She was being nice because she wanted you to join the yoga center," Jodi says.

"So, do you want to hear my joke or not? Because really, given the fact that I've been replaced, you can see how my ego might be a little fragile right now," I say.

"Go ahead," Jodi says, knowing I will anyway.

"Okay. So this woman finally gets up the nerve to tell her very best friend that she's having an affair. And her best friend is open-mouthed and surprised silent for a moment before saying, "You? You're having an affair? I can't believe it! Are you going to have it catered?!""

"Well, Syd, for the past few weeks you've been telling me about the grace of the guru. Maybe you could ask the guru to grace you with better jokes," Jodi tells me.

But Margot is smiling and then says, "Actually, I think it was pretty funny. And as long as I have to co-chair the country club comedy night, I'm thinking that after Donna does her shtick with her puns, you can follow her with your top ten favorite jokes!"

"Please tell me that you're having some professional comedians," I say to Margot as we begin getting up from the table.

As I look around the room, I see whispers of conversations between tennis players and golfers and business associates. I think about the gossip that passes for conversation and connection, the quick cautious glances to other tables and then the resuming of talk amid the furtive looks. No different than what we did at our own table. And I think to myself that we are all caught up in a cosmic comedy and tragedy called life, where one's own group plays starring roles and reduces all others to merely walk-ons.

I realize that I bring a different part of myself to the Om Guru Center. A better part of myself. A more loving, open and compassionate self. And I vow to get to know that self better, and to take her with me not only to the Om Guru Center, but also to the other places in my life.

Even the country club.

Chapter Nineteen

Lying on the deck soaking up the summer sun, I think back to what my sociology professor once said. He told the class that if you always sleep on your left side, you see the world from that point of view. But if just one night in your life you slept on your right side, you'd see things from a totally different point of view. Even if you never went back to sleeping on your right side again, your world is forever changed, because you've experienced perspective.

After two months of going to the Om Guru Center, I think that's what I've done.

I always thought that the life I was leading was the only kind of life to lead. I was so materially focused. So weight focused. But practicing yoga, becoming a devotee of Gurujai, spending time with other devotees, my perspective has forever changed.

Still, not everyone is thrilled. I haven't played Mah Jongg in ages, and things feel sort of strained with my friends—even with Jodi. I guess I never realized how much we bonded around things like dieting and shopping. I've been trying to let go of my self-absorbed focus on weight loss, instead meditating, as Gurujai invites us, on the well-being and peace of all of humanity. And for the past couple of weeks I've been going with some other devotees of the Om Guru Center to a soup kitchen in Chicago where we perform *Seva*, selfless service, by feeding the hungry.

When my focus is on working for the benefit of others, I am able to let go of my own preoccupation with my body size. How have I lived my 43 years in such a cocoon, worrying about caloric intake while so many people are hungry?

I'm not weighing myself every day anymore, and I'm trying to learn that my self-worth is not related to the numbers on the bathroom scale. As the Om Guru lineage teaches, our bodies are merely a physical container for our infinite soul, allowing us to move through this incarnation toward the attainment of true knowing, and self-realization.

And between listening to Kali during yoga class and hanging out with Montana, I've begun making even more changes in my life. I've become a vegetarian.

At first I was a bit nervous. I mean, after years of dieting, skinless chicken breasts and lean turkey have become my safety net. But spending time with the devotees of the Om Guru Center, which practices vegetarianism as part of the lineage, and listening to Kali and Montana, I decided that as part of my spiritual path, I would honor the sacredness of all life by loving, and not eating, the animals that roam the Earth.

But trust me, it's not so easy to become a vegetarian, especially in the summer time with the smell of steaks and hamburgers on barbecues wafting throughout the neighborhood. And in a moment of deepening friendship I admitted to Montana that I often drove through Dunkin' Donuts after our soy chai dates for a hazelnut coffee with Sweet'N Low. She made me promise, not to her, but to the energy of the guru, that I would stop putting "that poison," as she calls it, into my body.

"Your body is a temple. Are you going to fill it with unhealthy fake sugar or nature's own sweetness?" she had asked.

I wanted to ask if she had every tried fake sugar because if you haven't tried it, don't knock it, but I figured she had a point.

She also made me promise to give up all diet sodas. When I had first protested, telling her that to me diet soda was like water, an absolute necessity, she had asked me, "Syd, why do you think the word 'die' is in diet?"

So I'm trying, for the first time in my life, to eat chemical-free and diet-free, filling up on granola, fruits and vegetables, tofu, garden burgers and peanut butter.

Gary wasn't thrilled with me last Friday night, though, when I had to meet him downtown for a dinner with an important client and his wife. We had met at a popular steak restaurant, and there were no vegetarian options on the menu. I had improvised and asked the waiter to bring me a Caesar salad, and for dinner some sautéed green beans, asparagus and a baked potato.

The client's wife kept telling me how "good" I was being and how jealous she was that I was able to stay on my diet. Apparently, she had just come off of Weight Watchers and was furious at herself that she had regained most of the weight she had lost in the spring.

I told her that I could relate. That I had been on Weight Watchers and Atkins numerous times, had stints with the Cabbage Soup Diet, South Beach, and a host of others, and every time I lost weight, I eventually gained it back.

"You should see my book shelf—it's a testament to how many diets I've tried," I told her.

As she was biting into her filet mignon she asked me what diet I was on now, and how did I manage to have so much willpower?

I told her that I recently became a vegetarian as part of a spiritual path. And then I felt Gary kick me under the table.

When we got home that night I asked Gary why he kicked me like that. He told me that he didn't want me to talk about my obsession with the Om Guru Center and Gurujai with his clients.

"Obsession? Since when is this an obsession?" I had asked him. We had just sat down in front of the TV, getting ready to watch an episode of *Lost* on DVD.

"C'mon, Syd, I don't mean it in a bad way. Whenever you begin something new you tend to get a bit carried away. It'll pass."

I was so mad I wanted to yell at him and kick him right back. But—and kudos to me—I simply inhaled deeply, exhaled, and said, "If I seem obsessed to you, perhaps you are merely witnessing my own intoxication with the realization that I am following my true bliss."

Gary had looked at me and smiled, saying, "You know what true bliss is? Biting into the juiciest New York strip dripping with béarnaise sauce."

"Well, I hope it was worth it," I said to him, "because when you bit into that juicy New York strip, you also bit into all of the cow's karma, and all of the violence that led to that poor cow's slaughter. And now you've absorbed that negativity and violence into your own body."

Gary looked at me like I was insane.

"Dear God, you sound like Rachel did before her bat mitzvah, when she used the whole Torah portion about animal sacrifice to manipulate us into getting her a dog."

I leaned over and patted Levi, who had made himself comfortable sitting on the floor, his head resting on the couch. One of my finest accomplishments was teaching Levi that the only furniture he was allowed on was the leather couch in the basement.

"Well, maybe she had a point. And besides, do you realize that 'dog' spelled backwards is 'god'? Maybe there's something to that," I said pondering the possibilities.

Gary hit the pause button and said, "Is this for real, Syd? Because I'm telling you, you could have a future as an actress. You'd be great; they'd give you a role and you'd spend months living as that character, working on your art."

I remember him laughing and pulling me over, but I wasn't going to be dismissed that easily.

"Gary, this is for real, and you need to understand that. I'm changing, and you don't have to change with me, but you have to respect my being and my process," I had told him.

He threw a pillow at me. I threw it right back.

"That's what I'm saying—who talks like that?" he had asked. "All of a sudden everything is a process, everything is by the 'grace of the guru.' I swear, Syd, sometimes I think you've lost your mind."

I looked at Gary sprawled out on the couch, remote control dangling from his hand, and said, "I have not lost my mind." Then I thought for a moment and corrected myself. "Or rather, I am trying to lose my mind."

Gary looked like he might call 911 at any moment. I could imagine his call. "*911? Yes, I need a dispatcher sent to 109 Cherry Street right away. The problem? By the grace of the guru, my wife has gone off the deep end. What's that? Ah, no, we don't have a pool in our backyard. Not that deep end. I mean in the figurative sense.*"

"I think you've just proven my point," he had said. "What does that mean, you're trying to lose your mind?"

I took a deep cleansing breath and tried to explain. "That's part of the goal of meditation. To lose your mind. You know, to let go of the constant chatter, the jumping from one thought to the next without ever noticing the preciousness of just this moment, of witnessing the power of the mantra. When you lose your mind, you can come to your senses and just breathe into what is."

The frame of *Lost* stayed paused, with a shot of Jack scanning the horizon of the island they couldn't get off.

"Well, it seems like more than just being with what is," Gary had said to me.

"What do you mean by that?" I had asked, reaching for a Dove chocolate from the candy dish on the coffee table. I had realized that green beans, asparagus and potatoes didn't fill me up the way a good steak did.

"If you're trying to just be with what is, was it necessary to remodel the upstairs office into a cultish meditation room?" Gary had challenged.

I saw what he was getting at, but he was missing the point. I should explain.

After my first Satsang, I decided that I would begin my meditation practice at home. I had gone to Barnes and Noble the next day and found myself in the Eastern religion section, where I saw lots of different books on various types of meditation. I figured that there was a proper way to begin this whole meditation practice, and I wanted to get it right.

But there were so many ways to meditate! It wasn't a whole lot different from standing in front of the diet section in the bookstore. Granted, the goal was nirvana and not weight loss (though if you asked me about the difference a few months ago, I would have sworn that weight loss and nirvana were synonymous,) but still, there seemed to be so many different methods. I wanted to make sure I found a book that was in keeping with the philosophy of the Om Guru path.

On the bottom shelf I saw the book *Meditation for Dummies* and thought maybe that was generic enough for my use, but just as I was bending down to look at it I saw a meditation book by Swami Baba. It was like finding a compass that gave me direction. His name gave me the security and stamp of endorsement I needed. It was like my own private Good Housekeeping Seal of Approval for meditation.

I bought the book and spent most of the day alternating reading Gurujai's *Finding Yourself, Finding Your Bliss*, and Swami Baba's book, *Sit Down and Meditate*. I wanted a foundation, and I wanted it quickly, and so I read and read. And what I realized immediately was that I needed to set up a room to serve as my sacred space for meditation. I walked around my house looking at various options.

The library, with its floor-to-ceiling ladder and overflow of books, might serve me well, I had thought. Perhaps the wisdom in all of the collected writings would penetrate me by osmosis while I was meditating. But then I had looked at the titles that lined my bookshelf: *Thin Thighs in Thirty Days, Lose Weight Now, We'll Tell You How*, and *Sleek and Slender*, and I thought maybe that shelf wouldn't be so helpful along the spiritual path. I eyed a few more shelves—legal thrillers, murder mysteries and chic books galore. I decided that the library didn't really give off the vibe I was looking for.

The living room wasn't private enough, nor was the family room, and I didn't want to meditate in the basement. I just didn't see myself meditating there; the space spoke to me of popcorn and movies and long-abandoned Scrabble games.

The sunroom held a moment of possibility, but I thought the windows and the sounds of the neighborhood would be distracting.

Despite the delightful rays of sunshine that filtered through our bedroom window in the morning, I knew that wouldn't work at all. I needed space, and I couldn't afford sharing that space with Gary. Ditto for Rachel's room, where I would undoubtedly be tempted away from my search for the Ultimate to cleaning out her drawers. For a moment I considered redecorating the guest bedrooms, but that would involve getting rid of wallpaper and reupholstering, so I let that idea go.

Then I walked into the upstairs office. Mahogany built-in shelves on the left, a marble fireplace on the right, and in the middle a floor-to-ceiling sliding door leading out to the second floor deck that wraps around to the left and connects with our bedroom. The back wall boasts a large desk housing a computer and some desktop filing shelves that were more for show than for use. Actually, the whole room was more for show than use. Years ago Gary used to do some work there in the evenings, but with the advent of laptops, if he brings work home he prefers to sit in the family room or the basement office.

When Rachel was younger I would use the office to organize the many things I volunteered for: room parent, PTA, school fundraising activities and committees, along with the country club projects that kept me busy; the fashion shows and charity events that were scheduled throughout the year. But now the office was no longer needed as much. It became a place to house something—a form to be filled out or a subscription to be renewed—until it could be completed and mailed. It became a weigh station.

So when I walked into the office, I saw the space with new eyes. I thought that perhaps the space could be transformed—reincarnated, if you will—to a meditation room that could be fit for a swami.

I had a new decorating project, and I threw myself into it with abandon.

In more ways than one. I was so busy spending two full weeks getting the meditation room decorated that I never managed to actually sit down and meditate.

But I wanted to get it right. I figured that if everything was just so, if all was in order and tastefully done, my perfectly appointed meditation room would ooze with spiritual accoutrements that would guide me into meditation transcendence.

So I rearranged.

And I shopped.

At the Om Guru Center after Satsang one night, I went into the gift store and bought a meditation cushion and a small, round Indian rug to set my meditation cushion on. It was woven into geometric designs in threads of gold, maroon, green and burnt orange. And then I bought a framed 8 x 10 picture of Gurujai on a mountaintop, and her maroon robe brought out the maroon in the Indian rug. I also bought a 5 x 7 framed photo of Gurujai sitting in meditation. I bit the bullet and bought a statue of Lakshmi and Hanuman, and just when I was about to pay I saw an off-white distressed wooden oar with the mantra *Om Namah Shivaya* written across it. *What better way to infuse the room with blessings,* I thought as I pointed to the one I wanted, and the devotee working in the gift store took it off the wall and rang it up with the rest of my purchases.

Later on that week, when I was running some errands at the mall, I happened to stop in Pier One Imports, and couldn't believe my luck. Or rather, my auspicious timing in shopping.

There I stumbled upon a beautiful incense holder made of sandalwood shaped like a lotus flower. They also sold Himalayan incense, and I stocked up. I put them in the office along with the items that I had bought at the Om Guru Center, and continued foraging through stores like a squirrel looking for nuts.

Running an errand at Target, I found myself in the back of the store where, unbeknownst to me, they had an Asian import section, and I found the most fabulous meditation table. It was low and wooden with OM engraved all around the border, and the legs were carved with tigers. It was perfect to hold my deities and incense and the photo of Gurujai meditating. Wandering around the displays, I also found a red-painted floor vase etched with tigers and trees. I placed some bamboo sticks being sold in bunches in the vase, and the feel was very Indian, very ashram. So I bought it all.

And then I went to work.

I placed the meditation table in front of the sliding glass door, and placed my deities, incense and Gurujai photo atop. I found the faux candles I had bought at Prana Yoga and placed one beside the photo. In front of the table I laid out my Indian rug and placed my meditation cushion upon it. I found a hammer and nail and hung my 8 x 10 beautifully matted and framed photo of Gurujai on the mountain top above the shelves on the lefthand wall. Then I hung my oar etched with the mantra above the desk, and I placed the red wooden floor vase filled with bamboo sticks in the far corner of the fireplace.

I was happy with it, but it wasn't ready yet. I went on searching.

One afternoon I went to TJ Maxx for a pair of beach flip flops, and just for fun I decided to look at the home goods.

I couldn't believe it! When did spiritual novelties become so popular? I saw a shelf with Buddha heads and statues of whom I now know is Ganesha. I swear if I had passed these statues last spring I would have thought it was a strange-looking elephant, and would have chalked it up as a TJ Maxx item representing their discounted and slightly irregular merchandise. But now I knew this was not merely an odd elephant. This was sacred! This was Ganesha, remover of obstacles! And there was a big Ganesha sitting on the floor!

I picked up the Ganesha and turned it over to look at the price.

It was only $14.99. I don't even want to tell you how much more I paid for my little Ganesha at the Om Guru Center.

I bought him. I figured that like shoes, you can never have too many Ganeshas. After all, there are lots of obstacles that need removing. So, along with a really cute pair of navy blue flip flops with a daisy of rhinestones decorating the space between the first and second toe, I bought my pal Ganesha.

I took him home and brought him upstairs to settle him into his new room where he could get to work removing obstacles. He looked right at home sitting in the lefthand corner in between the end of the bookshelf and the beginning of the meditation table. Then I displayed my *Sit Down and Meditate*, along with both volumes of *Finding Yourself, Finding Your Bliss,* on the center bookshelf. I walked into the doorway of the room to survey.

I impressed myself.

Nearly two weeks after I began my meditation project, I was ready to meditate. I lit the incense, turned on my faux candle, turned off the lights, prostrated before my meditation table/altar, and sat on my cushion to meditate.

Breathing in I recited the mantra in my mind, and breathing out I recited the mantra in my mind, letting it sail along the breath, bringing me closer to the divine that radiates within and without.

But then I realized that the only way I had to monitor how long I was sitting in meditation was to turn my head and look at the small desk clock. This would not do. I decided I couldn't meditate until I had a meditation timer that could guide my practice sessions. Luckily this was on a Wednesday afternoon and I was due back at the Om Guru Center the next evening, so I would wait to meditate until I could purchase a proper meditation timer.

The next day, when I stopped into the gift store after Satsang, Sarasvati was working and I told her what I was looking for. She was a huge help, and showed me a CD that was just for meditation. Each track was a meditation bell signaling the beginning of meditation, and a set number of minutes of silence for meditation followed by a meditation bell ending the sitting session. The shortest track was five minutes, and the longest was 45 minutes. You could just put on the desired track number to coordinate with how long you wanted to sit.

I told Sarasvati that I would take it, but I hated to put a CD player into the meditation room, as I thought aesthetically it really didn't work.

I'm telling you, the Om Guru Center thinks of everything. Sarasvati smiled at me and brought out a beautiful conch shell that was really a CD player. It was perfect, and I could put it on my meditation table, where it would not only be useful for timing my meditation, but I thought would make a statement as well.

I brought it home later that evening and placed it on the meditation altar. I loved how it looked. Everything was perfect!

But I was too tired to meditate, so I promised myself I would start the next morning, which I did.

I took the fact that Gary didn't say too much about my redecorating the upstairs office as a sign that Ganesha was doing his job and removing all obstacles, and by the grace of the guru silently supporting my spiritual exploration.

That was, until the night of the steak dinner where I ate no steak.

"Okay, Gary," I had said. "I am trying to be with what is, but there's no reason why I can't improve upon what was. None of us really use that office anymore. I transformed that space into something sacred; a room for me to meditate, a room for me to just be."

Gary sat up, and Levi moved over to him, willing him to pet behind his ears.

"A room for you to be what, Syd? What is it you're looking for all of a sudden?" Gary asked, looking at me seriously for the first time in a long time.

I took a breath and tried to think of what to say. How could I make him understand how empty my life began to feel after Rachel left for college? Of how much I thought about that horrific accident ending Brad Jackson's life, and giving Kevin Mann a second chance? How do I speak of baby Rae, and the release of grief I experienced sitting at Lincoln Elementary school? Of how much it affected me that night we went to Bar 23 and refused to really see the homeless man asking for help? How when I heard that Scott Someone speak, I knew he was speaking to me. Of what it's like for me to sit with Montana and Candace at the Om Guru Center, to be part of something bigger than myself.

How do I tell Gary that the Syd Arthur he knows, the Syd Arthur he loves, has spent 43 years sleeping through life, and now wants to be awake? Awake to the world, as it is moment to moment, and to take her place in that sacredness? How do I tell Gary how much I want to release my spirit and let it soar?

I didn't know how to answer his question in a way he would truly, really hear, but I tried. I looked at him, and I opened my mouth to try to explain, but then nothing came out.

I couldn't form the words. They got caught in my throat like pecans in molasses, and they couldn't break free. And then, before I knew it, I was crying. Silently at first, and then I couldn't stop.

It was like another dam had burst and I was crying and shaking, my heart pounding like it was going to erupt. I remember the sound of Gary dropping the remote on the coffee table, and the pause button must have been hit inadvertently because all of a sudden the TV turned on with Jack shouting orders to the plane crash survivors, and then I was engulfed in Gary's arms, sobbing. And he was stroking my hair and kissing away my tears, and murmuring things I couldn't really hear over my crying, but I knew, after twenty years of marriage, that they were the things I needed him to say.

Afterwards, after I had stopped crying, I tried to explain. I told Gary that I needed to explore this spiritual path, and that it gave my life more meaning. I told him he didn't have to join me, but I needed him to support my journey.

And he had hugged me and told me that he loved me, but made me promise not to pierce my tongue or get a tattoo, and that if I learned the *Kama Sutra* I would call him home from work early and he'd be more than happy to take part in that portion of my spiritual seeking.

He asked me if I wanted to talk more, but I told him I didn't. I felt exhausted from crying so hard—weak and empty, the way you feel after the stomach flu, when everything held inside you is released and you know there is nothing left to throw up. But it felt good, too, like I let go of all the toxins I'd accumulated from years of walking through life with my eyes closed.

Seeing how tired I looked, Gary had asked me if I wanted to go to bed, but I told him no, I wanted to just relax now and watch that episode of *Lost*. I was committed to seeing what led to these people surviving the plane crash and ending up on this mysterious island, and if, how, and when they'd get off and find their freedom on another shore.

Chapter Twenty

"I really want something cold," I tell Montana as we stand in line at Starbucks still sweating from the Power Yoga class we just finished. The line inches along as the baristas call out drinks that sound like heaven: Venti Espresso Iced Caramel Macchiato, Grande Java Chip Frappaccino.

I turn around and look at Montana behind me. "Don't those sound good? I think we should order something different today," I say, hoping she'll jump on my bandwagon, or at least let my bandwagon roll along into something cold and mocha-like.

Montana lets out a smile, but also a sigh that lets me know she's not jumping on board. "Syd, you've just spent 90 minutes cleansing your body, sweating out the toxins and heating up your chakras. There's nothing to be gained by ordering an ice cream masquerading as a coffee drink. Your system needs to cool down slowly and naturally," she advises me. "Let's order a cup of Zen green tea."

I'm about to challenge her, but then I stop myself. These past few months I've discovered so many new things thanks to Montana. And since I want to be more like her—spiritual, free and earthy—I agree with her, and offer to treat.

As we sit down with our mugs I try not to look at the customers claiming their mocha Frappaccinos, and instead watch Montana as she pulls her long hair to one side of her shoulder and sips her hot tea.

"I'm really going to miss Kali's yoga classes when I'm in India," Montana tells me.

I stir my tea bag around in my mug. "It's going to be strange going to yoga without you," I tell her, knowing how much I'll miss her.

"I feel like we've known each other forever. I can't believe we only met this past March," she says.

"Well, in this life we just met in March. Who knows how many other lifetimes we've spent together doing the Sun Salutation and drinking tea?" I ask, taking the tea bag out of my mug and finally taking a sip of my drink. I watch the tea bag seep through and wet my napkin.

Montana smiles at me and puts her hands in *Namaste* position and says to me, "And the student becomes the master."

I decide to ignore the drink orders that are being shouted, and instead drink in this moment with Montana. Drink in the calmness and the energy that I've discovered both through yoga, Gurujai and this new friendship. I know that come September, when Montana leaves for India, I'm going to wish for these times, the ease in which Montana leads me to new ideas, new ways of seeing the world and new ways of being in the world.

"Okay, listen," I say excitedly, perking up even without my java. "My birthday is in a few weeks. Let's do something to really celebrate before you leave."

Montana looks at me oddly and asks me the date of my birthday.

"August 20th," I answer, wondering if maybe I came on too strong. Or if maybe devotees of Om Guru, like the Jehovah's Witnesses, don't celebrate birthdays.

"Get out of here!" she says, hitting my shoulder. "August 20th?"

"Yeah, I'm going to be 44 years old," I tell her.

A grin forms on Montana's lips. I push my tea away, making room to put my elbows on the table, and rest my chin in my hands as I look across at my friend who is almost a decade younger than I. Montana folds her hands over her chest and just shakes her head, the smile still there.

"You know, 44 is the new 33, so you can stop looking at me with that silly smirk," I tell her.

"Well, if this isn't auspicious, I don't know what is," Montana says, looking at me.

"What's so auspicious?" I ask, knowing that in Om Guru the word "auspicious" is used as frequently as "calorie" is used in diets.

"Okay, Syd, are you ready for this?" She leans in close to me, with her hands holding on to the front of the table. "The minute you said your birthday was in August, I just had this feeling—" She shakes her head as her voice trails off and then returns with exuberance. "Gurujai's birthday is August 20th! Can you believe it? You and Gurujai have the same birthday!" She takes the palm of her hands and slams them on the table. "Born under the same sign of Leo on the same auspicious day. This is so exciting, Syd! This is big. This is really big, this is—"

I cut her off. "Auspicious?" I say, leaning back in my chair and folding my arms over my chest.

"Syd, I'm really serious," Montana says, leaning in closer. "And yes, we're going to celebrate together," she says, smiling.

"Great!" I say. "I know this is going to sound a little crazy, but you seem to help bring out the crazy in me."

"I take that as a compliment," Montana says as she plays with her tea bag on her napkin.

"As well you should," I tell her with a smile. "So anyway, when I was a teenager, I used to love to go to Six Flags. I'd go on the huge rollercoaster—you know, the one where you can see the top of the Sears Tower? Let's go there for my birthday. We'll go on all the rides, and we'll eat corn dogs and nachos, but the calories won't count because calories don't count when you eat them on your birthday," I explain. "Oh, and we'll pretend the corn dogs are really tofu dogs," I add, having forgotten for the moment that I've become a vegetarian.

She is smiling at me, but she is silent, so I continue. "And you know, not only do calories and meat not count for the birthday girl, but junk food becomes natural and organic for the birthday girl's friend," I say, waiting for her to get on this bandwagon, given that she let the first bandwagon, the one offering up ice cream flavored coffee drinks, ride on by. "So, what do you think?" I ask her, waiting.

Montana reaches across the table and covers my hand with hers. "I am going to celebrate your birthday with you. And if you want to go to Six Flags before I leave for India, we can do that. But we can't do it on August 20th," she tells me in no uncertain terms. "That's not how we're going to celebrate your birthday."

"Gosh, Montana, " I begin. "You do know it's common etiquette that the birthday girl gets to pick what she wants to do on her birthday, don't you? And you do know that if on my birthday I tell you I want to order a Grande Mocha Frappaccino with whipped cream and a cherry, you have to buy me one, right?"

Montana laughs for a second to appease me, and then she pronounces, "I am going to take you away for your birthday. I hadn't planned on going this year because of India and all, but now—"

Leaning in closer to me, she begins talking excitedly. "We're going to the Om Guru Ashram in the Catskills for a big weekend retreat where Gurujai will be celebrating her birthday. It's a very auspicious retreat where we all pay homage to the guru and celebrate her birthday and you can stand in line for Darshan where you'll meet Gurujai and receive *Shaktipat,* where Gurujai will transmit her spiritual energy to you and awaken your dormant kundalini."

She says this with barely taking a breath.

"Talk about your birthday! This will truly be a Birth Day. You'll be reborn into your true essence, taking your part in the cosmic play of the universe," Montana says with what I can only call ecstasy in her voice.

I take a deep breath and then I get ready to tell Montana all of the reasons why I can't go to the Om Guru Ashram for my birthday. "First, " I begin, "I can't go because Gary has already planned a dinner with our friends on the 19th, and—"

Montana puts her hand up and interrupts me. "This is not a time to be telling me why you can't do something. This is one of those moments, Syd. One of those doors that open for a moment, and that if you sneeze and keep your eyes closed for a second too long, you're going to miss. One of those moments where you need to stop thinking and answer with your heart, where you need to say YES! Yes! to the spiritual yearning inviting you to wake up! Yes! to the possibilities of knowing the ultimate truth! Yes! to unleashing your kundalini energy, to letting it uncoil and bring you to the cosmic explosion of ecstasy! Are you going to tell me that you'll have to say no to this because Gary has made a dinner reservation?"

"Okay, when you put it that way, I'll think about it," I say, smiling.

But Montana does not return the smile. "I'm serious, Syd. This is an auspicious sign. You have to go on this retreat with me. It's time. It's meant to be. All you have to do is say yes, and I'll take care of the rest—"

I stop listening. My heart is pounding. I can feel the blood coursing through my body, coming out in my ears, thumping me awake.

"Yes," I say, cutting her off. "Yes."

Montana gets up and hugs me, and I hug her back, tightly, holding on and not wanting to let go. Not wanting her to leave me and go to India.

We spend the next half-hour talking and making plans over another cup of Zen tea. She explains that the three-day retreat will start on Friday the 19th and go through the 21st. Her plan is for us to fly into LaGuardia and then rent a car and drive up to the Catskills.

By the time we leave Starbucks I still haven't figured out how I'm going to tell Gary about my change of plans, but there is no doubt in my mind or my heart. I will celebrate my 44th birthday at the Om Guru Ashram on a three-day retreat where Gurujai will celebrate her birthday, and I will be reborn, by the grace of the Guru, as she calls my energy and I awaken.

On the drive home, I feel free. Because the day is hot, but not humid, I turn off the air conditioning and open the windows. I shake out my ponytail and let my hair whip out the window in the wind. I change the radio dial until I find a song that fits my mood. I realize that Montana is right about seeing the auspicious signs as they arise. I turn up the radio and sing along with the song "I'm Free" from The Who's *Tommy:*

I'm free!

I'm free! And I'm waiting for you to follow me...

By the time I pull into my driveway, however, the song is over and Rod Stewart is wailing away, singing *Do Ya Think I'm Sexy?*

I let myself in through the garage door and see that Rachel's car isn't there. At least this means she didn't sleep into the afternoon. As I walk into the house I will the words to Rod Stewart's song to stop playing in my mind, and I let Levi out to pee.

Back inside, I put down my purse and see a note from Rachel on the counter. *Hi Mom, Went out for bagels with Tammy. Probably will go to the beach. Call u later, luv Rachel.* I fill a water dish for Levi and bring it outside, deciding to leave him in the yard while I take a shower.

Before I head upstairs I check the voice messages on my machine that are flashing. The robotic voice tells me "You have five new messages. *Beep.* Wednesday, 8:52 A.M."

"Hey Syd, it's Jodi. Just checking to see if you're going to make it to Mah Jongg tomorrow night. It's at my house. Okay, call me, bye. Oh wait, let me know if you want to go shopping with me at Neiman's this afternoon. Okay, bye."

"*Beep.* Wednesday, 9:33 A.M."

"Hello, Syd? Cynthia Goldberg calling. We'd love you to come to our planning meeting for next year's fashion show. You know we decided to schedule it in the spring instead of the fall. Took us months to make the decision, lots of sleep lost over it, I'll tell you, but now we're all set. So it's next Thursday, 11:00 at the club. You were marvelous with the auction items last year, and we're all counting on you again. Please call me and let me know if you can make it. Love to Gary. Bye bye."

"*Beep.* Wednesday, 10:18 A.M."

"Hey hon, it's me. Turns out my afternoon meeting is now a dinner meeting, so I'll be home on the later side. Talk to you later, love you."

"*Beep.* Wednesday, 11:07 A.M."

"Hi Syd, you must be out. Listen, your father and I are trying to decide when to go back to Florida. I know last year we weren't here for the High Holy Days, and I felt a little guilty about that. So we can wait to go back to Boca until after Yom Kippur, if you want. I know Rachel doesn't leave school to come home for the holidays, and I don't want to leave you alone. You know, unless you're maybe thinking of being with Jodi and her family? Not that we wouldn't stay here if you want us to. Most of our friends are going back early again this year—well, the ones who don't live there year round, which I think your father and I are going to do soon. Why go back and forth when our lives, except for you, of course, are in Boca? "

"*Beep.* Wednesday 11:09 A.M."

"Syd? Still me. I think we got cut off. Anyway, I'm your mother, I'll do whatever you want, so just let me know. Because between you and me, I think your father already has his bags packed and lined up some golf games. But Syd, one word from you and you know we'll stay through September. Call me. Oh, and I have some extra brisket from last night I want to bring over for you, Rachel and Gary—" Pause. "I just remembered. Are you still a vegetarian? Well, the brisket was delicious. Very tender, so maybe you can just eat it anyway. Oh, I have another call. Talk to you later, bye."

I take a deep breath, and decide I'll return the calls after my shower.

But after my shower, still thinking about going on this retreat, I decide instead to harness this spiritual energy and sit down to meditate. The longest I've sat so far at a given time is 25 minutes, and today I vow to sit for 45 minutes. For some reason, 45 minutes has always felt more earnest, more legitimate, like you're really a meditator if you can sit for that long. Like you are entitled to assume that identity when you can sit down in meditation for three-fourths of an hour.

Which, when I think about it, is really strange. I am still struggling with my changing identity, and my friends and family are, too. But somehow the world out there has received the memo, gotten the buzz, jumped on board.

How, I've been wondering for most of the summer, has the world gotten wind of my changing self—or, I should say, my changing Self? Somehow I've begun getting mail addressed to Syd Arthur from places I never knew existed (like The Self-Actualized Spa and Yoga resort in the Berkshires), been offered subscriptions to magazines I've never heard of (like *Nirvana News),* received catalogues never on my radar (like *New Age Merchandise for the Enlightened Consumer).* I get special offers for the latest edition of the *Bhagavad Gita,* postcards alerting me to special offers for trips to India, and invitations to meet with investment firms with a social conscience.

How have they figured out where I'm heading before I've fully figured it out? While I'm still searching, they've already found me as part of their target audience. I'm flattered, but confused. How do they know—and who, by the way, are they?

My old marketing courses come back to mind, and I'm sure that the fact that I take classes at Prana Yoga and that I've been going to the Om Guru Center has found its way into the mass database where personal information is sought and bought.

Before sitting for meditation to claim myself as a true spiritual seeker, I go outside to call in Levi. He doesn't want to come in. I try once again to coax him inside. "Levi, inside for a treat," I yell, but he just picks his head up to look at me and plops it right back down. I refill his water bowl and then I return inside, thanking my lucky stars, or my auspicious stars, that last fall we put in the Invisible Fence.

I go upstairs to my meditation room. I light my Himalayan incense in my lotus incense burner. I turn on my faux candle, walk over to my conch shell CD player and press the track for the 45-minute mark. I turn off the lights, close the door, and sit on my mediation cushion across from my meditation altar.

I begin reciting the mantra in my mind, *Om Namah Shivaya* on my in-hale, and *Om Namah Shivaya* on my exhale, and I will myself to stay with the mantra, stay with the breath for 45 minutes.

Even if it kills me.

Okay, I might have dozed off here and there, but for awhile there is nothing but the breath and the mantra and then, while I wish I could say "before I knew it, the end of meditation came with the sound of three chimes," I *can* say that despite it being harder than it looks I did manage to sit still—in body if not always in mind—for the whole 45 minutes. I feel like I have made good progress in my meditation practice; that my spiritual seeking is legitimate. That I have passed some invisible test I had devised that makes my decision to go to the Om Guru Ashram totally valid. I am no longer only Syd Arthur, long-time shopper, dieter, and organizer of domestic bliss, but now I am also Syd Arthur, spiritual seeker.

I am becoming more verbs.

Which reminds me of the time when I was a teenager and we had a guest rabbi at our temple. He was young with long hair and a beard and he looked like a hippie. I remember him telling the congregation that in the Torah, the true translation of God's name was actually a verb, not a noun. That God's name literally translated to: "I will be what I will be."

At the time this was surprising to me, as I was a good student of grammar, and I knew that a person or thing was a noun. I didn't understand what he was talking about. But now, thinking about this not as a student of grammar but as a seeker, I find this intriguing. God a verb? God changing and flexible and flowing in action? God like energy? God like Shaktipat?

Here I am going to the Catskills, the Borscht Belt, to take retreat in an ashram. Maybe the God I grew up with is there, too. Maybe the God I grew up with isn't even so different from the kundalini energy I seek to release, like a verb in action.

I head downstairs to make lunch. Montana turned me on to this all-natural, organic peanut butter, which I spread on my seven-grain bread. I once saw a loaf of 15-grain bread, but that just seemed overkill. I look at the phone, knowing I should return the messages, but though energized from my yoga and meditation, I lack the motivation to call Jodi about Mah Jongg, to phone Cynthia about the club's fashion show, to talk with my mother.

I pour myself a glass of vitamin raspberry water and turn on the TV while I eat my lunch. Rachel Ray is pounding a chicken breast in preparation for a Marsala dish. I've only been a vegetarian for two months, but I flinch at the screen. All that negative karma, all that pounding into flesh. I take another bite of my peanut butter and feel virtuous.

The phone rings and I check caller ID. It's Jodi, and I know I should pick up, but I don't. *I'll call her after lunch,* I promise myself.

The machine picks up: "Hi, you've reached us but we're not home, so please leave a message and we'll get back to you. *Ciao! Beep."*

"Hey, it's me again. You're not home yet? Where are you? Call me. Call me soon. I want you to go shopping with me. I have to get a new dress for our neighbor's daughter's wedding. Oh, and come play Mah Jongg tomorrow night; it'll be fun. I'm going to Neiman's around 2:30, after I pick Rebecca up from the pool. Okay, call me."

I haven't played Mah Jongg since June. And not once since Barbara Cohen started playing with us. Or with them, I guess I should say. Am I not an "us" anymore? How long can you sit out and still be a part of something?

I call Jodi back. She answers after the first ring.

"Hi," she says in her chipper voice.

"Hey there," I answer.

"So where were you all morning?" Jodi asks me. I rinse off my plate, using the sink brush to wash off the sticky peanut butter before I put it in the dishwasher.

"I took a power yoga class," I say as I bend down to start the dishwasher. Silence.

"Jodi, are you there? I ask.

"Yeah, I'm here," she answers. "Must have been some power class. What was it, like four hours long?"

I know she's pissed.

"Look, Jodi, I'm sorry I didn't call earlier. I went out for tea with Montana after class, and the time just got away from me."

"Tea? Tea? Since when do you go out for tea? What are you, British now? You, my dear friend, my best friend who I know better than you know yourself, are not a tea drinker. You do not go out for tea; you are a coffee girl.

I've known you for forever, Syd, and except for the time you had mono our freshman year of high school, I never saw you drink tea. Not once. Now, if you promise to go shopping with me this afternoon, I will take you out for a cup of joe."

I had planned to tell Jodi that I couldn't go shopping today. I really wanted to just get some things done in the house, and then maybe sit out on the deck again and read a book. But I knew that I needed to go with Jodi, that she needed me to spend the afternoon with her, so I tell her that I will meet her at her house at 2:30 and that we'll go shopping for her new dress.

Jodi thanks me by promising that in return she will buy me a Grande Mocha Frappuccino at Starbucks after we finish shopping. And Jodi, ever my best friend, asks, "And you'll want that with whipped cream, right?"

And holding the phone close to my ear, I answer her, "Yes, with whipped cream."

Chapter Twenty-One

At 2:15 I get ready to drive to Jodi's. I grab my purse, reapply my lipstick, and open the door to call Levi inside.

I don't see him, and he doesn't come.

"Levi, inside for a treat," I yell. Sometimes he explores under the deck and it takes him a minute or two to come around, but he always does, so I'm not really worried. I just don't want to be late.

"Levi, c'mon, inside, let's go!"

Nothing. I go outside in the yard and walk around the front, the back, the side.

"Levi, if you come in now, I'll give you some Godiva," I call. "Let's go, boy, where are you? Inside for a treat, Levi! Levi?"

Now I'm getting worried. Something's not right. I look at my watch. I've been calling him now for over five minutes, and he hasn't come. He always comes.

Now I'm scared. What if he's really lost? What if something's happened to him? I feel the fear rising through me. I make one more lap around the yard willing for Levi to appear.

Oh God, I can't find him.

I go back inside, grab the phone and take it outside. I call Gary's office. Jake answers and tells me that Gary is in a meeting. He must hear the panic in my voice. "Is everything okay, Syd?" he asks, with concern.

"No, no, it's not," I tell him. "I really need to talk to him," I say.

"Hold on, Syd, let me text him," he says. I keep walking around the yard looking for Levi. After a minute I hear Jake's voice. "Okay, Syd, here he is."

"Syd, what's wrong?" I hear Gary ask.

"Levi's gone, I've been looking all over the yard. He's gone," I cry into the receiver, feeling my heart racing.

"Calm down, Syd, I'm sure he's not gone. Did you look under the deck? He likes to go under the deck," Gary explains to me, as if I don't know this. As if I'm not home all day with the dog.

"Gary, I've looked. He's not here. What do I do? Rachel will be beside herself if something happens to Levi. He's never done this before. This damn Invisible Fence. Sure, it works for a while, but really, how can it keep the dog in the yard forever?"

"Syd, listen to me. You've got to get a grip. Even if he broke through the Invisible Fence, he probably didn't wander very far. He'll find his way back."

"How do you know that, Gary? There's a whole world out there. What if once he starts wandering he can't find his way back? Or what if once he starts wandering, he doesn't want to find his way back? Huh? What then?" I ask, my voice rising.

"Okay, Syd, this is what I want you to do. Get in the car and start driving around the neighborhood. He's probably just in a neighbor's yard," Gary tells me. "Check in with me on my cell and let me know what's happening. Have Rachel go with you," he adds.

"Rachel's out with Tammy," I tell him. "And Levi better be back here before she comes home. If I can't find him, you need to leave work and help me."

I hang up, get in the car, and drive slowly down the street, my window open this time not with the radio on, but with my voice calling out for Levi. Though it occurs to me that Levi himself might be singing the same song I was singing only a short while ago:

I'm free!

I'm free! And I'm waiting for you to follow me!

I drive down Cherry Street, looking into yards and calling his name. Some neighborhood kids come up to me, asking me if Levi is lost. I tell them yes, and they tell me they will look in their yards and around the street, and help me to find him. I thank them, and then continue down the street, turning left on Maple.

I think to myself how I never wanted this dog. About how I feed him things I shouldn't feed him to save calories, even though I know it's not good for him. But I don't want to lose him, not like this.

I continue down Willow Street, calling his name as I drive. There is no sign of him anywhere. My cell phone rings and I jump.

"Syd, where are you? I thought you were going to be here at 2:30," Jodi says with irritation in her voice.

"Oh, Jodi, I'm sorry. I totally forgot to call you. Levi's gone," I tell her.

"Oh my God! He died? When?" she asks me with shock.

I don't have time for this. I have to find Levi.

"No, no," I begin. "He's not gone as in dead, he's gone as in missing. He was outside, but somehow he got out of the yard and as we speak I'm driving around the neighborhood looking for him." I turn slowly down Birch Street willing Levi to appear.

"How the hell did he get out of the yard? " she asks.

"Jodi, I have no idea. All I know is that I have to find him," I tell her, not knowing where I should drive. If maybe I should go back home and see if he's returned to the yard.

"I'll come over and help you," she offers.

I feel like this isn't really happening. Like this is a dream. What if I never find Levi?

"Syd? Are you still there?" I hear Jodi ask.

"Yeah, I'm here. I just can't talk now. I have to focus. Let me look for him a while longer, and I'll let you know if I need help."

"Syd, are you sure? Are you sure you don't want me to come over now?" she asks.

"No, thanks. Let me just keep looking. You should go shopping for that dress. If I can't find him within the next half hour, I'll call you," I tell her.

"Okay, but how do you think he could have gotten out? He had his collar on, right? Why would he let himself get shocked all of a sudden?" Jodi asks me. "He does have his collar on, right?" she asks again, like a lawyer cross-examining a witness.

"Of course he has his collar on," I tell Jodi.

I had asked Gary just last night to change the battery for the Invisible Fence collar. The new battery comes in the mail. It had been sitting with the mail for the past week, and I was worried that the old battery in Levi's collar was going to die any day. Gary's always been in charge of changing the batteries in Levi's collar.

And then I pull over to a curb and turn off the car.

"Jodi, I gotta go," I say, and hang up. I call Gary, who answers after the first ring.

"Did you find him?" he asks.

"Not yet. Gary, you were going to change the battery in Levi's collar last night. You changed it, right?" I ask.

"Oh shit!" he says. "Oh shit. Syd, I'm sorry. I screwed up. I was just about to change the battery last night and then Rachel came home and asked me if I wanted to go for a run with her, and she's always so busy, I jumped at the chance. I remember hurrying to change into my running clothes, and then heading out with her. By the time we got back I totally forgot that I hadn't changed the battery. It's probably still sitting behind the bar." He sounds defeated.

I start the car and pull out of the curb and on into the street. "Oh, Gary, I don't know what to do. Levi could be anywhere."

"Syd, I really screwed up. If you don't find him in the next hour, call me and I'll leave work early. I have a company that's in the middle of a crisis, and I've got to make some client calls, but then I'll come home, okay?"

I want to tell him that this, this is a crisis of his doing. I want to remind him that I never wanted a dog to begin with, that he, along with my mother and father, had played right into Rachel's hands all those years ago—six years ago, to be exact; 42 in dog years. Instead, I remind myself that I have just meditated, that I am going soon to an ashram, that I am someone who seeks peace and calmness and the Guru's blessing. And so instead I tell Gary that I will call him with any news.

I make another search down the streets, stopping the car and calling out for him. The neighborhood kids tell me that haven't seen him anywhere. Little Charlie wonders if maybe he got kidnapped. He tells me, "Dogs can't yell 'Stranger Danger' if someone they don't know comes up to him and offers him a bone or something."

"We'll keep looking," Charlie's older sister tells me, and she takes Charlie's hand and leads him back to the group of kids running through sprinklers on the lawn.

I decide to go back to the house and see if Levi is there. Maybe he's just lying down under the big tree in the yard.

But when I pull into the driveway there is no furry dog under the tree, or under the deck, or anywhere. I call and call. I don't know what to do next, and then my home phone rings. I pick it up from the table on the deck where I had left it before embarking on my unsuccessful search. It's Jodi.

"Any luck?" she asks me through a not-great connection.

"No, I can't find him," I tell her. I see the landscapers across the street, and all of a sudden I am worried that Levi is injured somewhere. That he's discovered a new yard to lounge in and a lawn mower didn't see him, all flat and feather-like, and ran right over him.

"Do you want me to come over? I'm just parking and I'm thinking that this is probably a bad time to be shopping, what with Levi missing and me feeling so bloated. I probably shouldn't have had the girls' leftover Hawaiian pizza for lunch, because now I feel really fat, and I'm thinking this probably isn't the best time to be trying on a strapless evening gown. A muumuu, maybe, but not a gown."

Silence.

"And I shouldn't be complaining to you about any of this because Levi is missing, so I'm just going to shut up right now. And I'm just going to pull out of this really great parking spot I found right in front of Neiman's and I'm going to come right over and help you look for him, okay?"

"Okay," I tell Jodi. "Thanks."

I hang up the phone and walk again around the yard, willing Levi to appear. Willing him to come out of nowhere with his panting mouth that makes him look like he's smiling at you.

I go inside to get a glass of water. I take the phone from my hand, put it in its cradle, and see the answering machine flashing new messages. I press play.

"You have two new messages. *Beep.* Wednesday 2:22 P.M."

"Hey Syd, it's Margot. I know Jodi was going to call you about tomorrow night, but I just wanted to check in with you to see if you were going to play. Would love to see you. Oh, and wanted to tell you again how much fun Ralph and I had with you and Gary in the city last Saturday. Wonderful evening, though if Gary really wants some fabulous lobsta, you've got to take a trip back East with us one of these days. Bar Harbor in the summer. They sell lobstas along the street the way you Midwesterners sell corn. So I'm counting on you playing Mah Jongg tomorrow night, it's been way too long. Talk to you later, bye."

"*Beep.* 2:28 P.M."

"Yes, hello, uh, my name is Bo Jenkins. I'm looking for the owner of a dog named Levi. He's here with me, and, uh, he's just fine. Wandered into my yard a while ago, and has been making friends with my dog, Golden. Finally let me have a look at his collar and I got your phone number. Anyway, he's fine, and as I said, he's in the yard with me now. Please call me when you get this message."

I grab a piece of paper and write down the phone number he recites on the machine. I am so relieved. I take a deep breath and look at the clock; it's almost 3:45 already. Why didn't I think to check my messages while I was out searching the neighborhood? I dial the number and after two rings, he picks up.

"Hello?" he says.

"Hi, Mr. Jenkins? My name is Syd, Syd Arthur. I've been looking all over for our dog, Levi. I can't tell you how relieved I am that you called. Thank you. Thank you so much for finding Levi and for calling me."

"Well, I think it's the other way around—he found us, ma'am. But he's just fine. He's taken a liking to my dog, Golden. Levi's been trying to engage Golden in some chases, and Golden's been doing his best to keep up with him, but my Golden here, he's getting on in his years, just like I am, just like

195

eventually we all do. But what a pleasure it's been for me to watch Golden playing like that again. Gave them both some water and now they're just having a little rest."

"Well, thank you, thank you again. I was so worried I wouldn't be able to find him. I can come get him now, if you give me directions to your house," I tell him. "I'm on Cherry Street. In Highland Ridge."

"Yep, no problem. I'm in Highland Ridge, too, but I can see that Levi is quite the adventure seeker. He crossed a mighty busy intersection," Mr. Jenkins tells me. "I'm on Middle Way Drive—do you know where that is?"

"No, I don't," I tell him, walking over to the kitchen desk to get paper and a pen.

"Just take Cherry Street past Forest Avenue to Main Street. When you get to Main Street, you want to keep going straight through the intersection, but then bear left on Center Street. Now, take the second right off Center Street, that's Pleasant Road, but then immediately after you turn right on Pleasant Road there's a small street on the left, but it comes up quickly and if you're not looking for it, you can easily miss it. That's Middle Way Drive, and I'm number 8, last house on the left. Sits just at the base of the Highland Ridge Forest Preserve."

I write down the directions and thank him again, telling him I'll be right there. "Take your time," he tells me. "No rush. We're just enjoying the afternoon."

I hang up and hurry to my car, calling Gary while I back out of the driveway.

"I promise I'll change the battery as soon as I get home," Gary says.

I call Jodi. "Hey, it's me. Some older man found Levi and called me. I'm on my way to pick him up."

"The older man or the dog?" Jodi asks me.

"Very funny," I say. "Why don't you run back to the mall and shop for that dress? I'm fine, now. Crisis over."

I drive through the intersection at Main Street, bearing left toward Center Street.

"No, I decided I'm going to spend the next week on the Combo Diet again. Last time I did it, I lost five pounds really quickly. Maybe you'll go shopping with me next week when I'm thinner. I still have some time before the wedding. So listen, now that you've found Levi, can I just ask if you'll come for Mah Jongg tomorrow night? I'll brew you a pot of your favorite hazelnut coffee, okay?" she asks.

"Okay," I agree.

"Okay, good. I'll call everyone and tell them you're playing, and I'll make them promise not to tease you about this phase you're going through," she tells me.

I see Pleasant Road and turn right. "Listen, Jodi." I say. "I gotta go. I don't want to miss his street. I'll see you tomorrow night." I hang up and put the phone down in the cup holder.

Eyes open as I drive down Pleasant Road, I see how quickly Middle Way Drive comes up, how easy it is to miss this street. But I'm focused, and I see the sign in time to turn left, and slow down as I drive to the end of the road, to number 8.

Chapter Twenty-Two

Number 8 is the last house on the small street, with a side yard that slopes into the beginning of the Highland Ridge Forest Preserve. Mr. Jenkins's house is worn and weathered but still inviting, with a small front porch where an empty rocking chair sits. I park along the curb, grab my purse and throw my cell phone back in the inside pocket as I head to the front door. Just as I'm about to ring the doorbell an old man opens the door, and from behind him I see Levi barking happily with a beautiful Golden retriever by his side.

"Started barking the minute he heard your car pull up," he says as Levi comes bounding for me, licking my face as I bend down to pet him. "C'mon in," he says, and I follow him inside.

He is tall, with just a wisp of white hair and a strong, handsome face with sharp cheekbones and chiseled features. His eyes are blue, and there is a light in them, a sparkling glint that would seem to fit with a younger man, yet here they are, bright and radiant in an old man's face. He is dressed in baggy jeans and an old, faded denim work shirt tucked into his pants, which are held up by a worn brown leather belt. He wears hiking sandals, and it is clear that he hasn't bent down to cut his toenails in a long time.

"Thank you, thank you so much for finding Levi and calling me," I say.

For a moment I feel guilty about the fact that only the other day I googled the average lifespan of a Coton De Tulear, what with Rachel in college and me tied down by the demands of a dog. I remember being surprised to find that these little dogs live an average of 16 years. *That's another ten years,* I had thought to myself. *By the time I can go into the city for a day and spontaneously decide to meet friends for drinks and dinner without having to worry about who will take Levi out or who will feed him, I'll be almost 54 years old!* I had given Levi an extra snack of my pepperoni pizza that night. He gobbled it up happily, and I figured that with his sodium intake Levi might just come in below average in the lifespan curve.

But now with Levi clearly so happy to see me I feel guilty, and the fact that he ran away today makes me feel even more so. Like somehow Levi read my thoughts while I was googling and now he is paying me back.

I keep petting Levi, and then I stand up and hold out my hand, which Mr. Jenkins takes, and I am surprised by the warm firmness in his grip despite the wrinkles and veins that peek out from under his translucent skin.

"Really, thank you so much, Mr. Jenkins. I was looking for him everywhere."

"Call me Bodee. And I'm happy to be of help," he tells me as he leans down to pat Levi's head and then scratches under Golden's chin.

"Bodee. Now that's an interesting name," I say as I lean over to give Golden a pat. I don't want him to think that I'm not a dog-lover, that I'm someone who would welcome a shorter doggy lifespan.

"It's a nickname. Been my nickname since I was just a little tyke. My first name is Bo and my middle initial is D. Went to school with another boy my age whose name was also Bo. Our first grade teacher started calling me Bo D. to distinguish us, and then everyone just started calling me Bodee, and that's who I've been ever since."

"Well, Mr. Jenkins—I mean, Bodee—thank you again."

I feel I should explain. Let him know that I'm not a negligent dog owner. That this has never happened before. "We have an Invisible Fence at home. See, he has his collar on," I say, pulling at Levi's chunky red Invisible Fence collar.

"I thought that's what that was," Bodee tells me, nodding his head. "I've seen their ads and figured that black box in the front held the battery or contraption or whatever it is for the fence."

"Exactly! And it turns out that my husband, Gary, forgot to replace the battery and this battery is dead, so he was able to run out of the yard without getting that high-pitched sound that reminds him that he's too close to the perimeter. He went straight through the Invisible Fence because he was able to avoid the shock," I explain.

Levi jumps up to Bodee, who leans down to pet his head, and his face breaks out into a big grin. "He saw his opportunity for the freedom of adventure and he seized the moment! Figured that maybe there was a big world out there, bigger than the yard where he roams, and you went after that, huh, boy?" he says as he moves from petting Levi's head to rubbing his ears.

"C'mon in, sit down," Bodee says. "I was just going to make my afternoon tea. You'll join me, won't you?"

I watch Golden make himself comfortable in his blue checkered dog bed beside the fireplace. There is a cozy cream-colored couch with four blue-and-red woven pillows, and two old white cane rockers on the side with a small wooden table in between. A coffee table sits atop a classic oval rug braided in red, pink, blue, green and flecks of yellow. Levi jumps up on the couch while Bodee puts his hand on the rocker next to the couch, motioning for me to sit down. I feel like I have just stepped into a Norman Rockwell painting.

"Levi, get down," I say as I walk over to carry him off the couch. But Bodee waves me off and holds the back of the rocker, again motioning me to sit.

"Levi's fine up there, Syd. Leave him be. Let's let the dogs rest a bit while we have a cup of tea."

The last thing I want to do is have more tea, but I look at Bodee and his kind face and I don't want to seem rude, so I sit down.

"Nothing like afternoon tea, I always say. Shirley, my wife—she passed away a few years back—she used to say her favorite part of the day was our morning tea."

I'm thinking about the million little things I have to do, that I was planning on doing after going with Jodi to the mall. The million little things that somehow no matter what I accomplish during the day, I'm always left with. But he seems like maybe he's lonely, so I just smile and rock back in the chair.

"Yep, Shirley loved that morning tea, a fine way to welcome the day. But I love the afternoon tea. The way it just slows the day down a bit, let's you savor those moments that you'd otherwise miss if you're so busy trying to beat the clock," he says, standing to the left of the rocking chair.

I smile at him, glad I didn't tell him I couldn't stay because I have a million little things to do. There's something about him, and as I push my feet back and rock myself in the chair, I feel surprisingly comfortable. As comfortable, in fact, as Levi, who is now curled up cozily against a pillow, eyes only halfway open.

Bodee asks me what type of tea I like and I tell him that anything is fine, that I don't know the difference. That actually, I'm more of a coffee drinker. "Montana, a new friend of mine, has gotten me into drinking tea with her. I met her when I started yoga, and after class we have tea at Starbucks."

"A very fine tradition: yoga, tea, and friendship. Can't go wrong with that," he says with a grin.

I smile, feeling myself relax into the rocker.

"No, I don't suppose you can. Though a hazelnut roast coffee still has a special place in my heart," I say, smiling. "But Montana, she's a health nut, and she's been helping to change my ways. You know, instead of coffee, tea, instead of steak, tofu."

He chuckles and then says, "Let me make a pot of tea. You just make yourself comfortable."

"Here, let me help you," I say as I push myself out of the rocker.

At first it looks like Bodee is going to refuse my offer, but he looks at me intently, and doesn't. Instead he smiles kindly and motions me to follow him into the kitchen.

He fills an old kettle with water and sets it on the stove, turning on the flame. The kitchen is small and narrow, with white countertops and appliances that look to be at least four decades old. On the counter is a bowl of bananas, and to the side of the sink is a dish rack with some plates drying, and I realize that there is no dishwasher. A blue dishtowel hangs on the oven door, and in the left corner the kitchen opens only slightly to make room for a two-person round table.

"Nice to have someone to share tea with," he says, smiling.

I glance at my watch and realize that I won't make it to the pharmacy, or to the tailor's. But when Bodee looks at me again and smiles, I smile back and try to forget about those errands. And about the deli order for Rachel I forgot to pick up, the wine I was supposed to buy, and the facial I was supposed to schedule.

I watch as Bodee opens the cabinet and takes out a small Chinese porcelain teapot and two small teacups, both decorated with bamboo and dragons.

"How about we enjoy some green tea?" he asks. "Nice on a warm summer's day."

"Anything is fine, really," I say. "Please let me help you. Where do you keep the tea bags?"

He looks at me smiling, his blue eyes like melting liquid sapphire. "Ah, there is no tea bag," he says, and I look at him confused. "But not to worry," he laughs, "there is tea."

I watch him open another cabinet and take down a blue and white canister among a dozen others, this particular one decorated with images of rowboats being rowed across a river by Chinese men wearing hats. Bodee opens the canister and breathes in, with a satisfied *ahhh* when he breathes out. He passes the canister to me and instructs me to inhale.

For a split second I feel like I'm back in college at a fraternity party, where a guy that I don't know is passing around some new type of weed. I think of Bill Clinton, think of not inhaling, but Bodee is holding the canister to my nose, so I breathe in.

It smells good, sweet, like a fragrant bat mitzvah centerpiece. I look inside the canister. "What is that?" I ask. I wonder all of a sudden if perhaps I am a little crazy to be here in the house of a stranger who yes, on the outside seems friendly and kind, but who really could be a psychotic killer. I mean, whatever is in the canister is like nothing I've ever seen before—little dried round balls that could be some kind of hallucinogenic drug, for all I know.

I look back at the dish rack, where a sharp knife is ominously drying.

Bodee takes the canister from my hands and holds it up to his nose, breathing deeply.

"Can you smell the jasmine?" he asks me. "This here is Jasmine Dragon Pearl. A fine green tea it is."

"How can it grow in little balls like that?" I ask him, reminding myself that despite made-for-TV movies, psychotic killers are actually quite rare.

"Ahhh, they do not grow like that," he tells me as he pulls out a dried ball. "Each individual tea leaf has been hand rolled and dried by somebody, and then mixed with the scent of jasmine flowers." He holds it up to his nose. "What a beautiful aroma," he says as he hands it to me. I breathe in its wonderful scent again.

"That's amazing," I say. "I can't imagine someone doing that, though. It must take so long, hand-rolling each tea leaf. It must be such time-consuming dull work."

Bodee looks at me and shakes his head. "And I think, on the contrary. What magnificent work it must be! For someone gets to know the detail of each tea leaf, gets to lovingly roll it into a ball and mix it with the scent of jasmine, knowing that eventually, someone—perhaps close by or perhaps far-away—will one day savor the fruits of his labor, brought forth from the earth, by drinking the sweet tea."

"Well yeah, when you put it that way—" I say, laughing, and Bodee laughs right along with me.

We hear the whistle of the kettle, and Bodee turns off the stove. He takes off the top of the teapot and measures out the Jasmine Dragon Pearl tea, which he puts in the strainer that sits inside the teapot. He takes out a wooden tray and places the teapot and teacups upon it. Then he pours some water from the kettle into the strainer and puts the top back on the teapot.

I glance at the kitchen clock, and my muscles tighten. It's already 4:10. I need to get going. But how can I just leave? I can spare a few minutes for a quick cup of tea. And by the look of those teacups, those really small porcelain teacups, I figure one gulp and I'm out the door. One gulp and I'm done.

"Shall I pour?" I offer, trying to seem kind, but really trying to hurry along this afternoon tea business.

"No, no. We must let it steep for a few minutes before we drink it," he explains. He opens the pantry and pulls out a box of biscuits, which he arranges on a small plate and adds to the tray, along with two blue cloth napkins.

"Let's have our tea in the living room, keep the dogs company," he says as he picks up the tray and carries it. I'm surprised by his steady strength as he places the tray on the table between the rockers.

My cell rings, and I pick up my purse from the coffee table and dig out my phone. I look at the number; it's Rachel.

"Hi, honey, what's up?" I ask.

She tells me that she's still at Tammy's and that they are going to go out for dinner with some friends later, and then to a party, and that she will be home by 2:00 A.M. or she'll call me and let me know if she'll be any later.

"Everything okay?" Bodee asks me as I hang up the phone.

"Yep, fine. Just my daughter checking in," I explain. He smiles.

"Please, sit down," he says, motioning again with his hands. We sit, he in the rocker closest to the fireplace and where Golden is resting, me on the rocker to the left, near the couch where Levi is lying. "Let's let the tea seep just a minute longer, so we can enjoy the full flavor," he suggests, and I nod my head and smile.

I gaze around the living room, turning my head behind me, looking on into the small dining room with the four-person teak table set with red placemats and silver candlesticks with red candles, and suddenly I feel like there is nowhere else to be, and nowhere else to go.

Except, of course, the pharmacy, the tailor and the deli.

"I think now the tea is ready," he says. He gracefully pours tea for me, and then for himself.

I watch as he holds the teacup in his hand and then looks into the cup before sipping. I wait for him to sip, and then I follow.

"A beautiful tea, isn't it? Such a robust flavor, full of body and with a hint of sweetness," he declares.

"It is good," I offer. "It has a different flavor from the green tea I've had at Starbucks," I add. "Sweeter."

I watch Bodee sip his tea. He drinks slowly, and I try to match his unhurried pace.

"So tell me about yourself, Syd," he says as he eats a biscuit.

The biscuits look good, and I decide to try one. I break off a piece and put it in my mouth, chewing slowly. It feels like I have to chew slowly because everything about this teatime, it seems, is about moving leisurely. The biscuits are delicious. I take another sip of tea and the combination is wonderful, a mix of warm and sweet and buttery.

"Mmm," I say, trying to finish chewing my biscuit before I open my mouth. "Well, for starters," I say, swallowing the last crumbs of the cookie, "I'm usually a better pet owner." I look over to Levi, who has fallen asleep.

Bodee laughs and tells me that I am a fine pet owner, and that I made Golden's day by Levi coming his way and engaging him in play. "Golden is getting on in years," he tells me. "It's good for him to play with a younger dog, one who is full of life and vitality."

I'm again feeling a twinge—okay, more than a twinge—of guilt about the food I secretly feed to Levi, and the whole googling incident. I'm 100 percent sure that Bodee doesn't feed Golden foods from the junk food aisle, or look forward to his eventual demise.

Bodee looks at me and smiles, patiently waiting for me to tell him about myself.

"Okay, let's see. I'm married, Gary and I have been married for almost 21 years, and we have a daughter, Rachel, who's a sophomore at college."

Bodee smiles and sips. I take another sip of tea, and realize that it's going to take longer to finish the cup of tea than I figured. Even though the teacup is so small, the etiquette seems to be to take little sips very slowly.

"And let's see, what else. Well, I was born here. My parents still have a place here, but they're spending less and less time in Highland Ridge, and most of the year at their home in Boca."

Bodee nods, smiles, sips, and it seems as though he wants me to continue, and so I do.

I take another sip and say, "So not really much else. You know, same old same old," I offer.

Bodee smiles a smile that lights up his face, and then laughs. "Same old same old? Now what does that mean?" he asks, and he laughs some more.

I look at him and think to myself, *Maybe he's a little senile.*

Then he puts down his teacup and stares at me and says, "There can be no 'same old same old.' No man ever steps in the same river twice; for it's not the same river and he's not the same man. Heraclitus said that."

Okay, maybe he's a retired philosophy professor, I revise in my mind.

"So, tell me, Syd. Would you really explain your life as 'same old, same old'?" he asks with—what? A knowing. A knowing like I have when Rachel tells me nothing is wrong, and I absolutely know that something is wrong.

"I think there are a lot of changes in your life," he says, taking another small sip of tea.

I follow his sip. I realize that I have timed my sips to reflect his sips so that I don't finish my tea too quickly, in a gulp, and insult him. But I gotta tell you, this teacup is small. I mean, at Starbucks, their small is actually called a Tall. And you could probably put the equivalent of six teacups in one Tall. I guess it just goes to show that it's all relative.

"And what makes you say that?" I ask.

He chuckles, "Well, for starters, you've told me that you have been drinking more tea when you are a coffee drinker, and you're eating tofu instead of grilling steak, and I'm betting that your yoga classes are replacing your health club classes," he says as if he just said checkmate. Golden gets up, walks himself in a circle in his bed, and then settles down comfortably again. Levi is still dozing contently. "And I'm betting that Montana is quite different from your other friends."

"God, you're good," I say, picking up my tea to sip, but then realizing my cup is empty.

"May I pour you more?" he asks, already holding up the teapot.

I try to glance at my watch without seeming obvious. But Bodee catches me, and kindly asks, "It's 4:45. Do you have time for another cup, or do you need to be somewhere?"

I realize how my muscles tighten—clench, really—when I think of time. When I think of how it's getting late and I have to get home. But really, there is absolutely nothing I have to be home for. Rachel is out, Gary has a dinner meeting, and that leaves Levi. Usually I'm looking at my watch trying to figure out what time I need to rush home to let the dog out, but Levi is here, resting on the couch. There is no one I need to rush home for. It's strange.

I hold my teacup out. "I'd love some more," I tell him, and he refills my cup, and then refills his own. We both take a sip.

"So, life is changing for you. Tell me," he encourages.

"Okay," I begin. "But how about I offer you the Cliffs Notes version?" I say, breaking off a piece of biscuit and savoring once again its buttery sweetness.

Bodee holds his hands open as an invitation to begin.

"Okay, so you know my name, Syd Arthur, and that I was born here in Highland Ridge. My parents always called me their little princess, and as I grew up I aspired to all of the things I was supposed to aspire to in the world that I know—to get married after finishing college, start a family in a beautiful home, spend time at the country club, play Mah Jongg, go shopping, vacation in the Caribbean, and always and forever diet to get thin and stay thin. And you can probably see from the way I'm eating these biscuits that I break my diet just as often as I start my diet. Shall I go on?" I ask.

"By all means," Bodee says, beaming. "I want to see where all this is going."

"Well, first, it's most likely going to my hips, " I tell him, and he smiles.

"But seriously, whenever I try to explain something I'm always reminded of Ellen DeGeneres' book, *My Point...and I Do Have One*. I, too, have a point. It just takes me awhile to get there."

"Ah, but that is the beauty of afternoon tea. When you stop to create time and space, *voila!* You have time and space," he says, and I feel that even though he is old, there is agelessness about him.

I find that I am enjoying sitting with him, talking with him. My mind wanders off as I sip my tea and look at Golden wrapped in a ball unto himself while his master drinks tea by his side. Realizing that I lost my train of thought, I look back at Bodee.

"You left off where everyone is dieting," he encourages with a sly grin.

"Right!" I say, putting down my teacup. I glance over at Levi, who is still sound asleep.

"So, I dieted. I've tried every diet. Seriously, you could name any diet and I bet you I've been on it. It's amazing I didn't burn up enough calories to make me permanently thin just by jumping from one diet to the next. And along with the whole diet rollercoaster thing, I was taught, like most women I know, how important it is not to let yourself go. So I have standing appointments. You know, nails, facials, hair, the works. It's what we do. What we've been told to do.

"Do you realize what we women spend to keep up with what we're told? We buy, buy, buy, spend, spend, spend, and just when we think we've caught up to where we're supposed to be, how we're supposed to look, there's a new fashion season, another trend, and on and on it goes. So that's how I've spent most of my time. Well, of course I was also busy taking care of Rachel."

Sighing, I tell him, "She's going into her sophomore year of college at the University of Wisconsin in Madison. And after Rachel went to college last year, and that horrible car accident in our town, all of a sudden there was this emptiness, you know?"

Bodee is nodding his head, urging me to continue.

"I mean, I was still busy—I always have a million little things to do. But I felt this emptiness that all of the exercise and dieting and shopping and country club stuff couldn't fill. And without going into it all, I saw a homeless man on Rush Street in the freezing cold of winter and I walked right past him, and something happened to me. And then I ended up in the wrong lecture, an 'Introduction to Buddhism' instead of 'The Combo Diet'—"

I had been looking at Golden while I rattled all this off, and now I gaze back at Bodee, who is looking at me with amusement.

"Hold on," I say to him. "You haven't heard the latest. After starting yoga, and meeting Montana, I began going to the Om Guru Center and practicing meditation."

For the first time, Bodee interrupts. "And this would be when you began eating tofu?"

"Yep, that's when I became a vegetarian. So I've been going to the Om Guru Center, learning about the teachings and practices, but my friends are not happy with me. I've been missing our weekly Mah Jongg games to go to Satsang at the center, my husband thinks I'm acting weird, my daughter tells me 'interesting midlife crisis you're having.' But the thing is, I've spent my whole life striving for the perfect figure, perfect look, perfect house. And I'm starting to think that there's more to strive for, more that's out there."

I've confided in him the way you talk to a perfect stranger sitting next to you on an airplane. Bodee looks at me with a piercing gaze, and then breaks into his comforting smile and chuckles. I look at him, wonder if he's even following what I'm saying, or if somewhere in my monologue I've lost him.

Then he laces his hands together and says, "Sounds like you and Levi are very similar."

"Huh?" I ask. I look over to Levi, who perks his head awake at the sound of his name and then begins to lick his private parts. I look back at Bodee. "No, I have more manners than he does," I tell him with a sneer.

Bodee laughs a hearty laugh, and with an even bigger grin he tells me, "What I mean is that today Levi broke out of the area of freedom he was allotted to explore the wider world. It sounds like that's just what you've been exploring, the world beyond what you've been shown—the world beyond life as a princess in suburbia. It sounds like you're breaking out of your own Invisible Fence."

With a half smile, half smirk I ask him if he's a therapist.

"No, not a therapist," he answers, smiling. "Just someone who sees what's in front of him. And what I see is a woman who is embarking on an important journey, a woman who is breaking free from constraints."

For a minute there is just silence. But not an awkward silence, like you'd think, considering you're sitting in an old man's house who you've only just met, sipping tea and telling him your life story. No, this is a warm silence. A peaceful silence. A calm silence. A silence that, you know me, I had to go and break.

"Okay, and you want to hear about really breaking free and out of the protective fence? I haven't even told Gary yet. But for my birthday in a few weeks, Montana and I are going to go to the Om Guru Ashram in the Catskills for a retreat. I'm going to receive *Shaktipat*, when Gurujai will transmit to me her spiritual energy and awaken my kundalini. How do you think that's going to fly at my house?"

When Bodee doesn't respond I feel embarrassed, like he thinks maybe I'm insane.

"Once you take the collar off, who knows where you might roam and what you might discover," he says.

"Well, I'm going to make sure that Gary puts new batteries in Levi's collar when he gets home tonight," I say.

"Ah, yes, that'll take care of Levi here," he tells me. Levi's ears perk up again and he jumps off the couch and settles himself by Golden, pushing his paw in Golden's bed. Golden gets up and they sniff each other, and then Golden trudges off into the dining room with Levi following right behind.

"Levi will have new batteries in his collar, but what about you, Syd?

"I'm much more of a choker girl, really. Preferably white gold and with diamonds," I say.

"Ah!" he says with a clap of his hands and a wide grin. "Will she be a seeker of the jewel of enlightenment or a seeker of jewels?" he teases me.

"*Touché,*" I say, and then add, only half-kidding, "Can I be both?"

Instead of laughing at my attempted joke, he looks at me steadily and says, "Only you can answer that. Only you can find the right balance in your life. Just like only you can take off your invisible collar so that you can find what it is you're looking for."

Again there is silence, but this time I sit with it and let myself absorb the quietness that feels so full.

After some time I say, "So now you know my life."

"Well, the Cliffs Notes version, anyway," he says with his smile.

"Yes, the Cliffs Notes version. But what about you?" I ask.

We watch as Levi tries to make Golden chase him. For a minute Golden plays along, but then he lies down in the hall, and Levi lies down beside him.

"You have time?" he asks.

I smile and nod.

"How about the Cliffs Notes version?" Bodee asks.

I nod again.

"I grew up in South Bend, Indiana, a fine place to live. Helped my dad harvest the corn, and helped my mama bake cornbread. Worked in the fields, and eventually got into some construction work. But I always loved traveling to upper Michigan, loved to watch the seasons change there, and to sit at the shores of Lake Michigan. Met a girl when I was 19 years old, a girl who loved to pick blueberries in July, rake leaves in the fall, catch snowflakes on her tongue and wait patiently for the first crocus to pop up in spring. Her name was Shirley, and you know what I did? I picked blueberries with her in July, raked the leaves with her in the fall, caught snowflakes on my tongue right along with her, and kissed her when the first crocus sprouted up to bask in the early spring sunlight. And then I married her.

"We both loved Michigan and we particularly loved a little island in the bay between lower and upper Michigan where we spent our honeymoon. Powhatten Island, it's called. And when we found that a wonderful little bed and breakfast called The Powhatten Inn was for sale, we gathered our pennies, bought it, and ran it for fifty years.

"Wow. Fifty years? That's something!" I say.

"Sure was," Bodee says wistfully. "Eventually we renamed it The Firefly Inn, in celebration of them."

"Huh. I would never think of celebrating a firefly. I'm not a bug person." I pause then, and worry I've insulted him, so I add, "Not that I don't think that The Firefly Inn is a great name for a bed and breakfast."

Bodee smiles at me and tells me that the first year they ran the bed and breakfast they kept the original name.

"During that first summer Shirley and I would spend our evenings on the veranda rocking chairs watching the children run around the grounds when darkness fell, seeing how mesmerized they were by the fireflies that would light up with their spark. And time after time we would watch them find little jars to catch the fireflies. And I would go down the steps of the porch, gather the children around, and I'd ask them, 'Why are you catching the fireflies in those jars?'

"And they'd invariably answer, 'We're catching them because they light up, and they're neat when they light up.'

"I would tell them, 'They light up, they show their spark, and they fly free. But you catch them. And when you catch them they cannot let their spark light up the dark, they cannot fly free.' And then I would tell them that each one of them has an inner light, a spark that makes them special, and that if someone were to catch that, and not allow it to shine free, it would be lost to them and to the world. Because we need sparks. We need to shine our inner light. We all yearn to be free.

"And by goodness, they understood. I would have them stand with me facing the lapping shores of Lake Michigan from the sloping hill of the Inn, and I would count to three and then they'd release the fireflies and set them free. And Shirley, she would call them over to the veranda, and she'd offer them lemonade and oatmeal cookies and we'd all watch the fireflies light up the night."

"That's a beautiful story," I tell him. I watch him sip his tea, his eyes looking somewhere inward. Maybe he's back on that veranda, drinking lemonade with Shirley.

"Well, you know, Syd, it's a beautiful world out there."

And I nod my head but stay silent. We finish our tea like that, without saying anything but finding comfort in each other's presence, just like Levi and Golden, who are now both stretched out in the hallway.

"I should go home and make dinner, though after these biscuits, I better not eat anything too fattening," I say, feeling all of a sudden embarrassed that I would break the silence with a complaint about my caloric intake.

Bodee just smiles and says, "Have you ever heard the wise words of Lin-Chi?"

I shake my head no. I have no idea who he's talking about. To me, Lin-Chi sounds like it could be a yummy Thai or maybe Chinese dessert.

"Lin-Chi said, 'When hungry eat your rice, when tired close your eyes. Fools may laugh at me, but wise men will know what I mean.'"

I start thinking that maybe I'll order in Chinese tonight. Maybe some tofu fried rice.

Bodee continues to look at me, and I think he's maybe wondering if I understand Lin-Chi, if I am wise or a fool. I want to be seen as wise, so I say nothing, simply smile in solidarity with Lin-Chi's words while I think to myself that an order of vegetarian egg rolls sounds really good, too.

I take a last sip of my tea, and the warm sweetness of the amber liquid matches the feel of this unexpected afternoon.

"Thank you," I say. "Thank you for finding Levi and for sharing your afternoon tea with me." I feel a kind of gratitude that I'm not sure I understand.

Bodee looks at me, looks right into my eyes. "You're welcome," he says, with his eyes dancing.

I stand up and ask if I can help him clear the tea.

"Thank you, I'd appreciate that," he says.

I pick the teapot and plate of biscuits off the table and he carries the tray into the kitchen, while I follow behind. I watch him rinse the teapot and wash the teacups. I pick up the dishcloth and dry the teacups, handing them to Bodee, who returns them to the cabinet. We don't talk, just busy ourselves with the task, and it feels satisfying.

A loud truck rumbles down the street, and Levi and Golden begin barking in unison. Levi's barking always drives me crazy, and I walk towards him in the living room, telling him, "Hush, Levi, shhh."

Bodee follows me into the living room, laughing.

"What?" I ask. "What's so funny?"

"You are, Syd. How can you tell Levi to stop barking? He's a dog. It's his nature to bark."

"But it's so loud," I tell him as I try to still Levi.

"Then it's Levi's nature to bark loudly!" he concludes smilingly.

"You know, I have a friend whose dog barked so much that she couldn't stand it anymore. She and her husband bought one of those collars that make your dog stop barking," I tell him.

Bodee is petting Golden, who is now quiet, and leaning against Bodee's leg. "How does a collar make a dog stop barking?" he asks as he scratches Golden under the chin.

Levi is quiet now, and is lying down at the front door.

"Every time the dog barks, he gets a little shock from the collar. Pretty soon he learns to stay quiet to avoid a shock," I explain.

I see Bodee wince.

"Well, it worked. They were happy to have some peace and quiet," I add.

"Like a trapped firefly," Bodee says sadly.

I think about how happy my friend was when their dog finally stopped barking, but looking at Golden and Levi, I see Bodee has a point.

"Yeah, when you put it that way, it is sort of cruel," I offer.

"Syd, if there's one thing I've learned in this life, it's that you have to honor the essence, you have to honor that core spirit that resides in each living being. To ignore it, to disrespect it, to misuse it, to suppress it, is to go against nature herself, to show contempt for creation itself," he tells me with a quiet conviction that could turn red states to blue.

"You sold me," I tell him. "When Levi barks, I'll learn to applaud his doggy nature," I say teasingly.

Bodee walks toward the front door with a smile, giving Levi a pat. Then he turns back to me with his piercing blue eyes and says, "And as you continue your spiritual search, remember to applaud your inner nature."

My breath catches in my chest.

"No one has ever said something like that to me. I wish I had a tape recorder. Then I could play what you just said to my Mah Jongg group and maybe they'd stop giving me such a hard time," I whine to him.

"Ah, but Syd, you can simply remove the collar."

There is a moment of quietness that blankets the room, and then I smile and tell him that I really must be going. I remove the Invisible Fence collar, putting it in my purse and then pulling out the collar and leash I brought to bring Levi home.

"Before you go, let me give you some tomatoes from my garden out back," Bodee says, opening the front door where Levi and I follow him out.

"Oh, wait! Bodee! Golden's gotten out!" I yell as Golden squeezes past Levi and me.

"That's okay, he's fine," Bodee calls back as he heads toward the backyard.

I watch as Golden trudges toward Bodee while I follow with Levi pulling along the leash. I follow Bodee toward the garden, where he stands in front of the tomatoes, which are full and ripe and sun-kissed.

"You don't worry about Golden running away?" I ask. "I could never do that with Levi. Well, I guess you already know that," I add.

Bodee turns his head to look at me and says, "Ah! When Golden was younger, he liked to take off and run in every which direction, but he always found his way home. And now, Golden is content to stay by his old master, content to keep me company in the yard while I tend to my garden. Content to watch the cycles of growth."

He points out the produce he is growing—broccoli, carrots, radishes— and shows me where the pumpkins are planted. He invites me to pick some tomatoes, telling me that they are exceptionally fine this year, and I do. He offers me a small burlap sack to put them in.

"You know," I tell him, "I can never get my head around the idea that tomatoes are really a fruit. For my whole life I thought tomatoes were a vegetable. Then, a couple of years ago I was watching *Jeopardy!* and it turns out that because of the way the seeds are or something, a tomato is really a fruit. It just doesn't seem right, always throws me off.

"I love tomatoes, don't get me wrong," I say, not wanting to seem ungrateful. "I just can't imagine that it's really a fruit." I watch as Levi sniffs around the garden. Golden has found a warm, sunny spot near the broccoli and is lounging deep in the grass.

"That's the problem with labels," Bodee tells me as he picks a tomato and rubs it clean against his denim shirt. "Once you begin labeling, once you begin putting things in boxes, you risk losing the essence, the core nature of the thing."

When I don't respond he holds out the tomato to me and says, "Here, take a bite."

I want to tell him that I'm a fork-and-knife girl, that I don't like to eat in a way that has the potential to make a mess and squirt on the really pretty white imported Indian cotton hand-embroidered blouse that I'm wearing. But he's holding the tomato out to me, and I feel I can't refuse. So I take the tomato and carefully bite into its warm flesh, feel the squirt of the tomato open and the sweet liquid wash through my mouth, the little seeds mixing together giving it texture, and I luxuriate in its freshness, in the explosion of taste in my mouth. And then I look at Bodee, who is watching me intently.

"See? No fruit, no vegetable, only tomato!" he says, laughing.

And seeing that I have not spilled at all on my shirt, I do the only thing that makes sense, and I finish the tomato.

Walking back to the front yard, Levi happily at my side, I thank Bodee again not only for finding Levi, but for a lovely afternoon.

"It has been a lovely afternoon for me as well. Please come anytime and join me again for tea. Any afternoon. Golden and I will be here," he tells me, and I shake his hand, noticing once again its strength and firmness.

I give Golden a quick pat on his head and then I walk Levi to my car, open the back door to let him in, and get in myself. I start the car and open the windows. As I pull away from the curb I turn my head back to wave, and I see that Levi has his head out the window, barking his goodbyes to Bodee and Golden. I give another wave, and drive away.

As I drive back down Middle Way Drive, before turning onto Pleasant Road, I check the rearview mirror but I don't see Bodee or Golden. Levi has pulled his head back in the car and is resting on the back seat. I close the windows a little, and drive home.

A while later I feed Levi and then try to figure out what I should do for dinner. Chinese food isn't sounding as good as it did earlier. The peanut butter sandwich I had for lunch, I realize, along with the biscuits, has filled me up, and I notice than I'm not that hungry. In fact, I'm only thinking about dinner because it's dinnertime. But Gary and Rachel aren't here, and I'm not on anyone's schedule. I don't really need to make dinner. Still, I want a little something, but what sounds good? I look at the sack of tomatoes, and I realize that that's what I want for dinner. Sliced tomatoes with some goat cheese in my favorite Shitake Sesame dressing.

I slice the tomatoes, thinking about Bodee's garden, and I sprinkle them with goat cheese, pouring my dressing on.

I sit down and am about to turn on the TV for company, but for some reason I don't. I eat my tomatoes and goat cheese in silence, and I savor every bite.

And as I'm chewing, I hear Bodee quoting Lin-Chi, who is obviously not a Thai dessert but probably a great Chinese philosopher, and in my head I hear: *When hungry eat your rice, when tired close your eyes. Fools may laugh at me, but wise men will know what I mean.*

I rinse off my plate and put it in the dishwasher, feeling content, feeling very content. Then I notice the answering machine is flashing its messages.

I don't press the play button.

Instead, I breathe in the quietness of the house, and I go upstairs to meditate.

Chapter Twenty-Three

"Get out of here!" Donna says as she sets up her Mah Jongg tiles along her rack. Her long nails are painted a coral pink, and they are making *tap, tap, tap*ping sounds against the tiles and along her rack, followed by her new Tiffany bracelet, so that together it sounds like *tap-tap-tap clink! Tap-tap-tap-clink!*

"Donna, c'mon, wake up and smell the coffee! You think Celia lost all that weight from dieting? *Plleease!* She had lipo early in the summer, when she went back to Colombia to visit her parents," Barbara Cohen is explaining as she flips her perfectly highlighted hair to one side.

"Really? She wasn't even fat," Donna says as she reaches for a handful of cashews.

"Jodi, can I have a Diet Coke?" Barbara asks, and Jodi jumps up to get one. "Well, she was gaining weight. I mean, she told me that before she had kids she was wearing a size two, and when her third child was born she was wearing a size six, so you know, you've got to stay on top of things like that, take care of things while they're still manageable, before things are really out of control. I say good for her. But she really didn't want people to know that she had lipo. Told everyone she dieted all summer and with the heat in Colombia, the pounds just melted away. But she admitted it to me, and of course I promised I wouldn't tell anyone, that her secret was safe with me, so don't tell anyone what I told you guys, okay?"

"Of course, don't give it a second thought. We won't say a word, will we, girls?" Donna asks.

We all nod our heads in agreement, and I'm already thinking to myself that this Barbara is a piece of work. We do the passing in record time, and begin playing our third game of the evening.

"Here you are," Jodi says as she places a glass of Diet Coke beside Barbara. "Can I get anyone anything else?" she asks, and we tell her that we're fine.

But then Barbara asks if she can have a slice of lemon for her Diet Coke, and Jodi goes back into the kitchen, saying, "See how great this is when we have five players instead of four? Whoever's not playing that round can serve everyone."

I don't think that our foursome needed much serving. Barbara, it seems, needs a lot.

Jodi returns with a few slices of lemon on a plate.

"Thanks. Four crak," Barbara says, dropping the lemon in her pop and taking a sip.

"Five bam," I say, throwing out my tile.

"West," Margot says, reaching for a handful of cashews.

"Flower," Donna chimes in.

"Jodi, the pop is a little warm, Could you be a love and put some more ice in? Eight dot," Barbara says as she hands Jodi the glass and throws her tile in the mix.

I give Jodi a look, and she shakes her head for me to be careful. Then, when no one is looking, she sort of rolls her eyes and shrugs her shoulders.

"I think Celia looks great now. She's back to a size 2, so I know how happy she is."

Jodi returns the Diet Coke to Barbara, filled with ice.

"There are a lot of people doing preventative plastic surgery. I read about it all the time in the magazines. Why wait for a problem? Nip it in the bud, " Barbara explains, twirling her pop.

"Nine bam," I say.

"Green Dragon," Margot calls out.

"I'll take that," Barbara says, and we pass our tiles around so Barbara can expose the three green dragons on her rack.

"You know, I'm thinking of having a face lift for my 35th birthday," Barbara says.

"Are you crazy? Your face is lovely. Why would you even consider that?" Jodi asks, flabbergasted.

"I told you, it's preventative," Barbara says. "One crak."

"Six dot," I say, picking up a carrot, dipping it in the hummus and crunching a satisfying crunch. "They have anti-aging and anti-wrinkle moisturizer. I have a coupon for a new rejuvenating cream at Saks—why don't you try that first before you let someone cut into your face?" I ask, and this time Donna and Margot join Jodi in giving me a look.

Maybe I'm being hard on Barbara because I feel she is replacing me in my Mah Jongg group. Or maybe she is just so opposite of the things I'm learning in yoga, from Montana, and at the Om Guru Center that she's getting under my skin. Or, as I'm sure Barbara has noticed, my somewhat-aging skin.

Or maybe she reminds me of that part of myself—of my own drive to stay pretty, stay young, stay thin, as if that were all that mattered. I'm learning now that more matters.

"North," Margot says, as Jodi looks over her tiles and smiles.

"I see what you're playing," Jodi says. She walks over to Donna, who is busy rearranging her tiles, which she sets in two different patterns.

"What do you think?" Donna asks Jodi, wanting her to help her decide which hand to go for.

"Hey, no fair!" I yell. "You can't be helping Donna with her hand when you already know what Margot has in her rack," I declare. "Sit down," I demand, pulling up a chair. "Eat a carrot," I say, dipping it into the hummus and handing it to her.

Jodi takes a plate and sits down at the table. Donna is still debating what to discard and then cautiously throws out a red dragon, looking over at Barbara to see if she is going to claim it. Barbara doesn't and throws out a seven bam.

As I move my tiles around, pondering what to throw out, my bracelet knocks my rack, making a clanking sound. Barbara looks over at me.

"What an interesting bracelet," Barbara says in what I decide is a condescending voice. "Whatever is that?" she asks, as she plays with the clasp of the big heart-shaped diamond bracelet adorning her wrist.

"Seven dot," I say, throwing out a tile and shuffling the tiles on the table closer together. "It's a mala bracelet. It's used for mantra recitation, " I explain.

Barbara looks to the others and then says, "Oh, right! That's all part of why you haven't been able to play Mah Jongg on Thursdays. You've been going to some New Age temple or something."

Margot is still shuffling her tiles, debating what to throw out.

"It's not a New Age temple. It's actually quite ancient, part of a lineage of gurus that teach from the Hindu tradition," I say, feeling my heart pounding.

"Two dot," Margot says, throwing in her tile.

""Same," Donna says, throwing out another two dot. "Margot, can you pass the hummus?"

Jodi looks over to me, and she can tell that I am not happy with Barbara. "Syd's been going to yoga and meditating. You know, I keep hearing about how both things are supposed to be really good for you. Lowers blood pressure, helps you stay calm, in that happy place," Jodi says, and then adds, "And it can help you lose weight."

"Well, it's got that going for it. But Syd, isn't it, I don't know, sketchy over there? The people must be kind of weird," Barbara says. "Nine crak."

"Flower," I say, admiring my mala bracelet as I throw my tile in the center of the table. Then I look at Barbara. "Actually, the people at the Om Guru Center are wonderful."

"Soap," Margot says. "Can you pass the hummus this way?"

Jodi slides it over, along with the dish of carrots.

"Well, you wouldn't catch me in a place like that. Barbara looks at us and laughs, saying, "and it's a good thing, too, because I'm free on Thursday nights to fill in for Syd here while she's out meditating with the Moonies."

"They're not Moonies," I tell her.

"Okay, the Hare Krishnas," she amends.

"They're not Hare Krishnas," I say evenly.

"Okay, the people who are lost and searching," she says, taking a sip of her Diet Coke.

"One crak," Donna says with exuberance—her way of trying to lighten the tension.

"Mah Jongg!" Margot says.

Even though it is Margot who has won, while I only needed one more tile, I am happy that she has called Mah Jongg, am hopeful that the end of the game will take away the momentum of the conversation that is threatening the table, the Mah Jongg table where conversation is supposed to flow easily. We pay Margot what we owe for the game, and it's Margot's turn to sit out. We all busy ourselves mixing the tiles and then setting them up again on our racks.

"Can I get anyone anything while I'm sitting out?" Margot asks.

We all shake our heads no, but Barbara hands Margot her glass and asks if she can get her a little more Diet Coke. The game goes smoothly enough until Jodi brings up my birthday.

"So I know we're all going out for dinner on the 19th, the Friday before your birthday," she says.

There is an awkward silence because, of course, I am not friends with Barbara, and she was not part of the dinner group. Barbara tells us that she and her husband, Philip, are going to Lake Geneva that weekend, as if this were the reason she wouldn't be joining us.

"But we haven't planned the rest of your birthday weekend yet, and it's getting late, so let's come up with some fun ideas," Jodi says enthusiastically.

Clearly, Gary has yet to tell Dave about the change of plans, and so Jodi doesn't know that there will be no dinner. I think back to when Gary got home last night, how he dutifully changed the battery in Levi's collar and apologized for forgetting to do it the other day. He felt badly that I had had to deal with Levi running away. I tried to explain to him that it had actually turned out really well, that I met this really nice older man and spent the afternoon with him.

"Syd, if you're mad at me about the collar, just yell at me. Don't try to make me jealous by telling me you spent the afternoon at an older man's house," he had said to me.

"Not older as in Richard Gere older. Older as in he was probably uttering his first sentences just as the Great Depression descended," I had told him.

And then he had asked me why I spent the afternoon there. "Weren't you going to go shopping with Jodi?" he had asked.

I explained to him that it didn't work out, and that anyway, I stayed with Bodee to have afternoon tea.

"What is a Bodee?" he had asked.

I tried to explain, to describe Bodee and Golden and the small, old house with the sparse furnishings, the simplicity of drinking tea. He had just shaken his head and turned on the TV. I had picked up the remote control, turned off the TV, and set it back down on the coffee table. Then I told him that I had also had a conversation with Montana about my birthday.

"Great, what are you going to do, a sunrise Happy Birthday chant calling for the Guru's grace?" he asked me sarcastically as he picked up the remote control.

I had told him to stop joking around, that I wanted to talk with him about something important. And then I explained that I needed him to cancel our dinner reservation, and that I was going away for my birthday weekend with Montana to a retreat at the Om Guru Ashram in the Catskills.

Gary had looked at me like I was insane and then, in fact, had told me that I was insane. I had held my ground, told him my plans, and asked him to tell Dave so he and Jodi could call the others who were going to join us about the change in plans.

Gary took a deep breath and said, "You know, Syd, I'm an understanding husband. I didn't say a word when you took up yoga at that Prana Center, kept my mouth shut when you started hanging out with those loonies from the Om Guru Center who are so busy searching for whatever it is they're looking for that they forgot to get a job and earn a living. What do they do all day, sit like a pretzel and chant and expect the heavens to open up and reward them? C'mon, Syd, this is bullshit. Enough already."

I was getting pissed, and was ready to really give it to him. But then I thought of Bodee, and his validating words about applauding my inner nature. I was going to tell him about that, and try to explain how much I wanted to meet Gurujai and receive Shaktipat.

But when I opened my mouth, these were the words that came out instead:

"Enough already? Enough already? I'll tell you enough already! For the past 21 years I have stayed home while you have been out in the world. I've cooked, cleaned—"

That's when Gary interrupted with a big "EXCUSE ME?"

And I had to revise with, "Okay, I ordered in a lot, and Marina cleaned, but I supervised it all, and I stayed home with Rachel and I volunteered at her school and at the country club, and did everything a Jewish Stepford Wife is supposed to do, and you know what? I'm taking my collar off!" I had yelled.

"Uh, Syd, what collar is that?" he had asked, looking at my tank top and bare neck.

"The metaphorical one," I had answered.

"Syd, this isn't going anywhere, and I really want to watch the Cubs. Are we done now? Can we just forget all this and go to dinner like we planned?" he had asked.

"How many business trips do you think you've gone on since we've been married?" I asked.

"Jesus, Syd, I don't know," he answered, getting up from the couch and walking over to the bar.

"Hundreds and hundreds, right? Across the country, across the Atlantic? You've traveled so much for your work, and I've never said a word," I challenged.

He opened a Corona and took a sip. "That was work, Syd. I have to travel for work," he said, leaning against the bar and taking another swig from the bottle.

"Fine, but let me ask you this. Do you like working at Global Investments?"

Gary had put his beer down on the bar and looked exasperated. "You know I do, Syd, and look around you. This is the fruit of my working at Global Investments."

I had gotten up and was pacing across the family room. "But Gary, don't you get it? Everything in our life is set up for you to live out your nature, to do what you love. I want that chance, too," I tried to tell him.

"Syd, you have everything you could possibly want! What is it with you? Ever since you met this Montana woman—and now, I don't know, sometimes you act so crazy, talking about your kundalini and what Gurujai says. It's silly. Why would you want to surround yourself with all those lost souls?"

And then I had told Gary that I found it funny, really funny, that all the years I spent trying to get thinner, all the groups I joined, the programs I followed, the crazy rules I adopted to lose weight, to that, he never objected. But when I try things not to lose weight but instead to find myself, he balks.

Then I told him that I'm going to the ashram regardless of what he says. He took his beer over to the couch and turned on the Cubs, and I just stood there, waiting for him to say something.

Which he didn't. So I had gone upstairs, taken a relaxing Jacuzzi, and got ready for bed. During the 7th inning stretch Gary had come upstairs and told me that he didn't want to fight. And he told me that he bought me a fabulous birthday gift that he knew I would love.

I told him that the best gift he could give me would be if he would support me.

To which he said, "That's what I've been doing at Global Investments."

To which I said, "Not financially, but spiritually."

To which he said, "Dear God, first men are told we need to be financially supportive, then we're told to be more emotionally supportive, and now you want spiritual support? I don't even know what that looks like."

To which I said, "It looks like calling Dave and canceling dinner reservations and telling me to have a good retreat."

He had kissed me goodnight, and went downstairs to finish watching the game.

When I got up the next morning he had already left for work, but instead of leaving me a fresh pot of coffee he had left me a mug with a Lipton tea bag we had leftover from when Rachel had had strep throat in the spring of her senior year. Next to it he had made an XO on the napkin, so I figured that his sweet peace offering meant that he would call Dave and they would cancel our reservation.

But now it seems Gary hadn't done that yet, and I have to begin all over again at Mah Jongg. I bring my attention back to the game.

"Nine bam," Donna says, throwing out her tile. "I think we should do a spa day. There's supposed to be this fabulous new spa that just opened on Michigan Avenue. What do you say, Syd?"

"Six dot," Barbara says. "La Belle Femme. It's magnificent, but you'll never get in at this late date. You have to book way in advance."

I pick up my future tile, look at it and put it on my rack. I decide I have the most tiles for a hand with the winds, and so I start to throw away my tiles from the other hand I was contemplating, the 2, 4, 6, 8 under the evens.

"Four dot," I say. "I'm going to need to take a rain check for my birthday this year, guys."

"What are you talking about, Syd? What do you mean, a rain check? Jodi asks as she dips another carrot in the hummus.

Barbara is looking intently at her tiles, deciding what to do.

Taking advantage of the break in momentum, Jodi asks me again what

I am talking about. I watch Barbara drumming her fingers on the red Mah Jongg rack. Her emerald cut diamond is huge. Really huge. And I'm mad at myself because I really want it.

"Change of plans. I'm going out of town for my birthday weekend," I begin.

"What?!" Jodi exclaims. "What do you mean you're going out of town for your birthday? We always celebrate together."

Barbara breathes a sigh of relief as she moves her tiles around in her rack. It is clear that she has just realized a good hand to play, because she ignores the conversation that is going on and says, "C'mon, Jodi, throw a tile."

Jodi sighs, shakes her head, and says "Red dragon."

"Soap," Donna says.

"Four crak," Barbara says quickly, shuffling her tiles in her rack.

"Eight crak," I say, keeping up the rhythm.

"So where is Gary taking you? Flower," Jodi says, throwing out her tile.

"I'm not going away with Gary," I explain.

"North," Donna says.

"Soap," Barbara says.

"Eight dot," I say, putting the tile in the middle of the table. "I'm going on a retreat," I add.

"Oh! Dear! God! Don't tell me. You're going to spend your birthday meditating, is that it?" Jodi asks in a mocking tone.

Margot has been sitting silently watching the game, and now, upon seeing Jodi's look of exasperation, she heads into the kitchen and brings out the plate of M&M cookies. "Here, have one," she says to Jodi, passing the plate around.

Jodi takes one, and after taking a bite she says to me, "Do you remember what we used to call these cookies when we were kids? Party cookies. Operative word being 'party.' As in, when it's someone's birthday, you party, you celebrate; you don't sit in the dark reciting some voodooish words in search of some meditative trance."

"You sound like Gary," I tell her.

"And a wise man he is," she tells me.

"These are so good!" Donna says. "I love when they're soft and chewy."

Margot breaks off half a piece and closes her eyes. "These are really good, Jodi. But now that I've had sweet, I can't go back to salt. Is everyone ready to move from salt to sweet? Should I put the cashews and hummus away?"

We all nod our heads.

"Margot, on the counter by the fridge there's a bowl of nonpareils. You can bring those out too," Jodi calls.

Margot brings the bowl of chocolates and places them on the corner of the table, in between Barbara and me. Barbara promptly takes the bowl and moves them across the table. "I don't know about you girls, but I'm staying on my diet. Don't try to tempt me. Margot, will you be a dear and get me another glass of Diet Coke?"

Margot returns to the kitchen for the pop.

"Okay, Syd, you're not really going to spend your birthday at that place, are you?" Jodi asks.

"Yes, I am. It's important to me. And we can find another date to all go out," I tell her, hoping she'll just let it go.

"Where is this place?" she asks me.

"In the Catskills," I tell her.

"Okay, this is too much. The Catskills? Where our grandparents used to go for vacations, those Catskills?" she asks. "God, I think my great aunt had her honeymoon there. How can that be a place for an ashram? My Great Aunt Sophie would be turning over in her grave if she heard that," Jodi declares.

"Whose turn is it? I'm finding it hard to concentrate with all this chatter," Barbara informs us.

"It's your turn, Jodi," I tell her.

She looks at me and slowly shakes her head. "One dot," she says, throwing out her tile and picking up another nonpareil. "So you're going to go all by yourself to the Catskills for a retreat, and that sounds fun to you?" she asks me.

"South," Donna says.

"Mah Jongg," I say, picking up the south to complete my hand.

"Ugh! This always happens to me. I just needed one more tile," Barbara laments.

"What did you need?" Jodi asks.

"A five bam," Barbara answers, and Jodi exposes her tiles, saying that she was holding them for her hand.

We all throw our tiles in, and everyone pays me what they owe. Then Jodi says that before we start another game, she wants to finish this conversation. So I explain that I'm not going alone, that I'm going with Montana and that it's Gurujai's birthday, too, that there will be a big celebration. I see the hurt in Jodi's eyes.

"Syd, they'll be celebrating the guru. I don't think anyone will be bringing presents for you, or having you blow the candles out from a cake. We would do that for you. We're your friends," she says.

"Montana? You have a friend named Montana? Who would name their kid Montana?" Barbara asks.

"Apparently Montana's parents," Margot says. "Jodi, do you want me to serve the coffee?"

"No, I'll do it," Jodi says as pulls herself up from the table. She walks into the kitchen and gets five mugs. I get up and help her carry them. Then she comes back with the carafe of coffee and sets it down on the table along with the milk and Sweet'N Low. "And it's hazelnut, your favorite, Syd. Because I'm your best friend, even though you're blowing me off," she says. I can't tell if she's kidding or not.

"I once knew a girl named Savannah, but that's south," Barbara says.

"Well, I really don't think Syd is picking her friends based on their location," Margot offers.

"Well, this whole birthday celebration is going south, that's what I think," Donna says, sitting back down and taking a sip of her coffee.

I reach across for a nonpareil and pop it in my mouth, trying to bite off the white tiny balls with my teeth.

"You know what, guys? I don't want to have this conversation. I want you to tell me that you support me, that you're happy for me. We can all go out anytime; it doesn't have to be for my birthday. And Montana is leaving for India in September. She may be gone for a year. This is our one chance to go on retreat together," I say.

Jodi opens a Sweet'N Low and pours it into her coffee.

"Oh, goodness! India? She's crazy. That's like the filthiest country. It's more than third world. More like fourth world. Why on Earth would anyone choose to go there?" Barbara asks, dropping another slice of lemon in her Diet Coke.

Jodi sees me cringe and says, "Syd, I support you. You're only going to the Catskills for the weekend. It's not like you're taking off to go to India." Then she looks at me ands asks, "You're not planning on taking off and going to India, are you?"

I sip my coffee and shake my head no.

"Okay, then, I'm going to do with you what I do with Melanie. Allow the smaller things so she won't rebel against me with the bigger things. Pick my battles. If you want to spend your birthday on a retreat, then that's what you should do."

"Thank you," I say, adding some more Sweet'N Low. It occurs to me that though I love coffee, I have to add a lot of sweetener to compensate for its naturally bitter taste.

Then Jodi adds, "But when you get back, I'm making reservations at that great new French restaurant, Mistral. Oh. But you're still a vegetarian, aren't you? Well, they'll whip up something; the French can do wonders with leeks."

Chapter Twenty-Four

I can't believe that Rachel is now a college sophomore. It makes me feel old, because I can no longer say that Rachel is just starting kindergarten, has just entered high school, has just sent in her first college application. Well, that and the fact that in two days I will be 44 years old, which really is practically 45, and then the next big birthday is the big 50, and then, well, then you start getting things from AARP in the mail and then—God, I don't even want to think about then.

So today, like they teach at the Om Guru Center, I just need to be in the here and now. Not chase after the past (though I wouldn't mind being back in my 20s), not worry about the future (when do age spots really appear?), but just be in the stillness of what is; I'm still 43. I'm still 43. I'm still 43. Well, at least for another 48 hours.

The phone rings and I go into the family room to answer it.

"Hi Syd, it's Montana," she says.

"Hey, how are you doing? Listen, I'm all packed and ready for tomorrow. Okay, I'll admit I might have overpacked a little, but I bought some great new long Indian cotton skirts from Earthy Chic and I couldn't decide which ones to take, so I just packed them all!" I tell her. "Oh! And I packed a shawl like you told me, you know, in case I get cold sitting for the long meditations."

"Syd," she begins. But I interrupt her.

"Listen, I didn't have a shawl that would work at the ashram, but I found this cream- and-maroon checkered one at Saks. Who knew, right? And they had others, so just let me know if you want me to stop and pick one up for you. They're cashmere, and on sale," I tell her.

"Great, Syd. You sound all ready to go," she says.

I see a fingerprint smudge on the coffee table and walk over to kitchen to get some Windex and a cloth to wipe it clean.

"Yep, I am," I say as I spray the Windex. "Jodi and Gary still think I'm crazy to go at all, let alone on my birthday weekend, but Montana, I'm telling you, I know this is right. I know this is exactly what I need to be doing for my birthday this year," I say, wiping the smudge away.

I walk over to the bar and give it a Windex spray even though it doesn't need it. I'm rubbing the granite with a cloth when Montana tells me she is so glad that I feel this way.

"You are right. This is absolutely what you need to be doing," she tells me. "And I'm glad you feel it so strongly, because Syd, you're going to be fine going alone."

"What?" I ask as I stop wiping. I must have breathed in too much Windex and lost focus for a minute. "I'm sorry, Montana, what did you just say?"

"Okay, listen, Syd. I want you to sit down and take a deep breath, okay? A deep cleansing breath."

Silence.

"Syd? Are you there? Are you doing your Pranayama breathing?"

Okay, I'm not. I'm not feeling good about the direction of this conversation, and I am anything but calm right now. But I don't want Montana to know that I'm still more neurotic like than yogic like, and so I just wait a minute and lie that yes, I am doing my breathing.

"Syd, listen to me," she says. "I can't go with you on the retreat, but you will be fine on your own. You can still fly to New York tomorrow, get the car rental, and drive yourself to the Catskills."

I'm mad. After all I went through with Gary, with Jodi, with everyone at Mah Jongg, with my parents. You should have heard my mother telling my father what I was doing. They kept calling me *meshuggha*. Everyone is giving me a hard time about going, but I've put my foot down and made the decision to go anyway. I knew I had Montana beside me, and now she's blowing me off. For what? What possible reason could she have for not going with me to the ashram? It's my birthday, for God's sake. It's Gurujai's birthday, for God's sake, or Shiva's sake, or Vishnu's sake, or whatever. It's one thing to blow me off, but Gurujai?

"Montana, I can't believe you're doing this. We had this all planned. What possibly could have come up that now you can't go?" I challenge her.

"I'm in the hospital on an IV," she says.

I had not planned on this answer. "Oh my God, Montana, what happened? Are you okay?"

"I will be. I had to be admitted in the middle of the night, and the doctor said I have to stay here for at least another 24 hours. I told her that I had to be at a retreat on Friday, but she was adamant that even if I were able to leave the hospital, she didn't want me to travel this weekend.

"But what happened?" I ask her.

"Well, I just have this stomach thing going on, and I couldn't stop vomiting. I even fainted, I was so out of it. I barely remember calling 911, but I must have, because the paramedics came and took me to the hospital. They're still running some tests, and trying to rehydrate me. I keep telling them I know what's wrong, but they won't listen to me."

"Montana, what do they think is wrong?"

"Oh, who knows? They're talking about salmonella poisoning, but I'm telling you that's not it. This happens sometimes," she tells me.

I sit down on the bar stool, trying to absorb all of this as willingly as the Windex cloth.

"This has happened before?" I ask her. "You've gotten sick like this before?"

"No, no. Not to me, but to other devotees. Before a retreat or some other auspicious occasion. It's a purification of the Shakti energy. It's my body getting rid of all the negative karma. It's my body's attempt to help the more subtle bodies, a cleansing of the spiritual body to be more ready to receive Shaktipat and to allow the kundalini energy to flow through my body more freely. Really Syd, my vomiting is really a blessing. Wait just a second, Syd."

I hear her talking to a nurse who is telling Montana that they are going to add more fluids to her IV bag.

"Okay, Syd, I'm back," she tells me.

"So wait," I begin. "Did you tell the doctor this?"

"Oh yeah, I told her. But she didn't seem receptive to what I was trying to explain. Guess it's just not her karma right now to be open to a spiritual understanding of the way in which the body can respond to the world of the sacred. But this is fairly common," she tells me, seeming not at all worried or concerned.

"This is common? Other devotees have gotten sick like this before a retreat?" I ask her, and she tells me yes.

I'm ashamed of myself that I think that this could be a quick way to lose a few pounds. Sign up for a retreat, let the negative karma out over a toilet, and *voila,* you're spiritually cleansed and physically more svelte. A sort of spiritual bulimia, if you will.

Not for the first time, I'm relieved that people can't read minds.

"So the doctor doesn't believe that that's why you got so sick? She thinks you have maybe salmonella? Why is that?" I ask her, wondering if it's too early to pour myself a nice cold glass of Chardonnay.

"Oh, because of the ovo-lacto vegetarian drink I made myself yesterday morning. You know how they ask you everything you've eaten or drank in the last couple of days? Well, when I mentioned this delicious health drink I made yesterday morning for breakfast, they sort of jumped on this, and so now they're doing tests. But I keep explaining to them it's just my body's way of preparing me for the retreat through the purification of the Shakti," she tells me adamantly.

"So what was in this ovo-lacto vegetarian drink?" I ask her as I open the bar fridge and pull out an open bottle of Toasted Head. I think of Jimmy Buffet's song "It's Five O'clock Somewhere." I pour myself a glass of the Chardonnay and take a sip.

"Oh, the usual—a couple of raw eggs, soy milk, organic strawberries and bananas. And I sprinkled in some wheat germ, too," she tells me.

I almost spit out my wine. "Raw eggs?" I yell into the phone. "Raw eggs? Montana, you can't eat raw eggs, that's how you get salmonella poisoning!" I shriek into the receiver.

"Now you sound like the doctor. No, no, no. I do this at least twice a month, and I never get sick. It's the timing of it that lets me know what it is. I had sat for a long meditation yesterday in preparation for the retreat, too. This is all about purifying my body for the energy I would be receiving at the ashram," she insists.

If this is true, I can only imagine that my body is a failure. Late this morning I had two slices of cold cheese pizza and now I am drinking wine, and I've got to tell you, I feel fine. My body's not rejecting a thing, not cleaning out a morsel. I mean honestly, I've even been a little constipated. There's no getting rid of the old to make room for the new.

I take a deep breath, which I know Montana would be proud of. "Don't you think that maybe all these times you've had that ovo-lacto-whatever drink, you've just been lucky that you haven't gotten sick? I mean, you have to admit, eating raw eggs is kind of like playing Russian roulette—your version is just more like Russian omelet."

Montana only laughs, telling me that when I see for myself the incredible spiritual power that infuses the ashram, I'll understand more fully. I'll be able to see the world and events in a different way, in a way that incorporates the work of the divine, the work of the kundalini force within.

And when I listen to her, there is part of me that is listening as Syd the devotee, who wants to believe and suspend judgment, and part of me as Syd the suburban housewife, who is thinking *this woman is nuts!* And then I realize that when I talk to Jodi, or Gary or my parents, maybe this is how they hear me?

"Okay, but Montana? I really think you have salmonella," I tell her. "You should start drinking orange juice in the morning, and scrambling your eggs."

"Syd, this isn't what's important right now. What's important is making sure you have all the information and the directions you need to get to the retreat tomorrow."

I take another sip of my wine, savoring the crisp, cool liquid. "What, are you crazy?" I ask her, and then feel bad for saying that, because really, at this moment, I'm thinking maybe she is. "Montana, I can't go to the ashram without you," I tell her.

"Of course you can. You have to. You'll be fine," she says in a voice so strong it belies the fact that she is lying in a hospital bed with an IV drip.

"But Montana, I can't picture going by myself to an ashram where I won't know anyone, won't know what to do, where to go, what to say. And on my birthday, no less!"

"Listen to me, Syd," Montana says in a serious tone. "You are going to go on that retreat. You say you won't know anyone? Everyone there is a devotee of Gurujai—they're your people, Syd. They're your spiritual family! That is where you belong, especially on your birthday!" she says emphatically.

For some reason when she tells me this I can't help thinking about the driving trips we used to take to Florida when I was little. When we would stop at a hotel in some rural town for the night, my mother would take out the small phone book in the hotel and count how many Jewish names she saw in that town. I guess that was her way of finding her people.

"But Montana," I begin, and then she stops me.

She tells me that my spiritual path is spread out before me, and all I have to do is follow it. She tells me that I should hang up, sit down and meditate, and that by the grace of the guru I should open myself to receive Shaktipat on my birthday. She makes me promise this and then has me write down the directions to the ashram and the information for the rental car. Before we hang up she has me recite the mantra with her 44 times, in celebration of my birthday.

When I hang up, I get ready to meditate, like I promised Montana I would. But before I do, I gulp down the rest of my Chardonnay.

Chapter Twenty-Five

The sky is dark with menacing clouds overhead. I spend the first half of the drive listening to Jackie Mason's comedy routine. It seems like a good way to honor the past energy of the Catskills, a salute to my Jewish upbringing. But by the time I'm exiting the highway and driving down the one-lane country road sprinkled with farms and rundown houses, I am well into my Om Guru CD with its chants of mantras and Sanskrit hymns of praise to the guru. I am feeling more confident; I am feeling like a real devotee of Gurujai. I am ready to follow my spiritual path where it is leading me.

At a red light I look to my left, where there is a group of people gathering. They are all Hasidic Jews, with their big black hats, peyos and long beards. For a minute I am confused. I am looking for my new people, my new community, but all of a sudden I am back in my ancestral *shtetl.*

Oy vey.

I look again and they are walking down the road, and at the next corner I see more Hasidic men, all strolling down the street in their long black coats and sensible black shoes. The signs all around me are in Hebrew, and I try to reach back to my Hebrew school days to see what they say.

I have no idea what they say, but I'm proud nonetheless that I recognize all of the letters and some of the words. And it hits me that this is Friday, late afternoon, and they are getting ready to usher in the Sabbath. As I continue driving, I see the remnants of this once thriving Jewish community. The Nevele, the old orthodox resort hotel, is still there. I remember hearing about it from my Aunt Selma and Uncle Abe. But the days of Grossinger's and The Pines are long gone. In fact, many of the old Jewish resorts have been bought and converted into ashrams. I wonder if there is any old brick and mortar out there lamenting how the building has converted, which is what my parents think I am doing.

Every sign I see is in Hebrew, and I start to wonder if maybe I'm lost. But I continue down the road, following Montana's directions, and keep the Om Guru CD on for continued inspiration and strength. But in deference to the orthodox Jews walking, I turn the CD down and keep my windows closed.

Finally I see the street, and I take a left and travel down a winding road up toward the main building of the ashram. I am awed by its size and beauty.

I follow the signs for devotee parking along the road just as the skies open and the rain begins to fall. I'm sure if Montana were with me she would tell me why this is an auspicious sign. But all I can think is that I'm going to have to carry my duffel all the way back to the entrance in the rain, and that my hair will frizz. Apparently there is no valet parking at an ashram.

The narrow road finally breaks off to the left into a large parking area. Which is filled.

And I mean really filled. It's like being at the mall on the day after Thanksgiving. I keep driving up and down, willing a space to appear. When I finally find one I park the car, turn off the engine, and just sit there. Not just sit there in a meditative way—more like in a *what the hell am I doing* way.

It's pouring now, and I have no umbrella. I can't decide if I should wait to see if the rain will let up. When I check my watch I see that the welcoming session is going to begin soon. The rain continues to pelt my car, and I decide I should probably just make a run for it. I open the car door, take a deep breath, and start running as I splash through the parking lot puddles and ruining, I'm sure, the really cute brown leather sandals that I am wearing. By the time I run up to the front of the main entrance I am wet, chilled and rethinking this whole retreat.

But just as I am standing at the front entrance hall, two amazingly beautiful young women dressed in saris, both with perfectly straight long brown hair that looks like it hasn't had any contact whatsoever with the elements falling from the sky, open the door and motion for me to come inside.

"Namaste," they both say in unison with sparkling smiles, and I say the same to them. They would be perfect in a commercial for whitening strips. The foyer is immense and opulent; marble floors and high ceilings, with huge portraits of Gurujai framed on the walls, and large statues of deities scattered about with fountains and velvet benches and chairs along the walls. A few people are sitting, and others are walking down the long hallway.

"You are here for the retreat?" one of the women asks.

"Yes, and I hope I'm not arriving too late," I say, thinking that Montana really should have booked us on an earlier flight. I hate cutting it so close.

"We are glad you are here," the other woman says. "You can check in later at reception, after the welcoming ceremony. I'll bring your duffel there now, and it will be waiting for you. That way you can go and get settled in the meditation hall. Just follow the corridor all the way down and then turn right. You'll see three sets of big double doors—that's where the welcoming ceremony will be taking place," she explains.

I thank her, and they both flash me another set of their perfect pearly whites.

I stop and use the bathroom, which is as lovely as the one at the Four Seasons Hotel. Then, still chilled and wet with rain, I walk toward the meditation hall and stop when I see a large group ahead of me all waiting to enter the hall, and, like at airport security, taking off their shoes.

The chill has now spread throughout, and I find myself fighting against the idea of going barefoot to enter. The air conditioning seems to be on full force, and all I want to do is wrap myself up in my new cashmere shawl and take a nap. I also realize now that Indian cotton, while it looks lovely when pressed and ironed, does not do well after being soaked by the rain. It's sheerness only serves to wrinkle and soak through into your bones. I am so cold that it feels more like December now than August.

I follow the crowd making its way into the large double doors, and when I find a little bit of space right before entering I remove my shoes and place them with the hundreds of others on one of the shelves. I feel like I should get a shoe check—you know, like a coat check. I hope after the welcoming ceremony is over I can find my shoes again.

It's really chilly, and I'm wondering what I am going to do when I walk in. Where will I sit? Will I know what to do? Will I freeze the whole time?

And when I enter the meditation hall, all my worries fall away.

The marble floor, which I assumed would be cold against my bare feet, is heated. Every single tile is warm, and that warmth flows through me, warming me, welcoming me. The hall is massive and beautiful and crowded. At the front is a huge stage surrounded by beautiful fresh flowers, with the sides of the stage roped off in gold velvet. In the center of the stage is a velvet maroon chair with legs low to the ground, and to its side is an altar with pictures of Bhagawan Mulka and Swami Baba. Surrounding the chair are large peacock feathers.

I wonder what time the doors opened. You have to be here really early, I'm assuming, if you want to sit up close. Then I notice that the front maybe 15 or 20 rows are filled with what appear to be Gurujai's attendants. The men are dressed in white robes and the women in stunning saris. There are two huge TV monitors at either side of the hall, so you can watch Gurujai up close no matter where you are sitting. Even if it's in the cheap seats. Correct that—I mean the cheap cushions.

I find a row to the right and sit down on the meditation cushion, spreading out my skirt over my legs and taking out my new shawl. The woman to my right smiles at me, and says *"Namaste"* before resuming her meditation posture.

Soon the music starts, followed by chanting. During this time I find myself being swept up in the energy, swept up in the devotion. I look around the room and think *I am here, I am part of this,* and I feel that somehow I have arrived. I have arrived at my destiny, am walking along the edge of spiritual bliss, of spiritual awakening.

Then above the chanting I hear the distant music to the theme song from *Sex and the City,* and it's coming from my purse.

Shit, I forgot to turn off my cell. I try to discreetly reach into my bag and turn off my phone. But when I close my eyes again and sway in rhythm with the chant, I feel like Carrie, Samantha, Miranda and Charlotte are now watching me, judging me, as they sit in a trendy New York bar and sip their cosmopolitans.

All of a sudden the chanting stops, and the equivalent of a drum roll—in this case maybe a harpsichord roll—begins, and the room falls silent. A group of eight, four women and four men, walk to the stage area and then divide themselves on either side of the empty chair, sitting down on golden meditation cushions. And then Gurujai walks in, and there is total silence as the people in the hall put their palms together and bow their heads.

Gurujai stands on the stage, her arms outstretched, and she is utterly lovely. "I welcome you all here with great love, and I welcome you to wander in the boundless love of this universe."

I feel goose bumps, and I know that they are not from the rain, but from the place of possibilities. From the idea that maybe, after all of these years of living in the material world, there is another world out there, a world where I can connect to the sacred. A world where my worth is not weighed on the scale but in knowing my true nature, in meeting my true self, and of merging with the absolute consciousness of the universe.

Gurujai asks us to meditate with her for the next 20 minutes, "to infuse the room with our joyful energy." As I sit in the quiet stillness, I feel wrapped in the warmth of my shawl and in the warmth of community.

I hear the end chime of meditation, and slowly open my eyes. Looking around, I see everyone is wide-eyed, their focus up front with Gurujai. She is beaming from her chair, wrapped in a maroon robe and a white, fuzzy hat. She is glowing.

"Can you feel the power of Consciousness? Can you feel the vibrational energy pulsating all around us from the strength of our collective meditation?

From the power of our love and devotion radiating out from our hearts and merging with the universal Consciousness, the universal oneness?"

No one raises their hand to answer. I'm assuming this is a rhetorical question.

"This, this is the power of true devotion. This is the energy of the self-merging with the limitless Self. This is touching the Truth."

Though there are literally hundreds of people in the meditation hall, there is not a sound. Everyone is focused with rapture on Gurujai. I am, too, but the fact that I am noticing that everyone is in rapture means, I guess, that I am not totally focused—that I still have this need to check out the scene and see what's happening.

"What are the qualities that serve as the foundation of a spiritual life? It is to practice true devotion with discipline, commitment and determination. That is what we are doing here together today, and what each of you must do at home, when you sit for your daily meditation practice, and when you chant the mantra. By the grace of the guru, with discipline, commitment and determination, you can meet your own inner guru, meet your own true self."

People are beaming; the words are as if water to a people in the desert. And somehow it all feels familiar, as if these words, these ideas, are as old to me as time, are quenching my thirst. Maybe in a past life I was a devotee. Or maybe I was even one of the guru's attendants. Or maybe I was the guru herself. This whole idea of discipline, commitment, and determination, of practicing it here so we can take it home and practice it daily, it feels so familiar, reverberates so strongly. I must be farther along on the spiritual path than I realized. I continue to listen to her as she talks more about the foundation of spiritual practice.

And then, shit. It hits me why it sounds so familiar. It sounds like the foundation of every damn diet I have ever tried.

No matter which diet it was, the emphasis was on discipline, commitment and determination, of practicing the rules daily so you can become who you really are: your true self, the thin person within waiting to be revealed.

But then I think of Montana and how she told me, before I left for the retreat, that the accumulation of negative karma can try to sabotage your spiritual progress by pulling you back to old ways of thinking, to unwise and unskilled observations, so I vow to let go of my skepticism of the merits of discipline, commitment and determination, and try to think instead of maybe Moses climbing Sinai to hear the word of God. He had to have these qualities, didn't he? To hike up that mountain in what, bare feet? Thin little sandals? He had no leather hiking boots or hiking pants, no wick-away hiking shirt, no backpack and water bottle, no Power Bars. When you think about it, what did Moses have, really, but his discipline, his commitment and determination to hear the word of the Lord?

Granted, he could also have benefited from the practice of pranayama breathing so that when he saw that his people had made a golden calf in his absence he could have just taken a deep cleansing breath instead of having a tantrum and smashing the tablets upon which the Ten Commandments were written. Still, I guess it was his discipline, commitment and determination that led him back up the mountain to tell God that he sort of screwed up, and could he get another copy of those ten rules?

"And so, even though I am celebrating my birthday with you all tomorrow, this celebration is really about celebrating our collective rebirth every day; our rebirth as we come closer to merging with the Absolute, as we come closer to realizing the Truth, and we become our true Self. Tomorrow, as I offer you all the blessing of Shaktipat, the awakening you experience may be like a bolt of lightning for some of you; for others it may be more subtle, like the soft opening of a rose. And both are real and powerful. Both are imbibed with the spiritual energy that makes the rivers flow, the tide come in and go out, the thunder roar, the sun shine, and the Earth spin.

"When we touch the divinity within ourselves, we realize that we are part of the whole. Like a wave forming, we breathe in, and like a wave reaching the shore, we breathe out. We are that wave; we are a manifestation of that vibration. We are a drop of water, a speck of sand, a pebble. And we are the ocean, the continents and the tallest mountain. We are Mount Everest! Do you see? If you pour a drop of water from a cup into the ocean, is the drop of water still part of the liquid in your drinking cup, or has it become the ocean itself? We are that drop, and we are the ocean, because we are divinity itself. But we have to become conscious of that, we have to know our greatness, know our divinity, to actualize our True Self and to live sacred lives."

Her words resonate. The images she is using evoke a feeling of connectedness in me, a feeling of being part of something greater than myself, of being part of the cosmic energy, or as Montana calls it, the cosmic dance. Gurujai talks a little longer, and her voice feels soothing and melodic to me, like a lullaby.

We end the welcome session singing *Hare Rama Hara Krishna,* and I know the words from the old Beatles song. Then we are told the plan for the evening—dinner, and following dinner a special performance of a section of the *Bhagavad Gita* where Lord Krishna instructs his disciple, Arjuna, on the nature of the universe, God and the Supreme Self, by a group of devotees on a year-long retreat at the ashram.

By now my clothes are dry and I am warm, but a shower sounds great, and I'm hoping I have time to clean up before dinner. But I don't. It takes a long time to exit the meditation hall. There is no big rush for the doors, but rather a slow-moving almost meditation-like pace that speaks of being here now, not rushing somewhere else. And so slowly, like the idea of letting the ego go, I am letting go of the wish for a warm shower. I am evolving, wrinkled in clothing, but hopefully smoother along the edges of my soul.

Miraculously, or, by the grace of the guru, I find my sandals, and they are not ruined from the rain, just maybe a hint lighter in the leather. I make my way over to reception, and wait in a long line to check in.

I mean really long.

This is not, I tell you, a short line.

And no one else seems to mind. Everyone is just smiling and smiling. Some have their eyes closed and seem to be in some kind of meditative state. Others are talking quietly with one another. I figure I might as well use the time to call Gary and tell him that I arrived here safely, but as I take my cell out of my bag a woman standing behind me taps me on the shoulder and tells me that cell phone use is prohibited anywhere but in your room, and even there, it is discouraged. She says this kindly, like the way a really patient mother might tell her young child that she really shouldn't be sticking peas up her nose.

I put the phone back in my purse and continue waiting in line.

Finally, after close to an hour, it is my turn to check in. I am given a folder filled with the words of various chants, a schedule for the retreat, a history of the ashram, and a list of rules. I am given my duffel bag, which the welcoming attendants had dropped off earlier.

"I see you have requested a single room," the woman in reception who is helping me says.

"Yes, that's right," I tell her. Montana had been somewhat annoyed with me when I told her that I wanted my own room. She is trying to save money given that she is taking off for India, and a single room is double the price—and let me tell you, the retreat itself is rather pricey. But I told her that I don't do well with room sharing, that I needed my space. In the end I think she understood, though she had commented, "You don't really need your space as much as you need to create space inside, in your heart." I had told her that was beautifully said, but it didn't change the fact that I wanted a private room—a suite, if they had one.

"Yes, well, you will be in a triple for this retreat," the woman says to me with a pleasant smile.

"No, I'm sorry. My reservation was for a private room," I explain.

"Yes, you requested a private room, but we can't always guarantee that."

She must see my face fall, because she tells me not to worry, "The grace of the guru works in mysterious ways. It is in your karma to have a triple," she tells me again.

Hey buddy, I want to yell, *it may be my karma to have a triple, but it's on my reservation form to have a single.*

But I take a deep breath, and she does the same. We stand there for a moment, breathing together.

"Listen, I've never been on a retreat before. I wouldn't be comfortable sharing a room with strangers. I'm sure there must be a single room available somewhere. I'm happy to pay extra—"

But she interrupts. "No, really. There are no available single rooms, but not to worry. The guru provides."

I don't know what that means, so I just stand there. Does this mean the guru will provide me with a private room?

"And you won't be sharing a room with strangers," she begins to explain, and I am momentarily relieved. There must be a room for me after all.

"Every devotee of Gurujai, every retreat participant, is part of this great family of beings. We are all connected and all protected by her grace," she says as she hands me a key. "Never question how the retreat unfolds. Be willing to change your expectations, to lose your ego, for all this play of consciousness is happening for a reason, and in time, all is revealed."

And after that I simply ask, "Does the room have a private bathroom?"

And thank God, I mean thank Gurujai, she nods her head yes.

Chapter Twenty-Six

I press the light on my travel alarm clock and see that it's almost midnight. If I fall asleep now, I can get four and a half hours of sleep. If I miss the 5 a.m. Guru Gita chant I can pull off an extra hour of sleep, but in any scenario there is little chance of having time to blow dry and straighten my hair.

I know that I'm on this retreat to look at the bigger picture, but I feel better looking at the bigger picture with perfectly straight hair, especially on my birthday. But alas, I'm learning that sometimes you just have to let go.

I can hear the soft snoring of Gwenda, a devotee from New Hampshire, and I try to let her rhythmic breathing sounds lull me to sleep, but I'm unsuccessful. Even though the room is dark, I can make out the image of Christine—I mean Savarna—sitting in her bed and doing mantra recitation using her long mala bead necklace.

Five years ago Christine met Gurujai for the first time, and when she requested from the guru a Hindu name, Gurujai gave her the name Savarna, which means "daughter of the ocean." Christine—that is, Savarna—had told Gwenda and me that she knew then and there the great powers of Gurujai. "I mean, what a perfect name, right? I was captain of my high school swim team."

When I found myself about to challenge this logic—after all a pool is not the Atlantic—I heard Montana's voice telling me to stop judging, stop challenging and just open up and start loving.

Okay, but Montana? How do you do that?

Take Savarna. She is so devout. She is so sure. And I realize that when I see this, I am either jealous because I want to be like that, or I write her off as a nutcase. When I met her last night, she told me that it is fate that she lives in New York City, because the proximity of the Om Guru Center to her apartment and her job means she can attend the center every morning and evening. She only associates with other devotees, except for at her job, and all of her vacation time is spent here at the Catskills. She is saving up to go on a three-month retreat at the Om Guru Ashram in India. She told Gwenda and me that she has done past-life regression and that in one of her past lives she was a great Hindu saint.

I just looked at her and said, "Wow, a Hindu saint, that must have been cool," and she seemed to happily accept this response because she had said to me, "It was one of my greatest lives." I was going to ask her what her other lives were like, but I was already stressing about having to share my room with two women, and somehow learning about her other lives and inviting them in made me feel like the room would then really be too crowded.

But the food—oh my God, the food here is amazing. Seriously, even if there is not an ounce of you, a morsel of you, that is seeking a spiritual path, you should come here anyway just for the food.

It is heavenly, mouthwatering, delicious and abundant. And of course it's all vegetarian and so good that while you're eating it you don't even think of the steak *frites* you haven't eaten now in months. For dinner I sampled the red-lentil dahl soup, raisin sun slaw, and tabbouleh. I feasted on the potato eggplant maharaja, the millet chickpea casserole, the curried vegetables, and ginger brown rice. I topped it all off with a slice of carob-almond cake and a chai. If I could have someone cook like that for me every day, I would die happy. But probably not for a very long time because the food is so healthy, and at the same time so delectable, that my body would respond with health and vigor into three-digit numbers, I'm sure of it.

That's the problem with my own heritage. What do we Jews eat? Potato latkes, brisket, matzo ball soup, noodle kugel. The fat and sodium are the main event—the food itself, an afterthought.

I hear Gwenda shifting in her sleep, her snoring stopping now that she is resting on her other side. I glance at my alarm clock again; it's 12:03. It's my birthday. I'm 44 years old now, and I need my sleep—I can't squeeze by on only a few hours like I did when I was younger, when I was in college like Rachel.

I can't believe Savarna is still doing her mantra recitation. I should do that tomorrow. I'm probably not getting the full effect of this whole experience unless I do all of the practices, and considering I'm already thinking of blowing off the morning *Guru Gita,* I can't afford to let other things go. I'm sure Savarna does every practice, performs every austerity. Maybe what I need is to ask Gurujai for a Hindu name, too. Maybe if I had a spiritual name I'd manifest spiritual qualities in the world. I wonder if I asked Gurujai for a name, what she would give me?

I hear rustling and doors being open and closed. I try to wake myself up, but I'm caught between a dream where someone is calling me Sajna and another voice is calling me Syd.

"Syd, are you awake?" I hear a voice ask. At least I think this voice is calling me Syd and not Sajna. "Syd?"

I fight to open my eyes, and it takes me a minute to remember where I am. I blink myself to semi-wakefulness and see Gwenda standing next to my bed, her cropped blonde hair wet from the shower.

"Oh, I'm up—I don't think my alarm went off. What time is it?" I ask, fumbling for the clock on the bed stand.

"It's 5:15. I didn't know if I should wake you. The *Guru Gita* started at five, but I'm not going to the meditation hall until the morning meditation at 6:15. I wasn't sure if you meant to stay sleeping, or if you wanted to wake up," she explains.

I sit up in bed, wiping my eyes awake. "Thanks, Gwenda. When I couldn't fall asleep last night I figured I'd blow off the *Guru Gita*. Oh. Sorry, that sounds sort of disrespectful. I mean I figured I would miss the *Guru Gita* and be fresh and awake for the meditation, but I must have turned my alarm off and forgotten to reset it," I explain.

"Hey, you know what? It's my birthday today," I tell Gwenda, because it feels weird not to tell someone it's my birthday. It feels weird to not have Gary waking me up with kisses and cards and presents.

"Happy birthday! Hey, you and Gurujai have the same birthday! That's gotta mean something, don't you think?" she asks.

"My friend Montana seems to think so. She was adamant that I celebrate my birthday here this year. Maybe we should ask Christine—I mean Sarvana—what it may mean." I look over at Savarna's bed and see that it is made and that she is gone.

Gwenda sees me looking over and tells me that Savarna left early this morning to make it to the *Guru Gita*.

"How does she do it?" I ask. "When I finally fell asleep, sometime after midnight, she was still sitting up in her bed doing her mantra recitation."

Gwenda runs her fingers through her drying hair. "That's what people say, you know. After meeting Gurujai, after receiving Shaktipat, you have more energy than you can imagine," she says. "That's what I'm hoping for today. That when I receive Shaktipat, I'm forever changed, and that I have a renewed sense of purpose in my life. And I wish that for you, too. What better gift could you receive on your birthday than the blessings of the guru and the awakening of the kundalini?"

I have to stop myself from saying that I saw this great Marc Jacobs bag at

Bloomingdale's that I wouldn't mind receiving all gift-wrapped and presented to me along with my morning cup of hazelnut coffee.

"I'm going to jump in the shower and get dressed. Are you going to stay here? Do you want to walk to the meditation hall together when I'm done?" I ask her.

"Sure. I'm just going to go outside and take a little walk around the temple. I'll be back here in about a half an hour, and then we'll go together," she tells me. "She opens the curtains above my bed. "What a beautiful day—the sky is so blue. Blue like the blue pearl of meditation, you know? This must be an auspicious sign. Like the rain last night was to clean away all the negative karma and prepare us all to receive Shaktipat today."

Gwenda leaves and I head into the bathroom, preparing to get ready for the day faster than I ever have before. By the time Gwenda returns I am dressed but don't have time to finish drying my hair to its usual straightness. Maybe this is my auspicious sign, to let go of what I think are necessities and let in my own true nature as manifested in hair that actually has a natural wave that I've spent my life trying to tame straight.

Gwenda is right; the day is gorgeous, sunny and warm. There is a brilliance to the beautifully landscaped gardens, as if everything has been washed clean and new and is now basking in the warmth and light of the day. And it's nice finding a friend in Gwenda, someone to walk with, and someone who knows it's my birthday.

She points out the temple she walked to this morning, and the Garden of Grace, where statues of great saints and prophets and deities are depicted amongst exquisite flowering plants and shrubs and blossoms. I promise myself that I will walk through there later, when I have some free time, to reflect and maybe connect with the great masters of the world. Maybe one of them is Sarvana in the incarnation of the great Hindu saint she once was.

"I saw people already lining up at the meditation hall," Gwenda says. "We should head up there and wait for the doors to open," she suggests, and I agree.

The ashram is huge. Think Sandals Resorts, but for every tiki bar and smoothie stand, think shrine and deity; for every swimming pool and hot tub, think fountain and Shiva surrounded by burning incense. And instead of resort guests wandering around in their beachwear, think devotees in saris and robes. As we're walking toward the great meditation hall, I see a huge white tent far off on a hilltop. I point to it and ask Gwenda if she knows what the tent is for.

"It looks like someone's having a big wedding, or maybe a great cocktail party later," I venture.

Gwenda follows my gaze and then tells me that actually the tent is for a month-long silent retreat that a group of devotees are doing.

I look at her to see if she's serious, which she appears to be. "A month-long silent retreat? You mean to tell me that for a month they can't talk? For a whole month?" I ask, thinking who could stay quiet for so long?

Gwenda tells me that they offer this retreat every summer, and that she is planning on doing it next year.

"Really? You could imagine being silent for the whole month of August?" I ask her, thinking I could never do it.

Gwenda smiles. "It's supposed to be very powerful. Your meditation practice really deepens on that kind of retreat," she offers.

"Still," I say, "That seems really hard. You really can't talk at all, for the whole time?" I ask again.

Even though there is no way I could imagine taking an entire month without talking to sit in meditation, I am riveted; like slowing down to see a horrible accident on a highway, you know you shouldn't look, but you can't help it. That's what this month-long silent retreat feels like to me, a horrible idea that is thoroughly captivating my imagination.

"I wonder if you're allowed to laugh on the retreat?" I ask, thinking about the sleepovers Jodi and I used to have when we were kids, when we would dare each other to see who could keep quiet and not laugh, which of course only served to send us into roaring fits of giggles.

Gwenda looks at me and says, "I don't know. I guess if the laughter is from a deep and authentic place, if it comes up spontaneously in meditation, then you're probably allowed to laugh."

There are many devotees walking, some performing sun salutations, others sitting under trees meditating, and still others burning incense over a big sand pit with Shiva in the middle.

We make our way to the meditation hall, and once again the crowds are waiting to enter. Today I make a promise to myself not to be impatient, to wait, like everyone else seems to do, as if they have all the time in the world. When Gwenda and I get close enough, we take off our shoes and place them on the shelf. We go through the double doors and scan the large hall to decide where we should sit. Gwenda points to a row of meditation cushions on the left with good views of the stage.

She points out the famous people who enter the hall—actors and singers that I never knew were part of Om Guru. I'm tempted to tell you who they are, but Gwenda tells me that it is ashram etiquette that their privacy be protected.

But think legal dramas and country music.

There is a lot of energy in the room, and I am impressed. It's only around 6:00 in the morning, breakfast is not served until after our first meditation, and there is not a coffee cart in sight. This is pure, raw energy of the spiritual kind, not the caffeinated kind.

Soon the familiar music starts, followed by a chant that I am not familiar with called *Jyota Se Jyota*. From my bag I pull out the folder I was given at reception and find the words to the chant, happy to see from its translation that the chant asks for the Guru's own flame burning in her heart to kindle the flame of divine love in the devotee's heart.

I close my eyes and will my wick to be kindled. That has to be better than the candles of the birthday cake I'm missing today, right?

After the chant we meditate, and then Gurujai emerges. Like yesterday her voice soothes me as I listen to her talk about divine love, about the one heartbeat of the universe in its many vibrations.

By 8:00 I have found my bliss back in the dining hall over a breakfast that is absolutely fabulous. All of this spiritual talk and ritual has made me hungry—for nirvana, sure, but also for the whole-wheat banana pancakes and blueberry scones.

After breakfast I have an hour before we meet again in the great meditation hall. I decide to walk around inside the main building, and find myself confronted with the most beautiful gift shop I've ever seen.

I walk in and my senses respond immediately. There is the smell of burning incense, a CD playing a version of *Om Nimah Shivaya* that I've never heard before, but love instantly. And there are fabrics, wonderful fabrics. Silk scarves with Shiva, long, beautiful saris with 14-karat gold thread, the price tag reflecting that thread. A large locked case of jewelry, and shelves and shelves of earrings, necklaces and bracelets. There are jewelry boxes from India, along with teas and imported pillows. There are shelves of books and pictures everywhere of Gurujai, Swami Baba and Bhagawan Mulka. There are statues all over, small, medium, big, and bigger. There are chimes and CDs and everything you could ever need for meditation. There is a rack of yoga clothes, and another with T-shirts—some of Gurujai, some with the mantra, others with pictures of deities and saints.

I want it all.

I am also feeling like I should maybe be sitting in meditation, either in the temple or in the meditation cave that is supposed to be infused with spiritual energy that takes your meditation to a whole new level, a whole new consciousness. And I promise myself I will, this afternoon. But now I am captivated by the gift store, and I cannot leave.

I want to shop.

And this is what I buy:

• An Om Guru calendar for the New Year complete with pictures of Gurujai and the ashrams (both in the Catskills and in India) and infused with beautiful quotes about traveling the spiritual path.

• A pocket size book of Gurujai's *Lessons for Living Your Bliss.*

• A T-shirt with *Om Nimah Shivaya* in the front and a picture of the Om Guru Ashram on the back.

• A silk scarf with Shiva (I thought I'd get more wear out of that than the sari I tried on which was, I have to say, simply amazing on me after the saleswoman patiently helped me put it on. Gary's great helping me with a zipper on my dress, but somehow I don't see him being able to negotiate around a sari).

• And my big-ticket item. I fall in love with the white gold bracelet cuff engraved with *Om Nimah Shivaya*—which, while not inexpensive, I figure is invaluable in meaning.

I think of the MasterCard commercial where they give the prices of all these items, and the last thing they say is something like, "spending a day at the ballpark with your son, priceless." Well, when I looked at the price of the bracelet I didn't really see the dollar amount. Instead I heard in my head, "wearing the mantra around your wrist and infusing your being with spiritual energy, priceless."

Plus, I rationalize, it's my birthday.

So I make my purchases, and by the time I drop my shopping bag off in my room it's time to return to the meditation hall for the beginning of Gurujai's birthday celebration, and then for Darshan, where I will receive my first Shaktipat.

Everything at the ashram is done so beautifully and so fully. It is organized, inviting, and lovely. The flowers are magnificent, the entertainment is great, and the food is outstanding. Really, they could outsource some of the Guru's attendants as bar mitzvah consultants.

Though as of yet, I've seen no Shiva sculpted out of chopped liver.

During the birthday celebration the children of the ashram come out dressed in the cutest little outfits—the girls are in white summer dresses with pink sashes, and the boys are in blue sailor shorts with white shirts and little jackets. As rehearsed, they come out from both sides of the stage, and, facing Gurujai, they sing her a song. I have no idea what it means, but it's sweet and melodic. The children then sit in a semi-circle around Gurujai, who is dressed for her birthday in a gold robe with a matching hat. The stage is filled with flowers of every kind, and the scent makes its way through the hall and makes me feel intoxicated with happiness.

Montana was right. This is where I needed to spend my birthday. And when we sit for meditation, I think I see it. The blue pearl that I've heard about, the brilliant blue light, tiny as a seed, that appears during deep meditation, representing the home of the true, inner self. *I got it,* I think to myself. *I got it.* And when meditation is over, I find myself anticipating meeting Gurujai, and receiving Shaktipat, more than ever. Montana would be proud. I find myself waiting eagerly for my true Birth Day, for my true awakening.

I'm thinking about all of this while those in Gurujai's closest circle are presenting her with readings and poems, as a group of lithe attendants dressed in beautiful saris, perform dance after dance celebrating the cosmic ecstasy of the universe, depicting the release of spiritual energy as they end their final dance at the feet of Guruaji, in prostration.

I twirl my new bracelet on my wrist and smile.

And then when I look up again, I see the male attendants surrounding the Guru, telling her that they have a special birthday surprise for her. They explain how we all love the stories she tells us about her childhood in India, and about the tigers she loved so dearly, especially the baby tigers.

"And so, Gurujai," one of the white robed male attendants says, "The least we can do for you, who has graced us with celebrating your birthday with your devotees here in the States, is to bring a little India to you."

Gurujai claps her hands in excitement, and I'm thinking, *curry. I bet they're making some fabulous curry dishes for lunch,* but I'm wrong. I hear a squeal of excitement when the back double doors of the meditation hall open and what do I see? Well, I'll tell you, it's not an Indian chef bringing pakora appetizers and naan breads filled with potato and peas.

I must be hallucinating, because I swear when I turn my head to the back of the meditation hall, I see baby tigers coming through the double doors, and there is no leash. I repeat—there is no leash.

I start to count—one, two, three, and yes, there it is, four baby tigers are now moving down the meditation hall guided by a host of attendants/trainers who seem perfectly comfortable walking beside them, pressing them on toward the stage to where Guruaji is standing and beaming and clapping her hands. There are loud gasps of excitement in the hall, and for a moment I am caught up in the excitement of it all, too. They're adorable, these baby tigers, truly adorable.

One of the attendants picks up one of the baby tigers and places him (I don't really know if it's a him or a her—wouldn't want to get close enough to the baby tiger to determine its sex) in her arms with a baby bottle filled with milk. Gurujai sits down holding the tiger the way you would hold a little baby, and begins feeding the tiger the bottle.

They need to make a poster of this. This is the cutest thing I've ever seen. This is incredible. Talk about a birthday surprise! I can honestly say I have never known anyone who received such a gift, and I, like the rest of the devotees in the hall, are making cooing sounds, enjoying the scene like one big extended family.

And then the other baby tigers start roaming around, and we are all captivated, all watching where they will go and what they will do. There are attendants standing in different places throughout the meditation hall, but the tigers are given space to roam.

And then it hits me. The tigers are given space to roam. Are they nuts?! They're tigers—the baby part seems insignificant. Instead of hearing a chant in my head, *Jyote Se Jyote* or something, I hear instead, *Lions and tigers and bears, oh my! Lions and tigers and bears, oh my!*

Somehow I've gotten off the spiritual path and onto the Yellow Brick Road, and I want someone—the wizard or something—to keep me safe, because all that I can think right now is that I am sitting down with a crowd of people while tigers are wandering the hall.

I'm the kind who screams when she sees a spider, so you can only imagine that my heart is pounding so hard I think it may burst. I scan the room again, wishing I could spot Gwenda, but I don't see her. I look around trying to gauge others' reactions. Everyone seems to be doing fine. No one looks particularly scared or uncomfortable. On the contrary, people look happy.

I realize that despite how I'm feeling inside, I probably look pretty much like everyone else on the outside. The question is, are they scared like I am, or are they really fine?

Soon the baby tigers are gathered up and led out of the hall. Then one of the attendants takes the microphone and tells Gurujai that they have another surprise for her. Gurujai again claps her hands together, waiting to see what is coming next.

The attendant speaks to both Gurujai and the devotees. "You, Gurujai, are a rare jewel. To be in your presence is to know awe, and to be enlightened by your wisdom is to know nirvana. What is rare is very cherished, as is attested by the hundreds and hundreds of devotees gathered here to celebrate your birthday. And in keeping with bringing a little bit of home to you, a little bit of India here to you, we have something that, like you, is precious and rare."

The side door on the right of the stage opens, and in walks an older Indian man with a huge tiger. Thankfully, this time on a chain.

There is a collective gasp, and the attendant continues to usher the tiger up on stage. "This is a very rare white-and-black-striped Bengal tiger, and we feel both its preciousness and beauty represents what your devotees feel for you, Gurujai."

Gurujai hugs her attendant, and then walks over to the Indian trainer who is holding the massive tiger. They talk quietly with each other in their native tongue, smiling and laughing. Then, while the man is holding the tiger's chain, Gurujai begins petting the tiger and murmuring soft words in its ears, whereby the tiger lies down at her feet. The trainer whispers something in Gurujai's ear, and again, she claps her hands together with joy.

While the tiger is still lying at her feet, she tells all of us that the tiger's trainer has just told her that this afternoon after lunch, every devotee will have a chance to pet the tiger outside by the lily garden. The entire hall begins clapping, and the tiger stands up and is then led out of the hall.

The door to the right of the stage opens again, and for a moment I worry that maybe it is a lion or a polar bear, but in fact it's a large table lined with a white linen cloth being rolled in by a group of attendants, with a huge birthday cake—the size of a wedding cake, really—alight with candles. Then the entire hall sings "Happy Birthday" to Gurujai, and I am only momentarily miffed that another birthday cake, this one for me, isn't being rolled out.

And then it's time for Darhsan, for which we've all been waiting.

And it seems like we will have to wait some more. The hall is packed, and in Darshan, you wait in line, patiently of course, to meet Gurujai and to receive Shaktipat.

I'VE BEEN waiting in line now for over an hour. I look at the devotees ahead of me, trying to ascertain how much longer until it is my turn. I can't determine how much longer it will be, but at least now, as I slowly move up in line, I can see some of the devotees receiving Shaktipat.

What I see is that first the devotees talk for a moment with one of the attendants. Some of the devotees appear to be handing over gifts. Shit. No one told me that I was supposed to bring something. What could they be bringing? I do a mental survey of what I have with me, shopping on myself, so to speak, to see if there is anything that I can offer up when I meet Gurujai. There isn't. Maybe I could send something later. She seems to like hats— maybe I can stop at Madam Hatem at the mall when I get home. They have great hats. But wait, I see some other devotees getting ready to meet Gurujai and they don't seem to be carrying gifts. It must be optional.

Gurujai seems to be spending just a minute or so with each devotee, some a bit longer, others shorter. The devotee approaches her and the attendant whispers something in Gurujai's ear—maybe whatever the attendant is asking the devotee before the actual meeting is now being shared. Then the devotee kneels before Gurujai's seat, and Gurujai takes some long peacock feathers and taps them three times on the devotee's head while she murmurs some words to her, as if in prayer. A moment of conversation continues, and it looks like sometimes a devotee is handed something before exiting off to the left.

The line continues to move at a snail's pace.

"Daaad, It's taking too long—I'm tired of waiting. When is it going to be our turn?" a little boy, standing behind me, whines to his father.

It's like I've found my kindred spirit. That's exactly how I've been feeling in this ever-so-patient line of devotees.

The father bends down to his son, who can't be more than six or seven years old, and says, "The waiting is what makes it so special and so sweet. What could be more wonderful than waiting to see Gurujai? The longer we have to wait, the more time we get to be excited to see her and connect to our spiritual yearning," he explains as he hugs the boy close to him. "It makes it that much sweeter when it's our turn."

The father seems to me so wise, and so kind. Still, I wouldn't mind cutting to the front.

I continue watching the ritual of Shaktipat, trying to see how the energy is getting transferred. Clearly the peacock feathers play an integral part, like an energy conduit. And I'm curious about the words she is saying, and why with some people she is quick and with others she spends a longer time.

I want to be in the latter category.

Finally, when there are only about eight people before me, I realize that I should probably have been meditating, or praying or doing something spiritual while waiting in line.

And I'm nervous. All of a sudden my heart is pounding and my hands are shaking. Is this supposed to happen? Is this part of the whole energy transformation?

I try to take some deep breaths to slow down the pounding in my heart.

And, as if in a dream, Gurujai's attendant is motioning me to come closer. I move up to the first stair of the stage, where the attendant is standing. "Welcome, and how are you?" she asks me.

"I'm fine, thank you," I tell her. I am watching the person before Gurujai being tapped with the peacock feathers, as another devotee stands behind her, waiting her turn.

"What is your name and where are you from?" she asks me.

"My name is Syd Arthur, and I live on the North Shore of Chicago, in Highland Ridge," I tell her.

She smiles at me and I just smile back.

"And have you been to the Om Guru Ashram before?" she asks me.

"No, this is my first time," I explain, and this seems to make her face light up.

"Wonderful!" she says. "Many lifetimes have conspired for this very moment to occur," she tells me, her smile widening. "When it's your turn to receive Shaktipat, I will escort you up, and I will introduce you to Gurujai. You can kneel on the step right below where the Guru is sitting."

"Okay, thank you," I say, looking at the many wrapped gifts on the stage and feeling a tightening in my stomach, feeling like I've arrived at a birthday party without a present.

And then it's my turn. The attendant tells Gurujai my name and where I'm from and that this is my first time at the ashram. I just stand there, and then I remember that I'm supposed to kneel, so I do. I look intently into Gurujai's face, into her eyes and into her big, wide grin. I want to get everything out of this, every nuance in her gaze, every bit of spiritual energy that she is offering—I want it all.

I bow my head slightly as Gurujai raises the peacock feathers. She utters some words that I take to be Sanskrit while she hits the feathers three times upon the crown of my head. The last line she utters I know well. It is the mantra, and I realize that my eyes are now closed, and that the world has fallen silent, and I feel the muscle of my heart soften and open.

And when I look up to meet her eyes, she is already looking past me, at the next devotee preparing to meet her. Another attendant is already ushering me off to the side of the stage, and I feel like it's over too fast. I want to refuse to get off the stage. I need more confirmation of what I felt. I need to make sure I got what I'm supposed to get. I need more acknowledgment. Didn't she hand something to some of the devotees?

The attendant is kindly but firmly waving me off stage, but I stop for a moment and look back at Gurujai, willing her to understand that I need more. And as I look back at her, our eyes meet, and she smiles a radiant smile.

She is motioning me back! She understands! She knows I need more! Of course she knows, she's the Guru.

The attendant puts her arm out, motioning for me to return to Gurujai, and when I do Gurujai smiles at me again, and I look so deeply into her face and into her eyes that I feel we are locked in an energy so great and deep that it rivals the force of an ocean's tidal wave. And then she bends down and picks up a small gold box, smiles and hands it to me, and holds her arm out to the attendant to usher me off the stage.

I follow the attendant and descend the stairs gripping the box in my hand, waiting to find a private space to open the precious gift that Gurujai has given me. Well, along with the precious gift of Shaktipat. After finding my shoes

I walk outside and find a quiet space, and while I want to rush to open it, I want to savor the waiting—the way the father in line told his little son to savor the waiting. But my curiosity overwhelms me, and taking a deep breath, I open the box anticipating a powerful and transforming spiritual object.

It's four pieces of chocolate.

My heart deflates. Four pieces of chocolate? That's not spiritual, that's caloric. That's my weakness. That's what I try to avoid. That's what I feed to Levi to save calories.

I decide to take a walk before lunch to ponder this. I know I felt something powerful—the peacock feathers, the Sanskrit, the powerful gaze and eye contact, the opening in my heart. And then I wanted more, and Gurujai knew that, right? She had to know I needed more, because she had me come back, and she gave me something and here it is, so what does it mean?

As I walk I find myself in the Garden of Grace, and I take my time in the warmth of the sun looking at magnificent statues. There's Shiva, Vishnu and Brahma, Ganesh, and Durga, the eight-armed warrior goddess who represents the universal Shakti, the divine Mother. And there's Jesus, and the Virgin Mary, and Muhammad and the Buddha, and there's Moses. I stop in front of Moses and smile, feeling like we go way back.

And then I realize that this garden holds the answers. This garden, full of the representations of the great spiritual traditions rooted firmly in the earth like the magnificent flowers blossoming in its soil, is about the unlimited ways of opening to the sacred. Rather than looking at one religion as holding the answer, all religions can hold the answer, because the truth is the truth. Different labels, maybe, different paths, sure, but truth is truth is Truth.

I sit down at the side of the garden and begin to meditate, and the word that I keep hearing is "love." I am filled with a lightness I've never felt before, not even at my thinnest moments. And when I open my eyes I experience such gratitude, such a welling of emotion. The gentle breeze caresses my face and carries the fragrant smell of blossoms in the air. And I breathe in its sweetness, suffused in the glory of all that is.

And then I pull out Gurujai's gift in an attempt to make sense of the symbolism. Fattening chocolates, yes. But what does it really mean in the spiritual realm? Perhaps the blessing of Shaktipat is to learn how to open up to the sweetness of life, to take it in and imbibe it and then manifest it to the world.

And so, right then and there, I open the small golden box, and eat the chocolates.

And since I understand that they represent the sweetness of following a spiritual path, I know, deep down in my soul, that the calories of the chocolates don't really count.

Chapter Twenty-Seven

It was very sweet. Gary surprised me with a birthday dinner with our friends when I got home after the retreat late that Sunday. I tried to explain to them why it was fine for me to pet the Bengal tiger that, after all, was on a long leash. How I knew I was protected by the grace of the Guru, and that it was a great experience in letting go of culturally induced fear.

"Uh, Syd?" Jodi had said. "I don't think fear of tigers is culturally induced. Fear of spinach caught in your teeth? That's maybe culturally induced, but I'm fairly sure that fear of tigers is pretty instinctual."

I knew better than to try to explain the whole experience at the ashram over dinner. I just went with the flow, cause that's what I'm all about now. Well, that's what I want to be about now.

And anyway, I didn't know how to even begin to try to explain the experience. It's like trying to introduce someone to a new language, culture and philosophy all at the same time. And in little bursts in between the martinis, appetizers, entrees and desserts. So, realizing that it was fruitless to try to convey to them what it meant for me to be on a spiritual retreat, I figured I would regale them with a joke I had heard at the Saturday night dinner at the ashram, before heading to the Yajna, the sacrificial fire ritual that we performed in honor of Gurujai's birthday late into the night, reciting Vedic mantras while wood, fruit, grain, oil, yogurt and ghee were poured into the fire as an offering to the Supreme. That, I didn't think they'd want to hear about, but one of my infamous jokes? It just might make them all more comfortable as they bit into their dinners of salmon, chicken and steak while I twirled my vegetarian pasta around my fork.

"So I was sitting at dinner with some other devotees—" I saw the look my dinner companions gave each other, and I revised my speech. "Okay, so I was sitting with some other people who were also on the retreat, and I was telling them how I heard that there was a month-long silent retreat and that I couldn't imagine not being able to talk for a whole month. And this guy said that he had done it the other year, and that it was actually great. Then he told me this joke about a seeker on a silent retreat."

I saw Gary looking at Dave and shaking his head, and then Margot said that if the joke's good, I can add it to the repertoire that she plans for me to showcase at the country club comedy show she is organizing, "without a lot of help from my dearest friends, at this point." I smiled at her and then continued:

"Okay, so there was this devotee who was going on a four-year silent meditation retreat. He was taken to a small hut where he would stay for this silent retreat alone. He was told that every year he would be visited by the most important attendant of the guru, and that at that time he was allowed to say two words.

"After the first year of his silent retreat, the attendant came to the hut and told the devotee that he had completed his first year of the retreat, and was now allowed to say two words. The devotee looked at the guru's attendant and said, 'Bed hard.' The attendant returned with a thin mattress.

"After the second year of the four-year silent retreat, the attendant returned and told the devotee that he had now finished the second year of the four-year silent retreat, and was once again allowed to utter his two words. The devotee looked at the guru's attendant and said, 'Need pillow.' The attendant returned with a pillow.

"Another year goes by and the attendant returned, telling him that he had completed his third year of his four-year silent retreat and was now allowed his two words. The devotee looked at the guru's attendant and said, 'I quit!' And the guru's attendant looked at the devotee and told him, 'Well it's about time—all you've done since you've been here is complain!'"

So, I don't mean to complain now, but this brings me to my next dilemma. How do I tell Gary that despite my realization back in the Garden of Grace that the truth is the truth, I don't want to go to services for the High Holy Days this year? That year after year, the prayer book fails to speak to me? That despite me being all about finding the sweetness in life, I don't want to sit in temple for Rosh Hashanah, even with its traditional wishes for a sweet new year, ushered in with apples and honey?

It's funny. When you're little, you can't wait to grow up and be an adult, where no one can make you do anything you don't want to do. But here I am, 44 years old and feeling like I can't really make the decision not to go to temple. That somehow that action, or more correctly that inaction, seems to be even more of a statement than spending my birthday at the ashram.

How do you allow yourself to move away from what you've known in the past, to create a different future? Am I so bound by tradition that I'll just go through the motions so that, while I know I'm already rocking the boat, I don't sink it?

What do I owe my family, and what do I owe myself?

It was with these questions that I found myself calling Levi to the door, removing his invisible collar, putting his leash on and taking him out for a walk. Though it's warm outside, I can feel the September air—the way that despite the heat from the sun, the gentle breeze holds the hint of the smell of leaves about to begin changing, and the way the angle of the sun seems to speak of crisper days ahead.

In the few weeks since I've been home from the retreat, I find myself enjoying more alone time. I still see my friends, of course, and I had to say goodbye to Montana, which was hard. We spent a wonderful afternoon together before she left. At first she was insistent that we go to Six Flags, like I had wanted for my birthday. But I knew how little time she had before leaving, tying up loose ends with her job, preparing and packing for India. So in the end we went out for lunch at this wonderful Indian restaurant where I was able to talk with her about my experiences at the ashram, and then I went to her house to help her finish packing.

Since I've come back from the retreat I find walking Levi very relaxing. And I try to emulate him on his walk. You know, like the old cliché—stop and smell the roses. Or, as in the case with Levi, besides stopping to smell the roses, stopping to sniff other dogs' poop, but in some way that's very spiritual, you know?

The whole idea of constantly turning to only what is pleasant and avoiding what is unpleasant is the antithesis of a spiritual path. A spiritual path, as Kali always tells us in yoga, is about being with what is in the here and now and knowing that everything is constantly changing. That once we find that place within our meditation, that place that is not pulled by external circumstances, we find our inner peace.

So I watch Levi trying to experience everything in the here and now, and I try to be patient as he pulls me yet again to a patch of grass that he seems to find utterly fascinating. I let go of the idea that this will be a power walk, that I will be burning any calories of significance, but I see that getting out with Levi and appreciating the day allows me to have a powerful walk.

I find myself walking further than usual with Levi, but I am enjoying the day so much that I continue onward. And a little while into the walk I realize where I am heading, where I've been walking toward without being fully conscious of it. I wait at the light to cross the busy intersection on Main Street.

And continue walking toward Bodee's.

Turning on Middle Way Drive, I walk down to the end of the street to Bodee's house. Levi and I bound up the porch steps and I start to ring the bell, but Levi is pulling me off to the back yard. I ring the bell anyway, but let Levi pull me across the side yard out to the back, where Bodee is bending over his garden while Golden is resting under a tree.

Golden gets up when he sees us and lets out a small bark as Levi pulls me to Golden. They greet each other in a pleasant display of sniffs and happy tail wagging.

Bodee looks up from his gardening with a smile and says, "Hello, Syd, what a lovely surprise! Just checking up on my broccoli." He stands up and wipes his hands on his jeans to clean the dirt off before reaching out to shake my hand. "Beautiful day, isn't it?" he asks.

"Gorgeous," I agree, as I try to hold onto the leash while Levi is trying to engage Golden in play. I bend down and try to pet Golden while at the same time I'm trying to untangle Levi's leash from his back left paw, all the while he is jumping with excitement to be back at 8 Middle Way Drive.

When I accomplish this, Bodee bends down to pat Levi on the head. "I remember when Golden was young and had the kind of energy Levi has. Time passes," he says, but not in a sad way, more in a factual way, like you might say the phone is ringing.

"You'll join me for my afternoon tea?" Bodee asks, and I tell him that I would love to.

"C'mon, boy, time to go inside," Bodee calls, and Golden follows his master into the house while Levi and I follow suit.

I take off Levi's leash, letting him wander the house with Golden, and follow Bodee into the kitchen. He fills the kettle with water and puts it on the stove to boil.

"I was thinking of Tie Luo Han today. What do you think?" he asks me as he opens the cabinet and takes out a canister, this one red and yellow with dragons.

I smile at him and say, "I have to remind you, if it's not coffee, I'm pretty clueless."

He chuckles and says, "Yes, I remember you telling me. A cup of coffee while you rush through your day, right?" he says kindly, with that same twinkle in his blue eyes. He hands me the canister as he takes out the teacups and sets them on the counter.

"Yeah, that about sums me up. If anyone were to ask me what the greatest invention during my lifetime was, I'd have to say the drive-thru: drive-thru coffee, drive-thru fast food, drive thru ATM machines," I tick off.

"It sounds like you live in your car," Bodee says, chuckling. "I hope you at least open the windows to breathe in the fresh air," he teases me. "If you're not careful, you just might drive-thru your life."

I smile as I watch Bodee take out the same tray and then hand me a plate with a box of biscuits. I open the box and arrange a small row of biscuits on the plate and place it on the tray. While we wait for the water to boil, Bodee opens the canister and shows me the tea.

"This here is Tie Luo Han," he says, and I peer in. It looks like long, brown strands. "It's a type of Oolong tea from Fujian," he tells me as he measures out the tea, puts it in the teapot strainer, and then pours in the water from the kettle. He places the teacups on the tray, which I carry as I follow him into the living room. I set down the tray on the table, and he places the teapot on the tray.

"Let's wait another moment before pouring," he says. "The tea needs some time to steep and reach its full flavor."

Golden and Levi are both lying down in front of the window where the afternoon sun is filtering in. I, too, feel the warmth permeating this house.

Bodee pours the tea, and then looks into his cup. I do the same. It's a golden reddish liquid, which seems perfect for welcoming the fall, just around the corner. When Bodee takes a sip I follow suit, and the tea tastes smooth and sweet. I know now not to take big gulps to finish, but rather to take my time with little sips, to taste not only the tea, but also the taste of slowing down, of conversation, of simplicity.

Bodee puts down his teacup and smiles at me.

I put my teacup down too, and say, "I'm guessing that there are no drive-thru tea shops?"

Bodee pretends to shudder.

I break off a piece of the buttery biscuit and ask him how he gained such an appreciation of tea.

"Ah, a wonderful story that takes me back quite some years," he begins. "My wife Shirley and I had been running the Firefly Inn for close to 10 years when we had a most interesting guest. His name was Ji Hwang, and he was a Chinese businessman. He stumbled across Powatten Island after doing business in Michigan one year, when he wanted to add a few days to his business trip for some relaxation. What a nice man Ji was. His business took him all over the world, but after discovering Powatten Island he came back many, many times. Shirley and I loved when he came to stay with us. A chess player like I've never seen, I'll tell you," Bodee says, laughing. "Only beat him twice in all of those years, but even losing to him was a pleasure!"

I smile as I take another sip of my tea. "I never learned how to play chess,"

I tell him.

"Never too late to learn. A fine game it is," Bodee says, chewing a biscuit and wiping some crumbs from his jeans. "So in the morning and afternoons at the Inn, Shirley and I would put out different coffees and teas along with fresh baked pastries and fruit. Well, Ji took one look at the tea bags that were set up in our tea case, and asked if we'd mind if he brewed a pot of his own tea. Well of course we didn't mind, and in that first pot he offered a cup to Shirley and myself, and it was simply exquisite. And on his visits over the many years he came to the Firefly Inn, he would bring us wonderful teas from all over China, and he'd tell us about the places that they were from. Like this one, for instance, that we are drinking now, is from Ooyee Mountain, and it's called a blue tea because the mountain is made from blue-gray color rocks that contain many minerals."

I take a sip, and try to imagine this mountain.

"But more than teaching us about the various teas and the correct way to prepare a pot, he taught us how to really sit and enjoy a cup of tea. How to slow down and let the tea define the space, to let the tea soothe not only the taste buds, but the soul," he explains.

I take another sip, willing it to smooth my soul.

"And soon every visit he was bringing Shirley and me many kinds of tea, and before long we were preparing tea the way he taught us, and offering it to our guests in that way that Ji showed us—with reverence, with tranquility, with a slowing down and a savoring." His eyes are looking at me, but I can see that his mind is back at the Firefly Inn, drinking tea with Shirley and their guests. Then he chuckles and says, "Our afternoon tea time became so famous on the Island that guests from other inns would come just to sit over tea!" he tells me happily.

"Where is Ji now?" I ask him, eating the other half of the biscuit that I had broken off earlier.

"Don't know," he says.

"You didn't keep in touch after you sold the Inn?" I ask him.

Bodee sighs deeply and says, "No, he stopped coming about five years before we sold."

"Why? What happened? Why did he stop coming?" I ask, feeling sad, wanting Ji to be a yearly fixture at Bodee's Inn.

Bodee looks at me and is silent for a moment. Then he tells me, "We never knew when Ji was coming until he called and made his reservation, and sometimes he just popped in without one. It was always a delight to have him as our guest. Sometimes he came every year, sometimes even twice a year. Other times it could be a couple of years without hearing from him, then all of a sudden he'd turn up."

"But you must have had his address, from his credit cards, or in your records from the Inn," I say, not wanting Ji to be lost to Bodee.

"He was a world traveler, used to say wherever he had his tea was his home," Bodee tells me. "I think the last time he came to the Inn, he knew he wouldn't be back. He was getting older, and I don't know, maybe he was sick. He never let on that he wasn't well, but I think he knew this was his last visit to Powhatten Island," he says with a faraway look in his eyes.

"Why do you think he knew he wouldn't be back?" I ask him.

Bodee smiles at me and says, "You see the teacups we are drinking from, and this teapot from which we are pouring?"

I nod my head yes.

"These were Ji's teacups and teapot that he always traveled with. And that last visit he gave them to me. Told me to always take time to savor my afternoon tea."

I look at my teacup and then back to Bodee.

"Did he say anything else?" I ask him.

Bodee smiles and says, "Yes. He told me that my chess game was still in desperate need of improvement," he says, laughing, "And he was right. Thing is, I never found another chess player like Ji."

I smile at Bodee, but then my smile fades and I ask him, "Doesn't it make you sad? You never got to see him again, and you never learned what happened to him."

Bodee picks up the teapot and refills our teacups.

"Well, you know, Syd, Ji is here with us now. He has passed on his love of tea, and his understanding that drinking tea is also about creating the time to stop and sit, to reflect, to experience the moment. And in our sitting together for tea, Ji is here. He is in the tea leaves, in the teapot, in the teacups. In the conversation and in the quietness. Like the tea itself, Ji has seeped into the space created when we stop, and when we sip," he tells me—no, more like instructs me.

I'm quiet for a moment and then say, "I understand what you're saying, but don't you wonder what happened to him?"

But Bodee shakes his head and says, "What's to wonder? The details change, but the story is the same. He is either alive or dead. And if he is alive, his circumstances have changed so that he doesn't come to Powhatten Island anymore. Or he is dead, which is the eventual fate of us all. And so what is there to know? Is it helpful to wonder about the many possibilities of what happened to Ji, or is it enough to be grateful for all of the times Shirley and I were graced with his company? All that we learned from him, and all we were able to share with others through the tea we offered at the Firefly Inn during our cherished afternoons."

I look at him and say, "I suppose that's true. I mean, it's nice to think that we are drinking from his teacups. That he passed them on to you." I take another sip of tea. "I really like this Oolong tea. It has such a sweet aftertaste," I tell him, savoring the flavor on my tongue.

Bodee smiles at me and says, "Just like Ji."

Chapter Twenty-Eight

"Yes, I'll have a large hazelnut with two Sweet'N Lows," I tell the woman at the Dunkin' Donuts drive-thru. She asks me if I want anything else with that—a donut, maybe? And I want to yell, "Yes, of course I want a donut! What's not to want? Preferably a strawberry frosted with sprinkles." But instead I tell her that no, I just want the coffee.

Which is, of course, a lie.

But here's the truth. I've been feeling a little lonelier these past few weeks with Montana in India. Even though I know other devotees at the Om Guru Center, it hits me how many times I ran things that seemed strange to me at Satsang by Montana, who allayed my worries with reassurances. Sometimes I worry that there is a more questionable side to the whole Om Guru lineage, sometimes it just seems so out there, but then I realize that it is most likely my ego trying to cling to the familiar in a last ditch effort to keep me wrapped up in illusion.

At least, that's what I'm told.

But as I am wavering a little in my spiritual quest, Gary pounced on this opening last week with reasons why I must go to services on Rosh Hashanah. I tried to explain to him how our synagogue offered not one iota of spirituality for me, that I experienced the prayer book as dry as the Maxwell House *Hagaddah* we used at Passover. But Gary told me that was beside the point. "We're Jewish, and these are the High Holidays," he said simply.

The woman hands me my coffee and I drive out of the drive-thru thinking back to that conversation and what unfolded next. It was later that afternoon at yoga, and I was talking to Janet Rosenbaum, a woman I had met in earlier in the summer. Luxuriating in the cool lobby following our blistering hot yoga class, I told her about my predicament. I knew that she meditated and followed a spiritual path, so I figured maybe she could tell me how she deals with her husband or other people challenging her decision not go to synagogue.

" Oh, but I love going to synagogue," Janet told me as she sat on the couch putting on her socks and shoes.

I stared at her, dumbfounded.

"I—err—I just figured—I mean, I know you meditate and, uh—" I stammered. "I mean, I thought you went to a Buddhist center or something," I said, trying to find my balance.

Janet finished tying her shoes and looked at me, smiling. "I do, and I also go to a synagogue that really speaks to me spiritually."

I thought she must have been kidding. A synagogue that spoke spiritually? The synagogues I knew spoke culturally, politically, ethically, but not spiritually.

Janet continued, "You know, Syd, there is a beautiful spiritual tradition in Judaism, but you have to look for it. It has to be in the right place with the right teacher and the right community."

We talked together for a while, and she invited Gary and me to come with her to The House of Shalom for Rosh Hashanah. It was in a western suburb, about an hour's drive, and I was sure Gary wouldn't go for it, but at dinner that night I broached the subject.

"Why would we drive an hour when our temple is a mere ten minutes away?" he asked.

"You're always talking about our people wandering in the desert for forty years before they could enter the Promised Land, so what's an hour?" I answered.

"Look, Syd, we pay our annual dues to our temple and we get our High Holy Day tickets for services. We don't need to make this more complicated."

I scooped a forkful of tofu and rice and popped it in my mouth.

"Dr. Seuss once said, 'Sometimes the questions are complicated and the answers are simple,'" I shot back.

Gary took a bite of his burger, using his napkin to wipe away some ketchup that had gathered in the corner of his mouth. "So now you've gone from quoting the guru to Dr. Seuss? I can't tell if this is progress or not."

Seeing my lips tighten in frustration, Gary told me that even if he wanted to give me the simple answer and go with me to The House of Shalom, we didn't have High Holy Day tickets to get into the services there. I explained to him that Janet said they don't have tickets for the service—anyone can come and all are welcome.

That made Gary even more wary of the temple, claiming he'd never heard of such a thing, reminding me of an episode of *Curb Your Enthusiasm* where

Larry David is standing in front of the temple for the High Holy Day service trying to buy a ticket from members of the congregation, resembling a Cubs' fan outside of Wrigley Field looking for a scalper.

I SIP my coffee while I maneuver my Range Rover into a long line of cars at the Mobile station, waiting to get my car inspected, and think back to Rosh Hashanah. In the end, Gary relented and we went to The House of Shalom for services. On the car ride to temple I explained to him what Janet had told me, that there were different options for prayer and reflection at the synagogue, different forms of worship going on in different rooms under the same roof.

"Sounds more like a movie theatre," Gary had said, to which I replied, "Not a bad idea considering you prefer James Bond while I'll take a romantic comedy any day."

At the temple Gary decided it was all a bit too much for him and he was going to attend the traditional Rosh Hashanah service in the main sanctuary. I sat with Janet in the smaller sanctuary in the mystic renewal service with Rabbi Jacob, a traveling rabbi who, Janet had explained to me, is a frequent teacher at their temple. I had asked her what a traveling rabbi was, because at first all I could picture was an orthodox-looking rabbi driving around town ringing doorbells and trying to sell Bibles. But she told me that Rabbi Jacob taught study groups all over the Midwest called "Torah as a Spiritual Path." When she shared this, I kept picturing the floor plant we had in our house when I was growing up called a Wandering Jew.

I move up a little in line, reminding myself that next year I should come earlier in September to get my car inspected to be ahead of the rush. I'm glad I have the large coffee to keep me company while I wait.

My mind drifts back to the service with Rabbi Jacob. I was blown away when I first walked in. The lights were low, and the chairs were arranged in a semi-circle with Rabbi Jacob sitting behind a conga drum, with green plants (though I don't believe they were Wandering Jews) flanking him, along with the same faux candles I had bought at Prana. He welcomed us with palms together at his heart center, and invited us to sit together in community while we spent the next 15 minutes in mindful meditation.

I thought I was going to *plotz*. I had to remind myself that I really was in a temple, and not back at the ashram.

After the meditation he beat the drum and the room began chanting— beautiful chants, not in Sanskrit or Hindi, but in Hebrew. The words were printed on a sheet so that everyone could follow along, though after a few rounds, just like at the Om Guru Center, the chants reverberate in your very being and the words become increasingly familiar and the room is swaying with the vibrations.

Never, and I mean never, have I seen this type of worship at a temple. Some people were standing up and swaying, their hands in the air as if reaching for God. Others had their eyes closed, radiant smiles emanating from their faces.

I know how to do this now, how to lose myself in the moment and imbibe the space. Om Guru helped teach me how.

We chanted: *Rabbah Emunatakha,* which means "The divine flow is abundantly present in our lives," and we chanted *Nayr l'raglee d'va-recha, v'ohr leen-teeva-tee,* which means "Your word is a lamp to my feet and a light to my path." We also chanted *Shalom,* which means "peace," over and over, and Rabbi Jacob instructed us to place special emphasis on the "om" part of "shalom" as the universal expression of oneness in the world.

For a moment it was no longer about temple versus ashram, and my heart relaxed in a place that went beyond "this" or "that" to simply "yes."

As I watched Rabbi Jacob chanting and drumming, I kept thinking to myself that I should ask him what *Hagaddah* he uses for the Passover Seder, because I know it's not the Maxwell House one, I know it must be rich and robust—like a good coffee, yes, but full of meaning and openings to connect to the sacred.

I TAKE another gulp of my coffee, grateful there are only three cars ahead of me now, and that Dunkin' Donuts serves their coffee so hot it stays that way for a good, long time.

I keep remembering Rabbi Jacob's talk at the service. It wasn't a sermon, like I'm used to—it was a group discussion of the First Book of Samuel about Hannah, who was married to Elka'nah. Rabbi Jacob explained that Hannah suffered because she had no children, while his other wife, Penin'nah, had many children. He told us that in Hebrew the name Hanna means "grace" and the name Penin'nah means "pearl," implying that Penin'nah was a necessary irritant to Hanna, who in the end had the ability to contribute to what was precious and beautiful. Because of the pain Hanna experienced from being barren, she cannot eat or speak. Going to the city of Shiloh for the yearly worship and sacrifice to the Lord, Hanna began weeping and praying to God for a child that she vowed she would give back to God. The priest, Eli, saw Hanna and thought she was crazy and drunk, for though she was praying to God, she was only speaking in her heart; her lips moved but her voice was not heard. When the priest accused her of drunkenness, she spoke to him out loud and told him what she was doing. Rabbi Jacob explained that in Hanna answering Eli out loud, she was literally speaking truth to power. When Eli understood, he supported her prayers and said, *"L'chi lehsalom,"* which means "go toward wholeness."

After this Hanna's face was totally transformed, even though nothing around her had changed. She was able to live out her name, for in the act of speaking her truth, she experienced and received grace. Hanna was then able to take in sustenance and was nourished both physically and spiritually. She conceived, and, as she vowed, she lent her son to the Lord. Her child was Samuel, the first prophet, and Samuel in Hebrew means "God Heard."

THE GAS station attendant knocks on my window, and I startle. I open the door, give him my registration, and walk to the little waiting room in the station. I continue thinking about the discussion that followed.

Rabbi Jacob invited us to talk about how we go about transforming, how we go about becoming who we were created to be, but haven't yet become. He asked us what it meant to live out our names. I remember thinking that maybe it was good that Gurujai didn't give me a Hindu name. Maybe it was my karma to live out the meaning of Syd Arthur, and to transform into whom I was meant to be.

MY CAR, like myself, is fresh and inspected for a New Year. I have a funny amount of time before I have to be at Satsang. I haven't been back to play Mah Jongg since that Thursday last month, and I know that soon I will have to make an appearance again so my friends won't be too frustrated with me. Glancing at the clock in my car, I decide I have time to drive to Bodee's to say a quick hello.

I pull in front of his house and walk up the porch steps and ring his doorbell. I hear footsteps, and then he answers the door.

"Hello, Syd, what a nice surprise," he says motioning me to come in. "Where's Levi?"

I follow him inside and tell him that Levi is home, that I'm on my way to Satsang at the Om Guru Center and had a little time before I had to be there.

"I hope I'm not intruding," I say.

"Not at all," he tells me. "I welcome your company."

I see Bodee is looking at the cup in my hand, and I realize I am still holding my coffee.

"Perfect!" he says. "It is past afternoon and I have already had my tea."

"And I need my caffeine to keep me going," I tell him as we take our seats in the two big wicker rockers.

Bodee tells me about his garden, and the salad he had with his early supper featuring the vegetables he picked that afternoon. I tell him how much I loved eating the food served at the ashram in the Catskills, how fresh everything was, and how delicious, but I also shared with him some things I didn't like.

I tell him how protected Gurujai was—always surrounded by her attendants, yes, but also with people who seemed to be like security guards. I tell him how she held private meetings on the grounds with the famous devotees on retreat, the actors and singers, but there was never an opportunity for anyone else to hold those private meetings with her.

"Why is that?" I wonder with Bodee, who shakes his head along with me that he doesn't know why this was so.

I take a drink of my coffee, now cold, and Bodee sits with me, just listening. I don't know why it's so easy to talk with him about things. It just is.

"Are you religious?" I ask him.

He smiles at me and tells me that he wouldn't call himself religious per se.

"You know, Syd, I think there is not enough religion in the world to unite us, but just enough to divide us, and that is something that I don't want to take part in," he explains. "But that doesn't mean that I don't believe. I do believe."

I take a last gulp of my coffee and ask him what religion he is, what he does believe in.

"I was raised as a Christian, but I wouldn't call myself a Christian now," he explains.

"What would you call yourself, then?" I ask him.

He pauses for a moment, and then looks at me intently. "Well, Syd. I guess I would call myself a Bodee," he says with a smile.

I smile along with him, because his smile is contagious. I think back to something that Scott Someone said at that "Introduction to Buddhism" class when Jodi and I were trying to attend the lecture on the Combo Diet. I remember him saying that Buddha sat under a bodhi tree when he attained enlightenment, and that the term Bodhi today refers to one who is awake or one who has attained enlightenment. I smile to myself, thinking that Bodee is pronounced just like Bodhi. I wonder if he knows that?

He clears his throat then and tells me, "There are so many people, Syd, who are searching for something. They want to feel that their life has meaning, that they are a part of something bigger than themselves. And that's fine. But so often they are searching outside for what can only be found inside. They are looking to emulate others, to be Christ-like, for example, if we are looking at the faith into which I was born. But if we're so busy trying to be someone else, how can we be who we truly are? What if Jesus was running around trying to be Moses?

I interrupt him, saying, "I get it—we wouldn't have gotten the sequel!"

He looks puzzled for a moment, and I jump in to explain. "If Jesus was trying to be like Moses, we probably wouldn't have ended up with the New Testament. We'd only have the Old."

"Yes, yes. That's what I'm saying!" he says excitedly, leaning closer to me. "We have to be who we are, live out our name, so to speak. In Judaism, the tradition in which you were born, there is a wonderful story by Rabbi Zusya, a great Chasidic master of the late 18th century. Rabbi Zusya said to his disciples:

"I fear only one question when I stand one day before the Heavenly court.

"If God should inquire of me, 'Why were you not more like Moses?'

"I will answer, 'I did not have his courage.'

"If God were to ask, 'Why were you not more like Isaiah?'

"I will answer, 'I did not have his talents.'

"If God should ask, 'Why were you not more like Maimonides?'

"I will answer, 'I did not have his genius.'

"But the truth is, God will not ask me those questions at all. God will ask a far more difficult question.

"'Zusya, why were you not more like Zusya?'"

I smile at him and say, "I love that. I've never heard that before."

Bodee presses his feet against the floor to give him momentum. I watch him rock rhythmically back and forth. I try to match his rocking, and he says, "You know, every spiritual tradition offers great wisdom. The trouble I see people getting into is when it becomes their God versus someone else's God, their rituals versus someone else's rituals, their path as the only source of redemption, the only path to liberation, and when the trappings of religion become more important than the path itself. But real spiritual awakening, it doesn't work like that," he tells me as Golden pokes his head onto Bodee's knee. Bodee stops to pet Golden and continues. "It's about this," he says.

I watch him petting Golden, waiting for him to finish his thought, to tell me what it's really about. But he doesn't say anything else. He just keeps petting Golden, who contently rests his head in Bodee's lap.

Finally I break the silence to ask Bodee to tell me what he was going to say. But he looks at me with a bewildered expression, and I think to myself that he's older—maybe his short-term memory is going? So I remind him what he was just saying, before Golden had walked over.

"You started to say 'it's about this,' but then when you started petting Golden, you didn't finish your thought."

And then Bodee is looking at me with a huge grin and laughing. I pray silently—to whom, I'm not so sure anymore—that he isn't becoming senile.

"But I did finish my thought," he tells me, scratching Golden behind the ears. When he sees I'm not following, he tries to explain. "When you are awake, Syd, awake to every moment that presents itself, then you can respond skillfully to whatever is in front of you with kindness and compassion informing your actions. And what was in front of me a moment ago? During my conversation with you, Golden came to rest against me, which I know is his way of wanting to be patted and loved. And so that is what I did. In that moment, when Golden showed his love and devotion to me, I responded by showing my love and devotion to him. And Golden couldn't care less if I go to a church, a synagogue, a temple or a mosque. He doesn't care if I go on a retreat at an ashram, if I meditate or recite Hail Marys, if I go to confession. All he cares is how I respond in the moment, in real time."

I reach over to pat Golden too, because I don't want to appear to be acting without kindness or compassion. I don't want to be seen as someone who doesn't act in what Bodee calls 'real time.' And I say to him, "I wonder if I'm getting caught in the trappings?"

Bodee smiles, saying, "Only you can be the judge of that."

I look at my watch on the same wrist as my mantra cuff bracelet, and realize that I have to get going if I'm going to be on time for Satsang tonight. I thank him once again for his company, and he tells me that he looks forward to my visits.

I stand up, picking up my now-empty coffee cup and asking where I can throw it away.

He looks at me and says that he will take it, that he will put it in the recycling. And I wince a little, because I usually only recycle the newspaper and pop cans, and I feel guilty. First Al Gore, and now Bodee.

But Bodee only smiles when he takes my coffee cup, saying, "Who knows what this cup will become in the future!"

And before I leave, he hands me some broccoli he picked earlier from his garden.

Chapter Twenty-Nine

"I don't get why they have to wear those little skirts," Jodi says. "You'd think that with the women's movement, field hockey would have thrown those plaid monstrosities in the fire along with their bras and invested in some cute running shorts, you know?"

We both drink our lattes while we watch Melanie at her field hockey game.

I watch the girls running all hunched over with their sticks, trying to score a goal by hitting the yellow ball into the net. "This is an orthopedist's nightmare," I say, thinking of the back problems these girls could develop because of the posture this game necessitates.

"Or an orthopedist's dream," Jodi counters. "Just think of all the houses, vacations and jewelry a field hockey team provides."

"GO HIGHLAND RIDGE!" the crowd of teens watching up on the bleachers yell.

"How can this be Melanie's last season?" Jodi asks. "How is it that Melanie is going to be in college next year?"

I zip my jacket, feeling the chill in the air as the sun goes down. "How is that when Melanie starts college, Rachel will already be a junior at Madison?" I say.

"And what about us—how have we become middle-aged? We were just in high school together, Syd. We were just filling out our own college applications," Jodi says nostalgically. But then she is back in the here-and-now as she screams, "That's it, Melanie—go, go, go, go!"

Melanie runs the ball down the field, makes a beautiful pass, and her teammate scores the goal. As we're jumping up and clapping, screaming things like, "Way to go, Highland Ridge, let's get this win!" I see Jodi wipe a tear from her face.

"Hey, are you okay?" I ask.

"Yeah, I'm just going to miss her so much. I can't believe that when I pass this field next year, she won't be here playing on it."

As I put my arm around her in an attempt to reassure her, I think about the tree I passed earlier in the day, the one at the intersection of Sycamore and Main Street. It's coming up on the one-year anniversary of the car crash, and the dried up bunches of flowers tied on the tree have been replaced with fresh bouquets. Brad Jenkins dead almost a year now; Kevin Mann a college freshman.

"You'll be okay. Sure, it takes some adjusting, but you're going to be fine. And I'm here for you whenever you need me." I'm looking at her with tenderness as I say these words. I'm thinking of Bodee, of his practice of seeing what is in front of him and acting with kindness and compassion in real time. And I wait to see the fruits of my effort by imagining that Jodi will respond with a big hug, telling me I'm the most understanding and best friend that a person could have.

But she doesn't.

Instead she looks at me and says, "Syd, I love you, but please understand that you're the last person I want to take advice from about Melanie leaving for college."

Okay, this is not what I was expecting. I look at her and open my mouth to talk, but she holds up her finger for me to wait.

"Listen, no offense, but after Rachel left, your way of adjusting—the yoga and the meditating and the ashram scene? Okay, that is so not for me. I'm not planning on having a mid-life crisis at all, let alone one that puts me at some guru's feet. I'm thinking that I'll take more vacations, add a Mah Jongg game in the afternoons, and see mid-day movies. And you're welcome to join me in one or all of the above," she tells me.

We hear a cheer from the bleachers on the other side of the field at the same time the crowd on our bleachers lets out a collective groan as the other team scores a goal, bringing the score to 1–1.

"Hey, I came to Mah Jongg last night," I remind her.

We hear the spirited yelling of Highland Ridge fans, and join in the screams of support.

"C'mon, girls, get hungry," we hear their coach yelling." Get hungry!"

"Yeah, speaking of hunger, what am I going to make for dinner tonight?" Jodi asks. Then she looks at me and says, "That's one thing I envy of your empty house. You don't have the pressure of the family dinner. Whatever I cook, someone is sure not to like. All you have to do is cook for you and Gary. That's easy," she says. "And you can go out anytime and not feel guilty about leaving the kids home," she adds. "That's one thing I'm looking forward to when both kids are in college."

I tell her that's true, but since becoming a vegetarian, dinners are a little tricky, and Gary and I rarely eat the same thing unless I make his favorite pasta with vodka sauce.

"Yeah, well, you brought that on yourself with this whole spiritual thing you've got going on. You make things hard for yourself."

I start to protest this last comment, but Highland Ridge has just scored again and we are all busy cheering, and then I just decide to let it go.

We're both drinking our lattes, warming our hands on the still warm cup.

"So did you have fun playing last night?" she asks.

I hesitate a moment before answering. "I did, but I gotta tell you that Barbara Cohen drives me crazy. Really, I don't know how you can stand playing with her every week." I look at Jodi and add, "I know I'm being harsh, and that it's not healthy to gossip, but I swear she stands for the opposite of what I'm striving for."

Jodi turns back to look at the game and says, "Well, she's got something going for her that you don't."

The crowd is screaming, and Highland Ridge is in position to score. We are cheering wildly, and Highland Ridge does not disappoint, making the goal and bringing the score to 3–1. As the crowd settles down I tap Jodi on the shoulder and prepare myself for what Jodi was about to say.

"What, Jodi—what does Barbara have going for her that I don't?"

And Jodi puts her arm around me and pulls me over and says, "She has every Thursday night free for Mah Jongg."

And I give her a nuggie, taking my fist and rubbing her head the way we used to do when we were kids, and we laugh until we hear the referee blow her whistle three times signaling the end of the game and the win for Highland Ridge, and then we are standing up on the bleachers cheering.

As we walk toward the field to congratulate Melanie and her teammates, Jodi drops her empty cup in the garbage, but I pull it out. "These can be recycled," I say. "There's a recycling can over there. I'll be right back."

When I return, Melanie is already telling Jodi that she's just going to go home and shower quickly, that there is a party she is going to and they'll be ordering pizza there for dinner. Jodi pulls out her cell and calls Rebecca. I'm listening to Jodi's side of the conversation and see her face soften to an immediate future she had not foreseen. When she hangs up, she tells me that Rebecca has been invited to her friend Marianne's house for dinner and a sleepover.

"No one's going to be home tonight," Jodi says. "And since I planned on them being around, or them maybe having a friend over, Dave and I made no plans. Are you and Gary around? Do you want to go out for dinner or something?"

"Yeah, sure," I say. "I'll call you when I get home. I say good-bye to Jodi, wave to Melanie and walk over to my car.

As I drive home I think again about how fast life flies by, how if you don't really open your eyes, really wake up to what is happening, you can find yourself at the end of your life asking, "Where did the time go?"

I know that Jodi thinks that this past year I've acted a little crazy, and I know that my other friends, and Gary and my parents, think so, too. But am I the crazy one, wanting to find more meaning in my life? Or is our culture itself the chief loony of the societal asylum? I mean really, when you think about it, what is it that we're told? To find happiness in buying more and more goods? To find bliss in losing weight? Doesn't there have to be something more?

Granted, I'm not convinced the Om Guru Center is the answer for me. All this talk about the grace of the guru is getting—I don't know, maybe a little stale, a little overdone.

It's sort of like all the diets I've been on. After a while you realize that maybe it's not the right meal plan for you. I'm thinking that I might want to explore something other than the Om Guru Center, but I'm committed to continuing my spiritual search. I need to fill up something within myself that can't be filled with more Mah Jongg games, trips, jewelry, clothes or weight loss. And I don't mean to put Jodi down for thinking she can find her happiness in those places. Maybe it will work for her. But at the end of the day, or at the end of my life, I don't want to find myself wearing the T-shirt I see everywhere that says *The one with the most toys wins*. I think that maybe winning, if you were to call it that, would be to live out your name, as Rabbi Jacob talked about, and become awake.

I pull into the driveway and see that Gary's car is already in the garage. I walk in the house and call, "Hi, Gary, I'm home."

"In the basement," I hear him yell back.

I hang up my coat, let Levi outside, and head down the stairs, where I see him sitting in the office at his computer. I stand beside him and give him a hug, and he reaches one hand around me without taking his other hand off the keyboard and squeezes my side.

"Oooh, you feel thin," he says, and for the first time I can remember this isn't a cause for celebration. What I detect in me instead is a little irritation. I'm searching for real meaning in my life—or maybe he didn't get the memo?

"I'm just about done with this report," he tells me, typing away.

I watch him for a moment and realize I can't blame him for focusing on my weight. It's what I've done forever. Just because I'm trying to shake up my life, I can't expect everyone to figure out where I am at a given moment, right?

"Listen, you and I are going to have dinner with Jodi and Dave tonight, is that okay?" I ask.

"Sounds great," Gary says. He finishes the sentence he's typing, presses save and then swivels around on the chair saying "all done" as he pulls me onto his lap. I let my head rest on his shoulder.

"How about Thai?" I murmur into his shoulder, breathing in his Georgio Armani cologne.

"How about sex?" he answers me.

I pick up my head and look at him, asking, "How does that even compare?"

To which he answers "I agree" as he puts his hand under my shirt, cupping my breast.

I decide that I shouldn't tell him that what I meant is how can you compare old, married sex to a delectable order of Thai rolls and curry puffs, to the exotic scent of basil fried rice?

So when he moves his head to kiss me I kiss him back, but in my mind I pretend that I am in Thailand, sitting at a bar drinking some glamorous Thai drink and wearing a long traditional Thai dress but with no underwear underneath. And this gorgeous guy comes in—

Gary picks me up and carries me into the guest bedroom downstairs and lays me on the bed. He undresses me so sensually that I decide that the gorgeous guy who has just walked into the Thai bar can be Gary—and as Gary moves his fingers expertly over my clit, I pretend that he is doing this while we are sitting in that Thai bar, his fingers sliding up my thigh under this long traditional Thai dress (I break away from my fantasy for a minute to remind myself to Google "Thai dress" later to see if there's actually a real name for them, like the Indian sari). And when this strange man, who out of love and devotion I have decided is Gary, realizes quite happily that I have no underwear on, and because we have had so many festive Thai drinks and are both quite drunk and therefore uninhibited, I let him finger me under the bar, feeling my wetness spread. The other customers at the bar are unaware of what is happening between us, and this only adds to the illicit passion.

Gary is on top of me now, and with an empty house he lets out one loud moan after another, with me following suit. And I think to myself that I have to remind Jodi of this part, that an empty house also means sex anywhere you choose, and as loud as you want.

Though I have to admit, Gary and I rarely have sex outside of the bedroom, and sometimes the groans we make while we're having sex have more to do with the meteorologist on the news in the background saying he's predicting rain for the entire weekend.

As we're getting up and walking upstairs to take a quick shower and get dressed, Gary says to me, "So you think Thai sounds good?" and for a moment I worry that the fantasy I concocted in my head I had somehow said aloud. I look at him, feeling embarrassed, until he says, "Did you make a reservation?" and I remember we are talking about Thai food, and so I tell him no, I'll call Jodi and have her make one.

AN HOUR later we are driving with Jodi and Dave to the city for an 8:30 reservation at Thai Ginger. Jodi and are discussing what appetizers we want to order as we find a parking spot a few blocks from the restaurant. As we're walking, I see a disheveled man with a tin can in his hand. "Spare some change?" he asks.

I look at him.

"Spare some change?" he asks again.

I stop to open my purse, get out some money, and drop it into his can.

"Thank you, bless you," he says.

Gary, Jodi and Dave have stopped to look back at me, and I quicken my steps to catch up with them.

"You know, Syd, those people—" Dave begins, but I cut him off.

I don't want to hear him tell me why I shouldn't give money to someone asking, so I smile at him and instead say, "I know, Dave. Those people are no different than us."

And I walk into Thai Ginger feeling an opening in my heart, and a growl in my stomach.

Chapter Thirty

As sweat drips down my face while I try to hold the Warrior Three pose, I come to a realization. You know how if you skip a day of your exercise routine it's harder and harder to get back on track? Well, it's the same with meditation. Miss a day or two and you just might stop meditating altogether.

So right now I guess you could call me a really lazy seeker. You'd think that after receiving Shaktipat this wouldn't happen, that I'd have boundless amounts of energy and would reach nirvana in no time.

I used to hit a dieting plateau—now I think I've hit a spiritual plateau.

That first week or so after the retreat, I felt energized. But lately I find myself wondering about all this devotion to this one person, this Gurujai. Is it really for real? But it feels like if you ever voice a doubt you're told that it's either your ego holding on or your karma burning up, and that in any case, by the grace of the guru you will see the light and find the riches within.

Well, I've certainly seen the riches without—the sprawling ashram, the elegance of the local center, the gift shops. Let's face it. If you're trying to merge with the Absolute, do you really need all of this stuff?

I know I sound cynical. It's just that in a way I'm feeling a little foolish, like I jumped in too fast with my eyes partially closed and my wallet open, and now I'm rethinking. I'm planning on talking to Kali after class, and guessing she would call this rethinking "discernment," encouraging me to go deeper and learn from the wisdom within.

But do I have that wisdom? I mean, I only had two out of my four wisdom teeth ever come in, and they were both impacted.

You'd think that when I came across an article about Gurujai and read an expose on the ashram—read about the sexual allegations, unsavory characters and money laundering—that I would have been devastated. I wasn't. And I wasn't sorry that I had spent these past five months involved with the Om

Guru Center. In fact, I felt like I learned a lot.

I learned that I wanted to follow a spiritual path. I discovered meditation, and a new way of looking at the world. But I also learned that this wasn't the spiritual path for me. And I discovered that while I might hunger for a wise and authentic guru, just as importantly, I have to be a wise and authentic disciple.

So now I'll continue my search a little wiser.

But what am I going to do with all of the Om Guru merchandise? I wonder if I ever do merge with the Absolute and find my bliss, if they have garage sales in nirvana?

"I UNDERSTAND what you're saying," Kali says as she rolls up her yoga mat after class, after the other yoga students have left and I've had a chance to tell her my thoughts.

"You're looking for a spiritual path that doesn't have so many rituals, isn't focused on revering a living person, doesn't have all of those deities to keep track of."

"Yeah," I say, shaking my head and redoing my ponytail. "The thing is, I know I want to follow a spiritual tradition. I just don't feel that the Om Guru lineage is right for me." Kali walks across the studio, turns down the thermostat, and heads to the stairs, motioning for me to follow her down.

We open the door at the bottom of the staircase and walk into the Prana lobby. "Ah, such bliss," I think to myself as I savor the cooler air. I go to the cubby to get my shoes and Kali follows me over. Janet is heading out and we give each other a wave.

"Syd, just don't throw out the baby with the bathwater. Your search is a noble one, and it's good to trust yourself on these matters. From what I hear you saying, you're looking for simplicity, for the essence. You should explore Zen," she tells me.

I put on my coat so I won't get too chilled by the change in temperature, and I turn to face her.

"But I don't know anything about Zen," I tell her.

And Kali breaks into a wide grin and says with exuberance, "That's perfect! If you already don't know anything about Zen, you're practically a Zen Master!"

"I don't get it," I say to her, moving to sit down on the couch.

She sits down beside me and says, "Exactly!"

"What are you talking about? I'm telling you that I don't understand."

Kali puts her hand on my shoulder and gives it a squeeze. "You don't understand. That's it. That's Zen."

When it's clear that I really don't understand, she tells me, "In Zen, there is nothing to understand, and no one to understand it. That is enlightenment."

I stand up, getting ready to go, and say, "Kali, that makes no sense. I think you've lost your mind."

She leans over and hugs me, not seeming to mind that we are both sweaty. "Syd, you are absolutely right. You are so Zen!"

I put my head in my hands and shake it back and forth. I look up to say something, to respond, but I'm so confused by the conversation I end up not saying anything.

Kali looks at me and says, "That's what Zen's all about. Losing your mind. Moving beyond words and concepts, becoming awake, enlightened. Sit here for a minute—don't leave yet."

She gets up from the couch and goes over to the front desk, taking out a brochure and walking back to me. "Here, have a look," she says, handing me the brochure. "Just about five miles down the road is a Zen center. You should go there, check it out. It's a wonderful place, truly. Go. Try. See."

I take the brochure from her, turning it over and looking at the print.

"Now don't go stuffing it in your bag and forgetting about it," Kali advises. "Honor your search. Honor your questions. Honor yourself. Go, try, and see."

I admire Kali, I trust her, and so I tell her that I'll go, I'll try, I'll see.

Chapter Thirty-One

And here it is, the end of November, and for the past month I've been going, I've been trying, and I've been seeing. I'm experimenting with Zen, with having a beginner's mind, a mind willing to let go of all the clutter of preconceived notions and beliefs about life. I'm inviting in emptiness, an only-don't-know mind, a be-here-now mind.

I like the notion that Zen is not about your rational mind—in part because I've never been the most rational person, as Gary likes to point out, but also because I feel I am changing so much, and in Zen there is room for change but without the idea of an "I."

My parents, Gary, Jodi, my other friends, they keep telling me that my mid-life crisis has been going on too long. That I should just go back to being Syd, to enjoying my charmed life the way it's always been, and I've had to push against that. Zen encourages the letting go of the construct of "I," the construct of "me" that we create for ourselves. So if there is no real Syd, maybe they'll all just stop pestering and leave "me" alone. That way, I figured, I'd have more time to sit in zazen, which is what the all-important meditation practice is called in Zen. It involves total concentration of your mind and body.

This time, as I prepared to sit zazen, I didn't have to start from scratch. After cleaning out all of my Om Guru belongings and boxing them for storage, I kept the things that I felt transferred into any meditation room, regardless of the particular spiritual tradition. Like the altar, the conch shell CD I use for timing my meditation, and the incense and candles. But I decided to put my meditation cushion in storage because, as they showed me at the Zen Center, in zazen you use round meditation cushions called zafus, and most people sit their zafus on a zabuton, a rectangular cushion that sits beneath the zafu. And I want to get this all right, so I figured I should invest in the Zen meditation cushions.

In Zen meditation I learned to sit with my eyes slightly open and focused downward. This really helps with the whole falling-asleep thing that can happen so easily in meditation.

Instead of reciting the mantra, I learned to count my breaths. I practiced opening up to the present moment, without judgment. I'll tell you, though, Zen is a stickler for sitting still no matter what. If you have an itch during meditation, don't scratch. Your knee is aching in the half-lotus position? Don't budge. The point is to be in the moment, until it changes to the next moment, and then that's where you should be. Don't push away, don't pull toward, just sit, just breathe, just be.

I tried, and was doing pretty well, I thought. But then I had this conversation with the woman on the other end of the toll-free number I was calling from the *Zensational* catalogue I picked up at the Zen Center a couple of weeks ago. It went something like this:

"Hello, this is *Zensational,* how can I help you?"

"Hi, I wanted to order a few items from your catalogue."

"Wonderful. Just give me the item numbers, please," she said.

"Okay, item 4329, and 4330—"

"One moment," she had said. "Okay, that's the zafu and the zabuton, is that right?"

"Yes," I had confirmed.

"And what color would you like that in?"

"I'll go with the black bottom and the forest green top," I told her.

"Wonderful. And what else?" she had asked.

"Well, I've been debating about splurging on the Buddha on the lotus throne," I tell her.

"A wonderful addition to any home. Can I have the item number please?"

I had paged through the catalogue to find the Buddha and then told her "B968."

"Wonderful, and what else?" she had asked.

And I said, "Boy, for a tradition that's all about nothing, there's so much to choose from."

And she had said, "Excuse me? Is there anything else I can help you with?"

And I answered, "I don't know. What else would help me reach enlightenment on the quicker side?"

To which she replied, "Just give me the item number first," and I said, "I like the little Zen sand garden with the rake," and she said, "the item number please," which I gave her. And then I told her, "I think it's okay to buy all of this because I'm not going to be attached to it, like they teach in Zen, and anyway, I know it's all an illusion, but still it's nice to have little reminders that point you toward the emptiness of nature, you know?"

But instead of talking about the Zen notion of emptiness, the profound understanding that nothing is truly solid, that all is impermanent and ever-changing, she just asked if that was all, or did I want to give her another item number.

So I told her that that was it. And then she said that because of the number of items I ordered, as a special offer I could purchase the Zen writing board for 50 percent off the original price. "It's on page 22," she had told me.

I had quickly found the page and read about the Zen writing board. It looked fun. It was a blank board sitting on a picture stand and came with a little bowl to fill with water and a paintbrush. When you wet the brush and use brush strokes on the board, the water becomes like black paint, only to disappear again in a short while, rendering the board blank again—inviting creativity and action, knowing it was only for the moment and would soon disappear to its original nature.

"Sure, I'll take that," I told her.

After she told me the total and I gave her my credit card information, I asked her when my purchases would be delivered. When she told me 2–4 weeks, I told her that I was all about Zen and being in the moment, accepting what is with patience and no judgment, but really 2–4 weeks was just too long. Couldn't I pay extra to get a rush delivery?

After she added the extra shipping cost so I could receive my order in 2–3 business days, I felt the need to tell her that I know I've contradicted the Zen philosophy by rushing an order, but she told me that customers do it all the time. And was there anything else she could help me with?

When I hung up, I realized that between the buying, the rush order, and the added deal in the end, I was being rather un-Zen like. Buying, rushing, wanting more.

It's so hard to let go of that consumer in me, you know? Like somehow to find enlightenment I need the tools of the trade for whatever path I travel. But the Buddha, he didn't have a catalogue store like *Zensational* and he became enlightened. *Maybe I don't need all of this,* I thought. But when the package came a couple of days later I was thrilled with my purchases, and decided that as long as I knew that all was subject to change, I was okay and in good shape.

At least spiritually in good shape. Physically, I have to tell you, I could be getting more exercise. Other than yoga, I've been spending my time doing kinhin, which is walking meditation in the Zen tradition. I promise you, you could do kinhin 24/7 and you would not lose weight. Trust me, it's the slowest walking I have ever seen. I think you quite possibly can gain weight from it, because whatever you would be doing instead of walking meditation, even sleeping, you'd have to be burning up more calories.

I've been to the Zen center every week, and I still can't get used to this kin-hin. It's all about breaking up the sitting meditation in order to stretch your legs and give them some relief as well as practicing mindfulness in motion. Everyone walks in a large circle, and you're supposed to synchronize your steps with the inhalation and exhalation of the breath in the slowest possible steps I've ever seen. You're supposed to feel every muscle involved with the step—how the heel touches first, then the arch of your foot, then the ball and finally, finally, the toes.

I showed Jodi how we do walking meditation, and even though she thought it was crazy, that she could never make herself walk so slowly, she is cautious about saying anything critical of my exploration of Zen. She loves Zen because the group meditation and teaching is on Tuesday afternoons and evenings, meaning that I am once again available for Thursday night Mah Jongg, and for Jodi, that's her version of bliss.

For my part, I've loved learning more about Siddhartha, the historical Buddha. Loved learning about his early life in the palace, with riches of every kind, and his decision to leave the luxury that was his life to seek enlightenment. He knew that he could spend his entire life closing his eyes to the inevitable fact of suffering and death. Could spend his entire life feasting on the finest foods, drinking the finest wines, with every possible comfort if he stayed cloistered within the palace walls. But after leaving those palace walls and seeing that in fact, life was full of suffering and eventual death for everyone, he was determined to find his own answer to life and skillful living. Siddhartha was convinced that there was a way to end suffering and to reach an enlightened state, an awakened state.

It didn't happen right away. He had to travel different paths, including living as an ascetic, sort of like a spiritual anorexic who was all about denial of the flesh. But he learned that either extreme—a life of self-indulgence like that in the palace, or a life of self-denial as practiced in the forest—was not the answer. And in the end he discovered the truth for himself, through the Four Noble Truths that Scott Someone talked about at the lecture last year, and through the Eightfold Path, the Middle Way. And under that Bodhi tree he sat still meditating as he was tempted by greed, fear, attachment, doubt, by lust and delusion. And watching it all without moving, without grasping, he put his hand down on the earth as witness to his enlightenment, to his awakening. To his realization of the way things truly are, the oneness and interconnectedness of all things.

I really like Buddha. I like the teachings, what they call the dharma, and the community of fellow practitioners, or the sangha. I like the idea that even though there is talk about the historical Buddha born Siddhartha, that the idea is more about discovering one's own Buddha nature, one's own Buddha-hood. The Buddha within. That the Buddha was just a man, that the word "Buddha" means one who is awake, and that we all have the potential to become awake.

I also think the idea of bodhisattvas is pretty cool. Bodhisattvas exemplify the ultimate form of compassion. It refers to those who become enlightened, who become awake, but rather than flowing off into this eternal state of merging and bliss, they vow to be reborn into the endless cycles of life and death so they can help others reach this enlightened state, which is what the historical Buddha did when he spent the rest of his life teaching and guiding others.

So I think I'm clicking with this whole Buddhism thing. It all makes sense. Or most of it makes sense.

I made the mistake of sharing some of my confusion over Thanksgiving this past weekend. Sharing your new spiritual seeking with family members can be challenging, but offering up your own doubts in their midst is just plain stupid, as I found out at my in-laws' Thanksgiving table down in Longboat Key.

All was going well. We met Rachel at the Bradenton airport late Wednesday night and drove to Arlene and Fred's house, where my parents would also be staying. By Thursday morning I was happily seated in front of the TV with Rachel and Gary, watching the Macy's Thanksgiving Day Parade. The weather was beautiful, and the Gulf of Mexico provided lovely, gentle waves that I could hear lapping and match with my breathing as I had sat for early meditation on the guest bedroom deck that morning.

Once again Nancy, Evan, Joshua, and Jenny were spending Thanksgiving at their friends' time-share in St. Martin, so that left just Gary, Rachel and me, along with my parents, at Fred and Arlene's. I was happy to be in Longboat, happy to be enjoying the warm Florida sunshine. My mom was thrilled for us to all be together, and when she arrived early Thursday she came in bearing her brisket and lasagna and insisting that she help Arlene in the kitchen despite the fact that Arlene was adamant that she had everything under control.

And everything was very pleasant. Rachel was the center of attention, what with Gary and me and two sets of doting grandparents. She was happy to chat with everyone, knowing that tomorrow Tammy was flying in so they could spend the weekend together. There was so much conversation that there was really no need for me to bring up my spiritual quest at Thanksgiving dinner.

So why bring up Zen? I don't know. I was in the moment, and I guess I forgot that I wasn't at the table with a group of devotees, or the Zen sangha, with Montana, Kali or Janet Rosenbaum.

"I'm really enjoying learning about Zen," I said after Rachel told us about her philosophy class. "It's really more a philosophy than a religion," I had added.

Silence.

"Have you ever read anything about Zen?" I asked. When there was no answer, just some headshaking, I had said, "That's fine, really, because you can't really teach Zen through words."

"Hmmph," my father had grunted. "A philosophy you can't explain through words is no philosophy."

My mother, wanting to keep the tone light, had said, smiling, "Well, at the bookstore I always see books about Zen. Some are even bestsellers, so there must be something Zen conveys through words."

Then I told everyone that I wanted to share a story I heard at the Zen Center that really explains Zen.

"Harvard was offering a class on Zen. For the final exam, the students were handed those Blue Books to answer the question *What is Zen?* It was spring, and the classroom windows were open. One student picked up his Blue Book and instead of writing anything or answering the final exam question, he made his Blue Book into a paper airplane, stood up, and flew the airplane out the window. He got an "A."

"I wish I were taking that class instead, Rachel had said. "It sounds easier than learning about Kierkegaard."

My father said, "You're sure this was at Harvard?" and my mother had said, "At least you're not involved with the crazy guru anymore. If you had stayed there any longer, your father, Gary and I would have had to hire one of those deprogrammers to get you out of that cult."

"It's not a cult. It's just not for me," I told them.

"On the campus kiosk by the Union I saw a flyer for an Om Guru meeting," Rachel said.

I swear you'd think a bomb had just exploded at the table, sending the green bean casserole flying. "STAY AWAY!" my mother implored, grabbing Rachel's hand.

Even Gary was alarmed by my mother's intensity. "Estelle, calm down," he had said. "Rachel's not worrying about finding her inner true self, are you, honey?" he asked sarcastically.

Rachel had smiled and said, "No, but a boyfriend would be nice."

And Arlene had said, "Why I bet they're lining up at your door, a beautiful girl like you."

"They'd be crazy not to," Fred had agreed.

"Speaking of crazy," Arlene began, "I don't like Gary having to worry about you going to those strange places. It's not right. Gary works hard all day, and when he comes home you should be there to support him, cook him a meal."

"Mom," Gary had interrupted, trying to break her momentum.

"No, darling, it's true. I've talked with your father about it too, right, Fred?"

But Fred had said, "Arlene, not now. Let's just enjoy. Look, Syd and Gary are happy. Let's not mix in."

But Arlene continued, telling me that it wasn't right that I cooked so little these days for Gary. That just because I've become a vegetarian, it doesn't mean I shouldn't be making Gary a roasted chicken or a leg of lamb.

"Actually, tofu is really healthy," Rachel had offered, but Arlene wasn't willing to give up so easily.

I tried to tell her that I do cook, and Gary tried to explain that really, everything was fine.

But then Arlene asked Gary when the last time I cooked him some beef stew was and Gary had said, "Mom, Syd never cooks me beef stew because I've always hated beef stew."

Arlene said, "No, you love beef stew. I used to make it for you all the time," and she was so busy insisting on this that she missed the eyes that rolled between Gary and his father.

When Arlene had calmed down—and passed more turkey to Gary, saying, "you better eat it here while you can"—she asked me, "Would it kill you to make him a chicken?"

And I had said, no, that it wouldn't kill me, but it sure would put a damper on the chicken's day. Then I remembered the Zen principle of connectedness, that what hurts me would hurt someone else, so be kind in this world.

So I tried to reassure Arlene that Gary was eating well despite my personal decision to become a vegetarian, that the fridge was stocked with animal products for him, that it wasn't like I wouldn't sit with him at the table while he was eating his grilled steak.

"Following Zen principles, or any philosophy, can be challenging in real life situations," I explained. "Just like the Buddha taught, you have to find the balance, the Middle Way." Then I told them about a Zen Monastery in New York and the dilemma they faced.

"One of the greatest tenets in Buddhism is the prohibition against causing harm or killing anything. Well, at this monastery there was a roach problem.

Now in Zen centers you sit on the floor for meditation and for the teachings. And you don't wear shoes in the centers. So having a roach problem was difficult. But they couldn't call the exterminator to get rid of the roaches, because that would violate such an important tenet."

Rachel put down her fork and said, "Mom, this is not a story to be shared while we're eating."

"Just let me finish," I said. "Eventually the problem got worse, and fewer and fewer people were showing up as a result. So in the end they decided to call the exterminator to get rid of the roaches so people would come to the monastery again."

My mother-in-law said that if a Zen monastery could break their own law and kill the roaches, why don't I let her help me plan a nice weekly menu for her son that includes meat, fish and fowl?

My final mistake was sharing with them the very confusing part of Zen for me, the koan practice. Koans are like Zen riddles that can't be answered by the rational mind. Instead they must be understood intuitively. Koans are tools to help you move through the stages toward enlightenment. And I think I need a tutor.

So I started telling everyone about koan practice at the Zen center. About some of the more famous koans, like "What is your face before your parents were born?"

I think I was discovering that night that I could probably write a book about how to stop the flow of conversation without really trying (or being mindful), but at the time I just couldn't help myself. I was thinking of all the Zen questions that had been floating around in my mind, and out from my lips they came.

"Like there's this famous koan, 'Mu.' A Zen master asked this guy Joshu, 'Does a dog have Buddha-nature?" and Joshu replied, 'Mu!'"

My father had said, "Someone should have taken Joshu to a farm when he was little. So that he'd know that a cow says 'moo' and a dog says 'arf, arf.'"

So I explained to my dad that it wasn't spelled "moo," but "Mu." That in Chinese, "Mu" means "no-thing."

And dad had said, "and that makes a difference because?" But when he saw that I looked upset, he said to me, "Okay, princess, give me another one. Throw another koan at me."

And so I said, "Okay, this is a really famous Zen koan. See if you can come up with an answer without your rational mind."

My mother was leaning with her elbows on the table, looking excited by this new game. My mom is a game show nut, and I think she saw this as the next game show hit.

I looked at my dad and said, "What is the sound of one hand clapping?"

He looked at me for a moment, and then smiled and said, "That's easy. The sound of one hand clapping? On Broadway they call that 'a flop.'"

And with that I knew there would be no encore from me. I willingly let the conversation move to other topics, without me taking starring role. That is, until Arlene was talking about the high divorce rate and the sanctity of marriage and looked at me and said, "And I remember a little bit about the story of the Buddha. Didn't he leave his wife and son to go look for salvation?" she had asked.

I had answered, "Well, Jesus was more about salvation. Buddha was more about enlightenment."

Arlene had shaken her head and said, "Either way, Buddha just up and left his wife and son for his own selfish reasons. That's not a *mensch,* Rachel. That's not the kind of husband you want."

"Well, he left to discover the Truth for the benefit of all humanity," I offered. "He had a good reason."

But Arlene only looked at me, saying, "Tell that to Mrs. Buddha."

And my mother, trying to keep things light and breezy, said, "How could I have forgotten this!" She jumped up from the table and went to her purse, and came back carrying a little red book.

"I found this at the bookstore last month, after you told me you were interested in Zen. I thought you'd like it," she said.

She handed it to me, and I looked at the title. It was called *Zen Judaism: For You, A Little Enlightenment,* by David M. Bader. I showed everyone the cover, and we all laughed at the figure of a man with a yarmulke and tallit sitting in the lotus position. I looked through and read a few selections, to everyone's delight. Even Arlene's.

Here's one of my mother's favorites:

"Let your mind be as a floating cloud. Let your stillness be as the wooded glen. And sit up straight. You'll never meet the Buddha with posture like that."

And one of my father's favorites:

"Thou shalt not bow down before false idols. You may, however, rent a Buddha statue for your Zen-theme bar mitzvah."

And one of Arlene's favorites:

"There is no escaping karma. In a previous life you never called, you never wrote, you never visited. And whose fault was that?"

And one of Fred's favorites:

"The Torah says, 'Love thy neighbor as thyself.' The Buddha says there is no 'self.' So maybe you are off the hook."

One of my favorites:

"If there is no self, whose arthritis is this?"

One of Gary's favorites:

"Wherever you go, there you are. Your luggage is another story."

And one of Rachel's favorites:

"To practice Zen and the art of Jewish motorcycle maintenance, do the following: Get rid of the motorcycle. What were you thinking?"

And as we read this little book over dessert, we were all laughing and having so much fun I realized that Zen had done its Zen-like thing. We were like the jolly, fat Buddha called Maitreya, the laughing Buddha, with big smiles and, as a result of our huge dinner, even bigger bellies.

And in the end I had realized that even though early on in the evening I may have sort of put my foot in my mouth (which I actually might really be able to do with my newfound flexibility from yoga) by bringing up my spiritual quest and my exploration of Zen, it actually turned out to be an evening of Thanksgiving.

And Arlene got to enjoy watching her son feast on turkey and brisket, her idea of the yin and the yang of life.

Chapter Thirty–Two

Gary pushes through the front door, almost running me over as I straighten the rug in the foyer. He is slick with sweat from his run, his Under Armour shirt clinging to his stomach, outlining the six-pack abs that come way too easily to him. I console myself that his body did not bear a child. The soft flesh of my stomach speaks of carrying our daughter for nine months. Well, that and white raspberry chocolate cheesecake.

"Syd, what time is it?" he asks, trying to catch his breath. "I'm trying to shave off a little time on my run."

I look at my watch, and then remember that it won't tell me the time. I bought it in Longboat Key at the cutest little boutique. It's a great watch with a wide brown leather band and big round face. But the face is colored in like the shores of a beach, with water and sand, and instead of the numbers and hands to keep the time, across the face of the watch it just says NOW. Which is really cute and quite a statement, but if you actually need to know what time it is, you're out of luck. I walk into the kitchen to see the clock and tell him it's 8:34. He follows me and tells me that he still has his speed.

Leaning against the fridge, glass of water in hand, he asks me what I'm going to do on this Saturday morning. I tell him that I have some errands, and that I wanted to go and see a movie this afternoon, did he want to join me?

"Sure," he says. Before turning to go upstairs for his shower, he asks me if I picked up his dry cleaning, and I tell him that no, I haven't had a chance yet. Gary walks back over to the fridge and pauses in front of the door. He puts his finger on a note card held up by a Bucky Badger magnet where I have written the words to a Zen poem. And he reads it out loud to me.

"Sitting quietly
Doing nothing
Spring comes

and the grass grows by itself."
"I know, isn't that beautiful?" I ask.

"It may be beautiful, but sitting quietly and doing nothing is not going to pick up my suits now, is it?" And with that, he turns to go upstairs.

AT THE movie, as Gary and I are buying our popcorn, I look at the oversized packages of Milk Duds and M&Ms and think of this visiting Zen teacher, or roshi, who came to the center last week. He was a Korean Zen master, and he talked a lot about Buddhism becoming so popular in the West. One of the things he talked about was the tendency for Westerners to turn everything into a commodity—even religion, where the trappings of spirituality have become a marketing sensation. I immediately thought of *Zensational* catalogue, and all of the things that I bought to accompany me on my Zen path, all that I had purchased during my involvement with Om Guru. All of the things that are sold at the ashrams and centers and funky little boutiques like the one in Longboat.

"It's all dharma candy," he had said with his heavy accent.

At first my ears perked up, wanting to know more about this dharma candy—wondering what was it, where could I buy some, and was it like a truffle?

But as this old Korean Zen master kept talking, I understood what he was saying. Dharma candy wasn't a treat to eat. Rather, he was referring to the enticements we get caught in, the glittery beckoning merchandise, the trappings of spiritual traditions—the necklaces, bracelets, and clothing, the statues and knickknacks, the accessories of a spiritual life that, like candy, may be tempting, but don't come close to the true nourishment of a spiritual path.

I follow Gary into the theatre. While Gary uses his BlackBerry to check his emails, to be in constant technological communication, I think back to last Monday, when Levi and I had stopped by Bodee's to enjoy the beauty and simplicity of slowing down and communicating face to face.

As we sat drinking black tea by the roaring fire, we talked. Levi tried to entice Golden to play, but Golden just lay at Bodee's feet, feeling the warmth of the flames.

I continued telling Bodee about what I was learning in Zen, which I had been sharing with him during my visits over the past couple of weeks. And I told him about the Zen Judaism book that my mom had bought me. "I memorized the perfect one for you," I had told him.

"Drink tea and nourish life. With the first sip, joy. With the second, satisfaction. With the third, Danish."

As he chuckled, I told him that I had bought him a few things from the store when I had gone shopping earlier. I took from my grocery bag some

Danish, and a small crate of clementines. He smiled such a radiant smile, and I felt so at home in his small, simple house, sipping tea and watching the flames in the fire dance.

Later that day, before leaving, I told him that while I loved going to the Zen Center, loved learning about and practicing Zen meditation, that I still wasn't sure if this was IT for me. If maybe there wasn't another Buddhist path that I should explore.

Bodee had looked at me and said, "Learning to know yourself, to be awake to life, you must know when to listen to the stirrings of your heart and when to take action or inaction. Know what is necessary, and what is distraction."

I had told him that he sounded like a Zen master, answering a question with a more puzzling riddle.

He smiled at me and said that what had guided him in this life was to be mindful to what is right before him, to honor the seasons and cycles of life, to live with an open heart, and with compassion. "That is all there is," he had said, "and that is everything."

As I left that afternoon, I drove home with Levi thinking about Bodee's words. And I checked my watch to see if I had time to pick up the dry cleaning, or had the dry cleaners already closed? But when I looked at my watch, the time it told me was NOW, and what came to my mind was the chant that concludes a day of Zen practice:

>"Let me respectfully remind you
>Life and death are of supreme importance.
>Time swiftly passes by and opportunity is lost.
>Each of us should strive to awaken. Take heed.
>Do not squander your life."

And I vowed to take heed and went home to meditate, putting off once again picking up Gary's dry cleaning.

Sitting in the movie beside Gary, munching on my popcorn, I watch the images flash across the movie screen, watch the drama and the laughter and the tears, and I think about that Zen chant, the admonition not to squander your life and to wake up.

I don't want to live out the rest of my life like an actor in a movie, reading the lines I've been fed. I don't want to live in the illusion that all of this is real and solid. I want to touch the edge of life, twirl in the fullness of the empty nature of all things, dance that cosmic dance and leap into the interconnectedness of all things. I want to step out of the movie screen and let go of the costume and greet the world and myself by becoming alive and awake.

But when the movie ends and Gary asks me if I liked it, I don't know how to tell him my realizations, so I just say, "Yeah, it was good," and Gary says, "I liked it too," and we walk out of the theatre following the crowd out into the mall.

I want to tell Gary, "We need to wake up!" But I don't know how, so I instead I just ask him if he remembers where we parked.

Chapter Thirty-Three

Hanukkah and Christmas are only a week away, and then, another New Year. I can remember last year using the holidays to motivate and monitor my dieting attempts, my goal of weight loss. Well, this year I'm all about gaining—gaining wisdom, insight, and ultimately, enlightenment.

But just like my dieting attempts, I'm still looking over my shoulder to see if there's maybe a better way, an easier way, a faster way. Atkins, Weight Watchers, South Beach. This year I'm learning the tenets of Om Guru, Zen, and now here I am driving to an all-day seminar in Milwaukee on Tibetan Buddhism. Just to check it out. See what it's about.

There was a flyer on the announcement board at the Prana Yoga Center, and I thought, *why not?* Apparently the teacher and best-selling author is an American lama of the Tibetan Buddhist tradition who is now called Lama Ningma. He looked nice in the picture, this big American in Buddhist robes.

Fortunately the day is crisp and clear and the traffic is light on this early Sunday morning. As I drive down Interstate 94 I find myself feeling happy and free. I'm getting the hang of this spiritual seeker business. No longer do I worry about traveling alone, or walking into a center or a talk by myself. Siddhartha did it, and so can Syd Arthur. That's what I keep telling myself.

I find the church where the seminar is being held. It's old and gothic looking, and inside the chapel is filled with stained glass windows depicting scenes from the New Testament—images of Jesus and Mary, of crucifixion and salvation. The pews are about three-quarters full, and I sit down on a bench about halfway from the front.

On the stage sits Lama Ningma. Despite his size, which is tall and broad, he is flexible, sitting in a full lotus position as he meditates. He has tight curly hair and a pleasant face. There is something familiar about him, though I can't put my finger on it. Maybe I knew him in a past life in Tibet. Maybe we were yak herders together.

There is a mix of people here—the Birkenstock crowd, the artsy folks, and just your average Joe types who look like they could be on their way to Starbucks after the seminar, or maybe they just came from their kids' basketball game.

We wait for Lama Ningma to begin the seminar as the clock ticks past nine, which is when this was supposed to start. But he doesn't. He just continues to sit in meditation, and who are we to stop him? He's probably on a different level of consciousness that maybe comes with a different time zone, maybe Cosmic Standard Time.

At 9:15 he very quietly starts to chant, in Tibetan, I'm guessing, and his voice is a low, soothing baritone that vibrates throughout the room. When he finishes his chant he spends a few minutes looking around the room, taking everything in.

He clears his voice and I find myself anticipating his words, willing him to impart the insight of Tibet to us Midwesterners. As he smiles, this is how he starts.

"What did the Dalai Lama say to the hot dog vendor in Central Park? 'Make me one with everything!'"

There are appreciative chuckles, and then he says, "So did you hear about the new Buddhist vacuum cleaner? It comes with no attachments!"

More appreciative laughter. I'm thinking that Margot could have signed him up for the country club comedy night.

"That's what Buddhism is really all about—interconnectedness and oneness, all the while understanding impermanence and nonattachment."

Then Lama Ningma begins talking about his own spiritual quest, and what led him to become an American lama. He explains that he was born in Philadelphia, and as he's talking, I realize that we are probably about the same age.

"Before I became a lama my name was Harold Nussbaum, and I was a pretty typical kid, for the most part. Except I played football, which is not typical for a nice Jewish boy, as my mother repeatedly pointed out throughout my childhood. In fact, when I was just a little kid I used to hound her to let me play, and she would tell me, 'Harold, Jews don't play football.' So when I went to talk with the coach in fifth grade, I told him my dilemma. I explained how much I wanted to play football, but that being Jewish, it was against the law. Because that's how I heard it. I figured that there was some law on the books that my mother was talking about that restricted Jews from playing. And the coach looked at me and told me that it didn't matter if I was Jewish, I could play football, and he gave me a permission slip to have my parents sign.

"Well, you can imagine my mother's response when I told her that she was mistaken. That the coach had said that Jews could play football, there was no law forbidding it. She looked at me and said, 'Harold, you don't understand. It's too dangerous. You like football so much? Become a sports agent.' But my father, he said, 'let him play,' and I did. From fifth grade all the way through high school, and my mother, she learned to let go of her worry, about the 'what ifs' in life. To let go of her preconceived ideas.

"And I tell you this because this is what Buddhism is all about. Letting go of the preconceived notions, of the fears that hold us back. In fifth grade I was already learning that you have to hold firm to who you truly are, and what your yearnings are about, because even those who love you the most will hold you back because of their own fears, their own beliefs."

I flash back to my comparative religion course, my *I Ching* class. Of how I stopped pursuing these interests when my parents and Gary discouraged it. And then it hits me—I know why Lama Ningma looks so familar. When I look at him, part of me sees Harold Nussbaum, the primordial Jewish boy that every Jewish mother wants her daughter to date. "What a success," I can hear my mother whispering. "A best-selling author." But what I'm seeing is a wise Buddhist teacher telling me about Avalokiteshvara, the bodhisattva of compassion, and about the Tibetan Buddhist path to enlightenment.

And one of the best things I hear him talk about is the Tibetan Mantra of Compassion, which he has us chant with him to a beautiful melody. The Tibetan words are *Om Mani Padme Hum* and the translation is "The jewel is in the lotus." How Lama Ningma explains it is like this: The lotus flower blossoms in the murkiest of waters. We are like that lotus flower. Within each of us is that jewel, that blossom. And even though our lives may be filled with murkiness, at any point we have the potential to bloom. Our hearts can open and flower even in the darkest of times.

Later, as the day is coming to a close, I see that someone has wheeled out a table full of Tibetan wares. There are bright colored Tibetan prayer flags and turquoise earrings. My eye catches on an ornate bell resting beside an odd-shaped object of some sort. The objects intrigue me, so I pick them up.

The woman who has wheeled out the table says to me, "Beautiful, aren't they? Wonderful meditation tools."

I smile, because I don't really know what they are used for in meditation, but since I have yet to let go of my ego, I'm too embarrassed to ask her their function.

"Yes, lovely," I say. Then, thinking about my most recent purchases from *Zensational* catalogue and how I'm trying to follow the Buddha's teachings of not desiring and craving so much, I think to myself that maybe I'll just buy the bell. I could ring it before meditation and feel all Tibetan-like, as if I'm meditating in a cave high in the Himalayas instead of in an office-turned-meditation room in Highland Ridge. But I don't really need that other thing.

"I'll take this," I say, handing her the bell and opening my purse to dig out my wallet.

The woman looks at me with a puzzled expression. "You want this, too," she says, picking up the object that had been sitting beside the bell.

"No," I counter, feeling like I'm finally learning to want less, finally learning about letting go of too much attachment. "Just this," I say, handing her the bell.

Her quizzical look becomes soft as she tells me that the two are only sold together.

"What is this, a buy-one-get-the-other-free?" I ask.

"Do you know what this is?" she asks, not unkindly.

I hold the bell and ring it.

"This is not an ordinary bell," she explains. "This is a bell—" she holds out her hand for me to give it to her, "and a dorge." She picks up the other object. "The bell and the dorge are used in many Tibetan rituals. The bell symbolizes the feminine principle, the wisdom of emptiness, and the dorge—what the Tibetans call the *vajra*—represents the masculine principle, that of compassion expressed through skillful means."

She picks up the dorge and brings it to the bell, which she gently hits to produce a chime. "The union of these two principles is the enlightened mind," she explains. "You can't have one without the other—that would be like cultivating wisdom without compassion, or compassion without wisdom. Traveling the spiritual path to enlightenment, you need both. You need compassion and wisdom." She holds up both and brings them together again. They come as a pair.

I'm sold.

Driving home from Milwaukee late that afternoon, my bell and dorge wrapped in tissue in the passenger seat, I think of the things I learned today. The mantra of compassion, the history of Tibet and the Tibetan people, the wisdom, compassion and philosophy of non-violence that are the cornerstone of Tibetan Buddhism and the Dalai Lama's teachings.

And I am salivating at an interesting little nugget that is truly proving food for thought. When Lama Ningma was talking about his time in the Himalayas, he told us about his everyday life there, and about his fondness for yak burgers. That gave me the courage to raise my hand and ask the question of all questions.

"How could you eat yak meat? Aren't all Buddhists vegetarians?" And Lama Ningma had answered that no, not all Buddhist are vegetarians, and not all Buddhist monks are vegetarians either.

"Some are and some are not. Tibet is an arid, dry land where it is quite difficult to grow crops for any sustainability, so meat is considered a staple." He went on to explain that as a rule, Buddhists who are not vegetarians prefer to eat meat, then chicken, and last, fish. The reasoning is that one yak, say, or one cow, can offer his life to feed many people. A chicken, while giving his life, can only feed a few people, and a fish, even fewer.

So when I get home that night I walk into the house and yell for Gary to come down and get his coat, I want to take him out to dinner.

As we get in the car I drive to Delmonico's, this wonderful steak house a few towns over. Gary is looking at me quizzically but not saying anything as we are escorted to a table for two. I order a glass of merlot, Gary gets a scotch, and then the waiter comes back to take our order.

"I'll have the Caesar salad, and the New York strip with Béarnaise sauce, medium rare, please."

Gary puts his order in and then takes my hand and asks me, "Is this your way of telling me that your midlife crisis is over, and that you're done with this whole spiritual quest thing?"

I take his hand and tell him, "I am not having a midlife crisis. I've learned that just because Harold Nussbaum's mother told him he couldn't play football because he's Jewish, he can. And just because I grew up like a princess, it doesn't mean that I have to stay sheltered behind the palace—I can follow a path toward the jewel of enlightenment. And just because I'm practicing Buddhism, it doesn't mean that I have to be a vegetarian."

The waiter brings our dinner over and I bite into the juiciest New York strip I have ever had. I look at Gary and say, "I may not have reached nirvana yet, but I'm telling you, this is heaven." And I take another bite.

Chapter Thirty-Four

"I hope they're wrong about the snowstorm we're supposed to get," Jodi tells me as she gets in the car for our after-holiday sales shopping excursion. "I'm sick of snow already."

I pull away from her house and remind her that it's only the second week of January. I drive down Main Street and take the exit onto the highway.

"Thank God Dave and I just made reservations for Barbados next month. I'm getting too old to be in this cold weather," Jodi says as she turns up the heat. "When are you and Gary going to Aruba?" she asks me.

I tell her we're planning on going in the spring, when work isn't so crazy for Gary.

"Well, at least you should go visit your parents in Florida for a handful of weekends. You look pale. You need a tan."

I get off the exit ramp for the mall and drive to the parking lot looking for a good parking space.

"Nobody points anymore," Jodi says to me. "What's gotten into people? How hard is it for someone walking to their car to point and tell you where they'll be pulling out from? It's just common courtesy."

"Compassion in action," I say.

"You turn everything into a Buddhist dictate," Jodi tells me.

I spot a space that's not close, but not all that bad, and pull in. We walk up to the Nordstrom's entrance and pull the door open.

"Let's look here first," Jodi suggests. And we do.

We look at Nordstrom's, and then Saks, Neiman's, and finally Victoria's Secret. I ask Jodi if she remembers when we used to buy all of the sexy lingerie as we carry our Pink sweatpants up to the register. We peek into Bloomingdale's and then we carry our shopping bags into the Cheesecake Factory, where I order blackened chicken fettuccini.

"So how are you liking breaking your diet?" Jodi asks me.

I tell her that I'm not on a diet, and she says, "No, I mean breaking the whole vegetarian thing," and I tell her that I think I've discovered that my true nature is as a carnivore.

We spend most of the lunch talking about Melanie's college applications, about where she's been accepted, and from where she's still waiting to hear.

"And when all of this is done, when Melanie is really away at college, and then Rebecca will be gone before I know it, what am I going to do?"

I smile and sit patiently with Jodi. She talks about this every time we go out now, and I want to support her, want to be there for her.

"Change is inevitable," I tell her. "So just open to that. Live in the moment." I think that I'm giving her good advice, sage advice.

But Jodi takes a bite of her chicken sandwich and says, "I'm not about to just live in the moment. I need a plan. Dave and I are thinking of buying a place in Florida. I mean, once Rebecca is in college, what's the point of staying here for the winter? Who needs all this cold?"

I take a bite of my pasta and say, "If you find your center, it doesn't matter what's going on outside of you—whether it's hot or cold, whether you're north or south."

Jodi puts down her sandwich and looks at me.

"You know, Syd, I love you, but I liked you better when you were superficial, you know? You were just more fun. And you know what else? I miss dieting with you. It's bad enough to diet, but dieting without your best friend just plain sucks. Tell me again why it is that your New Year's resolution is not to diet anymore. I don't get it."

I tell Jodi again about why I'm letting go of dieting. "I've been talking about it with Bodee—"

Jodi interrupts me. "Yeah, and that. Don't you think it's kind of odd to be taking dieting advice from an old man that you drink tea with?"

I smile at her, thinking about Bodee. He has taught me so much in his simple, humble and knowing way. He asked me once why it was that I didn't think I could trust my own body, its own wisdom, to guide me in knowing when I'm hungry, what I'm hungry for, and when I'm full and have had enough.

"If you're searching for your own True self, for the Buddha nature and the wisdom within you to guide you toward your own enlightenment, do you think you have to turn to someone else to tell you how to nourish the container of your soul?" Then he reminded me of Lin-Chi's dictate: "When hungry eat your rice, when tired close your eyes. Fools may laugh but wise men will know what I mean." And that's what I've been doing, following my stomach cues. Trusting myself.

I tell Jodi this and she says to me, "This from the woman I've spent many an evening with eating raw cookie dough and pepperoni pizzas."

"Like I said, Jodi. Everything changes. Even my eating."

When the waitress comes over to see if we want dessert Jodi says no, but I order a slice of the cookie dough cheesecake with a cup of coffee.

"See!" Jodi says when the waitress walks away. "You can't trust yourself—you're ordering cheesecake! You do remember how many calories are in that, right?"

"I do. But I'm hungry for something sweet and creamy, and that sounds good to me. So I'm going to eat it without guilt and without judgment. I'm going to eat it mindfully, and enjoy the sweetness of the moment," I explain, thinking fondly of the small box of chocolates Gurujai had given me.

"A moment on your lips, a lifetime on your hips," Jodi quips.

"You gotta let in the sweetness," I tell her as the waitress brings our coffees and my dessert.

Jodi reaches over for the Sweet'N Low and says, "See, I do let in sweetness." She empties the artificial sugar and stirs it in her coffee.

I take a bite of my cheesecake and sigh with delight.

"That looks really good," Jodi says.

"Are you hungry for something sweet?" I ask her.

She tells me she's always hungry for something sweet.

But I say, "You know what I'm discovering, Jodi? I'm not always hungry for something sweet. I'm not insatiable. Once I decided that I could listen to my stomach and eat what I'm hungry for, it turns out I'm hungry for a whole bunch of things at different times. Sometimes salad, sometimes pizza, sometimes fruit and sometimes cheesecake." I take another bite.

"The real question, Jodi, is what are you hungry for?"

She picks up her fork and takes a bite. "Oh my God, that is sooo good," she coos.

"Help yourself," I say, pushing the plate between us. We sit in silence enjoying the cheesecake, the sweet texture on our tongues. After a few more bites I realize that my stomach is full and I put down my fork.

"What, you're not going to finish it?" Jodi asks.

"I'm full, I've had enough," I tell her, feeling comfortably content.

"Since when did fullness figure in when you're breaking a diet?" Jodi asks.

"But that's just it, Jodi, I'm not breaking a diet. If nothing is forbidden any longer, there are no restrictions to break. When I know I can eat whenever I'm hungry, and eat what I'm hungry for, I find myself in a calm place, in a really good place. A place where I'm no longer suffering."

"I don't know, Syd, I don't think I could ever trust myself to eat without restrictions. I need those rules."

The waitress brings the check over, and we both open our wallets to pay.

"If you think about it, every diet we've ever been on, we follow the rules, but then we break the rules, and end up where? Yelling at ourselves, gaining back the lost weight, blaming ourselves and then starting yet another diet. I'm not a fan of that anymore. I'm learning to love myself, to trust myself, and to honor my body, which houses my soul."

Jodi is looking at me with her mouth agape. "Take me with you," she says.

I lean over excitedly. "On the spiritual path? You want to come with me to the Zen Center next week?"

But Jodi is shaking her head no.

"C'mon, Syd. With a speech like that, you must be practicing to be a guest on Oprah. And I'm your best friend. I want to go with you. Maybe Oprah will be giving away spa packages to the audience."

"You're crazy, Jodi," I tell her as I stand up from the table.

"Maybe, but not as crazy as you," she says, putting her arm around me.

Chapter Thirty-Five

The snowflakes are fluffy, and as I call Levi in he comes bounding toward me with snow covering his nose, his paws. He looks so cute that for a moment I forget what a pain in the ass it is to have a dog. But I remember quickly as he rushes into the house leaving little puddles of snow over the floor that Marina has just finished mopping.

I try to catch him, to wipe off his paws, but he's already heading into the family room, plopping himself down on his favorite spot on the rug. I head back into the kitchen to finish the tuna melt I just made for myself. I realize that I'm eating fish, the least preferred food for the Tibetan Buddhists, but I do love a good tuna melt.

Levi gets up, follows me into the kitchen, and sits beside me as I savor the melted cheddar seeping into the tuna, the perfect bite with tomato. He cocks his head as if to say, "I suffered through your bout with vegetarianism, I deserve a little tuna, too." I look at him and he looks at me, and he wins.

I break off a piece of my tuna melt and give it to him. He licks his lips happily. I watch the snowflakes twirling out the window, and if this were December, I would smile, because everyone loves the first few snowfalls. But this is the first day of February, and I've already had enough snow for one season. I'm ready for warm sunshine and the beach. Jodi's leaving for Barbados next week, and I want to pack myself right into her suitcase and go with her. I want to lie on the beach, drink a margarita, enjoy a spectacular dinner with a view, and then spend the night in the casino playing slot machines.

Which I realize is a very un-Buddhist fantasy, but still, I bet Buddha would have loved Barbados.

As I'm finishing up my tuna melt Levi is still staring at me, willing me to give him another bite. But I'm trying to follow my own hunger cues now, and my hunger cues are saying that I want to eat the rest of my tuna melt without sharing. So I finish it without making eye contact with Levi, and then I go to the fridge and tear up a piece of cheddar cheese on a plate for him. I figure that if I'm following my inner wisdom to guide me in my eating, I should try to honor what Levi might need, given he can't reach the fridge.

I look at the clock and realize that I have the next two hours completely unscheduled. Mah Jongg is at my house this evening, and I've already made the guacamole, cut up the veggies, prepared the dip, and baked the fudge brownies. I decide to put Levi in the car and go visit Bodee and Golden. I know that Levi loves his visits there, and I think I'm feeling a little guilty that I didn't give Levi more of my tuna melt. I look at the dish of cheddar cheese that he's left untouched, and realize that it was probably the tuna he was after.

Pulling in front of Bodee's house, I get Levi from the car and begin walking toward the front door when I scream. I run over to Bodee, who is lying on his back in the side yard, flat out in the snow.

""Oh my God, Bodee! Bodee!" I yell, running toward him. *Don't let him be dead,* I think over and over in my mind. I reach him and kneel beside him. "Bodee!" I shout.

He picks his head up from the snow and looks startled to see me. I worry that he has had a heart attack. I pull out my cell phone, ready to call 911.

"Hello, Syd!" he says with a smile. His voice sounds strong. His speech isn't slurred. I don't think he's had a stroke.

"Are you okay?" I ask, breathless, while Levi pulls on his leash to hunker down in the snow with Bodee.

"I'm fine, Syd!" he says, petting Levi.

"I was calling you, you were lying there, I thought—" but Bodee cuts me off.

"You thought I was dead, did you now?" he asks.

And when he says this, I keep myself from saying, "Yes, I thought you were dead," because that just sounds—I don't know. Not rude, necessarily, but sort of ominous.

Bodee sits up and says, "Lying in the snow with my hat on, I must not have heard you calling for me. I'm sorry if I scared you." He pulls himself up to standing.

"What were you doing?" I ask, relieved to see that he is in one piece and looks fine after all. "Really, Bodee, are you sure you're okay?" I ask again.

Bodee pats my head the way he would pet Golden or Levi, and tells me, "I was just enjoying the snowstorm and the washing of snowflakes on my face. Shirley and I used to do this all the time. Sometimes we'd make snow angels side by side," he says, looking up into the afternoon sky. "And sometimes we'd just lay there and catch snowflakes on our tongue," he says wistfully. "Nothing like a beautiful snowstorm."

We start walking toward the front door, and I tell him that I was just thinking the same thing, except that I think snowstorms should stop by mid-January, or the end of January at the latest. "I mean, after the holiday season the snow just gets old, and cold, and overstays its welcome," I explain as we head inside where it is dry and warm.

Bodee and I take off our coats, hats and mittens, and hang them on the hall tree. "Nature can never overstay its welcome, Syd," he tells me. "It's finding the beauty in each moment of the cycle."

"Well, my best friend Jodi is finding the beauty in escaping the cycle. She's flying to Barbados next week," I tell him.

Bodee smiles and gets ready to light a fire. He kindles the wood, producing a warm blaze that takes the chill out of the day.

"Where's Golden?" I say, realizing that he didn't run to the door when Levi came in. I had taken off Levi's leash, and I realize that I can't find him either.

Bodee sees me looking around as I call out to Levi. "Levi's probably gone to find Golden. He's been slowing down a lot, and has a hard time jumping off my bed, where he sometimes rests during the day."

I follow Bodee into his bedroom, and see Golden lying on the bed. Levi is cuddled right beside him.

"Is Golden sick?" I ask, feeling worried, and thinking that maybe I should ask Bodee if he wants me to take Golden to the vet for him.

Bodee pets Golden and says, "No, he's not sick, he's just old. But he loves to sit by the fire. Here, let me carry him off the bed." And he carries Golden to his doggie bed by the fire, while Levi jumps off the bed and follows them into the living room.

Golden curls up on his checkered cushion and looks at the colored flames. Levi seems to sense that Golden needs some quiet, and so he lies down on the hardwood floor, right beside Golden.

"Are you sure you shouldn't be taking him to the vet?" I ask.

"There's no cure for old age, Syd. It's just part of the cycles," he explains. "Let's warm up with our afternoon tea, shall we?"

I follow him into the kitchen, waiting for him to begin his daily tea preparations. But just as he's about to fill the kettle with water, he hands it to me.

"Why don't you make our tea today?" he asks, smiling. "I'll supervise."

So I fill the kettle with water and put it on the stove. I open the cabinet with the tea containers and look to him to tell me which one to pull out.

"How about we have some ginseng oolong today," he says, pointing toward a red and yellow canister with Chinese letters on it.

I open the canister and see tea that looks like little raisins. I remember where the porcelain teacups and teapot are kept and get those out, along with the tray and the biscuits. When I look up at Bodee he's smiling at me.

"Okay," I say, "how much do I measure?" I hold the canister in one hand and a measuring spoon in the other.

"Just under two teaspoons," he tells me, and I measure the rolled leaves dusted with what Bodee tells me is powered ginseng root, and pour them in the strainer.

I hear the kettle whistling, and I think I surprise Bodee by turning off the burner but not pouring the water into the teapot right away. Bodee smiles at me, and I say, "See, I've been watching," and he says, "Yes, you have."

After a minute or two I pour the water into the strainer, over the tea, and I carry the pot on the tray into the living room, setting it on the table as Bodee and I take our seats in the wicker rockers, waiting for the tea to steep.

As we sip our tea I find my tongue and taste buds come alive to the crisp, balanced flavor of the tea. Bodee sips and tells me that this tea originated in Hunan, China, and it soothes me to know this.

I look over to Golden, who is sleeping all curled up in his bed, his golden hair matching the flames of the fire, and Levi's fur, cuddled beside Golden, matching the snowflakes outside.

"You know what, Bodee?" I say to him, and he says," What's that, Syd?"

And I take in the fullness of all that is around me and say, "Barbados be damned. I'm right where I want to be."

Chapter Thirty-Six

"Syd, I don't understand this at all. I thought all of this would be out of your system by now," my mother is saying into the receiver. I have the phone cradled against my neck as I busy myself organizing my scarf drawer in my walk-in closet. I know this is a mistake, that my neck will hurt triple its baseline of pain, but once I start organizing, I can't stop.

"Mom, relax. It's not like I'm going to Tibet. I'm just going to Vermont for a week," I tell her, folding a Hermes scarf that I had totally forgotten about.

The other week I attended a talk at the Prana Center by a Buddhist teacher from the Vipassana tradition known as Insight Meditation. She was hosting an initial Dharma talk, followed by a weeklong class on this type of practice, and I signed up.

I was taken with the practice of cultivating a calm mind through sustained attention, and of deep reflection and insight into the way things really are. I liked that the teacher, Geneen Horwitz, grew up Jewish, and would sometimes explain a concept in Buddhism followed by a parallel example in Judaism that was new to me. Like how *Ayn Sof* in mystical Judaism refers to "The One Without End," so similar to the experience of the transcendence of Buddha's enlightenment.

One of the women taking the class with me, Lexie Shuman, said that there were a lot of us "JuBu"s out there, like she and Janet Rosenbaum. I had asked her what a JuBu was and she looked at me and said, "A Jewish Buddhist. There's a whole bunch of us. Even some books written about it."

At the end of the seven days, Geneen passed around a brochure about an Insight Meditation Center in Vermont, where two founding teachers of Vipassana Meditation in the West would be holding a seven- day silent retreat for beginners, one in May and the other just the following week. I don't know what happened, really. But I stayed after that final class and read the brochure and everything in my head was saying, *Why in the hell would you ever go on a seven-day silent retreat, in freezing Vermont, no less,* and my mind added, *then again, why would you listen to me, you're supposed to lose your mind and come to your senses,* and before this blew into a full blown migraine I listened to my heart and signed up for the retreat.

When I turned in the information sheet to Geneen and said that I was going to buy my ticket for Vermont, she had looked at me and said, *"Mazel tov,* Syd."

"BUT VERMONT? In this cold? Why would you go there? You don't even ski. And thank goodness you don't, because you should hear the stories I hear about Edith's kids who went to Aspen last year and I tell you, there were more broken bones and cracked ribs. Why anyone would think it's fun to slide down a mountain, I don't know," my mother tells me.

I shake out a Burberry silk scarf and smooth it as I fold it back in the drawer.

"Well, mom, you don't have to worry. I won't be skiing in Vermont." I'm tempted to explain Kinhin, the slow walking meditation, to reassure her that no possible injury could ever come of that, but I don't even know how to begin trying to explain walking as slow as possible in a circle for an hour to a woman who barrels through life to get where she's going in record time.

"Then why, Syd, why? Chicago has had such a snowy winter. Your father and I miss you. And we have warm sunshine and fresh-squeezed orange juice waiting for you. Your father and I will wait on you hand and foot, princess. Why aren't you coming to visit?"

My neck is reaching a new level of pain, so I pull myself away from my scarves and move to the chair in the corner of the bedroom to sit and to give my neck a rest by holding the receiver now in my hands.

"Mom, I told you I can't come this week to visit because I'm going on a retreat in Vermont," I tell her for what seems like the millionth time.

"Why, Syd? What is it you're looking for?" she implores.

"I told you, I'm looking for nirvana."

My mother lets out a grunt.

"Is that all, Syd? I'm telling you, your father and I found nirvana years ago. It's here in Boca. Now pack your bathing suit and get yourself to O'Hare and you can be here for dinner," she says. "Well, we won't necessarily make the early bird special, but still, we can have dinner."

Eventually we hang up—me to finish organizing my scarf drawer and then to pack for the retreat, my mother to put her head in her hands, wondering what she did to deserve a daughter who would pick the cold and silence in

Vermont over the warmth and chatter of Boca.

When I had told Gary about my plans earlier in the week, he just stood there looking at me. When I asked him what he was waiting for, he said, "the punch line."

I told him there was no punch line. That like Janet Rosenbaum, and Lexie Shuman, I was part of a whole group.

"A whole group of what, loonies?" he had asked.

But I explained that what she meant was that there was a whole group of people who had been born and raised Jews, but who were also following a Buddhist path. "They call us 'JuBu's," I explained.

Gary had said, "There must be a group of JuBus in Florida, then, since that must constitute half of their homeland. Why don't we spend the week in Boca, like your mother wanted, because anyway, I promised Evan I'd come play golf with him, so we can kill two birds with one stone."

And it hit me that that expression is definitely not in keeping with a Buddhist mindset of compassion, but I didn't think Gary would be interested in my musings.

"I bet there are even retreats in Boca for JuBus, though I can't imagine they'd be silent. That would truly take a miracle," he had said, and I had to agree.

"Oh, but this Lexie Shuman told me a funny joke," I had said.

Gary had put his hands up, but I insisted. "No, it's really funny." I told him. When he didn't protest, I began.

"A priest walks into the barbershop and says to the barber, 'I'd like a haircut.' And the barber says, 'Sure, no problem,' and he gives the priest a haircut. When he's finished, the priest says to the barber, 'How much do I owe you?' And the priest says to the barber, 'For you, a man of the collar, there is no charge.' So the priest thanked him and left. The next morning when the barber went to open his shop, he saw a small bag of gold sitting at his door.

"Later that day a Buddhist monk came into his shop and said, 'I'd like you to shave my head.' And the barber said, 'Sure, no problem.' And after he shaved the monk's head, the monk asked, 'How much do I owe you?' And the barber said, 'For you, a man spreading the teachings of the Buddha? There is no charge.' So the Buddhist monk thanked him and left. When the barber went to open his shop the next morning, he saw a small bag of rubies sitting at his door.

"Later that day a rabbi walked into the shop and asked the barber for a haircut. The barber said, 'Sure, no problem,' and cut the rabbi's hair. When the barber was done, the rabbi asked, 'How much do I owe you?' And the barber said, 'For you, a learned man of the Book? There is no charge.' So the rabbi thanked the barber and left the shop.

"The next morning when the barber returned to his shop, he saw a long line of rabbis waiting at his door!"

Gary was amused, I could tell, but he just looked at me and said, "Do you think you'll learn any better jokes on the retreat?"

And I said, "Well, if the retreat is all in silence, there's little chance that I'll be able to expand my repertoire."

And he said, "I hope Margot isn't serious about you taking part in the country club's comedy night."

And in preparation for the retreat, I simply looked at him and didn't utter a word. Not one little comeback.

Chapter Thirty-Seven

I shut off my iPod, though the words to the Indigo Girls' song "Galileo" still play in my mind: "*How long till my soul gets it right. Does any human being ever reach the highest light—*" The taxi stops in front of the massive brick building set upon a hill, home to the Insight Meditation Foundation. I gather my purse, my duffel, and pay the driver, thanking him. He asks me if I need any help, but I tell him no, that I'll be fine. I figure it won't look so good to be entering the retreat center with someone carrying my bags. It might give the wrong impression.

The taxi pulls away, and both the wind and the reality of where I am hit me hard. I survey my surroundings. The large expanse of land is covered in patches of ice and there is a stillness that cuts through the internal chatter of my mind saying *Really, Syd? Do you really think you can make it through a seven-day silent retreat?*

I look up past the main building and on up to the snow-capped mountains outlining the horizon. I take a deep breath and then exhale, watching my cold breath melt into the air.

I walk up the stone path that leads to the massive front door and step inside. The first thing I see is a large, standing Buddha. I feel like I've found a friend. I smile at this statue, knowing that he can't smile back at me, but all the same feeling comforted by his presence. I walk across the long corridor, looking for where I'm supposed to check in, but when I see a few other people walking in their stocking feet, I realize that I have forgotten to remove my shoes. I rush back to the front hall, quickly remove my shoes, and hope that no one realizes my faux pas. But then I wonder even if they did, would it be so bad? They can't really say anything to me, can they? It is a silent retreat, after all.

I head back down the corridor, this time shoeless, with my duffel bag and purse flung over my shoulder. The registration for the retreat is set up in the dining hall. I make my way to two long tables where there are a handful of people checking in. I wait until it's my turn, and then give them my name.

"Welcome, yogi Syd," the woman checking me in says. "I see in your application that this is your first time visiting us, and that this is your first silent retreat."

"Yep," I say. I don't want to say too much. I don't want her to think that I'm unsuited for a silent retreat.

"Well, we're glad you're here," she says sweetly.

I just smile.

She hands me a folder with information about the center and the rules of the retreat. I had already printed out the rules from their website, had read them at home and used them for my packing, but I was glad to have the ones she was handing me, in case there were any updates.

"Your room number is G104, a single room, as you requested."

Thank goodness, I think to myself.

"It's just across the courtyard to your right," she says as she points out the window. "But there's a map in your packet also." She pulls it out and highlights the building that my room is in.

I know from what I read online that the buildings are separated into male and female dorms, even for married couples. There is an oath of celibacy while on the weeklong retreat, regardless of marital status. The philosophy is that one's energy must be cultivated for meditation, and not for other purposes while in the midst of such intensive practice.

"And your yogi job will be cleaning pots after the evening tea," she explains. "That means that at 5:15, beginning tomorrow afternoon, you show up at the kitchen and work your yogi job until 6:00."

It could be worse, I think to myself. *I could have been assigned to cleaning the toilets.* But I stop this thought, and instead remember why it is that we are assigned our yogi jobs. It is to practice mindfulness in action, while offering up selfless service for the benefit of others.

"It's 3:00 now," the woman says, looking at the clock on the lefthand wall. "Our light tea dinner will be served at 4:30, and during that time the yogis on the retreat are allowed to talk with one another. The practice of noble silence for the weeklong retreat will commence at 5:15. Do you have any questions?'

I don't, but I rack my brain just in case, because if I have a question at 5:16 I'll be out of luck.

"Okay then, yogi Syd, if there are no questions, you're all set."

I start to walk away, but then realize that she didn't give me my room key. But when I tell her this she just smiles at me and says that there are no locks on the doors.

I'm about to tell her that this would be a thief's dream—no locks on the doors and no one can break the silence to claim a theft has occurred—but I don't because that just seems a very negative way to begin a seven-day retreat in the quest for enlightenment.

I go back to the front entrance, get my shoes, and then walk out the doors across the courtyard to my dormitory. The wind has really picked up now, and you'd think that coming from the Windy City this wouldn't bother me, but it cuts me to the core.

Which, when I think about it, is what I'm hoping this weeklong meditation marathon is going to do.

I find my dormitory and walk down the corridor to G104, about three quarters down on my right. I open the door and walk in. The room is sparse. The small space boasts a sink in the lefthand corner and a wooden platform with a sheetless foam mattress and a pillow in the back left of the room. A rough woolen blanket is folded at the bottom of the bed. There is a simple wooden chest of drawers and a chair across from the bed, and a small closet. The floor and the walls are bare. I go about setting up home.

First I dig out the set of sheets that I borrowed from Jodi. When I saw on the Insight Meditation Foundation's website about bringing your own set of twin sheets and towels, I realized I had no twin sheets. Gary and I have a king-size bed, and all the other bedrooms have queen beds.

But Rebecca still has a twin bed, so I had called Jodi to see if I could borrow an old set for the retreat.

"Sure, come on over," she had said. When I got there she held out two sets and said, "Do you want elephants in tutus, or penguins eating cookies?" And I picked the penguins eating cookies.

I shake out the sheets and begin making the bed. I stuff the pillow in the pillowcase and spread my cream fleece blanket on top. I'm thinking that the wool blanket they provide is going to be itchy, so I'm glad I have the fleece to cover myself with first. Next I unpack my clothes. The website had advised that clothes be for comfort rather than style, but I figured since the Buddha taught about balance and the Middle Way, maybe I could be comfortably stylish?

I unpack the leggings and Juicy velour sweat suits. It takes me about a minute. There is no little black dress to hang up, no linen pants to shake out the wrinkles. No tiny sandals or high-heeled shoes to line up in the closet. I take out the rolled warm socks I packed. Time spent in the main building and in the meditation hall is all without shoes, so I bought a ton of warm fleecy socks with non-skid soles.

When I had read about noble silence on the website, it recommended packing quiet clothes that wouldn't make noise during your movements. I had tried on my sweats, shuffled around in my bedroom, trying to see if they were quiet enough.

I finish unpacking and pull out my toiletry bag. This, I had realized while packing, was the most challenging. I had learned from the website that the Insight Meditation Foundation was scent-free. That many yogis are sensitive to scented products and chemicals, and so it is important that there be no perfumes or scented products of any kind.

I live for my Givenchy Amirage shower gel, lotion and perfume, for my Chanel Allure. But no, I had to honor the rules, so I left all that wonderful scent home. As requested, I brought unscented soap, unscented lotion, unscented deodorant and unscented shampoo.

And it scares me. I have no idea what I smell like without my fragrances. I line up my unscented products on the corner of the tiny sink. And then I open my toothpaste to smell the mint, and it reassures me a little.

I place my alarm clock on the windowsill and look out at the courtyard surrounded by mounds of snow and a small meditation labyrinth now lined with dead bushes. To my far right I see another Buddha statue, and I feel stronger. I look beyond the grounds and out to the line of mountains. I pull up the chair and look over the folder the welcome woman had given me. Most of the rules were what I had seen on the website. "Noble silence" means no talking or communicating of any kind—no reading, no writing, no phone calls, no eye contact. If it is imperative that you communicate due to an emergency, you may drop a note in the box located in the front hallway by the message board. Then I look at the schedule and I talk myself (silently, of course) into believing that I can do this.

Daily Schedule:

5:00—Bell ringers will circulate throughout the center to wake up re-treatants/yogis

5:30–6:15—Sitting meditation

6:15–7:30—Breakfast

7:00–7:45—Yogi Jobs

7:45–8:30—Sitting Meditation

8:30–9:15—Walking Meditation

9:15–10:00—Sitting Mediation

10:00–11:15—Yogi Jobs

11:15–12:00—Walking Meditation

12:00–1:00—Lunch

1:00–2:00—Yogi Jobs

2:00–2:30—Sitting Meditation
2:30–3:30—Walking Meditation
3:30–4:30—Sitting Meditation
4:30–5:15—Light dinner/tea
5:15–6:00—Yogi Job
6:00–7:00—Sitting Meditation
7:00–7:30—Walking Meditation
7:30–9:00—Dharma Talk (This is by the two teachers on the retreat. There is obviously no question-and-answer period, because we yogis will be practicing noble silence.)
9:00–9:30—Optional Tea

After reading the schedule, I think about the million little things that I always have on my To Do List, and I think that perhaps this type of To Do List could be really freeing. So I lace up my hiking boots (they had recommended hiking boots for the outdoor walks people are encouraged to take alone on a daily basis), grab my bag, and head out to explore the rest of the center. On my way, I stop and take a quick glance at the communal bathrooms, trying to assess the ratio of toilets and showers to yogis.

Back in the main building, I take off my shoes and jacket in the coatroom on the left and, in my stocking feet, set off to investigate.

I peek through the end of the coatroom and see a large room with hardwood floors and paintings of the Buddha on the walls. The plaque on the entrance identifies this as the Walking Meditation Chapel. Walking back through the coatroom and on out to the main hallway, I look to the right and see a large message board, the main way of communication on the retreat. The Daily Schedule is posted in the center, surrounded by Buddhist quotes from the various sutras and sticky pad notes asking for rides to New York at the conclusion of the retreat, or looking for passengers to drive to Boston.

To the left of the main entrance is a carpeted room that is used for doing yoga, and I see a few yogis in various postures. Farther down on the left is the entrance to the meditation hall, a large room with beautiful hardwood floors and windows making up the entire length of the left side of the room. Up front, on the altar, is a beautifully carved, bronzed Buddha with hands in the teaching mudra. A large Zen bowl is placed on the next tier, sitting atop a blue, red and gold pillow. On either side of the bowl are the meditation cushions of the two guiding teachers for the retreat. Freshly cut flowers grace both the left and right of the altar. The meditation cushions are lined up on the right side of the hall, with a few scattered about in various areas of the room covered with meditation shawls—some retreatants/yogis have already claimed their space.

I leave the meditation hall and explore some more. What hits me more is what I don't see than what I do see.

There is no gift store, no cute little earthy café, nothing at all to buy. There are no spiritual accoutrements, no dharma candy.

And though I've spent a lifetime shopping, a lifetime as a consumer, I am relieved. My body relaxes, lets go of the notion that I have to fill up from the outside and instead honors the idea that filling up comes from discovering what's there on the inside.

AT 4:30 I return to the dining room for the light tea and evening meal. Standing in line with other yogis on the retreat, I collect a cloth napkin, mismatched silverware and a mug. Then I wait in line at the buffet table. Even before noble silence begins, I can see that this foundation doesn't mince words. When they say "tea and a light meal," that's exactly what they mean. I've known people with anorexia who eat bigger dinners than this.

I sit down at an empty table feeling like a new kid at school during her first cafeteria lunch. A middle-aged hippie with questionable hygiene sits down across from me. He introduces himself as Todd, and tells me that this is his first time at the Insight Foundation. I tell him I'm Syd, and it's my first time, too.

"Well, let's be chatterbugs now, because then it's mum's the word," he says, and I smile. I don't really have anything to say to him, and I realize that it might actually be a huge relief to keep silent for seven days.

"So where you from, Syd?" he asks.

"North Shore of Chicago," I tell him.

"Cool. I'm from Rhode Island, Providence. Ever been there?" he asks, and I just shake my head no while I take a sip of my gingerroot tea and remind myself that I should save the headshaking for later.

Use your words, I say to myself, the way I used to say to Rachel when she was little and on the verge of a tantrum. *Use your words,* I say to myself again, *while you still can.*

"So Syd, you should totally come visit Providence. It's really a happening place, good energy, good vibe. I own a vegetarian restaurant there," he tells me.

"That's great," I say.

We both look down at our meal—crackers and peanut butter. We go about spreading the peanut butter on the crackers.

He breaks out of his hippie vibe and in an exaggerated Yiddish accent says, *"Oy vey,* this they call a dinner?"

I smile at him and imitate the overdone accent. "I wouldn't even classify it as a nosh. Would it kill them to put out some bagels, offer a *shmear* of cream cheese?"

We both laugh as we eat our crackers.

"This should be really awesome, seven full days of meditation," he says. "And a week after the retreat, I'm headed to Mexico for a weeklong yoga spiritual renewal vacation."

"Cool," I say, because it seems like the right way to respond.

"You should totally go on one of those vacations. It's like, mind-blowing, you know?"

I just smile and go back to sipping my tea. All of a sudden I feel really tired, and I find myself looking at the clock, wanting it to be 5:15.

A formal welcome is offered from a yogi who lives at the meditation center. He tells us that there are 75 yogis on this retreat, and that the energy from all of our intensive meditation will create powerful vibrations that we can all tap into.

"We practice mindfulness here—mindfulness not only on the cushion, but also in every breath of our day. We practice loving-kindness and gratitude. We ask that each of you do your part in creating the kind of environment that fosters an atmosphere of contemplation and reflection."

I look around the room at the collection of people on this retreat. There are people who look to be about Rachel's age, and others who appear to be in their seventies, and everything in between. The yogis, as they call us, are pretty evenly divided between males and females, though the group is overwhelmingly white.

I turn my attention back to the yogi speaking to us.

"So even in the bathroom, be mindful. Please be frugal in your use of toilet paper to help save our environment. And take no longer than three-minute lukewarm showers to conserve water and to make sure there is enough water and time for others. And we have some very sensitive plumbing, so be mindful of that. We ask that you not flush after every urination, but rather when the toilet looks like it needs a flush. It's fine to flush after bowel movements."

"You think?" I want to yell. But then I stop and remind myself of why I'm here.

He goes on to review the rest of the rules, and then explains how twice during the retreat there will be group interviews with the two guiding teachers, Craig and Cindy. "During that hour you will have a chance to sit with a small group of yogis and a guiding teacher to discuss anything about your process on this retreat. That is the only time noble silence will be broken." He hands a sheet around and has us sign up for our group interviews so that it works with a free hour we have during the day, when we are not doing our scheduled yogi jobs.

Then he hands us all a sheet with the words to the *metta sutra* on loving-kindness, and says, "Before our noble silence begins, let us all raise our voices to read this together."

After reading this sutra, I try to ignore the hunger pangs that the peanut butter and crackers didn't touch, and instead focus on my full heart as I follow the other 74 yogis in silence to the meditation hall for our first of many sittings together.

Chapter Thirty-Eight

I awake in the morning before the bellringer's sound, even before my alarm goes off. It's 4:30. Showers cannot be used until the bellringers signal the beginning of a new day, so I wait and lay out the things I will need. There are only three showers in the communal bathroom down the hall, and I want one. The minute I hear the distant ringing of bells across the lawn from my window I dart off with my unscented products and towel, wanting to beat out the other yogis.

As I rush down the corridor I think of the Dharma talk last night that yogi Craig gave. He talked about breaking the addiction to "I," to the illusion of a self. But the "I" is very much with me, *I* see already. *I* want to take a shower. *I* want enough hot water. *I* don't want to have to wait and be late.

Craig reminded us in his talk that this retreat was about practicing mindfulness at every moment, and I am becoming mindful that I am very much a creature of the "me" generation. I'm going to have to work on this.

I put my unscented products on the shower shelf, turn on the water and it bursts cold, so I move away until the steady stream becomes warm. And it feels so good—until I remember that I'm supposed to use lukewarm so I turn it down. But after a second I turn it a little warmer again, feeling guilty but no longer feeling so chilly. To expedite my shower, trying to keep within the three-minute shower framework, I have decided to forgo shaving my legs and my underarms. This is a first for me.

I'm out in a flash, or nearly a flash. I'd say I probably showered in five minutes, which is two minutes over the allotted time here, but a good 15 minutes faster than my average shower at home.

I emerge from the shower and see the bathroom slowly filling up. At first I think that everyone is mad at me, because everyone is staring down, looking away from where I am standing. But then I remember that noble silence

314

includes no eye contact either, so I chalk it up to that. I collect my things and walk back to my room.

I shake out my hair, and I miss the smell of my shampoo. I put on my lotion, and again miss the comforting scent of my fragrance. Instead I'm just left with me in the raw. I put on a pair of noiseless sweatpants and a zip-up sweatshirt. I am mindful of the fact that all is quiet. Meaning, I don't hear the drone of a single hair dryer. I rationalize that it would take forever for my hair to dry on its own, what with this cold chill of winter in Vermont, and that I'd be asking for a fever. Still, I know that under this reasoning is my own vanity, my own desire to have my hair just so.

So I plug in the dryer and the motor *vrooms* and bounces off the hardwood floor and the empty walls, and down, I imagine, through the entire meditation center. But it is only a sound, I reason, and not so different from the ringing of the morning bells. Like Craig explained last night, "All is impermanent. Things arise, and then fall away."

Like the sound of my hair dryer.

By 5:30 I'm back on my cushion in the meditation hall, and at 6:15 I'm waiting in a long line to enter the dining room for breakfast. While we wait I notice that other yogis like myself who are standing in front of the message board are reading the Daily Schedule that was up when we all arrived yesterday. The same schedule, the same sutras, the same ride board. I suspect that while we are all hungry for breakfast, we are already hungry for language, for communication, for something—anything—to read.

And it's only been a little over 12 hours.

As the line slowly inches forward I notice the blackboard hanging outside the dining room, and I tilt my head to read it, to be in some type of communication. It reads:

Good Morning ☺
Today's breakfast is offered with gratitude to the Earth for its bounty:
Millet
Granola (for topping only)
Bananas/oranges
Green tea

Now I realize how prudent is the recommendation to lose expectations. I was thinking maybe a mushroom-and-cheese omelet, home fries, English muffin and a hazelnut coffee.

I wait for the bellringer to signal the meal. People around me put their palms together and bow their heads. I do the same. And then I give a silent prayer of thanks for the food we will be receiving, and send wishes that all sentient beings be free from hunger.

With a heart that feels like it's opening I make my way though the line and stand at the table with the offerings. The board is right. There is exactly millet in a big vat, some granola with raisins, bananas and oranges and green tea.

What did I think? That they were going to surprise us with the chef's special for the main course? If not the omelet, then the French toast or the Belgian waffle?

I use the ladle to pour the millet into my bowl, and gingerly sprinkle the top with granola and raisins. I want to be mindful and take only my share. I grab a banana, and from the large pot spoon the green tea into my mug. I take a seat at a table where others are already sitting.

I am so hungry that I'm about to dig right in, but I notice that others are staring down at their food, maybe meditating on it, maybe saying a prayer, and so I close my eyes for a minute and repeat my earlier prayer before eating.

Oh God, what I'd give for a bowl of Fruit Loops right now, something crunchy and sweetened. But I'm hungry, and so I force myself to eat what's in front of me. And then I stop and think of all the people in this world who are hungry and have nothing to eat. And I pray that their suffering will be eased. And with each bite I take, I give thanks for what I have.

When I'm done, I get up to clear my dishes. I notice that there is a shelf with teas, instant coffee, and hot chocolate with a sign that reads "Please help yourself." And I feel happy that maybe later, when I take a break from meditation, I will make myself a cup of coffee or hot chocolate, and just sit.

I notice that people use any area they choose for walking meditation. There are people doing walking meditation in the hallway, and in the back corner of the dining room. My regular walking seems so fast, just my walking to get from A to B, and so I try to slow it down even when I'm not doing kinhin.

Because there is a 45-minute break for yogi jobs, but I'm not on until the afternoon shift, I have free time. I decide to bundle up and go for a brisk walk. Stepping outside, the cold whips at my bones and takes my breath away. I hesitate for a moment, thinking that maybe I'll just go back inside, where it's warm. But something forces me down the front steps of the building, mindful of any spots of ice. I zip my down jacket up to my neck, pull the hood over my hat, and stuff my gloved hands in my pockets. I head down the road to the right, constantly reminded of the flow of the breath as my exhalations appear and then disappear into the atmosphere.

I try to walk mindfully, noticing the bare branches, the mounds of snow and patches of green-brown grass that struggle to emerge in various spots. I gaze up at the mountains, and down at the road. And I walk.

The road is dotted with little houses, some more like log cabins, and you can see and smell the smoke coming from chimneys, the smell of a fire in the hearth. I keep heading straight and find myself walking down a hill. At the bottom of the hill toward the right is a partially frozen lake. It is beautiful, hovering beneath the surrounding mountains. I walk toward its edge and look at the frozen ice cover, and scan the parts of the lake where the sun has broken through the surface and cracked the ice, the water reflecting the sky.

I look down and think of what is below the surface, what is happening under the frozen layers. I think about what this lake must look like in the spring, in the summer, and in the fall. I think about the cycles of life—of birth and growth, of decay and death, and then birth again. I think of Bodee, of when I first met him and he asked me what was going on in my life and I said, "Same old, same old," and he said, "how could that be?" and recited that quote, "No man ever steps in the same river twice, for it's not the same river, and he's not the same man," and I understand it in a deeper way this time, a way that cuts under the protective ice barrier and moves down towards its depths.

Despite the cold I feel a heat well up in me, and I stand up straight, my arms spread to my side, and without speaking I let the universe know that I am alive, that my heart, like the icy lake inching towards spring, is melting and opening.

Back at the retreat I go through my day of sitting and walking meditation, of lunch (which, as the main meal of the day, is bigger and heartier), and of washing the pots after the evening meal. The woman I work with—I'd tell you her name, but because we can't talk I don't know it—seems nice. We have to use nonverbal communication to figure out who's going to wash and who's going to dry. To negotiate where we think the pots are supposed to be kept. But surprisingly, we do it fine, and before you know it we're in a rhythm.

That night when I'm in bed, I realize that I have not uttered a word in over 24 hours.

I find that I easily accept the routine, the sitting and walking meditation sessions, and look forward to the Dharma talks. I look at my sheets—Rebecca's sheets with the penguins eating cookies—and suddenly wish that the cookies were real, and that I could get in bed and gobble them up.

I wasn't prepared for the millet breakfasts and the practically nonexistent dinners. I know that monks in monasteries eat like this, but I just figured the food here would be like the food at the ashram—abundant and delicious with options. So once again I have to remind myself to lose my expectations, and to ignore my growling stomach.

I realize before falling asleep that I probably will lose weight this week, but it's no longer my goal. I want to follow what the Buddha taught, to practice mindfulness and balance. When the Buddha starved himself, he realized that denial was not the way, nor was a life of decadence. But a life of balance, of following the Middle Way—that was a path one could follow toward enlightenment.

So here I am, having given up the idea of dieting, letting go of the idea that my body needs to meet some ridiculous standard of perfection. I've been taking care of my body, listening to its cues, and for the first time that I can remember enjoying food and my body, no longer imposing self-denial followed by wild decadence.

How ironic, then, that I'm on a silent retreat where there's not enough food for me in the evening. From 1:00 on there is only the light evening meal of crackers and peanut butter, or tonight, yogurt and apples. So I'm back to craving food as if I were dieting, even though for once, I'm not. And I'm thinking there must be some meaning to this, but for the life of me I don't know what it is.

So I give up trying to figure it out for now, and I cuddle up with my fleece blanket on these cuddly flannel sheets, my head against an inedible cookie. And I pull the fleece blanket up to my nose, because I can still smell the mountain-fresh scented laundry detergent that the blanket was washed in, and it anchors me to something familiar.

THE NEXT morning, my routine still in place, I am back on my cushion for morning meditation at 5:30. Everything is feeling slower, more dreamlike. Sitting meditation, walking meditation, meals. I, like others, spend minutes standing in front of the message board reading the same notes, looking for anything new. After lunch there was a new message on the board about the Dharma talk this evening, and people remained huddled at the board craving any new piece of news or information to read.

On a retreat like this you begin noticing things you'd never look twice at in your ordinary life. Someone put a new Kleenex box in the coatroom, and I'm telling you, it was a big deal. When you are silent, with no reading or writing or eye contact, something this insignificant is now breaking news.

On the third morning we meet for our group interviews. I am with the guiding teacher Cindy and six other yogis. For the first time we are allowed to break noble silence and spend the hour speaking about our process thus far on the retreat. After introducing ourselves, Cindy has each one of us share with the group anything we'd like about our experience, and then she responds or offers advice to the yogi.

One woman talks about the crying episodes she is having during sitting meditation. A young man speaks of experiencing "intense realizations into the nature of things." Others speak of falling asleep during meditation, or of using this retreat as preparation for undertaking the silent three-month retreat offered each year.

When it's my turn I decide to speak my truth and not judge myself for it. I explain that I had spent a lifetime dieting and denying my hunger, only to break my diet and binge. But that through my understanding of the Buddhist path, and following a life of moderation and balance, I have stopped dieting. I have used my own inner wisdom to guide both my spiritual and physical nourishment.

"But here I am, trying to follow my own body wisdom, but I can't because there's not enough food for me, and I'm so hungry. I'm back to feeling deprived! And I try to remind myself of the people in the world who would be so grateful for the food offered here, and I don't mean to sound greedy, but while I'm meditating my mind is listening to my stomach growl, and I think of the irony of it all—when I finally decide that I am entitled to eat when I'm hungry, I find myself on a retreat that offers fewer calories than some of the strictest diets I've been on!"

Cindy tells me that most yogis bring some extra food from home, and that there is a shelf where you can label and store your snacks. She tells me that next time, I should be sure to do that.

I had wondered what all the food in the pantry off the kitchen was for, but I had figured it probably belonged to the yogis who lived here fulltime.

That night at dinner I fill my tray with my tea and crackers and peanut butter, and then get up to get a glass of water. When I return to my seat there is a wrapped granola bar on my tray. I look around, trying to figure out where it came from, but with the no eye contact rule, it's useless.

I sit down and finger the red shiny wrapper. *Who left this for me?* I wonder. I figure it has to be someone in our group interview session, but when I look up again, there is no one looking my way.

I pick it up and see that it is a cinnamon-apple granola bar, and my mouth waters. I don't know whom to thank, so I hold it in my hands before unwrapping it and send out a silent message of gratitude for being here, for being heard, and for being cared for.

After unwrapping it, I take a bite, and the taste is sweeter than the cinnamon, sweeter than the apple. What I taste is the sweetness of wisdom and compassion, of mindfulness in action.

Chapter Thirty-Nine

At the next light dinner the following day I put my tray down to get my water. This time when I return to my seat a chocolate-chip granola bar is beside my plate of cottage cheese and apples. I feel my lips move into a smile, and I stand up once again to see if anyone is looking my way, but they're not. I say a silent blessing of gratitude, and then I unwrap the bar and savor the soft yielding goodness in the blend of chips and oats.

What we practice on the cushion, hear in the Dharma talks, all comes down to this simple act of kindness from what I've now named my Secret Santa. In their evening talks, both Craig and Cindy talk about insight meditation as playing an important role in traveling a Buddhist path. The practice is all about developing a calm mind *(samatha)* through sustained attention, and insight *(vipassana)* through reflection. Rather than using a mantra for meditation, the focus is on the breath and cultivating a spirit of inquiry during meditation.

We are also learning and practicing *metta,* or loving-kindness meditation, where, starting with oneself, it is possible to cultivate love and compassion for all sentient beings. And I am learning but also practicing the truths the Buddha talked about and taking him up on his invitation to see if these truths hold true for me, to be a lamp unto myself. Namely, that the one constant thing in life is change and impermanence *(annica)*, the ceaseless beginning and ending all things go through.

As I finish my granola bar, I think about this concept. Like the table I am sitting at. It looks solid, but it's anything but solid. The table is made out of wood and nails that, when put together, for this time period, is a table. But if someone were to take the table apart it would go back to being the parts—the wood, the nails. And if a fire were to consume the room the table would now be a mound of ashes. The table would have ceased to exist, but it would have become something else. And that's true of everything.

And I am experiencing what the Buddha called dukkha, or a sense of dissatisfaction. The unpleasant sensations that so easily arise within us that we try to rid ourselves of. Even the dissatisfaction that arises from pleasant sensations, because even in their pleasantness we cause suffering to ourselves by either trying to hold on to them or feeling sad when the experience or the sensation is over. Like when Gary is giving me a great massage on my sore neck. I experience joy in the moment, but at the same time I'm already worrying that he will stop rubbing soon, tell me his hands are tired, or that he wants to read. And so even while I'm enjoying the massage the whole time I'm sort of ruining it by stressing about when he's going to stop rubbing and when the nice sensation will be gone.

But when you try to live skillfully and mindfully, when you take the calm and reflective mind that you are cultivating on the meditation cushion, or in the meditation walking, you can experiment with these skills in your own life. You can try to live in the world with mindfulness, compassion and wisdom, being grateful for the moment that you are in while knowing that the moment will change and you can stay awake for the next moment, and the next, until you ultimately become awake to your life.

AFTER THE final meditation for the evening I return to my room to get ready for bed. Back in the sheets with the penguins and the cookies, I acknowledge that a cookie sounds good, that I'd like to eat one. And I pay attention to my still-hungry stomach. But I don't do the add-ons of suffering that I've perfected so well in my life. I don't say to myself, *How am I going to get through the next three days without more food, and why did I sign up for this retreat anyway?* No, I say to myself, *This is what it feels like to have an empty stomach, and at some point, your stomach will once again be filled.*

And before I fall asleep I send positive energy to my Secret Santa for not only helping to fill my stomach, but also for filling my heart.

THE NEXT morning, day five, I'm standing in line for breakfast and jockeying for a space behind Todd. He's wearing a Grateful Dead shirt, and on the back of the shirt is a list of all the venues they played during their concert tour. I am dying to read something, and this will have to suffice. As I gather my silverware and pick up a mug, I am lucky enough to find one that's from Bob's Auto Body Shop in Detroit, and I busy myself reading their three different locations.

The days have their own rhythm now, and that would be S-L-O-W. Not S-L-O-W as in boring, surprisingly enough, but more as in slow motion.

I think back to when I had worked so hard to meditate in my house for 45 minutes. How now that time interval is like a hiccup. I've learned that I can sit, I can walk, and I can eat in silence. I can be patient. I can be hungry. And I can survive without fragrance.

During the retreat I have at times decided not to sit for a scheduled meditation or to not to walk the whole kinhin session. We are invited to be flexible, to listen to what we need. You'll find people stretching in the yoga room, or sitting in the dining room enjoying a cup of tea, or hot chocolate or coffee. And when I do take a few minutes to do the sun salutation in the yoga room, or to take a break and have a cup of coffee, it feels very powerful in a way that's hard to describe. The activity that at home would just be one of many, barely a blip on the radar screen of my day, is suddenly very significant.

In the late morning I decide to leave the kinhin session early and to enjoy a cup of hot chocolate. I head into the dining hall, passing the message board and glancing to see if there is anything new listed. I go over to the shelf and grab a mug, this one a PBS one, and that's all it says, "PBS Public Broadcasting System," so there's not much to read. I make my hot chocolate and take a seat facing the large window that runs the length of the back wall. I take a sip of my drink, and it warms me. In the back corner are two people doing walking meditation, walking slowly, slowly, the breath synchronized with the placement of each part of the foot.

I turn my gaze out the window, to the sunlight reflecting off the pockets of snow, the squares of bare pavement in the courtyard outside where the snow has been shoveled. The branches of the trees are mostly bare, with a few scattered leaves still holding on. There is a gust of wind, and I see a browned, yellow leaf twirl in the wind and settle once again on the ground. As I set my gaze on that leaf I become mesmerized. I watch the leaf get picked up with the wind, move on to bushes, back to the ground, and back up into the wind. It is as if I am watching a ballet, so graceful are the movements. It is like I am watching Rachel playing outside when she was little, watching her every movement, her features as familiar to me as my own hand. Watching that leaf is like watching the entire universe. That leaf has become everything, and I continue observing the leaf long after my hot chocolate is gone.

The wind carries it, and it moves willingly. The wind stops, and the leaf rests where it is. The wind starts up and it is suspended in the gust, making figure eights, sailing and soaring and resting only to be picked up a second later and set down on a mound of snow.

I hear the bell signaling the sitting meditation session will soon begin. I have been watching this leaf, I realize, for over a half an hour. It has grabbed my attention so fully and so totally. I find it hard to leave. I don't know what

I am going to miss. Where will the wind carry the leaf next? Where will it end up—what will be its fate?

Slowly I pull myself up from the chair and pick up my mug. I look once more at the leaf, and wish it well. And then I silently thank the leaf for letting me watch its dance of life.

LATER IN the day we are once again scheduled to be in our group interview to share our retreat experiences. I realize that I'm not in a hurry to talk. I have come home to my silence, and it wraps me like a soft, warm blanket just out of the dryer.

Still, I know I should participate. In a talk the other night, Craig said that in life there are three things you should do in every situation: Show up, be fully present, and be detached from the results.

So, following this dictate, I make my way to the group room upstairs and settle into one of the chairs arranged in a semicircle. A woman who looks to be in her late thirties or early forties, dressed in purple drawstring pants and a long-sleeved cream oversized sweater, offers to go first. She explains that for most of the retreat she has been focusing on something that happened this past August that she keeps turning over in her mind, and that she wants to share. Cindy encourages her to begin. It feels strange to hear voices again, but I turn to this woman, yogi Gail, and listen.

"In my front yard, in the right corner, there is a patch of dirt where a big rock sits. Every spring I plant flowers around this rock. The verbena seems to do the best—I think it's the unfiltered sun. Anyway, a few years back I bought a white cast Buddha statue and set it in front of the rock, on the patch of dirt, surrounded by my newly planted spring flowers. That first year I watched the Buddha sit among the flowering blossoms in the hot sun, sitting in his perfect lotus. He sat solidly through the thunderstorms with the strong wind gusts. Through hot humid days or cool, wet nights, he took it all. The Buddha would get wet, would dry out, and then get wet again. I watched while bees rested on his head, while a flower petal fell on his face, while the flowers grew so high that you could barely see the Buddha's face. I watched the Buddha sit in the middle of this patch, grounded in the soil, rooted in the Earth.

"In the winter, he didn't flinch in the cold—allowed himself to be buried in the snow, pelted by the ice, as if saying, 'I can take it.' And then when the snow became slush and the slush became moist soil for the spring planting, it would begin a new cycle."

"Sounds lovely," Cindy said, smiling at Gail.

"It was. That Buddha represented my spiritual quest. Every time I went outside, or when I'd drive home, that Buddha was what I looked for. But this is what happened.

"This past August I was driving home and I looked out the window for the Buddha, and I couldn't see him. I figured that I couldn't see him because the flowers had grown so high, so after pulling into my driveway I went out to look. I pulled the flowers away, expecting to see the Buddha sitting there as always, but he was gone. Someone stole the Buddha! It was horrible. I found myself getting angry, thinking, 'How can someone steal the Buddha?' But then I realized that that this thought presumed that the Buddha had been mine. And I knew that you shouldn't cling to the Buddha, not when you're learning about the impermanence of all things, not when you're learning about non-attachment.

"But on the retreat, I keep thinking about the Buddha statue. Even when I'm home, when I approach my house I look at the patch by the rock hoping that the Buddha will reappear. And when I'm sitting so long in meditation, I find my mind wandering to where the Buddha might be. And yesterday I was thinking that wherever the Buddha ended up, he must still be sitting calmly and serenely. And then last night I was thinking that whoever stole my Buddha, maybe needed it more that I did. Maybe a whole new path will open up to this person. Maybe this person stole the Buddha from an impulse to know the Buddha, and that's good. Maybe the person who stole the Buddha will become a great Buddhist teacher some day. So I know I need to let it go.

"This morning while I was meditating, another thought came to me. Maybe the universe sent someone to take the Buddha to teach me something. Maybe I'm supposed to practice letting go more, to see impermanence and nonattachment more deeply? And then, later in my meditation, I thought, 'Maybe no one took the Buddha. Maybe Buddha disappeared the way one who reaches enlightenment disappears into nothingness and everythingness.'"

We are all staring intently at Gail, and Cindy thanks her for sharing such a wonderful story. "Maybe the answer is all of the above," Cindy says to Gail. "Or maybe it's none of the above."

I'm glad that even though this is a time for sharing, there is still an abbreviated version of noble silence where only the person sharing talks, and the teacher responds. I'm glad I don't have to contribute to the conversation, because I don't know what to say.

"In a way," Cindy begins, "this is like the Buddha's teaching of the raft.

"The Buddha explains that if you make a raft to cross over to another shore, when you get to the other shore you shouldn't say that this raft was so helpful to me, I'll carry it with me wherever I go. The raft is a metaphor for the skillful teachings of the Buddhist path. But just like it's important not to get attached to unskillful behaviors or thoughts, so too, should we not get too attached even to those skillful ones. That we move beyond any attachments while knowing the wisdom of each moment. Thank you, Gail. Who'd like to go next?"

I realize that while I'm listening to everyone I'm not being fully in the moment, because I'm thinking about what I'm going to say. Part of me wants to tell them about the leaf, but I realize that there is really no way for me to convey what I experienced. That it really went beyond words, and that if I put it to words, I fear it might somehow lessen that experience. So when it's my turn, I say, "Ever since I told this group that I've been hungry on this retreat, that there's not enough food for me in the afternoon and evening, someone has been leaving granola bars at my seat. I'm assuming it's someone here, and I want to thank you for your kindness. I've felt taken care of. It makes me glad that I've stopped listening to the people in my life who avoid giving money to the homeless. Since I've begun meditating and following a spiritual path, I feel it is part of my practice to give, knowing that we are all interconnected. And now, being on the receiving end, I feel so much gratitude. So whoever you are, thank you."

IN THE taxi, driving to the airport after the retreat, I am overwhelmed. There is so much busyness—the taxi driver and his dispatcher, the radio turned up high, the sounds of honking cars. The airport is like an assault on the senses—the crowds of people, the food court smells, the security line, the announcement of gates and of final boarding calls.

Once you have a week to slow down, you realize how sped up is the world.

As I sit on the plane, looking out at the tarmac, I wonder where my browned yellow leaf is now, and wherever it is, I wish it well.

Chapter Forty

"Levi, c'mon boy! Let's go," I call, grabbing his leash from the hook in the closet and then removing his invisible collar. Levi is doing his happy jump, showing his excitement for an afternoon walk. Even though March is supposed to come in like a lion and go out like a lamb, sometimes it rebels against this expectation and decides to come in like a lamb. Which is what it did today. Here it is only the first week of March and the temperature is hovering in the low 70s.

I've been home from the retreat a handful of days, and I'm once again used to the constant chatter. Walking outside, I hear the crunch of a small pile of dead brown leaves that have withered up under winter's wrath. I forget to notice anything special about these leaves, let alone pick out a favorite. It's only when I see a lone crunched up leaf being blown down the street by the unseasonably warm breeze that I pull Levi to stop for a moment and watch the old leaf's trajectory.

Instead of going inside after our walk, I decide to put Levi in the car and drive over to Bodee's. I want to tell him about the retreat, want to shock him that I was able to stay silent for a full week.

As I turn down Middle Way Drive, Levi is already barking in anticipation. I pull up in front of the house and Levi and I get out of the car, Levi pulling on his leash to get to the front door as quickly as possible. The front door is open, leaving the sweet warm air to drift through the screen door. I knock half-heartedly, figuring my call "hello" will be enough to alert Bodee to our visit.

"Syd, is that you?" Bodee calls.

I push open the door and Levi bolts in the house. Bodee comes from the kitchen to greet us and bends down to pet an excited Levi, who is jumping up and down. Then Levi goes looking for Golden, walking through the living room, into the dining area, and then disappearing into Bodee's room to find Golden resting on the bed, probably needing help getting down.

Except that Levi walks out of the room with his tail down.

"What's wrong, Levi? Go find Golden," I say.

Then Bodee walks over to Levi and picks him up, carrying him over to his favorite spot on the couch. He sits beside Levi, petting his head and his ears. He motions for me to sit down and looks at me, his soft, wrinkled face gentle and strong.

"Golden died last Thursday, Syd," he says, as he covers his hand over mine.

"What? Oh my God, how? What happened?" I ask, not believing this could be so, not wanting to accept this news.

"Old age happened to him, Syd. It's what happens to all of us, you know," he says, and I notice that despite the grief he must be feeling, his blue eyes still shine with their twinkle.

I feel my eyes well up. Bodee sits with me, his hand still in mine, without saying anything.

Because, I realize, there's nothing to say. After a week of being on a silent retreat, I've come to know silence as a friend, have come to know that words aren't always necessary. And we sit like that for a while, my tears falling, our hands holding, and Bodee sitting there the way I imagine yogi Gail's white cast stolen Buddha sat in her patch of yard with the rock, taking it all, whatever life gave it, letting the flow of life happen.

Finally I just look at Bodee and say, "I am so sorry. I know how you loved Golden, how much joy he brought you. And Levi and I fell in love with Golden, too."

A smile spreads across Bodee's lips. "Yes, he was well loved, and he loved well," he says. "He was my faithful companion."

We sit like that for a while and Bodee talks to Levi gently, telling him how much Golden loved his company, and of how grateful he was to Levi that his energy touched Golden in these last months.

"Where did you bury him?" I ask softly. "I want to take Levi with me to his grave, so we can say good-bye."

"I had Golden cremated," Bodee says. "It's what Shirley wanted for herself, what I want for myself, and what I know Golden would want as well. To return to the earth in ashes of spirit, where they can scatter and settle where the wind carries. Being part of the never-ending energy of the universe, the ever-changing song of creation."

As I listen to him, I picture that browned yellow leaf I watched while on retreat, and I find myself telling Bodee now about what it was like to watch this leaf totally surrender to the wind. How fully absorbed I was watching this leaf—how the world, in that time, came down to that one leaf.

As I'm telling Bodee this his face glows more and more radiant. And I know he understands. And I know I understand.

We continue to sit in silence. Then Bodee looks into my eyes and pats my hand and says, "Golden loved laying under the maple tree in the back yard. He'd lie there so contently while I planted my vegetables, while I watered and tended to their growth. So I spread his ashes under the maple tree, and also spread some in the nature preserve, where he loved to walk with me and to explore. Now, Shirley? She always wanted her ashes spread over the water. Said she wanted to flow in and out with the tide. She used to say to me, 'Bodee, the Earth is three-quarters water just like our bodies. I want to go back to my source, like a baby floating in the womb.'"

It's seems an awkward question to ask, but I ask anyway. "Where did you scatter Shirley's ashes?"

Bodee's smile softens, and he tells me that he took a kayak out into Lake Michigan and spread her ashes in the water.

"Did you go back to Powhatten Island, to spread her ashes back at the shore by The Firefly Inn?" I ask.

Bodee shakes his head and says, "No, we were living here when she died. I spread her ashes off the shore of North Sandy Beach." He smiles at me and continues.

"The lake is always changing, always flowing, and on one shore sits Powhatten Island, another shore is right here, and Shirley? —She can flow in every drop, in every corner of that Great Lake, on every shore and no shore. That's what I'd like, too. Doesn't have to be Lake Michigan, mind you. After all, Lake Michigan today is different than Lake Michigan yesterday, and Lake Michigan tomorrow. Different fish, plants, sand, rocks. Always different, yet always Lake Michigan. It's the scattering of the ashes with love in a place that speaks to the still living, and a place that speaks to the cycles of existence. That's what makes the scattering sacred, a final act of love."

I give Bodee's hand a squeeze and rub my thumb over his hand, feeling the veins that pulse out from under his skin.

Bodee smiles at me, saying, "We are late for our afternoon tea. Why don't you sit here with Levi, and let me go and prepare it for us?"

I shake my head yes and watch him walk towards the kitchen in what I think is a slower than usual pace. I pet Levi, feeling grateful that his little heart is pumping, despite the food I have fed him over the years. I look over to the fireplace and see Golden's empty checkered bed and feel a twinge in my heart.

When Bodee returns he places the tray down on the table, and we take our places in the rocking chairs.

"Today we are going to have *Bai Hao Yin Zhen,*" he says as he picks up the teapot and pours the tea into our teacups.

"Where's it from?" I ask before taking a sip.

"From Fujian. And this tea is very special. It's a white tea," he explains. "Try it."

I pick up my teacup and smell the light, flowery scent, look at the pale, yellowish liquid and take a sip of the tea. "It tastes so sweet," I tell Bodee. "I don't think I've ever tasted a white tea. Actually, I don't think I even knew there was white tea."

I watch Bodee sip, and he tells me. "This white tea, what they call Silver Needle, is picked in early spring only for a few days out of the entire year, and only the buds are plucked. So brief, yet so delicious, don't you agree?"

I nod my head yes, and then Bodee adds, "Just like life."

And then, rocking beside Bodee, I feel the tears well up in me again. And without planning to, I find myself telling him about baby Rae.

He listens, and when I'm done he looks lovingly at me, saying, "You have known great heartache."

I look into Bodee's eyes, and I know he truly sees me, truly hears me, and my heart rests. But then my mind turns to Golden—to his absence in this house, to life moving so quickly, like the tide, never stopping, in and out, like the breath, until the breath ceases, and I worry that Bodee is going to be so lonely.

"What are you going to do, Bodee?" I ask, thinking of him losing Shirley, and now losing Golden. "What are you going to do?"

And Bodee smiles at me and places his hand on my cheek, saying, "What am I going to do, Syd? Well, we have just finished our tea, so come now and follow me into the kitchen. It's time to wash the teapot and the teacups."

And so we do.

Before I leave, Bodee leads Levi and me to the garden out back, and we stand next to the maple tree where Golden's ashes have been scattered. We stand silently, letting the soft breeze soothe us, feeling the weakening sun still bathe us in the warmth of the day.

I dig into my heart, trying to find blessings to say, mantras to recite, prayers to offer. But all I can see is Golden, and how he lived out his name— a golden treasure offering to his master companionship, unconditional love, and tenderness.

Before I can decide on how best to pay my respects, Levi sees a squirrel running up the tree and pulls the leash out of my hand while he's barking up a storm, trying to catch the squirrel, who has expertly run up the tree to escape Levi's would-be attack. And as we watch nature unfold around the maple tree, the cycles and challenges and joys, I reach for Bodee's hand and we both start laughing, watching Levi run around the maple trying to catch the squirrel.

Eventually Levi gives up, the squirrel having saved himself this time, and Levi plops himself under the maple to rest. It is then that I realize that I have yet to retrieve his leash.

I turn to Bodee and say, "Look, I'm not holding his leash and he doesn't have his Invisible Fence, but he's staying in the yard. What do you know?" Bodee bends down to pet Levi and says, "It's often when we think we can't leave that we run in all directions. Once we know we're free to leave, to explore, we often find the sacredness in where we've been all along."

Bodee gets up then and surveys the dead remains of his garden. "So much growth going on underneath during these long winter months. Come May, I'll be picking the first of the carrots," he tells me.

"I'll bring the ranch dip," I say, and Bodee looks at me and smiles.

"I'll look forward to that, Syd," he says. "I'll look forward to that."

"Me too," I say. "Me, too."

Chapter Forty-One

I pull into a spot in the parking lot of Chez Panache and glance at the clock. Only 10 minutes late—not too bad. Our Mah Jongg group is taking Donna to lunch for her birthday. Jodi, Margot, Donna and Barbara are driving together, but I had an appointment, so I told them I'd just meet them there.

As I walk into the restaurant, I spot the round table in the center of the room where my friends have already gathered. Before walking over to them I pause for a minute, watching them. I see the empty seat waiting for me, and though I want to walk over and claim my chair, there is another part of me that knows I can no longer occupy that space in quite the same way.

I've been spending time at the Buddhist Vipassana Center in the city for the community meditation and Dharma talks, and I like being part of their sangha, or community of seekers. I also enjoy my weekly Torah study group with Rabbi Jacob, where I am once again invited to experience the "om" in shalom. Lexie Shuman and Janet Rosenbaum are also part of that group, and between our yoga and study sessions we have grown closer over these months, talking and sharing in ways that feel truly nourishing.

Jodi looks up, sees me, and waves me over. I wave back to the table as I walk towards them, stopping by Donna to give her a birthday hug.

"Happy Birthday, sweetie," I say to her as I pull away.

Donna gives me a big smile and says, "This is so great! I love having our birthday lunches together!"

I take a seat as the waitress comes over to see what I'd like to drink. After I order I look back to my friends. "Sorry my appointment ran a little over," I say.

Everyone waves me off and Jodi says, "No, Syd, it's fine, really. We only got here a few minutes ago." She takes a sip of her lemonade.

"You look different," Barbara tells me. "Were you just at the hairdresser?"

"No, I had a dentist appointment," I answer.

She keeps looking at me and then asks, "Did you just have your teeth whitened?"

I shake my head no as the waitress brings me my sparkling water.

"Doesn't she look different?" Barbara asks the others at the table, and before they have a chance to answer she says, "I think you've lost weight."

Jodi, Margot and Donna are nodding their heads in agreement.

"You do look thinner," Margot tells me.

"Care to share your secret?" Donna asks as she spreads a roll with butter.

Before I can answer, Jodi tells them, "Syd is into this new thing she calls 'trusting her own wisdom.' Doesn't count calories, fats or carbohydrates, just tells me she eats when she's hungry and eats what she's hungry for and stops when she's full."

"Don't be ridiculous," Barbara says. "You can't lose weight that way. You have to go on a diet and stay on a diet if you want to lose weight." She looks longingly at the roll that Donna is eating.

I tell them that I'm not trying to lose weight anymore, that I no longer diet. "I'm just trying to feed myself in a loving way, and changing my love/hate relationship with food to one of mindfulness and gratitude."

"Yeah, if you wash that thought down with a few diet pills, maybe you'll have a fighting chance," Barbara says, sipping her Diet Coke.

"Well, with or without a change in your weight, you do look different," Jodi tells me, and everyone is nodding their head in agreement.

I think back to Rosh Hashanah with Rabbi Jacob, when he talked about how Hanna's face was transformed after speaking her truth and living out her name.

"So the other day Gary had lunch with Ralph and told him that you've become a JuBu—part Jewish, part Buddhist," Margot says. "It seems to suit you."

"Well, are you more Buddhist or Jewish?" Barbara asks with a bit of an edge in her voice.

I think back to last year, with Bodee in his garden. How I was telling him that I couldn't reconcile the fact that a tomato is really a fruit and not a vegetable. He had told me about the problems created by labels and stopped the conversation by having me take a bite of its essence, saying, "No fruit, no vegetable, only tomato."

Instead of answering, I just look at Barbara and smile.

Then I turn to Donna and say, "So tell me how you're feeling, birthday girl! Are you feeling celebrated?"

And she nods and tell us yes, and then shows us the diamond necklace that

Joel gave her this morning. We all admire it and tell her how much we love it before looking at the menu to determine what we want to order.

"I forgot my reading glasses," Jodi says, and immediately four pairs of reading glasses are offered her way.

"Oooh. I have such a choice. I'll borrow Donna's because they match better," Jodi says as Donna hands them over.

"*Oy vey,*" I say, laughing.

"You know, I'm the last of us to have needed reading glasses. At first I just couldn't read the phone book, so I just called 411. Then I was sure that the newspaper print size was smaller than it used to be, and that all of my magazines followed suit. Dave kept insisting that it wasn't that every print size had been reduced, it was just that I needed reading glasses. Well, I wouldn't go for his analysis. Finally, though, I realized Dave was right. When we'd go out to eat and I'd look at a menu, the only thing I could make out was Fish, Poultry, Meat, Pasta, as the headings. Couldn't see a damn thing under each section. Finally went out and bought a pair. Still can't get used to needing them, though. I forget to take them with me when I go out, and at home I can't remember what room I've left them in," Jodi complains.

I explain to Jodi that once you need reading glasses, the key is the plural in glasses—you need lots of pairs. "You need to keep a pair in your purse and in all the main rooms of your house," I explain.

"You can buy them in lots of fun colors. It's really like a fashion accessory," Barbara adds, taking off her pair and admiring them.

"Everything looks so good, "Jodi says. "Now that I can read the menu, I'm not sure what I want."

"Well, remember it's Donna's birthday and calories don't count on birthdays, right girls?" Margot asks, talking over her menu.

"The next Mah Jongg game is at my house and we'll make up for it by only eating carrots and hummus. No cookies, no candy, is that a deal?" Margot adds.

"Fine by me," Donna says. "But you know we never follow through with those plans." As she sees the beginning looks of panic cross over her friends' faces, Donna reverses her claim and says, "No, I agree with Margot's plan. It's my birthday, so let's order whatever we want, and we'll all go back on our diets after lunch and we'll eat carrots this Thursday at Margot's. Deal?"

"Deal," everyone says, though I busy myself taking a sip of my water so I don't have to be part of this whole diet conversation anymore.

When the waitress returns to take our order we are still making last minute decisions over the possibilities. Margot goes first and orders the coconut shrimp, Jodi decides on the grilled lime chicken breast over pasta, I order the quiche Lorraine, Donna gets the Acapulco chicken salad, and Barbara orders a small garden salad with a scoop of dry tuna and dressing on the side.

Our orders complete, I raise my glass and the others follow suit. "To Donna," I begin. "May you always know laughter, may you always know kindness, may you always know the love of your family and your friends, and may your life be filled with great surprises all along the way!"

"Here, here," everyone says as we clink our glasses.

"I'm getting old," Donna says as she takes a sip of her water.

"Hey, Donna, watch it. You're the youngest one here, so don't you go complaining," Margot tells her.

"We're practically the same age, though, I'm only six months older than Donna," Barbara offers.

"Can you believe our boys will be in the fourth grade next year?" Donna asks Barbara.

"No, I can't. It's going to be a whole different ball game," Barbara says. "In another year they'll be off to middle school and then we have to worry about everything—good grades for high school, bad influences. I don't know if I'm ready," Barbara tells us.

Jodi jumps in then and says, "Let me remind you that Melanie is graduating from high school next month. Next month! I can't believe she's going to college. I think she's ready, but I know I'm not." She brushes the hair from her face.

"Hey, at least she's going Indiana University. It's only a six-hour drive to Bloomington. If I want to see Nathan or Scott, I have to get on a plane," Margot complains.

"You spend your life raising them, attending to every need, the big ones and the little ones and all the in-between ones, and then they just pack up and leave. What's a mother supposed to do then? I mean, thank God that Rebecca will still be home for two more years, but really, after that? I don't know," Jodi says.

But Donna shakes her head and says to Jodi, "Think about it. You'll have more time for yourself. You can take more Pilates. Instead of picking up after school, you can schedule an afternoon massage. You can go to Michigan Avenue anytime you want! I think it's going to be great when Parker and Brittany are finally away at college. But that's not going to happen for a long time," she says, rather grudgingly.

Margot looks at Donna and says, "Listen, don't wish—"

But we all interrupt her because we know what she's going to say, what she has so often said. "Don't wish the time away because before you know it, they'll be gone, in just a snap they're off and on their own."

When we've finished, Margot looks at us all with a smile of resignation and says, "Well, it's true, you know." Then she looks at me and says, "Syd knows, and soon, Jodi, you'll know too."

We're all silent for a moment, and then Donna says, "Hey, you guys, we're celebrating my birthday. Can we all put on our birthday smiles and be happy?"

So we all give her our best picture smile, and then Donna asks, to no one in particular and to all of us, "Are you happy?"

And at first, no one answers.

Then Jodi says, "I'm happy with a small 'h.'"

And Margot says, "I'm happy on paper. I mean, I have everything I could want, and my boys are both successful men now. On paper my life looks great, but off paper, I do feel like something's missing sometimes."

"Well, I'm happy! I've kept on my diet and I'm down to my lowest weight since high school," Barbara shares.

"What about you?" Donna asks me. "Are you happy?"

And I smile at my friends, and say, "Yes, I'm happy. I've broken through my Invisible Fence and I've begun exploring both the outside world and my own inner self."

At first there is silence, and then Jodi spits out her lemonade and starts laughing. Soon everyone is laughing along with her.

"What?" I ask.

"Nothing, Syd. Really, I'm not laughing at you. I just feel like before we know it you're going to be off writing a self-help book for us trapped suburban women, hidden behind our white picket fences playing Mah Jongg and drowning in our Diet Cokes and overly perfumed bodies."

I smile at Jodi and tell her it would be a book that could be written in five words: "Just unlock the fence's gate."

"Oooh, Syd. Maybe there's a writer in you that you haven't met yet. Maybe you should try and write a book about all of your spiritual searching. I mean, you'd have to make it longer than five words. I mean, even short stories are longer than that," Donna says.

"A haiku is longer than that," Jodi adds.

I look at them and laugh and tell them that I don't think there's a writer within me waiting to come out, but there is maybe a painter.

They all look at me, and then Jodi says, "I remember you used to paint with watercolors when you were a kid. You were really good. You used to go that art school—what was it called? Acorn, that was it!"

The waitress brings the food, and I wait until we have all been served before I answer.

"Yeah, I used to love to paint. And then I just stopped after I started high school," I explain, while I take a bite of my quiche. It's warm, and the crust is the perfect amount of flakiness for me. "This is delicious," I say.

"Oh my God, this chicken is to die for," Jodi exclaims.

And Margot says, "Well, I'll die with you, because I haven't had coconut shrimp this good since I moved from Boston!"

Donna looks at Margot and says, "I'm so glad you like the shrimp, so then you won't be crabby about seafood in the Midwest. Now perch yourself closer and try a bite of my Acapulco salad." Donna offers her a forkful. "I know you love these kinds of salads."

Margot takes a bite and says, "Yum."

"Yum? That's all you got?" Donna asks, breaking off a piece of the taco shell holding her salad.

Margot stabs another piece of shrimp on her fork and says, "I'm having a whale of a time celebrating your birthday. How's that?"

"Oh, are you fishing for a compliment now?" Donna teases.

"Okay, enough of the puns. How's your salad?" Jodi asks Barbara, who is pouring on just a drip of dressing.

"Oh, fine, lovely," she says stiffly.

"Okay, so this painting thing," Jodi says. "When did you go back to it? And how did I not know that?"

I finish chewing a piece of quiche before I answer.

"I've been thinking about painting for a while, and then after I went on that silent retreat I felt the urge more strongly," I explain. For a moment I want to tell them about the partially frozen lake I would pass on my solo walks during the retreat. How the lake quivered in the sunlight nestled under the snow-capped mountains. About the browned, yellow leaf that I watched dance across the landscape. How those images welled in my heart, and how I wanted to express my experience of being in that moment, of how I wanted to paint those images.

But I don't tell them all that. I just tell them that after the retreat I went to the art store and I bought my supplies and I just started painting.

"I love it. When I'm painting, I don't even realize that time is passing. I look up at the clock and it's been three hours, yet it feels like it's just been a second," I explain. "You know, I could just wear my NOW watch, cause that's what the time feels like. Not 1:00, not 2:00, not 3:00, just NOW."

"I need something like that," Jodi says. "I need to find something to keep me busy. Once Rebecca gets her license next year she won't need me to drive her anymore. I'll lose my job as her chauffeur."

Margot pauses with a piece of shrimp on her fork. "You know, that's how

I used to feel with my knitting. When the boys were small, I used to love to knit. I'd knit them little sweaters and little hats. I remember it was so relaxing." She pops her fork in her mouth. "Oh God, these shrimp are good!"

"You should start knitting again," Donna says, chewing. "You could make us all cute scarves for Hanukkah." She takes a sip of water to wash down her bite.

"Well, I've got my hands full with Adam and Jill. I can't imagine finding the time to paint or to knit or even wanting to. When I have some 'me' time I like to get up and go. Go shopping, to the gym, go for a pedicure, play Mah Jongg, get a massage. That's what I do," Barbara says, biting off a forkful of lettuce.

"I wonder if our husbands go through any of this when the kids go to college," Jodi says. "I mean, do their lives change all that much after the kids are gone? Their routine is still the same, their identity stays intact." She sucks a piece of penne pasta off her fork.

"That's true," Margot says. "Ralph misses the boys, but when they left he pretty much continued to do what he always did."

"Well, that's like Gary, don't you think, Syd? Rachel went to college, Gary continued to go to work, and you became a spiritual psycho. And I mean that with love, but you know what I mean," Jodi says. When I don't answer she holds a fork full of pasta toward me and says, "Here, have a bite. You'll love the sauce."

I take a bite and tell her she's right.

"About the spiritual psycho stuff or the pasta?" she asks.

And I tell her about the pasta.

Jodi rolls her eyes, and I say, "Okay, I know what you're saying. I've done a lot of searching this year, but I needed to explore to find more meaning in my life. I didn't want to keep living a life where my goal was to stay on a diet and lose weight."

I look over to Barbara and say, "No offense," and she says, "Speaking as a size two, no offense taken."

I take another bite of my quiche and say, "I just knew, Jodi, that day last year when we sat in the Buddhist lecture—"

"By mistake," Jodi interrupts. "We went to that lecture by mistake—"

I interrupt her with a smile, saying, "Or by karma. I just knew that everything was leading me to that moment. And what I really love is that even though the Buddha is the epitome of wisdom and compassion, he doesn't ask that you take his word for anything he says. Instead he invites people to try things out for themselves, to see if a certain concept is true for them, to know their own experience. He teaches that we all have the potential to reach enlightenment, to discover our own inner Buddha nature. That we all have the potential to wake up! We just need to let go of preconceived falsehoods, let go of our attachments—"

Jodi interrupts me, saying, " Uh, Syd, I don't mean this meanly, but I've seen your meditation room. I wouldn't necessarily call that letting go of everything. You've bought quite a bit of knickknacks and whatnots, and I'd say that not only is that not letting go, I'd say you've got quite a new collection of spiritual *chachkis*. No disrespect meant," Jodi adds, smiling.

"No disrespect taken," I say, smiling back. Then I add, "It's true, you know. Everything these days is marketed and packaged for our consumer-driven society. Even spirituality has become a commodity. I've stopped buying all that stuff now. What's filling me up these days can't be bought at the store. It's found in the moments that make up our life, and being awake to those moments."

Donna looks at me and smiles and says, "Well, Syd. I'm just glad that wherever you're finding this inner bliss, you're finding it at times that don't interfere with our Thursday night Mah Jongg. It's been good to have you back."

"I know why you look different," Barbara says softly, almost in a whisper. We all turn to her and she looks at me. "It's not your hair, or teeth, or weight. It's not your makeup or your clothes. You look different because you're so content and at peace," she says.

I look at her and my heart softens. "I am," I tell her. "I am."

Barbara smiles at me, a slow smile that begins in the center and starts filling in along the corners.

The waitress comes back and clears our lunch, asking if we're ready for dessert. Jodi gives a slight nod to the waitress, who says, "Excuse me, I'll be right back." She gathers our dishes and disappears, reappearing moments later with a small chocolate mousse cake topped with strawberries and whipped cream and a single red candle.

We all sing "Happy Birthday" to Donna, and when we're done, Donna blows out her candle and makes her wish. The waitress pours us all coffee before disappearing again.

Donna does the honors of cutting the cake and handing us all a slice. When she passes one to Barbara, Barbara puts up her hand and says, "No, none for me," and Donna just puts the extra slice down in the middle of the table.

"This is fabulous," I say, taking a bite.

"Heaven," Margot says.

"To die for," Jodi adds.

"I'm *plotzing*," Donna *kvells*.

Jodi looks at Barbara sipping her coffee and says, "You should have some, it's really delicious."

But Barbara shakes her head no. I look over at Barbara, and then past her to another table to our right where two women are finishing their meals with a dish of raspberry sorbet.

I look at Barbara and think of the sweetness she refuses to let in, believing that her virtue comes from denying, from deprivation, from suffering enough so she can think she's won by fitting into her size two. And then I think that maybe for some, sweetness has to come in slowly, in stages, for it to be tolerated. I may not diet any longer, but I still remember calories. I have an idea.

"Barbara, "I say. "They have raspberry sorbet. See over there?" I ask, tilting my head over to the women on our right. "Low in calories, and so delicious. Your salad was small and hardly any calories. You barely used any dressing. Are you hungry for something sweet? Do you want to order a sorbet?"

Barbara looks at me and her eyes fill up. I watch as she quickly blinks the tears back.

"It's okay to let in the sweetness," I tell her gently.

I signal our waitress and order a dish of the sorbet for Barbara. While the waitress turns to get the order, Margot takes out the small gift box wrapped in silver paper with a silver bow on top.

"From all of us," Margot says, handing it to her.

"Oh, you guys, you shouldn't have," Donna says, taking it in her hands.

She carefully unwraps the package and opens the box, letting out a little squeal. "It's the earrings I fell in love with!" she says happily, taking out the diamond and pearl teardrops and holding them up to her ear. "Oh my God, I love them, how did you guys know?"

We all laugh, because she has taken each of us to see these coveted earrings at the jewelry store over the past few months.

"You've come home to mommy," Donna coos at them.

"Thanks guys, for the earrings, but also for this—for our time together and our friendship. It means everything to me," she says.

We all squeeze our hands together on the table, and a wave of nostalgia grips me for a moment. For years these have been my closest friends. We once had so much in common. But now there is so much that I am unable to share with them. I think back to the Passover Seder, about moving from Egypt, the narrow place, to the Promised Land, flowing with milk and honey. I find myself pulling away from those narrow places and moving toward a life that is sweet and sustaining. Just as the Buddha taught, everything changes, and I will have to experience these changes even within the friendships I had once counted on to never change.

The waitress returns with Barbara's sorbet, and we let go of each other's hands.

Barbara immediately removes the cookies that are placed on either side of the scoop of sorbet. She picks up her spoon and hesitates for a minute before taking a small spoonful.

I see her offer a tentative smile and I say to her, "That's right, let the sweetness in."

Chapter Forty-Two

I can't believe it's May. Rachel will be home in three weeks, and then she'll be officially halfway through college. What happens when she's finished? Feeling more confident with who I am, understanding now the need to trust myself, to follow my own heart, I am more able to wish that for Rachel, even if it takes her, logistically, away from me. And moves her toward herself.

I continue going through my closet, getting a head start on my packing for the trip to Aruba that Gary and I are leaving for this Wednesday. I marvel at the difference in packing for the retreat in Vermont versus the resort in Aruba. Instead of dressing for "comfort, not style," I'm packing for "style and screw comfort."

I take my stepladder to reach the top shelf of my closet filled with shoeboxes. I'm searching for my turquoise strappy Jimmy Choo high-heeled sandals, which look fabulous with my silk mini dress. As I search through the boxes an avalanche of shoes cascade to the ground, and for a moment my heels are like weapons. I jump off the ladder to get out of the way and sit on the floor to begin picking up the fallen shoes. As I'm sifting through matching pairs of shoes, my heart starts pounding. In one of the fallen shoeboxes, stacked away in the closet long ago, I find my poems and writings about baby Rae from when I was young. Hands shaking, I take out some of the old, folded papers and read them.

I am blown away.

The questions that I had posed about life and loss, about suffering and purpose and meaning are the same questions and yearnings that accompany me today on my spiritual path, be it on the meditation cushion, at the Dharma talks, in the discussions with Rabbi Jacob, or in the company of Bodee. The feelings and questions and yearnings after baby Rae's death have been waiting all these years for me to bring them to light, to allow them to thaw and flow through me.

I think of the Buddhist saying, "Wherever you go, there you are," and I know that it's true. I have traveled back to myself. My soul at the age of 10 is my soul at the age of 44.

On one sheet I see the watercolor painting I had done of lilac bushes hanging over a fence, and at the bottom, a haiku I had written:

Fragrant blossoms bloom
Stop now and breathe in their scent
Before they are gone

Though I've never meditated in a closet before, it's the only way I can think to pay homage to myself as a young girl struggling with pain and suffering and questions about God at a time when no one was able to talk to me about what I was experiencing. Sitting in my closet, the way a monk might sit hidden away in a cave, I practice metta or loving-kindness meditation, where I honor my parents and the suffering buried deep in their souls. I send them love as I understand that their focus on the external has been an attempt to save themselves from the terror of losing themselves in the internal.

I breathe in love and I breathe out love and I am filled with gratitude that 30 or so years after writing these thoughts they have not only survived within me, but have guided me in my spiritual quest, making me the Syd Arthur I am today.

The Syd Arthur going to Aruba on Wednesday, though—she I still had concerns about.

I hold the papers to my heart before putting them back in the shoebox, and stack everything back on the shelf, thinking about how this past month I wasn't at all sure I wanted to go to Aruba, despite the fact that it's one of my favorite vacation spots and we haven't made it back there for some time. I've been going to Bodee's at least once a week now, worried that he must be lonely with Golden gone. He's such a good listener, and I shared with him my hesitation about going on this vacation.

"The people I meet at the Vipassana Center, so many of them talk of their travels to Tibet, to Nepal, to Bhutan. And here I am, going to Aruba. I feel like a fake again when I hear them talking. Like if I were really a spiritual person I wouldn't be headed to the Hyatt Resort and Casino. I'd be headed for the Himalayas, like they are," I'd explain.

Bodee would look at me and ask me what I think traveling to the Himalayas would be like. "Do you think it's for you?" he'd say.

And I'd tell him, "I don't know. But when they talk about spinning prayer wheels at Boudhnath Stupa in Kathmandu, and when they talk about trekking to Tengboche Monastery to meditate at the base of Mount Everest, I think to myself, 'What kind of person am I that I'm picking slot machines, beach and wine over stupas, monasteries and yaks?'"

During our talks Bodee would ask me questions. Like once he asked, "Is a place sacred in and of itself, or is it something else that makes it sacred? Or, "Can a sacred place become defiled, and a defiled place become sacred?"

I would tell him that sometimes his questions reminded me of the confusing Zen koans, and he would laugh.

Just last week I told him, "I might want to travel to Nepal or Tibet one day," and he said, "I imagine that it's beautiful." And then I told him in frustration, "But I still love Aruba, and vacations like that."

He just looked at me and said, "Why is it one or the other, Syd?"

And I'd explain, "Because one seems so significant, like a pilgrimage, and one seems so superficial."

Bodee would tell me that I used to say things like that to him when I first met him. That I'd wonder if you could straddle both sides—could you be a spiritual person and still enjoy the comforts of suburban life?

I open a drawer and start counting out bathing suits. I start folding beach sarongs and shorts and decide I might as well just pack everything now and be done with it.

When Bodee and I would talk like this, he liked to remind me that I take such comfort in the Buddha's teachings about the Middle Way, about balance, so why was it so hard to think of myself as spiritual and suburban?

"In some ways," Bodee would explain, "It's easier to be a monk. You are surrounded in the monastery with other monks, where the routine and the rules are based on a community of spiritual living where you don't have to make those decisions that you so often wrestle with, where everyone is practicing in the same way, so there is nothing that you have to come up against. But to follow a spiritual path while living in a society often at odds with those practices, that you have to come up against time and time again—that is fortitude. That is strengthening and flexing your spiritual muscle."

Just the other day he asked me to tell him what I loved about Aruba, where he'd never been. "What's it like?" he had asked.

I told him about the divi trees that grew all over the island. Of how they're like a natural compass, always wind-bent and pointing to the southwest as a result of the trade winds that blow across the island from the northeast. Of the green and turquoise lizards and iguanas that if you saw in your house in Highland Ridge you'd put your house up for sale, but when you see them crawling by the pool, or under a table at lunch, they're just part of the charm. I told him of the flights of the pelicans along the shore of the Caribbean Sea. Of the soft sand on the beach and the thatch-covered huts that dot the sand in front of hotels for their guests.

And then I told him of one of my favorite spots in Aruba, the 100-foot-long natural coral bridge that arches 25 feet above sea level. Of how standing on the coral rocks and watching the turquoise sea crash against those cliffs with the constant winds of Aruba, I always felt so alive.

"I'd love to go there," Bodee had said to me. "It sounds beautiful, the image of the coral bridge against the sea. I'd love to go there." He smiled at me then, saying, "And that, my dear Syd, does not seem like a superficial place. It sounds alive and wondrous, and that makes it sacred."

I remember smiling at him then and saying, "Yeah, but I didn't tell you about the nightclubs and the casinos with their blackjack tables and their Wheel of Fortune slot machines. About the bars and restaurants—"

But Bodee had interrupted me and said, "What a perfect place, then. In each moment you are faced with the challenge of finding the Middle Way, and of finding your own balance."

As I take out some more flip flops, I think of how Bodee helped me to feel really good about this trip. That it's not an either/or situation.

I decide to finish the rest of my packing later—the linen that will wrinkle, my accessories. It's nearly 2:00, and I want to pick up Gary's dry cleaning and run some other errands. I'm in the mood to get everything done and to spend the weekend relaxing. I'm looking forward to meeting Kali, Janet and Lexie for dinner tonight and to celebrate it being Friday. We're going out for Indian food and planning a welcome home party for Montana, who is due to return next month.

I finish my errands, and even though I just saw Bodee the other day, I know that what with the trip, I won't see him for at least a week, so I decide I'll stop in. I'll be able to keep him company for afternoon tea.

I pull in front of his house and knock on the door. He always tells me not to knock, just to come in, but I'm always worried I'll startle him, so I like to knock. I see him dozing in his rocker, his chin down toward his chest, and so I knock a little louder.

When he doesn't look up I open the door softly and say, "Bodee?" He still doesn't budge, and for a moment I think about leaving so I won't disturb his nap, but something stops me. I let the door close behind me with a slight bang, hoping that the noise will rouse him, but it doesn't.

I walk over to him and put my hand on his shoulder. "Bodee, I came over for tea. I'll make it if you're tired. Bodee?"

I step away and look closer at him. I look down to follow the rise and fall of his chest, but I don't see him breathing. My heart starts racing. I call louder,

"Bodee! Bodee! Wake up!" But he's just sitting there, slumped over, and when I put my finger under his nose I feel no breath.

My hands are shaking as I pull my cell phone out of my purse and dial 911. The dispatcher answers and I can barely form sentences. I feel like this has to be a dream. This can't be happening.

"Hurry," I tell the voice on the other end, "hurry." I'm crying, shaking. I keep holding Bodee's hand so he knows he's not alone, that I'm here.

In the distance I hear sirens. I hear them coming closer, and then three paramedics—two men and a woman—burst in the door with a gurney and I move out of their way while they work on him.

I move back toward the dining area, looking at what they are doing and then looking away. I am shaking with cold, despite it being warm outside. I feel like my knees are going to buckle, that my bones are going to refuse to stay solid, are just going to let go.

And then the woman is coming over to me and putting a blanket around my shoulders. She leads me to the dining room table. "Come, sit," she says.

I let her move me toward the chair and guide me down. When I look back at Bodee, I see the frenzy has stopped. He is on the stretcher, but neither of the men is working on him.

The woman follows my gaze and holds my hand, saying softly, "He's gone."

I shake my head no, no—this can't be happening. I get up, and she doesn't stop me. I walk over to where the men are standing, with Bodee lying on the stretcher.

"I'm so sorry. There was nothing we could do. He was already gone before we got here. Your grandfather?" he asks gently.

I look up at him. "What?" I ask.

"Your grandfather?" he asks me again. And I shake my head no, saying, "He's my teacher and my friend."

They both smile at me, a sympathetic smile, and tell me that they're going to need some information, and could I help them contact his next of kin. But I tell them that he didn't have any next of kin, and that I would take care of everything.

"Can I have a moment alone with him?" I ask, and they all nod, with one of the men saying, "Of course."

They move to the other side of the room, and I kneel down beside Bodee. I've never been near a dead body before. My heart is pounding, but I force myself to slow down, and to breathe.

I put Bodee's hand in my hand, and lean in close to him. There's so much I want to say, but really, everything I want to tell him, to convey, is beyond words. So instead I look at his gentle face with his chiseled features and touch his soft cheek. And then I lean closer and tell him, "The Firefly Inn was the perfect name. That's what you do—you help others to find their own inner light and to shine and fly free. You will always be my Bodee, my bodhisattva guiding me toward enlightenment. Like the awakening of the Buddha under the Bodhi tree, you will always live your name. You are a Bodee."

I look up then, and the paramedics nod their heads. I look at his face one last time, and I see serenity, and I see peace.

I stand with them by the front door and answer their questions, give them the information they need, and make the necessary arrangements. When they leave, I stay behind in the silence, and in the emptiness that I know is also the fullness.

I sit down on the rocking chair I always sit on, and then I let go, and I cry and cry and cry until there are no more tears left. I just sit there rocking back and forth, saying, "What do I do, what do I do?"

And then I look at Bodee's rocker and I see him sitting there with his smile and I hear his chuckle. I feel him looking at me with his piercing liquid blue eyes, and I hear him say gently, "Syd, you know what to do. It is the afternoon, and it is time for tea."

So I get up and walk to the kitchen, put on the kettle, and open the cabinet with the canisters of tea. I pull one down and open the lid. I think it's the Jasmine Dragon Pearl, the green tea that we shared on the day I met him, when he told me how each individual leaf is hand rolled and dried and then mixed with the scent of jasmine flowers.

I pour water in the kettle and turn on the stove. I get out the tray and one teacup, and measure the tea and put it in the strainer, and when the water is ready I let it sit for a few moments before pouring it into the teapot. I carry the teacup and the teapot out to the living room, and place it on the table before sitting back down in the rocker. I let the tea steep in the teapot another minute before pouring the tea into my teacup.

I sit in the silence that blankets the room with a lump in my throat, and I try to allow the warm sweet tea to soothe the lump, to ease my soul. When I'm done, I hear the words creep back in my head, *What do I do? What do I do?*

I once again see Bodee watching me from his rocker, saying, "Have you finished your tea?"

And I shake my head yes.

"Then go wash the teapot and the teacup."

So I gather everything up and walk back into the kitchen to clean up. While I'm drying the teacup and teapot, I take down the companion teacup and examine their now-familiar pattern—the bamboo and dragons, the porcelain colors of red, yellow, blue and green. I think of Ji passing them on to Bodee and Shirley, to Bodee inviting me to share his afternoon tea. And I know, as surely as I know my name is Syd Arthur, that Bodee would want me to take the teapot and the teacups, and to savor the time set aside to drink tea, whether alone or with a dear friend.

So I take the dishcloth that is folded by the dish rack and open the drawer to find two others just like it, and I gently, lovingly, fold the teacups, the top of the teapot, and the teapot itself. As I am wrapping these precious items I am reminded of when Rachel was an infant, and I would swaddle my new baby daughter in her blanket just as tenderly as I am now wrapping the tea set.

Chapter Forty-Three

"Do you want to go for a walk?" Gary asks me, sitting up from his lounge chair and swinging his feet over to one side. I let the wind caress my skin, trying to cool the beads of sweat that dot my brow, that gather in my cleavage.

"Yeah, let's walk," I agree. I get up and tie on my sarong. My feet cave into the hot sand as Gary takes my hand and we walk towards the shore.

"Ah," we both say as the gentle waves wash over our feet, cleaning away the sand for a brief moment. "That feels good," I say as I walk a little deeper into the Caribbean, allowing the bigger waves to reach up to my shins before moving back again along the shoreline.

I look out at the people lounging on the rafts, letting the current gently move them. I watch the children building sand castles along the shore, laughing and then building again when a wave knocks the castle down.

"Another gorgeous day," Gary says as we walk down the beach, the sea on our left and the high-rise hotels on our right. Each hotel has its own beach setting, with color schemes for their beach chairs and towels, each with their own style of beach huts.

"It's beautiful out," I say, agreeing. When we arrived here on Wednesday the weather was picture perfect. Here it is, Saturday morning, and the weather is still picture perfect.

"Ouch!" I say, jumping to my right foot. Gary looks over to me.

"What's wrong?" he asks.

I pick up my foot to examine it. "Nothing, I'm fine. Just stepped on a sharp shell," I tell him.

"So after dinner tonight, I thought we'd go hear the band play on the beach, and then maybe a little blackjack. What do you say?" Gary asks.

"Sounds good," I tell him.

Gary stops walking and turns to me. "Syd, are you okay?"

"I'm fine," I tell him. "Let's keep walking."

We pass a father helping his little daughter put on a snorkeling mask. "I'm excited for Rachel to come home," I tell Gary as I watch the father guide his little girl into the water.

"Me too," Gary says. We walk more in silence and then Gary says, "It's been great being here with you, Syd. But you've barely talked about what's happened. You've barely talked about Bodee."

I don't answer right away, and Gary allows me the space to remain silent. I think it's like spiritual understanding by osmosis. Some of what I've been practicing all year seems to have just naturally rubbed off on Gary. Where once we talked endlessly about nothing, sort of like our own 24/7 version of Seinfeld, now we tend to allow more silence, which often speaks volumes.

"It's hard to talk about Bodee," I tell him.

"It'll take time," he soothes.

"Yes, but what I really mean is that words fail me when I think about Bodee. He goes beyond words, you know?"

Gary looks at me tenderly.

I smile at him and say, "I don't think you can really know what I mean. You never met him. I wish I had taken you there. I wish you could have sat with us for afternoon tea." A wonderfully cooling wave washes over my feet, splashing up to my knees.

"Well, I did meet him in a way. I met him through you, through your eyes," he tells me.

I appreciate Gary trying so hard to be with me in this. We continue walking down the beach, towards the Marriott hotel.

"And Syd, Bodee is with you, don't you think? Don't you think you carry him with you?" he asks lovingly.

I smile a little and say quietly, "More than you know."

Gary stops walking and faces me. "What do you mean, 'more than I know?'" he asks, confused.

I don't know quite how to tell him this. And since I didn't tell him initially, it makes it a little trickier.

"Let's keep walking," I tell him, letting my feet splash in the water.

Gary follows me and says, "C'mon, Syd, what do you mean he's with you more than I know?"

I look out at the horizon ahead and I see the California Lighthouse in the distance. I take a deep breath. "Okay, Gary," I begin. "The thing is, Bodee had no family."

"I know that," Gary says. "You told me that a long time ago."

"Right, but the thing is, I knew Bodee's wishes. I knew that he wanted to be cremated," I say.

"You told me that, too," Gary says as we pass by the crowded section of the beach reserved for Marriot guests.

"Yeah, but I didn't tell you that I picked up his ashes before we left for Aruba," I say to him.

He stops and looks at me. "You picked up Bodee's ashes?

"Yeah, I had to break through some red tape, but I got them," I tell him.

He looks at me open-mouthed and then asks, "Where are they?"

"Here, in Aruba," I tell him. "Keep walking," I say as I follow the shore-line. "That's what I meant when you said that I'll carry him with me, and I said more than you know."

"Wait, Syd. Where is he? I mean, where are the ashes?"

This time I stop walking. I turn toward him and say, "He's in our room. I couldn't imagine leaving for Aruba so soon after Bodee died. But I knew his wishes, I knew that he wanted to be cremated, and when I found out that this could all be done before we left, I had them prepare everything and I picked up his ashes Tuesday afternoon."

Gary's looking at me like I'm crazy, and he keeps starting to ask me questions but he can't manage to get out more than one word before stopping and trying again.

"It made it easier for me to go on this trip knowing that Bodee was with me. And these past few weeks, when I'd tell him about Aruba, he'd tell me how he wanted to go there one day," I tell him.

Gary puts his hand under my chin and leans my face up towards his and tells me, "I'm guessing that he meant that he wanted to come here alive."

I turn my head away and look out across the Caribbean toward Venezuela. I start walking again, gazing at the water, at how the sunlight plays upon the sea and the coral, turning some water deep blue while other sections look like green sea glass and still others are pure turquoise.

"Well, he didn't make it here alive, so I brought him dead." And then I laugh because it sounds like such a ridiculous thing to say, but it's true.

"I hesitate to ask this, but where exactly is Bodee?" Gary asks.

"Back at the hotel. In our room," I answer.

"Where exactly in our room?" Gary asks.

"Okay. The thing is, I wasn't sure how to carry him here, and I didn't want to bring an urn or anything. And with all of the airport security, I didn't know if I'd get in trouble bringing his ashes in a Ziploc—if they'd think it was some kind of weed, or maybe ashes from a terrorist bomb," I try to explain. When Gary doesn't say anything I continue. "And the other thing is, I wasn't sure legally if you're allowed to bring somebody's ashes out of the country. I mean, it's not like I had a passport for him or anything."

We keep walking, both of us kicking up the water as our feet slosh in the waves.

"You going to tell me where Bodee is?" Gary asks.

"Yeah, I'm getting there. So I figured that I should put him in my suitcase instead of in my carry-on, because I didn't want the airport security to see through my stuff and see the ashes."

Gary is taking in deep breaths now, and I can tell I should just cut to the chase.

"I put his ashes in an empty shampoo bottle," I tell him.

"What?" Gary asks.

"Well, I figured that an empty shampoo bottle would be able to hold the ashes, and you can't see inside the bottle, so it wouldn't raise any suspicions," I say. "When I brought the ashes home, I emptied out the little bit of Paul Mitchell shampoo that was left and let the bottle dry out. Then I took the funnel that we use to put the kitchen soap in the dispenser, and used that to get the ashes into the shampoo bottle," I explain. "At the moment, the shampoo bottle is in my Kate Spade tote bag," I add.

Gary starts to laugh, but then stops himself and instead says, "Do you know how crazy this is? Putting a dead man's ashes into a shampoo bottle and bringing it to Aruba."

I tell him that it's not crazy. That I needed Bodee with me, and at some point I need to figure out what to do with his ashes, but until then, he will stay with me.

"In the shampoo bottle," Gary says.

"In the shampoo bottle," I agree.

We turn around and head back to our section of beach. We walk in silence, because neither of us can figure out how to segue into a new topic after discussing Bodee's ashes in a shampoo bottle.

When we arrive back at our lounge chairs, I tell Gary that tomorrow I'm going to walk down the other stretch of beach where it's not so built up and it's quieter.

Gary asks me if I want a drink, and I tell him sure. I reapply my suntan lotion and settle myself back in my lounge chair. A few minutes later Gary returns with a cute little drink sprouting an umbrella. I think about Bodee saying that Aruba sounded like a wonderful place to practice balance, and so as I sip my island drink I let one leg dangle off the lounge chair and I anchor my foot into the sand, rooting myself to the earth.

Later that night I practice this balance even in the casino, trying hard not to get carried away by the sights and the sounds and the beat of wanting more, more and more. At one point I pull Gary away from the blackjack table and lead him out into the black night, onto the beach, where we kick off our shoes and let the cool sand breathe into the spaces between our toes. As we watch the waves caress the shore and the moonlight dance upon the sea, I let go of Gary's hand and began to twirl, my arms spread out to my sides.

"What are you doing?" Gary asks me

"Twirling like a whirling dervish," I answer.

"Syd, people are going to think you're drunk," he says.

"Drunk on life!" I yell out, twirling and twirling. "Maybe even drunk on death!" I add. "It's all the same, isn't it?" I ask. "Every birth is the death of something," I say as I stop twirling because I'm getting really dizzy.

Gary looks at me then. At least, I think he's looking at me. Everything is spinning around me, so I'm really not sure.

Gary takes my hands to steady me.

"I love you," I tell him.

He pulls me close then, and kisses me. "I love you, too. You're going to be okay, Syd," he says in a voice that's attempting reassurance. But what I hear is a little bit of a pleading in his voice, an urgency to know that I really am going to be okay, what with this whirling dervish thing and the fact that I had put Bodee in an empty shampoo bottle and brought him along to Aruba.

THE NEXT morning Gary and I enjoy the wonderful Sunday brunch buffet served outside, beside the lagoon where black swans glide over the silky water's surface. In the past, sitting at a buffet was an all-or-nothing event for me. I would have either hardly eaten at all because I was on a diet, all the while feeling deprived, or I would have eaten practically everything because I was breaking my diet, all the while feeling stressed about the weight I would gain and the diet I would need to start as a result.

Now, as I sit in this beautiful spot surrounded by every kind of food, I can practice balance, neither depriving myself nor overindulging. I check in with my stomach, with my inner body wisdom, to determine what it is I'm hungry for, and then I go about satisfying that hunger mindfully, joyfully and with gratitude.

"This is nice," Gary says between mouthfuls of his eggs Benedict.

"It is," I agree, as I spread strawberry preserves over my blintzes.

"So you're sure you don't mind if I head over to the golf course today?" Gary asks me as the waiter comes to pour us more freshly squeezed orange juice.

"Not at all. Actually, I was thinking of getting a taxi and driving over to the Natural Bridge," I tell him.

"You sure you don't want to wait for me? I'd go with you tomorrow," he tells me. But I reassure him that I'm fine going alone, and that I really feel like going there today.

After breakfast I go back to the room with Gary while he gets his clubs, and then walk out to the front of the hotel with him, where he meets up with a few guys he met the other day on the beach looking for a fourth for their golf game.

"Have fun," I say as he puts his clubs in the trunk of the taxi. Gary kisses me goodbye, and I tell him that I'll see him this afternoon. That I'll be back before he's done with his 18 holes, and that he can find me on the beach.

After his taxi pulls away, I walk back up to the lobby and stop at the concierge's desk.

"Can I help you?" the young woman at the desk asks with a smile. I smile back and tell her yes, that I'd like to get a ride to the Natural Bridge, and was there a car available to take me?

A frown crosses her face. "Oh, you must not have heard," she tells me.

"I'm sorry?" I ask.

She shakes her head sadly and says, "There is no more Natural Bridge. It disappeared back in September of 2005."

"What do you mean?" I ask. "What happened?"

"It collapsed. Apparently a crack had appeared at one end of the bridge several years ago. For thousands of years the pounding waves and strong winds formed that beautiful coral limestone bridge, and then in just one night that same wave action destroyed the bridge," she explains.

"I can't believe it," I say, "I loved that bridge. It's always been one of my most favorite spots," I tell her, trying to alter the landscape in my mind, to adjust to this new information.

"Yes, it was quite a tourist attraction. It's such a shame," she says mournfully. Then she smiles and says, "How about a snorkeling cruise instead? We have one that leaves at 12:30 and another that leaves at 3:00. We have spaces on both. Which one would you like?"

I shake my head no and tell her that I want to go to the Natural Bridge—and then I amend my words and tell her that I want to go to the collapsed Natural Bridge. She tells me she'll call a taxi for me, and I tell her that I'll be ready in just a few minutes.

I rush over to the elevators, wait for one to open, and move aside to let out the people dressed in their bathing suits ready for another day in the sun. I go in the elevator and press number 12, riding up to our floor. Back in our room, I gather a few things together in my beach bag and return down to the lobby, where my taxi is waiting.

As we drive out of the hotel the driver says, "You know the Natural Bridge has collapsed?" and I tell him that yes, I just learned what happened.

"Such a horrible thing," he tells me, shaking his head sadly.

He turns up the reggae music on the radio, and I lean back and think to myself, *is it horrible?* I love that bridge, there's no doubt. But why do we all think things are so solid? The bridge is here, and now it's not. An earthquake, a tsunami, a mudslide—these events magnify the fact that nothing is really solid. The Buddha was right. Everything is impermanent. The one thing we can count on in this world is change. Everything changes. To think otherwise is to invite in suffering.

"You having a good vacation here in Aruba?" the taxi driver asks me, interrupting my thoughts.

"Wonderful," I say. "I always love it here."

"You know our motto—'One Happy Island,'" he tells me.

"Yep," I say, happy when he begins singing along with a song, leaving me to return to my thoughts.

Why do we all think things are so solid? We see every day that life is impermanent, but we fight it every step of the way. We want things to stay the same, or we want things to change so that then, when things are just the way we want them, they'll stay that way forever.

We think we are solid, but like the bridge, we aren't solid. We are energy in motion, fluid, changing, living and dying. I hear again Bodee's voice: "No man ever steps in the same river twice, for it's not the same river, and he's not the same man."

I look out the window and watch the terrain of the island change. On this side, where the Natural Bridge stood, the island is much wilder in its beauty, undeveloped and raw, the gentle sea turning rougher against the rugged land and craggy mountains dotted with cacti, the sharpness of life piercing at your heart.

The taxi stops and the driver tells me he'll wait while I go out to survey.

"Take your time," he tells me. "Still good swimming coves all along the left shore," he says. "Isn't it something though, to look out and no longer see that bridge? Still can't get used to it."

"It really is something," I agree. "I won't be too long," I tell him as I get out of the car.

I walk up to the rocky land that juts out into the Caribbean and feel like I'm standing on a mountain. Here the wind takes on a new force, and you can taste the spray of the water, taste the salt that the sea carries.

I watch the waves crash against the land in such a force, a pounding force that carries the energy of the universe, the shakti of creation. I put down my bag and stretch my arms out to the side, and with the wind and the crashing waves it feels like I'm flying. There is no one around, so I yell out to the world a loud *OM,* feeling like I am part of that wind, part of this craggy rock, part of the roaring ocean.

I taste more salt on my lips and realize at some point my own tears have mingled in with the salt from the sea, and I couldn't tell you how much of those tears have to do with sorrow and how much of those tears have to do with joy. And I know that it doesn't matter, because sorrow and joy are conditions that arise and dissipate in cycles, just like the waves that form a bridge and then tear it down.

Everything that begins, ends, and all that ends, begins, and all that ever was, is no more, and all that is no more once again is. I see that in each wave, in each rush of wind.

And then I know.

I know why I am standing here, though it feels like I am flying in this rush of water and wind.

I know why I am standing here.

I pick up my bag, pull out my shampoo bottle, and talk to Bodee.

"You are everywhere. In the earth and in the sea and in the wind. You are part of the eternal nothingness, which is everything. You are embryo and fetus and child and old man and ashes and child once more. Everything changes, but the vibrations of love, of compassion, of wisdom beat in the heart of everything, if you just open your eyes and see clearly what is right in front of you. Thank you for teaching me. I know of no other way to show my gratitude and love than to set you free in the midst of this universal energy, to send your ashes into the ever-moving breath of life."

And then I begin pouring handfuls of Bodee's ashes into my hands and scattering them in the wind, letting them fall into the great waves of the ocean and onto the beach below and into the crevices within the limestone rock. And as I scatter Bodee's ashes, announcing him to the land and wind and sea, I let go. I let go.

I DON'T know how long I've been standing here. Maybe for just a few moments, and maybe for all eternity. My body feels fluid now, as if I myself am the rolling sea, as if I am ash floating upon wave.

Before turning away I hear myself say, "May all beings be free from suffering. May all beings be at ease."

As I walk back towards the taxi I look for somewhere to put the now-empty shampoo bottle. I pass a trashcan, but can't let myself throw it away. I walk a few steps down and see a recycling can. I smile and drop the Paul Mitchell bottle in, wondering what the next incarnation of the shampoo bottle will be.

Returning to the hotel, I run back up to my room, change into my bathing suit, and grab my straw hat. I head back down and out toward the beach. I put my beach bag and book down on the lounge chairs by the little thatch tree hut Gary and I have been using, leaving my sandals in the sand.

I walk toward the shore and head in the opposite direction of the hotels, down to the left, where the beach spreads out languidly, the water lapping at the sand leaving imprints that soon dry in the warmth of the sun. I gaze at the little footprints the sea birds have left, that will soon be washed away by the constant pull of the water against the sand.

A little ways down on the beach I see a lone divi tree. I decide to sit down under the tree to meditate. I pull the string of my straw hat snuggly under my neck so the wind doesn't blow it away.

I sit in the lotus position, watching my breath on the inhalation and watching my breath on the exhalation. Soon there is no "I" watching the breathing, there is only breath coming in and breath going on in unison with the sea, the breath letting go with the wave, and the breath returning into the ocean.

And I see a montage of images—everyone who has come before me and everyone who will come after me, and we are all different and all the same, and we are forever changing and merging and beating in the heart and heat of the universe.

I feel the sea coursing through my veins, and I imagine my blood flowing in the depths of the ocean, and I hear an infant cry out at her birth and an old man cry out at his death, and it is the same sound.

And I know that the greatest teaching is to move through life with your eyes open to what is right in front of you, to live mindfully with compassion and wisdom and balance.

I breathe this knowing into every cell of my being, even while I know that every second new cells within me are being born and old cells are dying. With every inhalation I breathe in gratitude and love, and with every exhalation I breathe out gratitude and love, and I sit this way for what again could be a few moments, or what could be eternity.

I SIT here under the divi tree feeling fully connected to this infinite universe, have become one with that boundless space, and then I feel a gentle hand on my shoulder.

"Syd, are you awake?" I hear Gary ask. He must have finished his golfing, and came looking for me on the beach.

I follow another cycle of my breath, inhaling and exhaling with the sound of the sea.

"Syd," Gary asks softly again, "Are you awake?"
I open my eyes and smile.
"Yes, Gary. I'm awake."

Acknowledgments

Many years ago I was having a conversation with my friend David Rosenberg when we discovered that we both loved the book *Siddhartha* by Herman Hesse. As we continued talking, David joked that he had visions of one day writing his own version of the book about a middle-aged Jewish man named Sid Arthur and his attempts to reach enlightenment. I told him I thought it was a fabulous idea, and that was that.

But David's idea stirred something in me, and continued to percolate. A few years later when I ran into David, I asked him if he planned to write his book. He shook his head no, explaining it was more a fun fantasy. I asked him if I could use his idea. I told him that I couldn't write Sid Arthur as a Jewish man, but Syd Arthur as a middle-aged Jewish woman seeking enlightenment? She I saw everyday when I looked in the mirror.

David told me I had his permission to use the idea, and some twelve years later, this novel was born. Thank you, David, for the inspiration.

My thanks to the tireless and wonderful Peggy Elam and Pearlsong Press for believing in this book and for giving it a home.

My sister, Judith Matz, spent endless hours on the phone with me discussing Syd. I wrote and rewrote, and she read and reread. Her insights and suggestions were invaluable, and her unflagging support gave me the courage to push ahead. She believed in Syd and she believed in me, and that has meant everything.

Ellen Barish lent her expertise as a writer and editor to help me shape the manuscript, and with her wit, humor and wisdom helped me to understand what Syd needed, and also what she didn't need. I am forever grateful to have shared the process with her; Syd and I both grew as a result of her efforts.

Rabbi Baruch HaLevi demonstrates flexibility, strength and spirit both on the yoga mat and off. I feel so fortunate to have his wise counsel, and his suggestions after reading the manuscript helped me to rewrite Syd Arthur on a deeper level. The only thing better than a latte at Starbucks is having a latte with Rabbi B at Starbucks.

My gratitude to my friends who served as readers and encouraged me to keep writing: Karen Imber, Phyllis Eidelman, Ellen Reifler, Sue Fligor, Todd and Rosalie Miller, Lisa Weisman, Amy Forman and Beth Kaiman, and to Judy Toner, Wendy Webber, Marjorie Patkin and Susan Yorks, who willingly listened to me talk about Syd and always offered encouraging smiles and words. My appreciation also goes out to Wendy Ruskin, who invited me into her home and patiently answered my questions about tea; her warmth and sweetness matched the tea that she poured. I so appreciate Becky Eidelman and her artistic skill in bringing my idea for the book cover to paper, and to Joanna Gammel, who brilliantly brought my book cover to life.

My enormous thanks to my mother, Lorraine Matz, who read the manuscript and told me that she loved both Syd Arthur and me. Thanks also to my dad, Joe Matz, who I would often call with a random question about the Chicago skyline or subway system when Syd was venturing from the suburbs to the city and I wasn't sure how to get her there, and to my brother, Bob Matz, for continuing to support my writing adventures. Thanks also to my niece, Laura Barhydt, for reading my manuscript and encouraging me on.

Barbara McCollough guided me as I navigated my own spiritual quest, and cheered Syd on as she navigated hers. It is my great fortune to have Barbara in my life; her wisdom and compassion have held me through the years.

Shelley Pouslen, Hanna Sherman, and Rabbi Alan Ullman are my Dharma buddies, Torah companions, and spiritual family. Their encouragement of this book, and of me, is one of my life's greatest gifts. I will forever be filled with gratitude to Rabbi Alan for offering me a path back to my Jewish roots while holding and honoring my Buddhist heart.

My heartfelt thanks go to Stacey Miller for her work in helping to launch this book.

My children, Allison and Matt, continue to inspire me, support me, and offer endless amounts of encouragement. They are my lotus flowers, infusing my life with such blossoming beauty and wonder. Thank you both for being who you are in this world.

And thank you, thank you, thank you to my husband, Steve, who, for the past few years as I wrote this book, allowed Syd to tag along in our marriage. I took her with us to dinner, on our walks, to the movies and to the Passover Seder. And Steve, ever loving and supportive, welcomed her into our lives. He read the manuscript, offered suggestions, and toasted me when I finished writing this book. Thank you for sharing your life with me.

And infinite gratitude to the Buddha and the teachers of the Dharma:
May all beings be free from suffering.
May all beings be happy.

About the Author

Ellen Frankel lives in Marblehead, Massachusetts with her husband, two children, and dog, Karma. Trained as a clinical social worker, she worked in the field of eating disorders in both outpatient and residential settings.

She is the co-author of *Beyond a Shadow of a Diet: The Therapist's Guide to Treating Compulsive Eating* and *The Diet Survivor's Handbook: 60 Lessons in Eating, Acceptance and Self-Care,* and the author of *Beyond Measure: A Memoir About Short Stature and Inner Growth.*

VISIT HER at www.authorellenfrankel.com.

A DOWNLOADABLE Book Group Discussion Guide for *Syd Arthur* is available on the author's website and at www.pearlsong.com/sydarthur.htm.

About Pearlsong Press

PEARLSONG PRESS IS AN INDEPENDENT PUBLISHING COMPANY dedicated to providing books and resources that entertain while expanding perspectives on the self and the world. The company was founded by Peggy Elam, Ph.D., a psychologist and journalist, in 2003.

Pearls are formed when a piece of sand or grit or other abrasive, annoying, or even dangerous substance enters an oyster and triggers its protective response. The substance is coated with shimmering opalescent nacre ("mother of pearl"), the coats eventually building up to produce a beautiful gem. The self-healing response of the oyster thus transforms suffering into a thing of beauty.

The pearl-creating process reflects our company's desire to move outside a pathological or "disease" based model of life, health and well-being into a more integrative and transcendent perspective. A move out of suffering into joy. And that, we think, is something to sing about.

PEARLSONG PRESS ENDORSES HEALTH AT EVERY SIZE, an approach to health and well-being that celebrates natural diversity in body size and encourages people to stop focusing on weight (or any external measurement) in favor of listening to and respecting natural appetites for food, drink, sleep, rest, movement, and recreation. While not every book we publish specifically promotes Health At Every Size (by, for instance, featuring fat heroines or educating readers on size acceptance), none of our books or other resources will contradict this holistic and body-positive perspective.

WE ENCOURAGE YOU TO ENJOY, enlarge, enlighten and enliven yourself with other Pearlsong Press books, which you can purchase at www.pearlsong. com or your favorite bookstore. Keep up with us through our blog at www. pearlsongpress.com.

Fiction:

The Fat Lady Sings—a young adult novel by Charlie Lovett
Fallen Embers (Book One of The Embers Series)—paranormal romance by Lauri J Owen
Bride of the Living Dead—romantic comedy by Lynne Murray
Measure By Measure—a romantic romp with the fabulously fat by Rebecca Fox & William Sherman
FatLand—a visionary novel by Frannie Zellman
The Program—a suspense novel by Charlie Lovett
The Singing of Swans—a novel about the Divine Feminine by Mary Saracino

Romance novels and short stories featuring Big Beautiful Heroines:
by Pat Ballard, the Queen of Rubenesque Romances:
The Best Man
Abigail's Revenge
Dangerous Curves Ahead: Short Stories
Wanted: One Groom
Nobody's Perfect
His Brother's Child
A Worthy Heir
by Rebecca Brock—*The Giving Season*
& by Judy Bagshaw—*At Long Last, Love: A Collection*

Nonfiction:

Fat Poets Speak: Voices of the Fat Poets' Society—edited by Frannie Zellman
Ten Steps to Loving Your Body (No Matter What Size You Are) by Pat Ballard
Beyond Measure: A Memoir About Short Stature & Inner Growth by Ellen Frankel
Taking Up Space: How Eating Well & Exercising Regularly Changed My Life by Pattie Thomas, Ph.D. with Carl Wilkerson, M.B.A. (foreword by Paul Campos, author of *The Obesity Myth)*
Off Kilter: A Woman's Journey to Peace with Scoliosis, Her Mother & Her Polish Heritage—a memoir by Linda C. Wisniewski
Unconventional Means: The Dream Down Under—a spiritual travelogue & memoir by Anne Richardson Williams
Splendid Seniors: Great Lives, Great Deeds—inspirational biographies by Jack Adler

CPSIA information can be obtained at www.ICGtesting.com

265134BV00001B/46/P